Night Ascending

The Guards of Nightfall: Book 2

Natasha Galan

First published in the United States in 2024
Paperback ISBN 979-8-218-50630-8
eBook ISBN 979-8-218-50631-5

Copyright © 2024 Natasha Galan

Special thanks to Miblart, Shana Grogan, and Natali Waters

This book is a work of fiction. Names, characters, places, and events in this book are products of the author's imagination. While they may be loosely based off those things presently or in antiquity, references to actual events, places, or persons—living or dead—is used fictitiously. And while the author has tried to remain concise in her use of such references, sometimes the internet can be a fathomless place, and the author asks for grace in these matters.

This book identifies with themes that may be considered strong by some readers. Caution is advised.

Dedication

To my first 99 followers on Facebook and 117 followers on Instagram. Without you I wouldn't exist. I am over the moon in gratitude for your support.

Chapter One

November 2021
Undisclosed location

She lost track of time.

The feat was nearly inconceivable for a vampire, because at an early age they were trained in unique ways to denote the passing of time. With their sensitivity to daylight a hindrance and in an era before clocks, one of those unique ways was to count the seconds in a minute. Before they reached an age where they could count, however, vampires were instructed to observe the path the moon made across the sky, and its phases to track the months. Months would coalesce into seasons, and spirited younglings would watch in wonder as leaves turned from shimmering green to rusted ember, their lives passing languidly, near to everlasting.

Yet where Kate was there were no windows to look through. No clocks. No electronics. No *electricity*. There was no schedule in which sustenance was brought to her. The temperature in the three-foot space she occupied never ranged far from freezing, and turned morbidly frigid when someone opened the single door. That detail alone led her to believe it was still winter, but she couldn't be sure. She was sure of nothing anymore. Because despite these perceptions she lost track of the seconds, the minutes, the days, the *weeks* she'd been stuffed in different cells with little but drywall, dirt, and concrete to keep her company.

She feared going insane.

Starvation would do that to someone, she supposed. She couldn't remember the last time she'd been nourished with blood or had a proper meal. *Creator,* but what she wouldn't give for one of Mora's homecooked monstrosities, laden with butter, cream, and salt. At this point Kate would settle for a stray crumb from a moldy cracker. A drop of perspiration from a leaky ceiling. A dehydrated bug carcass. Never again would she turn away from one of the elaborate sit-down meals, replete with different wines, various courses, and mouth-watering desserts. She could kick herself for flouncing away giddily to do whatever she thought had been more important as her father frowned in her wake.

I took so much for granted, she thought miserably, now too brittle, too weak to even lift her head from the dusty floor, let alone flounce. She moved her tongue from the base of her mouth to the top to somewhat pass the time, only to find the appendage stale and dry, so coarse it made her nauseous. Either that or it was the stench from her body. When was the last time she bathed? Not to mention the countless wounds she suffered, as the indurations in her body refused to heal. She couldn't even gather the tethers of her clothing together to make a rag if some water happened to seep in.

A tremor wracked her sunken form. *What did I do to get myself here?* She wasn't sure she could think back to the first step she'd taken against her foes, as time and memory morphed into something elusively vague. She was afraid she would succumb to the looming psychosis if she tried too hard, but then again maybe that was better than the constant state of bleak blackness in which she lived.

If she had the chance to go back to the time when she felt so justified, so sure, so righteous…would she change her trajectory? Before she so abruptly and brutally learned the entire time she'd been watching her enemy he'd been watching her? Before she knew Santiago had been waiting for the right moment to strike, to enact his own plan of decimation? What a fool she'd been to never suspect. To take no precautions. To not have one single inclination. To not think for a moment that she could be walking into a trap laid by her very own hands. *Naïve. Ignorant. Stupid.* The fateful night—Creator, was it over a month ago?—she'd met up with a handful of prostitutes to arrange a meeting with Santiago and then left to perform an independent patrol of the city, had changed her life forever.

In this moment it was easy to give into dismay as every

shiver, every wince, every breath brought with it unfathomable new pain. Her last interaction with Santiago had left her right hand crushed, her mandible broken on the same side, and several ribs broken, and in her depleted state she'd yet to recover. Vampires usually healed quickly, within a day or two, but she'd lost that ability weeks ago. She knew she had to be stronger than these consequences, but there were times when she felt she couldn't. Right now was one of those times. Right now she wanted to succumb. Right now she wanted to use what little breath she had left in her lungs to cry for help, to plead for mercy. But to whom?

There was no one.

She was alone.

In the beginning she sobbed and begged and prayed almost daily. The watchers who were supposed to guide her and The Creator who gave her life readily ignored such pleas. Her captors made fun of her wretchedness, and their constant sullying of her character drove her to muteness. And then, after The Guards' failed attempt at rescue, she fully gave up hope. Hope that anyone would hear her, much less free her.

Still, as the days and nights wandered somberly on, she couldn't help but think, Athair, *where are you? Why haven't you come for me?* She thought of her father so much; if she couldn't trust otherworldly deities to come to her rescue, she knew—at least she thought she knew—she could rely on her father. He'd always been there for her, his steady presence unwavering and unyielding in his protection of her.

But she'd quickly come to realize Santiago was too smart, too cautious, and too efficient in his villainous ways. Always one step ahead. She'd been moved four times since her initial capture, and Santiago regularly ordered his subordinates to destroy any evidence of her. One of the warehouses she'd been kept in had been burned to the ground, which set fire to the adjacent structures. An entire row in the warehouse district had been burned to ash. *Because of me. All of this because of me.*

What a *fool* she'd been.

If Kate had merely told someone of her plans instead of acting like she had something to prove on her own, she might not be where she is now. But where would that delusion get her in this particular moment? It certainly wouldn't excuse her from the aggressions of her captor. Because Santiago and his cronies wasted not a moment in their torture of her. Kate lost count of the number of times and the various ways she'd been tormented. The training she'd half paid attention to was useless against these stronger and more experienced adversaries. She'd lost all her strength, all her abilities, all her senses, all her motivation, weeks ago.

She'd failed everyone. *Everyone.* Even...even...

I'm sorry mother, Kate thought of the female she never knew, who'd passed just after Kate had been borne. Her father forbade others from speaking of her over the years, but Kate heard enough quiet murmurings to know her mother would never stand to be so manipulated and victimized as Kate was now. She could feel her mother's specter looking down on her in disdainful pity, could feel the reproachful curl of a sneer even from above. Still, in her darkest of moments, Kate dreamt fondly of her: how she sounded, what she smelled like, how she would laugh, what her likes and dislikes were, her favorite hobbies. Kate supposed that was the madness harkening, baiting her, taunting her with everything she would never have. *My family...my friends...my life as I knew it...torn to shreds because of me...*

Kate opened her eyes weakly, a fluttering of lashes that was the last of her standing will as the walls pushed in from all sides. She felt an ache clutch her heart with the same cloying talons that suddenly circled her throat. A fractured sob tore from cracked lips, and brittle fingers curled against the cold concrete. A hot tear trekked from the corner of one eye to dampen the dust that coated her cell, though her depleted body could produce no more than that single feat. Loneliness sunk its sharpened teeth into her flesh and the bitter cloud of sadness thickened overhead. She wasn't sure how much more she could endure...

I'm going to die here. Shamefully, wretchedly, and disastrously deserted. Long gone was the confident, vivacious, careless Kathryn Eithne MacNehhtonn, replaced by the shell of a female no one would recognize.

She had so many regrets, and too many started with not being a better daughter. More respectful. Cautious. Dutiful. More qualms plagued her, pulling her toward a stunning copper gaze framed by curling black hair which she always saw with the most crystalline precision. When it came to *him* she had the most regrets,

4

especially for what could have been…*if only*…

Time withered away again, though it was an illusionary concept anymore. Memories constantly intertwined with the perceptions of her current reality, taking her repeatedly to a place she yielded to in wallowing despair. What more could she do? She was too weak to stand. Too crestfallen to attempt any sort of noise or other movement. Any efforts to escape proved futile. Santiago and his associates had been ripping off her claws to prevent her from using them to pick the locks on the doors or dig through the walls for a while now, but Kate had the scabs from trying anyway. Her throat was raw from shrieking or weeping. She lost count of the bruises she had from throwing herself against doors or walls. She had no hope anymore. No determination. Everything positive and ambitious had been beaten out of her weeks ago.

I will never know my life from before.

The blackness of oblivion threatened, and she welcomed it as she so easily did anymore, wishing it would swallow her whole.

This is the night I wish when I close my eyes, I don't open them to this dimension.

This is the night I beg for death to become me.

November 2021
Warwick

Pacing. Pacing. Pacing.

Damian couldn't hold still. He couldn't stop thinking, but he couldn't center his thoughts. He felt restless. Livid. Revolted. Disappointed. The list went on and on and on. For weeks it had dragged on. And now after another night gone sour, another instance in which they'd yet again failed to garner any sort of lead, he was hardly controlling his emotions. He had no one or nothing to direct his anger at. His resentment at. His irritation at. No one had a solution to the problem. They kept failing, failing, failing. And Talorc… Talorc couldn't be bothered to be present for his own daughter, who had now been gone for thirty-three days, twenty-two hours, and thirty-one minutes.

Pathetic.

The disgust he felt toward Talorc returned tenfold and he had to pause by the fireplace to collect himself. The room he was in was a large one, an office in Talorc's manor they had been using as a meeting place, and it echoed with the crackling of the hearth. All The Guardsmales were present except for Vadin, who lay in the infirmary recovering from several stab wounds, none of which were lucky enough to make it to his heart. Unfortunately, compounding his healing was the fact that both of his legs had been crushed to mere fragments when he'd been run over by an enemy vehicle. Even with Lilith's medical diligence it was a difficult case that was still taking time to close. She'd gone back in once already to reset bones that were trying to heal inappropriately.

"In which direction did they go?"

Cyrus glanced at their captain, Ryder, from where they both sat in chairs before the desk, while Damian continued to linger by the fireplace. He was beyond verbiage, beyond rage, and he knew if he got too close to the phone he would explode. He couldn't comprehend the fact Talorc was on the other side of the phone, speaking from wherever the fuck he deemed more important than at home leading the fight to retrieve his daughter.

Noir, another Guardsmale, was the most remote, sitting in a chair across the room near one of the floor lamps. Their combined silence—which spoke of their uncertainty on how to appropriately answer—drove Damian closer to imploding, and he started his pacing again, trekking heavily across the blue oriental rug overlaying the shining hardwood floors.

"We don't know," Ryder finally replied.

"The truck just ran over Vadin," Cyrus added. He shifted in the tufted, brown leather chair, his massive frame swallowing the furniture whole. His thick legs were spread, and with a hand on his black beard, his shrewd brown eyes narrowed on the phone. As restless as Damian, he smoothed a hand over his bare head before sighing to say, "I went to him. Ryder was fighting off three vampires. Noir was trying to intervene."

A heartbeat of silence and then Talorc asked, *"And Damian?"*

6

"Pinned to the front of the Tahoe," Damian interjected harshly. "With a sword."

"He's lucky the grenade they planted underneath the truck didn't go off," Cyrus grumbled, his words rolling with thunderous ire.

It hadn't mattered, though. When Noir had found him…

Was that really just three days ago? Silence permeated the space once more. Damian's side ached at the reminder, where wraiths had pierced through his intestines with a sword—*a fucking sword*—and turned the blade so it caught in the grille of the Tahoe. He was lucky it hadn't severed his spine. He'd recovered from that injury a time or two and hated being confined to the bed while his spinal cord, vertebrae, and nerves regrew.

"How's it going on your end?" Damian asked, both rhetorically and cynically. He didn't care about any progress Talorc was making with the vampire covens, and he wanted Talorc to know. It had taken Talorc three days to catch up with them, and the lack of concern about their wellbeing sat ill with him.

Ryder sent Damian a shadowed look of warning to remind him to whom he spoke. Damian chose to ignore the pointed glance and instead thought, *what type of king abandons his family in their greatest time of need? What type of king runs instead of putting up a fight?* Nowadays, most of his thoughts on Talorc were less than pleasant. The male who had once been his friend, his liege, his guardian, his mentor, had become less than.

Talorc ignored Damian's implied criticism and instead asked, *"They are carrying swords now?"*

"They're getting creative." Cyrus shifted again, moving to place his elbows on his knees, the leather beneath him creaking.

"And smarter," Ryder added. "But now we know it's not just wraiths. Vampires and humans are involved too."

"There's only one way this could be going."

"Talorc, Kate…she has to be in bad shape," Damian said roughly, rounding back to the center of his thoughts. A nightmarish vision of her battered and broken body swelled to the forefront of his mind before he dissipated it with a little shake of his head. "We'll double our efforts. Ask for help from others."

"Vadin is in critical condition," Talorc replied. *"You must stand down for now."*

Wrath swirled like a tempest, and Damian cut piercing copper eyes toward the phone. "Stand *down*?"

Ryder shot Damian another warning look, this one sharper than the last, but as before, Damian didn't heed it.

"No one has seen her. No one has heard word of her. The places they could be keeping her… Creator, but the types of conditions she could be enduring… You know she has no food. No water. No bathroom. No comfort." The words pained Damian to say, because he knew in the depth of his soul Kate was so far beyond struggling and suffering. And as a soldier through the ages, he knew what enemies did to captured foes. "And *you're not here.* You've abandoned her just as much as you've abandoned us."

Ryder bowed his head while Cyrus closed his eyes, and Noir glanced out the window into the night. But Damian would not back down from this fight, would not cower from Talorc and his legacy. Yes, Damian had been with Talorc for centuries, and yes, Damian respected him, but what Talorc was doing was stupid. Senseless. Useless. The covens should *not* be the priority now, not when Kate was—

"You can save your judgement for another day, Damian," Talorc responded coolly. Damian knew if he were here, the temperature in the room would've plummeted to a near-freeze to show his contempt. *"When you lead, you may have an opinion on how I conduct myself."*

"I've led battalions, militias, and armies," Damian hissed, stopping in his pacing. "And never once did I desert the frontlines."

"I am doing something you cannot," Talorc replied icily. *"You do not have the leads I have, the connections, the birthright. I count on you five at home to do something better suited for your hands. Why do I have to explain this to you as though you are a youngling?"*

Damian bristled. "Are you so—"

"Enough," Ryder barked, the tone sharp even for him. "This bickering is baseless."

Damian resumed his pacing more fervently than before. He felt hot and tight, like if he didn't release the pressure in his chest he would succumb to full-fledged fury. He couldn't stay in this room, this manor, much longer. He needed an outlet. He needed his friend back. He needed—

"What is the status of the home front?"

Ryder leaned toward the desk. "Security is tightening on the manor. We have guard dogs now, which were extremely expensive by the way, and have hired a trusted vampire company to monitor the perimeter remotely. Before Vadin went down, he was reaching out to his contacts in the underground to see if there's any other way we can infiltrate the port; we still think that's our biggest lead. Damian has been trying to gather bodies for an international meeting, but most want to hear from you first."

"The local covens are ready for conflict," Cyrus added. "There shouldn't be any trouble mobilizing them."

"Scouting and recon is slow," Ryder continued. "Our enemy is well-hidden and well-guarded."

"Santiago doesn't stay in one place very long," Noir said, his voice barely carrying over the snapping flames. His slender frame molded into the shadows as if he were made from them, only just revealing distant hazel eyes. "He's difficult to pin down. People know of him but not enough to add to what we already know."

"And there is no talk of who he could be working with or for?"

None of the males replied, eliciting a sigh from Talorc.

"This is becoming more bothersome than anything," Talorc continued. *"But we have a set path. Continue your individual endeavors. Keep me informed on Kathryn. Do you have any idea where they have taken her now?"*

Ryder replied flatly, "They were headed north, but that means nothing."

There was a pause before Talorc said, *"I will stay diligent in my own ventures. Check in tomorrow morning with an update on Vadin."* He hung up without a word more.

Like the cork from a champagne bottle, Damian lunged for the door. *I can't stay here anymore.* He burst out from the suffocating confines of the study so forcefully the door threatened to retaliate, and his stride was long and swift as he headed for the foyer a floor below.

"Damian."

With the last ounces of his control, Damian halted at Ryder's voice. He turned only partly to look back at him and snap, "What."

Ryder closed the distance between them, while Damian held his ground. Ryder had been serving Talorc the longest, becoming the captain of The Guards of Nightfall because of his brutal efficiency on the battlefield and levelheadedness off it. He and Damian were stalwart friends, having been through every thick and thin, high and low, and up and over situation there could be. Today Damian's temper would only allow so much, and he didn't have the time for Ryder's bullshit, nor the introspection that would remind him of their camaraderie. He respected Ryder enough to listen and abide by him, but today…today he was at the end of his rope.

"You tread thin ice with Talorc," Ryder began, stopping a few paces away. The hallway was wide, but he still took up most of the space. The beige runner was eaten by his large boots while the sconces and paintings on the wall seemed to lean away from his commanding presence. "I know you're frustrated, but you're letting that get the better of you."

"He has no idea what we're going through. What *she's* going through." Damian gestured first one way then the other, his eyes wild, his rage barely under control.

"He knows. And he's right in his own account," Ryder told him, and Damian noted a hint of chagrin in his usually neutral tone. "He's utilizing his own unique abilities while we employ our own. Your resentment is clouding your vision and could interfere with your ability to fight."

"Never."

Ryder lifted a single brow. "Your behavior lately has been volatile, even for you."

Damian glowered at Ryder. "So says the male who can barely keep it in his pants over a human woman."

Ryder's stoic façade faded for a moment, revealing the annoyance he was keeping at bay underneath. "I'm only bringing this up because I want to reorient you to the present. You're getting ahead of yourself and losing sight."

"Roger that," Damian said sarcastically.

"Damian," Ryder chided once more. "Listen to yourself if you're not going to listen to me. Listen to how you sound."

Spitefully, Damian said nothing.

"You're acting no better than a youngling." Ryder's golden

eyes glinted with aggravation, a rare show for him, and his words fell heavy. "Baiting Talorc, or anyone else for that matter, is going to get you nowhere. I know you're worried about Kate, but you have to remember we *all* are. This isn't just about you. If you lose your head in this, Santiago and the wraiths will continue to take the upper hand."

"I get it, Ryder."

"Do you?" Ryder prodded. "You couldn't keep it together when we went for Kate at the warehouse. You cornered Claudia, throwing us all for a loop."

Not my finest work, Damian thought, grinding his molars together.

"Your reckless bickering with Talorc doesn't help. If he asks you to do something, you need to comply. He can see the bigger picture when right now our focus needs to be here. If you can't focus here, you are jeopardizing the mission altogether. And I know you are more sensible than that. Maybe not recently, but your resourcefulness and ability to maintain dominance on the battlefield is why I asked for you to be made all those years ago. Don't forget that. Don't make *me* forget that."

It was on the tip of Damian's tongue to tell Ryder to *go fuck himself.*

"I can't chastise you any more than I can punish you. But Talorc doesn't take insults lightly. And I know you respect him more than that.

"We'll get through this," Ryder continued. "We'll get Kate back. We're just behind the times and while we're paying for it now, hopefully it means in the future we'll be better for it."

Damian stared at Ryder, unwilling to give voice to his thoughts. They were still incredibly tumultuous, and he wasn't entirely sure what would come out of his mouth wouldn't be insulting. Instead, he turned and continued his trek, wanting to beat the rise of the sun back to his penthouse so he could try and channel his restless energy into something useful.

Maybe I can review the traffic cameras again, see where the car went off to. He stalked toward the hall that would lead to Talorc's garage. *Maybe I missed something...*

Night bled into dawn, and it wasn't long before Damian was

pulling his blue BMW M8 into the subterranean garage below his penthouse. The sky had lightened from a harsh cobalt to a softer cerulean, and for too long Damian lingered by the garage's opening comparing the shade to Kate's twinkling eyes.

They're not twinkling anymore, he thought morbidly as he moved in from the cold of the garage to the sheltered alcove of his apartment building, pressing a button to summon the elevator. The concrete echoed around him as he moved, and it reminded him too much of the emptiness that had settled in his chest since Kate's kidnapping. He swallowed heavily with the realization that he'd been unable to fill the void for weeks.

The elevator chimed faintly, signaling its arrival, and Damian crossed the threshold into the shining confinement. He closed his eyes as he leaned back against the steel wall after having entered a special combination on the keypad to get him to the top floor. *We failed her. I failed her.* The notion weighed him down, pulling him to depths that threatened to drown him. *Why can't we find her? What kind of leverage does Santiago have that we don't?*

His side ached in remembrance of being skewered to the front of the Tahoe with a sword. *Swords in this day and age. What the actual fuck.* While he was now almost fully functioning after the attack thanks to his enhanced vampiric genetics, his body still liked to remind him that it had barely been three days ago that he'd been incapacitated to the point where he let wraiths get the best of him. If it hadn't been for Noir he would've been killed. Or at the very least, captured and tortured, *and then* killed.

I failed her…

The elevator chimed again and opened to the small foyer to his penthouse. The black marble floors gleamed, as they were always kept pristine, and the small, gray sideboard beside the black door to his home boasted a small winter floral arrangement that the penthouse's staff maintained. The single light by the door gave off enough illumination that Damian was able to get his key out, place it in the lock, and open it after putting in the numerical code.

Automatically a light turned on overhead. Damian threw his keys to the small table he kept by the door and kicked off his shoes, forgoing the use of the shoe rack nearby. His curtains were drawn, shielding the spectacular sunlit view of the city from his sensitive eyes. He turned his sight to his home; the space which usually lent him comfort now was shadowed, reflecting the current state of his dismal and cheerless existence.

The penthouse was a ten thousand square-foot modernly minimalistic masterpiece. Perfectly polished concrete flooring swirled elegantly before him, though a corner to the right was laid with wide Brazilian cherry planks and boasted a small wet bar and black grand piano. Past the piano was a short hallway that led to five bedrooms, each with its own ensuite bathroom. Stretching to the left of the main space was the dining area and kitchen, separated from the large living area by a floor-to-ceiling electric fireplace that was presently turned off. Through another doorway off the kitchen was a den with an attached library, and another room which featured a projector and movie-theater seating. The entire place was encircled by a balcony, complete with hot tub, bar, grill, outdoor fireplace, and lap pool.

Lately, Damian was seldom home. Being here made him feel edgy, the comfort suffocating. Being at Talorc's was even more unsettling, as it usually led him to ire. The only place he could tolerate in longevity was on the streets, prowling for clues about Kate and her abduction.

I failed her.

Damian walked to the nearest space of sectional and sat down, placing his elbows on his knees and his head in his hands. He hadn't slept the last two days. Anytime he tried he had nightmares about what Kate might be enduring. Compounding his inability to rest was the fact that he hadn't fed for longer. Anymore he only fed to sustain himself at the most minimal level because he couldn't stand to be idle while Kate was out somewhere in Warwick—or Creator knew where—in whatever condition she was in.

Damian's fingers tightened around his hair as the rage he couldn't be rid of curled in his gut, writhing like a provoked cobra. What bones of hers had they broken? How many bruises did she have? Kate never cried—no she was too proud for that—but did she now? Did she think The Guard had abandoned her? Did her hair still carry the streak of violet or was it faded by now? Creator take him, but whenever he closed his eyes he heard her laughter, only for it to quickly turn into her withered shriek...

I failed her. Damian squeezed his eyes shut as the wrath

13

swirled from his gut and clutched his throat, and no matter how many times he swallowed it wouldn't let go. He ground his teeth together, his fingers scraping along his scalp. A hundred—no, a thousand regrets threatened to overwhelm him in that moment. A thousand regrets over the last four years, filled with denial, rejection, dissuasion, and unnecessary antagonism—

No. He lifted his head and opened his eyes, dropping his hands to hang between his knees. *I haven't failed her.*

He stood, shaking away that which mentally threatened him. He couldn't let those thoughts or feelings surface. They served no purpose. He had to move past this setback and focus on the present, the future. And Kate...Kate was his present. His best friend, his confidant, his ride-or-die... She was counting on him. Needed him. Ryder was right. He was thinking too much and letting the behavior of others get under his skin and affect his own.

Now, more than ever, my focus has to be Kate. I know she's counting on us. On me.

And I refuse to fail her.

Chapter Two

Date unknown
Undisclosed location

Time was now a phantom. It no longer was something Kate knew how to measure, for she'd forgotten how to count. It no longer was something she could reminisce on, because both her waking and unconscious thoughts turned murky, eventually leading to blackness. It no longer was something she could deduce from the opening or shutting of doors or the temperature of her environment, because she could not bring herself to care. What little vitality she had left leeched from her, and she'd nearly become a phantom herself.

What she was going through wasn't surviving. But it also wasn't death. No, Fate would never be so kind. So merciful.

What she suffered now was prolongation.

Santiago and his henchmen were prolonging her life for the sheer elation her torture brought them. And they excelled in letting her fester. Rot. Wallow. Every moment she was awake was another span of time in which she was tormented beyond her mental capacity. And for what? Because they thought she knew something? If only it were so simple. If she'd known something this would've been over a long time ago.

But she didn't. And it wasn't.

She gave up hope for a rescue. Whenever she was awakened to be brutalized the space was different than before, and she figured they were moving her nightly. One thing she couldn't fathom was why they wouldn't just kill her. She'd lost the will to live. Every moment she was cognizant she wished for death. Didn't they know she was a princess of nothing? She had no pull. No power. No one listened to her. No one beyond her father, her servants, and The Guard truly knew she existed. She had no friends. No relatives. She didn't matter. Why wouldn't they just let her die?

Kate just wanted to die.

She garnered she went from unconsciousness, to clarity, to madness frequently. The moments she could remember were fleeting, but distantly she heard herself crying, laughing, wailing. She was gracious her lucid moments were few and far between, because the pain...the pain...

The pain was a reminder she was still alive.

The pain was a reminder she could still feel.

The pain was a reminder though death was near, it was still so far away.

She stopped believing her father would scale whatever structure she was in and save her. Athair, Athair, *why have you failed me?* If she thought about how he abandoned her too long, it drove her nearer to the madness which called. *You've let me down. You've let me down the swiftest, the hardest. Because above all others I trusted you. My father. My own father...*

She stopped begging for dreams to take her away, to save her sanity. There were no dreams to be had; when she succumbed to oblivion the abyss was always black. Silently pleading to the watchers and The Creator continued to be pointless; they couldn't be pulled from their celestial palaces to see her well. It possibly had always been a fruitless endeavor. Kate lost her faith in so much, and her spirituality, it seemed, was suffering as well. For what otherworldly being could let one of its creatures descend into these dark, suffocating depths? Where was the empathy? Where was the concern? Where was the mercy?

There never was, nor would there ever be any.

Kate knew she didn't have much longer. She could feel it in her bones, in the sluggishness of her blood flow, in the muted electrical activity in her brain. Her mind, her spirit, her drive had been damaged beyond repair. She couldn't and wouldn't be, let alone remember, who she once was. She knew in her soul she would never be that female again. The life she once knew, once had, wasn't even a memory.

It was a work of fiction at best.

And what would she be known for? Being the spoiled daughter of Talorc, the fallen king of the vampires? She had no legacy of her own. She'd never made a difference to anyone or anything. She would be forgotten in time, as she deserved to be. She'd never been anything besides a waste of effort, time, and space.

Useless.

The only redeeming notion about her oncoming death was that she would finally meet her mother. She would pass through The Abeyance, as did all departed souls, and cross into Otherworld, where her soul would dwell for eternity. She hoped against hope her mother would be waiting for her. At the end of all her conscious moments, Kate would smile softly and welcome the ebon, picturing what her mother would say upon meeting her for the first time. She yearned for the faceless female to have empathy for her instead of disappointment, could try to understand that Kate held out for as long as she could…

She no longer feared insanity. She no longer feared death. Both were already upon her, and the darkness, the emptiness, the lonesomeness they brought wasn't so bad now that she'd learned to accept them. At least they weren't pain. Starvation. Coveting. *Cold.* So very, very cold. Those things were worse than anything else, and they were the blights that plagued her most, however fleeting they may be. She no longer felt things like embarrassment, or ambition, or optimism. She just *was*. A decaying carcass that took up space, used for the propagation of whatever the enemy wanted to produce.

At least where she was going, it would be quiet. It would be still.

No more pain, no more suffering, no more *feeling*.

Transient memories of times past swept up as though on a wave, threatening to submerge her with sentiment. She was desperate for the bliss brought on by the wayward recollections, tempted by the idea this would be the last she would have to endure. She allowed herself to drown in them, knowing she had to pay the price if she wanted salvation…

June 2021
Warwick

Kate stumbled out of the pool after Asha—Mora's daughter and Kate's best girlfriend—, laughing so hard she doubled over from a split in her side. She clutched her hands to her chest to keep her lime-green bikini in place, only a little buzzed from the moonshine she'd swiped from the pantry. A summer night twinkled above them, the moon new and the stars as old as time, and it was under their amused regard that the females fell into lounge chairs, wrapping themselves in fluffy towels. Neither could remember what was so funny but also neither cared, as the ebbs of the night carried them through in jovial bliss.

"I can't believe you did that!"

"I can't believe you *did that!" Kate fired back, wheezing with laughter. "We haven't done that since we were kids."*

"We used to do backflips off the top of the slide over and over and over again like it was nothing." Asha fell back in her chair, her hands on her stomach as she continued to laugh. "Now I'm pretty sure I pulled my back."

"I twisted my ankle," Kate said, causing Asha to lose herself to laughter once more. "Creator, we're so out of shape."

"Ugh." Asha reached for the pink moonshine they were sharing straight from the jar. She tipped it back to clear it to less than half and then said, "So out of shape."

She passed the jar to Kate, swaying slightly as she did so, her white bandeau bikini top slipping precariously. Kate giggled as she took it from her, tilting it back to take two hearty mouthfuls. She gagged, causing Asha to laugh once more, before she said, "This certainly isn't helping."

"Don't care." Asha snagged the jar back with a tottering sway, and both females dissolved into laughter once more.

Music thrummed from behind them at the outdoor bar area while a fire danced in the firepit between two long couches. The grill had cold hotdogs on it while the bar had two unattended plates of fries. Two beers had been left on the bar as well, their contents spent, next to phones that flared every once in a while with unseen notifications.

Kate whipped herself out of her towel as Gwen Stefani's Hollaback Girl *began to blare over the speakers. She jumped to her feet and began to dance, sliding to the edge of the pool in a less-*

than-elegant arc, causing Asha to choke on the moonshine in mirth.

"You're such a bad dancer." She struggled to sit up while sloppily arranging her top so it didn't cause a scene. "Careful you don't fall in too. Remember: old. *"*

Kate spun and swished her hips in a way that had Asha falling out of her lounger onto her hands and knees as she laughed, her towel forgotten on the ground. Kate laughed at her discombobulation, shimmying her way over to help Asha to her feet. The two clutched onto one another, grabbing each other's arms and screaming the lyrics into each other's faces as they danced, the rest of the world forgotten.

"Want to do the slide again?" Asha suddenly gasped, breaking away from Kate on unsteady feet. She reared back toward the pool and Kate grabbed her arm to stop her, and the two briefly broke out into laughter again.

"I love you so much," Kate told Asha, feeling a red blush of joy spread from her neck to her forehead.

"Love you too," Asha said, breaking away from Kate to scramble toward the slide. "I'm going for it!"

"I just want to float." Kate stumbled over to her inflatable, mumbling the lyrics under her breath as she shook her hips from side to side.

She was having too much fun to think about the trouble she was likely to be in with her father. Having returned from the nail salon later than what she originally told him, Kate was sure he was going to forbid her from leaving the manor again anytime soon. Even after sheepishly apologizing for their tardiness (of course while hiding Vietnamese coffees from Dim Sum Delights *behind their backs) the temperature of the house was still slightly cooler than usual—an obvious sign of her father's displeasure.*

She and Asha had holed up with blankets and popcorn in the in-home movie theater to watch the latest John Wick *movie to avoid him, but the females were never idle for long. When they'd finished, it had been Kate's rebellious idea to swipe some moonshine and roast hot dogs by the pool.* And it was a great idea. Who doesn't like hot dogs? Besides, I need to take advantage of the freedom while it lasts. Because it won't.

Kate walked to the edge of said pool, threw her float into the water, and then dove in, swimming languidly. She heard a

nearby splash that told her Asha had indeed gone down the slide, and Kate was just pulling herself through the bottom of the float to settle on top of it when an amused voice carried over the water.
"You shouldn't be drinking and swimming."

Kate swung her legs around so she laid comfortably atop her float while Asha broke the surface of the water, her eyes on the edge of the pool closest to the manor. Vadin was there dipping down on one knee, an elbow bent across said knee, as he winked at Asha. "You could drown. Might need saving. You know: mouth-to-mouth."

Asha and Kate both rolled their eyes so hard it floated them back. "I won't be counting on you, Mr. I'm-Scared-of-Water."

Vadin grinned, ascending to his full height, as Damian crept out of the shadows of the house, sliding the patio door shut behind him.

Kate's heart stopped and then began a staccato beat. Damian. Here. Tonight. *She couldn't stop a nervous hand from smoothing her hair, before restlessly moving to right the tiny triangles that covered her breasts.* I didn't think he was coming tonight. Was he supposed to? He never texted me. *Kate's eyes darted to her phone, and then back to him.* I checked. Didn't I?

She noticed immediately that he didn't spare her a look, his face tight but a mask of impassivity as he stood as still as stone with his hands in the pockets of his shorts. His dark hair curled around his angular face which boasted gleaming copper eyes and a sharp nose. His facial hair was neat, trimmed, a close beard and mustache combination that Kate had fantasized tickling the curves of her body too many times to count.

Though blaring music covered his footsteps, she would never not recognize his presence. Her skin always prickled while the fine hairs along her flesh rose and fire singed her nerves, right before his oceanic scent captured her senses and drowned her in him. *She faltered as the world burst forth with new life, new vibrancy, unabashedly captured by his lean, muscular frame.* Creator, *Kate thought as her body flared with a heat she couldn't control. Her very core panged with unrequited longing.* Why am I always like this around him?

She dipped her hands in the water and swished them so she floated as far away from him as she could get. I'm drunk. I can't be around him. *Who knows what I'll say. Still, a hunger settled in her chest, whispering to her to get closer instead.*

"I would brave the depths of any water for you," Vadin told Asha, and Kate groaned loud enough to shake the house as she spun in her pool float.

Asha swept some water toward Vadin, her long golden hair trailing behind her as she swam nearer to him. "You're stupid."

Kate gagged openly at the tone of Asha's voice; flirtation simmered just at the surface. The two had their flings here and there, remaining amicably civil in between trysts, never attaining anything more. Asha had once admitted to Kate she was glad it never turned into anything, as Vadin was too promiscuous for her tastes. Kate pointed out that she had no problem using him when she needed a private tête-à-tête, which made her just as promiscuous. Unashamed, Asha had grinned and refuted that Vadin never seemed to have a problem being used by her, either.

"What are you guys doing here? I thought you had training tonight."

"Done early." Vadin wiggled his eyebrows. "Came to see if you two wanted to go into the city."

Kate swallowed, again glancing at Damian. He stood near the bar staring at the muted widescreen TV showcasing a rerun of Friends. *Kate sensed restless unease from him, as his gaze flickered from the TV to the grill, the sound system, the fire pit—anywhere but the pool—while she stared at him brazenly. Her heart fluttered, and in her drunken state the butterflies that usually rushed her when he came around made her nauseous.*

"To go where?" Asha asked, sweeping long strokes through the pool. Kate noticed that Vadin watched her with narrowing eyes, his red-bearded grin turning mischievous.

"Wherever you want," he replied, obviously distracted by Asha's barely covered chest.

"We already went to the city," Kate cut in, spinning slowly on her float, which did nothing to help her nausea. She felt her fangs pierce her lower lip as her eyes trailed Damian's frame, astutely reminding her that it was due time she fed.

That explains the horniness, *she thought of the low coil she felt near her navel. She knew then and there she shouldn't be near him until she fed, and certainly not until after she'd sobered up. She wouldn't be able to control herself around him, and it was already getting harder and harder not to push him. She continually told herself that he would realize he wanted her as much as she wanted him one day, yet at this stage in their not-a-game, rampant hunger would only amplify her smoldering desire and arrogant confidence.* It can never be, *she reminded herself.* We're friends. Just friends. *And they would never be anything more than friends.* He's made it more than clear several times over. Which means no going into the city. Which means there goes my last chance at freedom. *Kate felt her mood souring quickly.*

"So?" Vadin asked, unperturbed by Kate's resistance. He was watching Asha as he spoke, and Kate could read the undertones of his emerald gaze easily. Her mood soured even more, irritated that Vadin had only one thing in mind and that it meant Kate would be relieved of her entertainment for the evening. "If we hurry we could hit up that dance spot you like to go to, Ash. It's only three."

"It's open until six, right?"

Vadin nodded, his grin widening to expose his fangs.

Asha looked at Kate, as if just remembering they were hanging out. "Want to go?"

Kate continued to spin with her float, her affect now flat. "No."

She could feel the look of dull indifference that Vadin shot Asha, almost as well as she could feel the look of apology that Asha returned it with. Feeling hurt, Kate maybe a little too drunkenly snapped, "You guys can just go."

"We came to get both of you," Vadin said, continuing to be unperturbed. "I thought it would be fun if we all went. Besides, Damian doesn't feel like being the third wheel tonight."

"Well, I don't want to be the fourth," Kate replied tartly, shoving herself out of her float. She drifted into the water and swam toward the ladder, pulling herself from the shallows with ease. As she wrung her hair with her towel and then wrapped it around her chest, she thought she heard a low rumble, but a quick glance at the sky revealed it was clear as ever.

"Kate where are you going?" Asha called, swimming to the edge of the pool to pull herself out. When she slipped Vadin grabbed her, and the two laughed, Asha losing herself to his covetous gaze.

Kate rolled her eyes, slipping her feet into her flip-flops as she swiped by Damian. As the fire within her flared, it took everything in her not to look at him. Ignore. Keep walking. Don't make eye contact. Creator, but it was getting increasingly difficult to ignore her feelings. How much longer could she pretend that his friendship was enough?

"Kate come on," Asha cried as Kate pulled open the sliding door and stepped into the air-conditioned room. "Don't be like that."

"Like what?" Kate stopped just over the threshold to pin Asha with a heated glare. "If you want to hang out with him it's fine, I don't care."

"You're being childish." Asha wrapped her own towel around her as she followed Kate, stopping a few feet away. The males made themselves busy looking at the TV screen as the females faced off. "Don't act like that."

"I'm not acting like anything." Kate's brow dropped to snarl her face with scorn. "I just don't want to go dancing. I was fine in the pool."

"Kate." Asha lowered her tone, her eyes turning pleading as she leaned toward her friend. "Just come with us. It'll be fun."

"For who?" Kate's eyes darted between Vadin and Asha. Asha well knew Kate's intimate desires concerning Damian...and how they would never come to fruition. That notion alone pissed Kate off even more, because she knew Asha was using her as a bridge to get into Vadin's bed. "I'm not stupid, Ash. I don't like being used to get what you want."

Asha glared at her. "That's low. I've never done that, and you know it."

Emboldened by drink, Kate replied, "You're doing it now."

"Kate," Asha turned pleading again; alcohol always made her a little whiny. "I just want to go out and dance. Have fun. I've been busy lately and you're always working out with Ryder. You've been taking it so seriously."

She said the last two words mockingly, and it stoked Kate's ire. "Well I don't want to go out," she said, her tone almost matching Asha's, causing the female to frown as Kate turned away. She tottered slightly, and Kate heard Vadin snort at her lack of footing.

"Shut up," Kate bit at him, her resentment and embarrassment getting the better of her. *"I know why you're here. Just take Asha and do what you so obviously want to do. No need to drag our sorry behinds with you."*

"Kate don't act like that—"

"Like what?" Kate asked Vadin, her eyes wide and unyielding.

"Like Asha said: childish," Vadin replied, slipping his hands into his shorts.

Kate glared at him like a ten-year-old but couldn't find a reply as her mind swirled. Instead, she turned on the lot of them and headed inside, slamming the sliding door in her wake.

An hour later Kate found herself miserable and alone at the kitchen island, sipping a warm mug of blood. Her earlier buzz had been displaced by her foul attitude, which blanketed her now in unreasonable sullenness. Her friends had departed not long ago to Bohemia, Vadin having acquired a reluctant Ryder and another one of Asha's friends to meet them there. Damian went as well, and Kate moodily assured herself that he would find a female to bed and bite.

Could have been you, her conscience prompted, and Kate wondrously got lost in a fantasy that replaced the faceless female Damian would find himself on top of later with visions of herself.

"I am relieved to see you are staying in."

Her reverie abruptly broken by her father, Kate lifted her eyes to watch Talorc head for the coffee pot that always held the brew warm and fresh. She grunted out a nonsensical response, lifting her mug to her lips. Freshly showered, her sage T-shirt had the words 'Hoeing Ain't Easy' on it with gardening utensils interspersed with flowers underneath, and her grey shorts left little to the imagination. Her long hair draped down her back to dry while her fuzzy-slippered feet perched on the bottom rung of the golden island chair. The forest-green upholstery beneath her was plush, yet Kate felt nothing but turmoil as she stared at the swirling gray veins of the marble countertop.

"I would have expected you to go out with them," Talorc commented, pouring coffee into his acquired mug. *"Summer is just starting."*

"You wouldn't have let me," Kate mumbled, not quite ready

to let go of her juvenile behavior from earlier.

Talorc paused after lowering the coffee pot back to the hot plate. "That is untrue, Kathryn. You know I give you plenty of leave."

"Only when you've had enough of me." Kate's tone was petulant before she sipped the blood that was now curdling in her belly.

Talorc frowned deeply. "Whenever you ask it, if it is within reason, I grant you freedom."

"Your version of it," Kate snapped back recklessly. "I always have to take someone with me. I always have to tell you where I'm going, when I'll be back, and give you updates along the way. I can never just have some space."

"For your own wellbeing," Talorc replied coolly, testing his black coffee. "There are always those that mean you harm."

Kate rolled her eyes, knowing her father hated it, but uncaring. "I have, like, three friends. I've never left Warwick. Up until a year ago you were still monitoring my computer usage."

"Not monitoring," Talorc rumbled, his own ire slightly piqued. "It was a measure of security."

"And an invasion of my privacy."

"I am aware you have no knowledge of anything outside of your current life, but there are many that would see me and mine own to harm."

Struck sharply by the truth of his former statement, Kate asked rhetorically, "Like?"

She knew the wraiths were an increasing problem. She'd heard the boys talking about them more recently and were working diligently to encourage her father to participate in their eradication. After months—truly, years—of stagnation and muteness from her father and no outward signs of him budging, Kate recently decided to take matters into her own hands. She'd begun to secretly concoct her own plan to put a stop to things before they could get started.

Flashing, Talorc's eyes moved from Kate to his coffee, as if memory swept him back in time. "You would do well to remain innocent."

"Says who!" Kate yelled, pushing back from the table. Her exasperation came to a head in that moment, and she glared at her

father. "Maybe in your opinion I can't do anything, but have you ever asked me *if I wanted more than the life I currently have?"*

"Why?" Talorc gestured about with his mug, indicating the entirety of the manor. *"What more could you possibly want?"*

Aghast that he would ask, Kate couldn't respond.

Purpose, *she thought dismally. She was tired of living a sad life, a pathetic life, an aimless life. Tired of dwelling on her worthlessness, which as of late led her to feel furiously resentful more times than not. Patience had never been a virtue of hers, and it irked her to be inactive to the point of stagnancy. She occupied her time at home by hiking, running, or exercising, and had a myriad of hobbies. But her father was right: she couldn't remember a single time in her life when she wanted for anything. She had the best education growing up: lessons in music, language, geography, mathematics, etiquette, and so much more, from the most gifted beings her father could find. She knew the* Elden Edicts, *the laws that sustained the vampires, by heart and could recite any with ease. She'd never lifted a finger in a day of labor. She had but to bat an eye and her father would provide her with the most whimsical of her desires. But it was all so...boring, anymore. She wanted more. She wanted* intention.

"You desire for not," Talorc reminded her, and his unfeeling tone made Kate angrier than she needed to be. "You ask, and you receive. You have everything you require right here. Others are constantly at your beck and call. You shop as if your very life depends on it. You are chauffeured around at your leisure. Tell me, Kathryn, what more could you possibly want?"

Choice. Independence, *Kate wanted to scream. Her father was right—she had everything she could possibly desire at her fingertips.*

And it made her want to rip her hair out.

"I guess nothing," Kate bit out sarcastically, jumping down from the kitchen stool.

"Kathryn," Talorc said, his tone edged with caution.

Irritated, Kate grabbed her mug a little too forcefully, the blood sloshing within. "What?" she nipped, turning flaring eyes to Talorc. "Going to tell me I'm being childish, too?"

Talorc lifted a single brow but said nothing.

Huffing, Kate made to leave the kitchen. She didn't want to deal with her father. She didn't want to be reminded of her confinement, how she would always bend to her father's will and how she would never truly know herself *because of it. How everyone else could always do what they wanted at the blink of an eye, but she would always have to ask. No matter how hard she pushed, no matter what she said, no matter how often she begged, it would never change. Abruptly she felt tired, and the fire that resounded within her receded, curbed by melancholy.*

Talorc said not one word in her wake, leaving Kate feeling hollow as wrathful tears burned in her eyes. For so many reasons they clamored, and for so many more she would not let them fall.

None of them are worth it. *She took the stairs to her room stormily with her mug of blood and her cell phone. She glanced at the screen, noting the time to be nearing five o'clock in the morning and a missing text from Asha.*

Miss you. Wish you were here. Not the same without your terrible two-step.

Kate ducked the screen away, refusing to reply. She was too tumultuous with emotions and knew her response would only ignite more anger. She felt volatile and vulnerable, and she trudged into her room on heavy feet, slamming the monstrous door as best she could behind her. She placed her mug of blood on her bedside table, threw her phone down next to it, then flopped belly-down onto her bed, shrieking into the linen.

If you don't want to be treated like a youngling then stop acting like one, *her conscience chided, and Kate grabbed a pillow to hug to her middle as she rolled over to glare at the drapery above her bed. Her brow softened a moment later as the tears she desperately tried to keep at bay began to slide out of the corners of her eyes.*

Just once, just once I wanted to be treated like an equal, *she thought.*

You need to change your behavior if you want to be taken seriously, *her conscience said softly.* The definition of insanity is doing the same thing over and over and expecting a different result.

I bet my mother would fight for what she wanted, *Kate thought, wishing she'd known the female for any span of time, even*

27

a short one. I bet my father wouldn't have told her 'no' in any capacity. If she was anything like the sparse rumors I've heard, she was denied nothing, the great love of his life…

Kate's melancholy returned tenfold, steeped richly in longing. Her tears began to fall like torrential rain, while feelings— about Asha, Damian, Talorc, bust mostly her mother—swallowed her whole, distancing her to a place she so rarely dwelled for fear it would overcome her normally jubilant nature. Every once in a while, Kate let herself mourn the female she never knew, yet if she did it too often it would do nothing but make her infinitely miserable, and that just wasn't Kate. On a night like tonight, however, wallowing in pity was easier than she wanted it to be— and she deserved it all the same.

That same pity sunk unrelenting claws into her then, ripping her from the undercurrent of memory to suffocate her with stifling self-loathing. *So much was taken from me for so long. I let myself be subjugated for so long. I have no one to blame but myself.*

If she had tears, she would've cried them, yet the pinch of dehydration was painful as her body worked to do something it no longer could. A wheeze of a sob seized her lungs, but Kate could only gasp as air, on muscle memory, manipulated her frame. She fell into darkness not soon after, exhaustion finally taking over. It was the only mercy she was granted, and she was eager for the claim it had on her, for it meant she had to feel no more.

Chapter Three

January 2022
Ursuline

T he night was cold and volatile, and reeked of death. A human lead had brought The Guard to a small, abandoned country house deep in the woods outside of a rural town about four hours from Warwick. They'd learned Santiago was supposed to meet his drug mules here and had planned to ambush him, but Damian and the others swiftly realized the lead was just another set up by Santiago. He *wanted* them here in this position, under the gnarled hand of his might.

Damian repressed a snarl and narrowed his copper eyes on his target. Santiago sat opposite just to his right, leaned back in a folding chair as if he weren't surrounded by five extraordinary vampires bent on his annihilation. The male wore a revolting smile on his face as he sucked on a cigarette, chatting with Ryder as if he hadn't a care in the world. Damian, on the other hand, pushed his tongue against the roof of his mouth to waylay his thoughts, his words, and curled his hands into fists to stave off the worst of his fury.

My chance will come, he thought to himself through the haze that lingered just at his periphery. *I'll get to Santiago. I won't fail her.*

Patience was indeed a virtue, yet one that Damian was slowly losing his grasp on. Because before him on the hard floor of the country house not only was Ryder's beloved, Taryn, but *Kate.*

It was surreal to think all their work could culminate in this moment.

It was damning to think they were still so far.

And now Taryn was involved. Damian glanced at Ryder and noted the male had turned pale, and his jaw was sliding from side to side as he held back his own aggression. Damian felt the rippling waves of ire from where he was standing, as they clashed and roiled with his own. He knew Ryder was beyond rage, toeing the precipice of rationalization. None of them thought they would be in this exact predicament, but that just went to show what lengths Santiago would go, teasing them with what he was capable of. He also knew however much The Guard wanted Kate safe, none of them wanted to endanger Taryn.

"Let me be clear, you will not find a way to take them both," Santiago said. "Either has been weakened to the point of rapid extinction. If you try to ensnare us, they both will be killed."

Damian felt his gut clench, then recoil. He glanced at Kate but couldn't bring himself to linger. When she'd been dragged down the stairs by two wraiths, her body *thunk*ing along every creaking step, he'd been rendered speechless, mindless. She was the very picture of horror, a living corpse. He hardly recognized her. If it weren't for the faintest trace of her lavender scent, he wouldn't have believed it was her.

Damian inhaled a steadying breath, drawing his eyes back to Ryder. *Focus. For Kate.* The male had pulled into himself, and shadows now lined his eyes, his mouth. Santiago had erred in making a beloved male choose between his soul and a dear friend. Santiago had erred in making *Ryder* choose. They would know blood this night. Damian's eyes flicked to where Ryder held his gun and watched as his gloved fingers discreetly repositioned themselves around the weapon.

It's about to go down.

Ryder opened his mouth to snarl at Santiago with nothing but fangs, "You can go fuck yourself." He raised his gun, trained it on Santiago, and fired from the ten feet that separated them.

Cyrus dove to cover the females while four of the countless wraiths converged on Ryder. Damian knew from their short standoff inside the country house there were five enemy vampires, including Santiago. There had been wraiths upstairs, on the main level, and if there was a basement he would assume there were some down there as well. Santiago had used some sort of cloaking ability to shield the wraiths' true numbers, usually telltale by their horrendous stench, so there could be more in the woods that surrounded the solitary abode. *Bring it.* Damian was itching for a fight, had been yearning for retribution since before they'd skewered him to the front of the fucking Tahoe.

Yet while wraiths were easy to kill, in high numbers they could be annoying. And they'd begun working together, going against their mindless nature, which could be even more so. The vampires that were present would prove to be even more challenging to annihilate, as it took increased skill and preciseness.

It was a vampire that came at him then, and Damian was whipped back to reality as he dodged a swiping knife, stumbling backward. He wore a Kevlar vest beneath his long-sleeved shirt so at least his heart would be protected, but as a vampire himself he still had to worry about being accosted with other weapons that would slow him down. A bullet to the brain would be cumbersome, an arcing throat slice would be disheartening, but a full decapitation could be fatal. If he avoided that, bleeding out, a stake through the heart, and the eventual sunrise, he could live to see this night through.

And be there for her. For Kate.

She needed him. And he could save her. *Finally.*

They could close the door on this gruesome chapter of their lives and move on.

Damian palmed his knife and voiced his frustrations in the rumblings of a growl, pushing forward with an elbow, followed by his weapon. The vampire hissed and jumped back, but not before crouching and pouncing at Damian like a leopard in an attempt to bring him to the ground. As other fights broke out around the open space of the house, Damian caught the vampire and together they toppled to the floor, rolling before crashing into a decaying wall.

Quickly, Damian recalled the layout of the structure: he had broken in through a side window adjacent to a fireplace. A living space sprawled the length of the house before ending at a curling set of stairs and a decrepit kitchen, where Cyrus had come through. Noir had broken in from the opposing side of the house, while Ryder and Vadin had come in through the front door. The house was crumbling, barely standing, and smelled of animal feces and rotting wood. There was a second floor to the home where Damian was sure the roof sagged in, while the walls and floors of both levels left little to the imagination in their decay. A porch was the preamble to the house, though was hard to traverse from the corroded wood. The structure had no running water or electricity and had been exceptionally hard to get to.

At least we won't be bothered by the police, Damian thought as he took a knee to the chin with a grunt. He grabbed his assailant's knee above and below the joint and twisted, eliciting a sharp curse and a striking move by the other leg. Damian flattened himself on the ground to evade it, then relinquished his hold to roll, propelling off the wall with his feet, before popping himself onto his hands and knees and springing to his feet once more.

It was instinctual: he looked for Kate in the spare moment he had. When she couldn't be found after a terse glance, he refocused on his foe. The vampire turned his back to the wall and lowered his stance to charge at Damian once more. Eager for the outlet of his anger and frustration, Damian adopted a similar stance and revealed a large set of fangs in a vicious grin.

"Let's go mother fucker."

The vampire, a large indistinct male that Damian didn't recognize nor care to, crossed the space between them in a single launching stride. Damian met the male in a clash that had his own teeth rattling, and they stumbled back several paces before crashing into a small table. Damian remotely heard glass shattering and felt the shards of it cutting into his jeans as they again rolled across the floor, through the seeping blood from the human lead Santiago had offed earlier. Damian felt no remorse for the loss of her life, had hated her the moment she'd surfaced in this godforsaken situation.

Worthless, waste of spa—

He grunted as the vampire kneed him in the chest, then pulled back his right fist to smash into Damian's face. Damian turned his head one way, then the other, then back again to miss several firings, and quickly grew bored playing dodge. On the fourth draw back of his opponent's arm he captured the male's fist, ripped his arm to the side, and headbutted him in the face. The vampire howled and reared back, giving Damian the leverage he needed to get his feet underneath him and kick the male away.

With another curling sweep of his legs, Damian got to his back without using his arms. He pivoted in a circle but was caught mid-turn by two snapping wraiths. One immediately sunk its fangs into his arm while the other swept him from his feet, and they all went crashing through the front door and onto the porch. Damian grappled for the hilt of his dagger strapped to his thigh, his fingers working with years of precision to unholster and handle it. He quickly stabbed the wraith who still had its jaw locked around his forearm through the neck, which was enough to dismantle the being from his person. The wraith fell back, baying its turmoil as it tried to staunch the flow of its blood while Damian swiveled on his back to the other wraith, who had leapt back into an assaulting crouch.

Damian had but a moment to ponder, *trying to save itself? How? Why?* Wraiths were mindless, soulless beings, humans risen from the dead to serve their master's whims. Those whims were born from strident hate and several millennia's worth of vengeance from powers far removed from Earth and the beings that inhabited it. The wraiths' main prey was humans, as they could feed on nothing else to survive. Damian had been fighting them for centuries, having been given his own second chance as long as he committed to a new purpose: protect humankind. He knew wraiths as well as his own self.

Focus. Find Kate.

The wraith he hadn't stabbed yet pounced on him and Damian rolled to his left, which unfortunately catapulted him down the rickety front stairs and sent his dagger spiraling into the darkness. He tucked his chin so he didn't bite his tongue, but wasn't able to get his footing until he rolled into the dirt at the bottom. *Unlucky that,* he thought, shaking out his hair as he sprang to his feet. He rotated his shoulders, but that was all he had time to do before both wraiths jumped from the porch.

Getting old, he thought drolly, his feet quickly getting him out of their trajectory. At the same moment he reached into a pocket on his vest and withdrew a gun to unload a full magazine into the closest wraith. With an expert hand he exchanged the mag for another, and in the two seconds it took to do so the former wraith disintegrated into inky vapor.

The other wraith skidded to a halt near a large SUV, and roared its fury as its fingers penetrated the hood of the vehicle. Damian frowned, curled an upper lip, and with one expert shot silenced the demon with a bullet through the skull.

Annoying as fuck, he thought, just as he was shot in the shoulder from behind.

Also annoying as fuck. Thankfully the vest had thick straps, and he turned toward where the shot had been fired to see the vampire he'd dispatched a few moments before standing on the porch. He was backlit by orange embers, and Damian had the startling sentiment that it faintly smelled like fire.

Kate.

Fear sliced through him, sharp and sickening. *Have to get to Kate.* He took a step, reaching for the dilapidated railing that bordered the stairs, his feet suddenly unsteady. *Is she still in there? She could burn...* He tucked his gun back into his vest and swallowed back the trepidation that sluiced over his limbs.

"Not so fast," the vampire warned, and Damian watched as he *disappeared.*

He couldn't process a second thought as a thick arm wedged itself around his throat from behind. His immediate reaction was to reach up and try to siphon a hand or at least some fingers at the crook of his enemy's elbow, but the vampire tightened his grip. Damian grunted, dropping his stance to offset the other male, but he wouldn't be thrown so easily.

"Think you're so great because you're one of *them?*" the vampire hissed, using his other hand to tighten his hold even more. "The elite five, The Guards of Nightfall: the vampire king's handpicked highwaymen, doing his dirty work since the dawn of time. Males of legend, whose battle prowess and warmongering transcend centuries. Only to be ended in this shithole."

Damian's vision blackened, and not because he was angry. The male actually had him in a hold that he couldn't get out of. He tried to slide his legs into a wider stance so he could throw the male over his shoulders, but the vampire had Damian's legs locked between his own. Damian tried again to drop his weight, but the male held him in place and wouldn't allow the counter.

"I'm going to peel the skin from your face like I did hers," the vampire whispered to him.

Damian felt his fangs pulse and his heartrate spike. *Kate?* He bucked against the hold the male had on him while black and white dots flickered across his waning vision.

"I'm going to pluck your nails off, one by one. When they

start to grow back I'll cut off the whole finger. I watched hers regrow once or twice. I started doing it just to see how fast she *could* regrow them. I lost interest after that; slow process and all."

Damian's eyes widened as he struggled to free himself.

"Did you know the longer you starve a vampire, the harder it is for them to regrow things? Oh," the vampire chuckled, as if recalling a delight. "Did you know that the organs regrow themselves *outside* of the body if they're still attached? I could show you. Don't worry though; I'll puncture both eardrums so you won't hear yourself scream. For her, I only did the one."

I'm going to kill him.

Saturated wrath overtook him. With the last of his strength, Damian threw his hips to one side and brought his fist and arm down like a sledgehammer into the vampire's groin. The vampire let go immediately and leaned forward as he reached to cup himself, and Damian pulled back his elbow to smash his nose through his face. The vampire reared back fully, clasping at his appendage with both hands, and Damian whirled while sucking in coughing breaths and reaching forward with both hands. He grabbed the vampire by the head and brought his face down to meet his knee one, two, three, four times before he threw him to the side, near the tree line.

Damian stalked toward his dagger while withdrawing his gun. The vampire was groaning and rolling onto his back, and Damian wasted no time in unloading the full mag of his gun into the vampire's genitals. He screamed in pain, which Damian silenced with a dagger through the tongue, then the back of his throat, and then the very top of his spinal cord.

Damian crouched down beside the male, pushing his dagger in farther as the male choked around the thick, steel blade. He writhed in the dirt, unable to move from the waist down as he bled out into the driveway, his hands flapping against Damian's shoulders in a sad attempt to free himself.

"I would have you meet the sun," Damian twisted the blade and the vampire shrieked as blood spurted from his mouth. He stopped flailing abruptly as his spinal cord was completely severed. "But that death would be too kind."

Damian pushed the blade until the hilt propped open the male's jaw, pinning him to the ground. The male choked on his own blood, unable to move his hands to free himself because of his new disability. Coupled with the bilateral femoral exsanguinations, it wouldn't be long until he fully bled out. He wouldn't be able to rejuvenate from the compounded injuries.

Damian slowly stood to his towering height, shaking off the last of his disorientation from being throttled. He rubbed a gloved hand over his throat and winced, knowing it would take a full day until the bruising would fade completely, but that was the least of his concerns. He looked back toward the house while he loaded another mag into his gun and saw Vadin locked in his own fight against a vampire male bigger than either of them. Lurching movement from his right had his gaze pivoting, and Damian saw two wraiths barreling from the woods, heading straight for them.

Oh fuck this.

With a precision he'd adapted over years of practice, Damian raised his gun and pierced the skull of the first wraith. Its body fell over the railing, crumbling to the floor, before evaporating into smoke. The other wraith propelled itself over the railing but instead of continuing for Vadin it slid to a stop and fixated its hollow gaze on Damian, its red eyes cutting through the darkness like cinders.

Briefly, Damian glanced behind the wraith. His nose picked up on it before his eyes: *fire.* The inner building was aflame, and with the way the house was it wouldn't be long before it succumbed completely to ash.

Where is Kate? Cyrus had to have gotten her. But what about Taryn?

Accessing another recessed holster, Damian drew the other dagger he kept with him and twirled it skillfully over each finger before gripping the hilt. The wraith wrapped decaying fingers over the porch railing before hauling itself over feet-first, and Damian shook his head with a shuttered grimace before launching himself at his newest foe.

Too late Damian noticed the creature carried its own weapon. The crowbar connected with his left knee with the force of a torpedo, and Damian crumpled to the ground on a bent ankle. *Mother. Fucker.* Bile rose in his throat before he forced it back down, and he rolled toward the stairs only to come face to face with his forgotten dagger. With a snarl he palmed them both, pushed through the pain, and jumped back to his feet while swinging a wide discharge with both weapons.

His aim was true, and maybe a little lucky as well. His first blade sliced the wraith across the chest while the other he raised a handbreadth more to slice up through the flesh of his foe's throat. Ruby blood spurted like a fountain, coating Damian in an arc, and Damian drove forward with both daggers and plunged them into the wraith's chest, effectively eliminating it permanently.

He turned back toward the porch just in time to see Vadin going back inside. Flames now curled from the windows in the front of the house, and Damian took a step forward to go after Vadin. He was halted, however, by a firm grip on his non-injured shoulder.

"Vadin is getting Ryder." It was Noir, and he was heaving with exertion and covered in various scrapes from his own battle. "The house is going to blow. There's an old oil tank out back. We have to go."

"But Kate," Damian panted, brushing sweat from his face. The heat from the flames licked at him, and he glanced back at the house just as a section of roof fell in. "Where's Kate?"

"Cyrus has Kate," Noir said. "Taryn is with Ryder. Now go."

Damian's racing heart sped up. *Cyrus has Kate. Cyrus has Kate!* His eyes flared as he nodded once; he didn't need to be told again. He took off into the woods, leaving the others behind without a second thought.

Damian ran as fast as he could through the trees, though his limp was pronounced. That damn wraith had gotten a good hit at his knee, which he was sure was close to dislocated, but he had to push himself harder, faster, further, to meet with Cyrus. It had taken them over a half an hour to access the country house from where they parked their cars at the library, the forest frolic not an easy one. Injured, it would take longer.

I have to get to him. To get to her.

Damian's breath sawed out of him in sharp thrusts, and he struggled to control the pattern through the elation and relief he felt. He had to focus a little bit longer, just a little bit longer. He had to endure. *She* needed him. He could finally help her. She was finally safe. He could hardly wrap his mind around it. He felt like shouting for joy, but he had to contain himself. He had to *focus*. Because beyond what he could believe or even fathom, they'd finally been successful this night.

Cyrus has Kate!

Damian pumped his legs with his newfound adrenaline, his arms syphoning at his sides. His hair blew back from his face, the blood of both himself and his enemies drying with his efforts. His wounds screamed for attention, but Damian wouldn't spare anything, not a single thought. *I have to get to her.* His breath left his lungs on trained exhales, passing through pursed lips. *She needs me.* Did he spot Cyrus? Or was the gleam of the moon playing tricks on his battered mind? He pushed harder, harder, *harder* still.

I have to get to her.

There. Just ahead. Through the trees he dodged on shaking legs. He could see them. Cyrus. *Kate.* A sound escaped him, one he didn't know was bred from joy or pain. It didn't matter. He was pulling up behind Cyrus, now beyond desperate to ensure Kate's safety and viability going forward.

She can't... No. Not after all this effort...

He refused to think like that. He was smarter than that, just like Kate was stronger than anyone gave her credit for. She'd *survived.* She was alive! As he swerved around tipping branches and tilted trunks, brittle bark cracking in his wake, he still couldn't fathom it.

The weather had turned in their favor with the wind at their backs and the clouds dispersed, making Damian feel like he made it back to the cars in record time. He burst from the line of trees and leapt over the small patch of grass that separated the library's parking lot from the forest, wincing when the movement jarred his battered knee. Cyrus had already pulled open the back hatch of his ancient behemoth of a Land Rover and Damian rushed to the posterior of the vehicle, his breaths lashing out of him like the winds of a hurricane.

"How is she," he demanded immediately, holding himself up on the bumper of the car with one hand while he helped Cyrus clear a space in the back of the vehicle for Kate.

Cyrus didn't answer, too busy with his task and holding Kate. Damian glanced over his hold to look at her, but Cyrus began to maneuver her into the confines of the vehicle which prevented Damian from getting a good look. He did notice, however, that she was completely naked, and with a clenched jaw he wrenched a utility blanket from the depths of the trunk to cover her.

"Let me get in there. I can pull her in. It'll be easier than pushing." Damian pulled himself into the SUV with a great effort to keep his knee from sustaining more injury. Cyrus paused in his endeavors and waited for Damian to situate himself with his back to the seats, and without saying a word they worked together to get Kate more carefully into the car.

Damian reached forward to slide his hands underneath Kate's back. He flinched at the feel of her shoulder blades cutting through her flesh, at the way her ribs protruded from the front and the back. His stomach rolled and then knotted as her shaved head lolled to her sunken chest, which he quickly covered with the utility blanket. "I got you," he told her softly as he reached an arm over the backseat to retrieve the first aid kit they'd brought with them, using his other arm to cradle her between his spread legs. "I got you Kate."

Cyrus carefully pushed her legs into the vehicle as Damian propped the kit next to him, popped the lid, and retrieved the flashlight within. The vehicle had no running lights, and he wanted to make sure she was as comfortable as possible for the ride to the cabin. He placed the flashlight in his mouth after turning it on and turned back to face her, only to be stopped dead in his tracks.

"Creator be..." Cyrus breathed.

Kate's legs were mere sticks; not even skin, just bone. Gaping, unhealed wounds lined her calves, shaped as if someone had taken a blade and dug until sinew was visible. She was missing an assortment of toes, and her right foot was curled inward at an odd angle. Her left knee was sunken, and the bruises...the bruises...

Cyrus peeled back the blanket slightly to bare a thigh, and revealed what were so obviously fingerprint bruises that Damian nearly retched. She also had fang marks of varying sizes and shapes puncturing her; some dragged down her sallow skin as if she'd tried to get away...

Panicking, Damian turned back toward the first aid kit and began tearing through the supplies. As he shifted, her head fell back, and Cyrus's sharp intake of breath had him turning back to reangle the flashlight on her.

Her hair had been shaved down to her skull, which was nearly visible beyond the thin layer of skin keeping it hidden. Her cheeks were so concave that he was sure they touched her fangs. The aforementioned appendages were shriveled behind parted lips that were as pale as her skin, and drier than the winter tree bark outside. Her crystalline blue eyes no longer sparkled but stared at the roof of the car in dull, sightless abandon. Dark circles hovered under her eyes, not to be confused with the countless bruises, scrapes, scabs, and gashes she sported in various stages of nonhealing.

She was…nothing. Damian faltered at tearing open medical supplies, lifting a trembling hand to her throat to check for a pulse.

He wavered, unsure if he wanted the truth.

"She needs blood," Cyrus said, pulling Damian from his nightmarish reverie. "And she needs it now."

Damian splayed two fingers just beneath her jawline, pressing against the carotid artery. Her pulse was thready and irregular, a staccato of beats he could barely feel. He quickly moved his hand to her chest to feel the rise of her breath and noted that it was similarly abnormal.

No.

She can't…

There's too much… She can't…

Without a second thought he brought his wrist to his mouth and tore at his muddied forearm, opening a wound deep enough to fount blood. *If she can smell blood, she will feed.* He pulled Kate into his lap so her head fell back against his bent knee and placed his wrist to her parted lips. *It's intrinsic. The nature of the vampire. All I have to do is offer.*

"Come on Kate," he urged in a whisper. "Come on."

Cyrus began opening bottles of sterile water and packages of bandages to tend to the worst of her wounds. Damian heard him let out a slow breath when he noted a particularly nasty wound on her ankle had maggots crawling in it. Damian wouldn't be deterred, and cupped Kate's chin and tilted her head to the side before using his thumb to prop open her jaw. His blood spouted from his self-inflicted wound haphazardly across her cheeks, her chin, before he appropriately angled the limb to align with her lips.

She didn't move.

"Come *on* Kate," he snapped at her. His own frantic heartbeat resounded in his ears, thundering so grievously it interrupted whatever thoughts he tried to string together. "You didn't make it this far to…"

Creator, but he couldn't finish the sentence aloud.

He pushed his wrist to her mouth and used his other hand to rub her throat in an effort to coax her to swallow. Too soon the wound at his wrist began to seal itself, and again he tore at his flesh, more viciously than the last time. Cyrus continued to bandage what he could, though he quickly used all the supplies they had.

She still didn't move.

"Kate!" Damian shook her slightly, frustrated and fearful and fucking *failing*. He wrapped his free arm around her shoulders and hefted her up, desperate to make her respond.

"Kate *please*…"

He felt his chest recoil and then expand before tightening once more. His breath continued to saw out of him and sounds that he was unused to making traversed his dried lips. *Kate please.* As he expended more and more of his blood, the injuries he'd sustained during the altercation clambered for attention, one after another, each louder than the last. But he paid them no mind. He couldn't. Kate needed him. She needed him. He couldn't fail her.

He had done nothing *but* fail her for so long…

"Kate…" Her name choked him, and he sputtered further, "*Please*…"

She still didn't respond.

Cyrus suddenly whipped his head up and looked around the car. He must have sensed something because he said, "I'm shutting you in. Hold on tight." He pulled the door to the trunk down and slammed it shut, enclosing Damian in with Kate.

A second later Noir piled into the backseat and Cyrus pulled into the driver's. With a roar the engine came to life and faintly, Damian was aware of Ryder's Porsche flying into action as well.

"She's not well," Noir said to Cyrus as Damian continued to silently plea with Kate to drink. "I don't think she'll make it."

Noir suddenly looked back at Damian, and Damian belatedly realized he must have made a sound of contempt.

"Taryn," was all that Noir supplied, and turned back to face the front of the now racing vehicle.

Not Kate, Damian thought in relief. *He's not talking about Kate. We have time. I have time.*

I can save her.

When his wrist again subsided in providing his blood, he rearranged Kate in his arms to sit her up, hoping gravity would pull some of his sustenance into her. He rubbed her chest, murmuring to her words he would never recall. With his other hand he palmed her forehead so her head stayed upright while continuing to vigorously rub her sternum, and then each of her arms, as if the added warmth would help stimulate her.

"How long until we reach where we're staying?" he called to Cyrus.

"Fifteen minutes. Need to avoid the town. The explosion alerted the force."

There was an explosion? I didn't even hear it. Shit. Damian redoubled his efforts, holding Kate to him so steadfast that each vertebra of her spine bit into the swells of his chest. Again emotion threatened to still him, but he pushed the sentiments away so he could focus on reviving her.

Because...

Because I have to.

He savagely opened the radial artery on his other wrist and put her head back against his shoulder while propping open her jaw once more. He shoved his wrist so hard against her mouth that not one drop of blood was forfeit. While he continued to murmur to her words of encouragement, he bound his other arm across her chest to hold her to him, so desperately afraid to let her go. He sloped his good leg over her own and let his other sprawl before him, allowing himself to be, to *feel* closer to her than he ever had. He lost track of time as they sat there, the world having faded around him to bear nothing but her.

Kate.

Kate...

The universe spun back into action as Cyrus pulled the Land Rover to a grinding halt in front of the cabin they were using for shelter while in Ursuline. A flood light spilled illumination across the gravel driveway as it was triggered by the movement, and another flickered on as Vadin pulled Ryder's Porsche to just in front of the door. Noir leapt from the car to go and help Ryder as

Cyrus came around to Damian and Kate, propping open the trunk with a tremulous hand.

"Anything?"

Damian merely looked at him, and by Cyrus's grim facial expression Damian knew he felt as haunted as he looked.

"Let's get her inside."

Damian allowed Cyrus to pull Kate to him, into his arms, before he slid over the rear of the car and dangled his legs above the ground. He used the side of the SUV to keep him upright as he tested his weight on his feet; finding all was well enough, he loped after Cyrus.

The stairs to the cabin were few, yet Damian grappled the railing as if he were climbing The Great Wall of China. He hobbled after Cyrus as the male struggled to open the door; when Damian approached, he relinquished the task to him and Cyrus took Kate over the threshold. Damian was hot on his heels, flipping light switches as he went, eager to return to his task of revitalizing the female.

Cyrus placed Kate delicately on the single couch in the sizeable living room and Damian dropped heavily on the floor next to her head. He wasted no time in opening his vasculature once more, and while Cyrus maneuvered Kate's head onto a pillow, Damian pressed his wrist to her mouth. Seeing they were situated, Cyrus left them to bound back outside, to do what Damian couldn't care less.

"Come on Kate you can do this," Damian insisted, moving his free hand to rub her chest once more. "I believe in you. We all believe in you. You've made it this far. *So far.* Believe in yourself now. We're here for you. *I'm* here for you."

A faint sound, a breath more than a cry, ricocheted between his ears. Damian's eyes flew open to their fullest extent as he said on an exhale, "*Kate?*"

He felt the feeblest of movements against his skin, her sallow lips brushing against his flesh. He hollered a sound of triumph as he turned to face her fully, putting his weight on his hip as he rubbed her chest with vigor.

"Kate! It's me, Damian!"

He felt the brush of her hand, so weak that he almost missed it. She tilted her head slightly toward the sound of his voice and the breath rushed out of him in a way that told him he had been holding it for only Creator knew how long.

"Yes! Me. *Damian*." He pushed his wrist to her mouth more urgently. "Take from me. You need it. Take it all. Everything. You have my *everything*."

Her lips retracted and then closed in on his skin. He felt her tongue brush once, twice, as if hesitant to indulge. But then, on a purely animalistic surge that was bred in survival, her fangs sluiced into his flesh, and she began to take from him in long pulls of necessity.

Damian felt the hot swell of tears in his eyes as he laughed. He moved his hand from her chest to her head, over the peach fuzz that had been left behind. He began stroking her forehead as she took from him, took everything she needed *from him*.

"Kate…" He laughed once more, the sound tumbling out of him uncontrollably.

We did it. Finally, blissfully, they were the victors. He closed his eyes, and the weight of everything he'd been holding onto since the start of all of this nonsense weeks ago lifted from his shoulders.

We finally did it.

Chapter Four

Present day · February 2022
Warwick

Damian flipped and ricocheted off the edge of his pool, beginning a new lap. He'd lost count how many times he repeated the maneuver. How long he'd been out in the brisk February air. How frequently the same thoughts crossed his mind.

How can she be so selfish? After everything we did for her? After everything I did for her? We went through so much for her. Endlessly. Every night was something different, something more dangerous, more challenging. For her. And this is how she repays us?

Over.

And over.

And *over*.

Creator take him, but three weeks had gone by. *Three weeks* and she hadn't made a single move to come out of her room.

He swam with even more fervor, his strokes a swirling tempest to match his mind.

The night after Kate's rescue, Talorc had met them at the cabin in Ursuline. He'd arranged safe transportation for Kate to come home after she'd stabilized enough to do so. The Guard each made it out of the battle at the country house to see another night, however Taryn had lost her life. Ryder spent three full days invoking the watchers to have her made into a vampire, with his pleas culminating in a visit from the almighty Oleander. The watcher relayed she would rise a vampire on the night of the new

45

moon, Ryder's wishes having been received—a feat in itself. While beloveds weren't rare, the making of a vampire was, as the watchers seldom made it of importance in this day and age. They were hardly involved in anything to do with Earth and its inhabitants anymore.

They're just as selfish as she is, Damian thought, and the bite of it had him feeling guilty, but the sentiment was fleeting. *They made us. They gave us purpose. And then they deserted us.*

Even The Creator, the god of them all, had abandoned them. By Its own hand It first made Earth, and eventually watchers to inhabit it. The Creator then fashioned humans, though shortly after became aloof of the progression of mankind and removed Itself, leaving the watchers in charge of Earth and all its facets. It fell to them to mind humankind and guide them through their unique life paths; they excelled in doing so, and in turn humans flourished. For centuries the balance between good and evil, right and wrong, light and dark—*duality*—was kept peacefully.

However, when the tyrant Adhamh began raising corpses from the dead to kill humans, the watchers had to turn to making vampires to defend them. The notion sat ill with the watchers at the time, but after they learned Adhamh was going as far as to bribe humans with immortal life after they sacrificed themselves to his plight, they had to act. With the mysterious help of what some whispered was magic, they learned of the tainted way Adhamh was creating wraiths and morphed it into one they could utilize on their own. They could think of little else to do, with no direction from The Creator, who continued to remain removed.

Yet they also knew the action could provoke It to come back and smite them all. But duality had to be maintained. And so, when all stayed silent from Astra, the watchers continued to make vampires—humans who died by natural death and pledged their new life to justice—and they were in turn able to curb the wraith population.

As vampires continued to triumph, time brought with it passivity and easy regulation. Within that time the watchers receded from their duties nearly altogether. Only through Talorc, who spoke on behalf of the vampire nation, was there continued communication. Yet after Talorc's wife was brutally murdered, he himself became removed, refusing to be the leader he was born to be. Simultaneously, the watchers became distanced and uncaring, resulting in mounting trouble and chaos on Earth, which left Talorc and The Guard in the position they were in now.

Oleander recently confirmed this burgeoning ordeal went beyond the politics of the vampires on Earth, beyond what even the watchers could currently comprehend; they were struggling to stay abreast. While they were immortal, omnipotent, and powerful beyond measure, their lack of interaction with the vampires and guidance of humankind saw them just as derelict as Talorc once was. It was only thanks to the budding war and the knowledge imparted to him by Oleander that Talorc was setting out for Canada once more…leaving Kate to rot in her room without any sort of encouragement or support.

What a fucking mess.

Damian met the other side of his pool and spun again, trudging through the heated water with angry strokes.

Talorc is leaving. Kate is wallowing. Ryder is encumbered with introducing Taryn into the vampire world. All the while the wraiths rage on, and Santiago—who disappeared into thin air at the country house—could still be at large.

The Guard's healing had come and gone, and Damian was eager to get back on the streets and start making headway into all that was left behind after their encounter with Santiago. Still, he found himself distracted by thoughts of Kate. *She's not herself.* The first week she'd been home she'd been too weak to get out of bed, couldn't even speak, and then one day he went to see her only to find her door locked and barred. He'd gone to find Mora who reported Kate had done the deed herself, and ever since she'd refused to see anyone. If it weren't for her soft lavender scent wafting from the other side, Damian wouldn't know if she was alive or not.

He gasped as he surfaced for air, propping himself on the concrete edge of his pool. He swiped a hand down his face and gently treaded water, his riotous feelings coursing through him like rapids. The cold night air bit his exposed skin, but he didn't feel it as he stared off into the distance, the flashing city alive far below his penthouse.

What can we do? What can I do?

He'd been going to her room two times a night every night

for the last three weeks. He'd talked with Mora and Asha and *anyone* to see what their thoughts were. No one knew what to do. No one had any insight as to what Kate needed. *Because she won't talk to us!* He almost had a mind to force himself into her room, only waylaid when Asha warned him otherwise. He'd snapped at her that he was her friend too, and he had a right to—

I just want to see her. To make sure she's okay. To let her know that we're here for her and she doesn't have to go through whatever she is alone.

Because he knew from his time as a soldier that whatever was going through her mind…

Was dark.

Fuck. He took a deep breath and started swimming again, his strokes more vigorous than the last set.

I just want to make sure she's okay.

A part of him he didn't recognize had woken after that night at the country house. While he knew his friendship with Kate was strong, the two of them hardly separable, this part of him was different. It haunted him. Pushed him. Plagued him. If he thought he hadn't been sleeping before, he was getting even less now. If he thought he'd spent too much time at Talorc's, now he couldn't get there enough. He had to be near Kate. To feel her. To know she survived wasn't enough. He feared if he went much longer without seeing her, he would go insane.

I need to feed, he thought, beginning another lap. *I still haven't fed since we've been back.*

I'll have to go to the store. There were banks for donors to give blood to the small population of vampires who didn't have others to feed from. Vampires could only feed from one another and gain enough sustenance to go one or two weeks without needing more. Feeding from humans didn't last as long and wasn't as strengthening. Purchasing blood from blood banks was a little better, but the sites worked with human butchers, who for a hefty price were swayed to give their leftovers to be mixed with vampire blood. Damian didn't necessarily like the taste of doing so, but he'd been operating in such a fashion for so long that it didn't faze him anymore.

I'll feed and then I'll head over to Talorc's. He continued his punishing pace. *Maybe tonight will be the night.*

Though he knew in his heart, in the pit of his soul, that this night would be no different from any other.

Time was still elusive to her.

She wasn't sure she would ever care to measure it again.

What was the point? For a being so pathetic, so worthless as she, what was the passing of time to mean?

As Kate sat in her window seat and stared through the pane in her darkened bedroom, her forehead pressed to the chilled glass, she couldn't even pass the thought that there was a point to anything anymore.

Worthless. Pathetic. Useless. Disgraceful.

Hopeless. Dark. Morbid. Plaguing.

Defiled. Hateful. Disgusting. Woeful.

No one wants you.

No one wants to be around you.

No one can stand your rotting presence.

The words, the feelings they invoked, had been swirling around her since the moment she regained cognizance. She didn't remember much about the first week she'd been home; everything spun together in a grey blur. She hardly remembered being forced to drink blood, broth, and water. She scarcely remembered someone cleaning her and bandaging her. She barely recalled the soft hands and murmurs of what she deduced was a medical professional as she spoke with Talorc after treating her. However, what she did remember with the most clarity was waking up and wishing she hadn't been looking at the ceiling in her room, feeling the presence of Mora nearby, warming from the light in her father's face, or sensing the cool aura of another—of *him.*

She wanted to go back to the last thing she remembered: being beaten and bitten by wraiths in a dirty basement somewhere that didn't matter. She wanted to go back to that time because, so badly, she wanted everything to end *there.* She wanted to go back to that moment to *beg* them to end her life. Because anything was better than being saturated in pitiful sympathy, which is what she had been withstanding night in and night out since she'd been home. She *hated* pity. She had been pitied and coddled and disparaged all her life. And though the manor was a place she was familiar with, filled with beings she was loved and cared for by, she felt like a phantom in a graveyard. She felt like she didn't belong. She didn't *want* to belong. She was beyond this. She didn't fit here anymore. In this place of comfort, of leisure, of painless respite. She... This was not her life anymore. She didn't *deserve* this life.

Worthless. Pathetic. Useless. Disgraceful.

She closed her eyes and tilted her head ever so slightly, the wisps of her uneven hair a barrier between her delicate skin and the cold glass. If she cared to listen hard enough, she could hear Mora downstairs talking with her father about how he shouldn't go back to Canada but should stay to be with Kate. It was an argument she had eavesdropped on so many times in the past three weeks that Kate quickly averted her hearing elsewhere, exhausted by it. The notion her father was so ready to leave her made her ill.

She could hear the servants, beings who were more friends than subordinates, about the house doing various chores. The same males and females she'd grown up alongside, who helped raise and care for her, she refused to see. She refused their comforting words and gentle touches of reassurance. She refused to speak to anyone. What was the point? She couldn't fathom why they would want to associate with such a broken being, one so engrossed in her trauma that she wished to be back in it. The very trauma that had become a part of her she didn't know how to dissociate from or think she ever could.

Hopeless. Dark. Morbid. Plaguing.

The three-story, ninety-thousand square-foot manor now had dogs in and around it, which frightened Kate and was part of the reason she didn't leave her room. She used to love animals, dogs especially, but their loud barking and constant growling startled her more than comforted her. She could hear horses, including her beautiful Rook, nickering softly while tucked away in the stables against the cold. So far from her mind was getting back in the saddle, along with many other things. She'd shuttered away that part of her life...

Woeful.

The subtle beeping of security cameras, alarms, phones, and other electronics made restless background noise, and Kate pinched her eyes shut harder and brought her hands up to her head to cradle it as she drew her legs up to her chest. It reminded her too much of the security Santiago had used to imprison her, to keep her secluded from the rest of the world. And thinking of Santiago had her remembering everything he did to her, every sordid detail…

Defiled. Disgusting.

Creator take her… She hitched in a breath and held it. Where was Its mercy? Why, why could no one show her mercy? Why did she have to live like this? In this painful, hateful place? It was so dark, *so dark*…

Please…take me…

Kate released her breath, knowing it wouldn't be long until her twice-nightly visitor appeared. *It doesn't matter.* He could come all he wanted, but it would just be another night she refused to open the door. It would be another night she refused to venture over the threshold. Another night she refused to bathe. Another night she refused to eat. To feed. To change clothes. To leave the spot she'd been solely inhabiting for now two weeks.

What was the point?

She didn't care if her wounds never healed. She didn't care if her hair never grew back. She didn't care if she smelled, was weak, or her clothes were rumpled. She didn't care if she starved to death. The only reason she didn't meet the sun in the morning was because her father locked the doors leading to the outside and she was too much of a coward to watch its rise. *Do I even deserve death?* Oh, the thought was there. Every hour, every minute, every *second*. Maybe she still would meet the sun. If she cared to.

But she didn't.

Why should she? Her father was leaving to continue his trek across continents to win the more ambivalent covens to his side in the growing war against the wraiths. *Too little too late, father,* she thought bitterly, her fingers curling around the short lengths of her hair. If her only flesh and blood couldn't be bothered to see to her, to make sure she was mending, why should she care about herself?

The others, that lost voice within her pleaded. *They care. Mora, Asha, Ryder, Cyrus, Noir, Vadin, Dam—*

She squeezed her eyes shut tightly and held her breath

again. *Do not think his name. Do not. Do. Not.*

Tears burned in her eyes, but in her continuously depleted state they wouldn't fall. She'd drank blood once since she'd been home, and it was only because she couldn't stand to hear Mora weeping from the other side of her closed door. Mora…Mora was the closest thing she had to a mother and although she loved her dearly with whatever piece of her soul still existed, Kate refused to be forced to prolong her life anymore.

For the way she was living had no meaningful existence.

She'd forgotten what life—what living—was.

It wasn't the time before her imprisonment because she would never fit into that mold again. It wasn't the time of her imprisonment because she had transcended past that physically. It certainly wasn't now. This was not her life. She was stuck. Stuck in some strange limbo of—

Worthless. Pathetic. Useless. Disgraceful.

Hopeless. Dark. Morbid. Plaguing.

Defiled. Hateful. Disgusting. Woeful.

She didn't want to come out on the other side. There was nothing for her there. *Here.* This was the other side and she *hated it.*

What. Is. The. Point.

She pulled at her hair, a long, slow groan pulling from dry lips. Everyone wanted her to pull through. To break through the wall of her suffering and be better, bigger, brighter. But that wasn't *her* anymore. Why didn't they understand? She would never be that female again. No amount of sympathy or caring would get her there. She didn't *want* to be cosseted. She didn't *want* to be doted on. Sometimes she thought she wanted vengeance, sometimes she could taste the tart tang of retribution, but they would be snuffed out in an instant by—

Worthless. Pathetic. Useless. Disgraceful.

Hopeless. Dark. Morbid. Plaguing.

Defiled. Hateful. Disgusting. Woeful.

And now she had *this* to contend with. New feelings. New sensations. Everything was so vivid and loud and nauseatingly odorous and sensitive and overpowering. Why couldn't anyone understand that she was overwhelmed? That the first week she'd been awake she wanted nothing more than to lie in darkness and silence? That her eardrums hadn't healed? That every caress reminded her of the rough hands that abused her? That every whisper sounded like a shout? That every smell reeked of the last dungeon she was forced to withstand?

Didn't they understand that all she wanted was to never feel anything again?

Why couldn't they just let me die?

The groan turned into a sob that produced no tears. Kate released her hair and slumped back against the wood of her window seat, tipping her head back to face the ceiling. The window was at least eight feet high and overlooked the garden she so studiously worked on in the summer nights but was now as dry and dead as her very soul. The soul that had once clamored for her to fight, to not give in to the—

Worthless. Pathetic. Useless. Disgraceful.

Hopeless. Dark. Morbid. Plaguing.

Defiled. Hateful. Disgusting. Woeful.

But how could she not?

What did she have to live for?

Nothing, she thought wretchedly, curling into herself once more. She placed her face down upon her knees and wept without tears, her arms tight around her bent legs.

I have nothing.

I have no one.

I am nothing.

I am no one.

Chapter Five

Talorc's gaze lingered on the orange glow that stretched along the horizon before shutting the heavy curtain to his private room. He could not displace a sigh before he hid his gaze behind tired eyelids and sat down at the black enameled desk in a plush leather chair. The Guard had held the front at home while he had been abroad, had been successful in their retrieval of Kate, but their edge was becoming precariously tenuous as the grip of whoever was guiding the wraiths steered them closer. Talorc could only fathom one reason: someone wanted his seat of power. That thought alone, never mind his thousands of obligations and responsibilities and dilemmas, made his bones weary and his spirit sag with exhaustion.

Yet his soul was on fire with a will stronger than it had ever been.

He knew his seat was a fragile one, and feeble if he were honest. His early tours of the surrounding covens made that obvious; though the more local ones were loyal, they murmured worries of disregard and fickleness to Talorc. And the more he reached out, the more he travelled, the regard became more coldly disdainful, as coven leaders turned their noses up at his attempt to communicate and rebuild rapport. He knew why, and he knew that it was deserved. He also knew if his precious daughter had not been taken from him, he would not be where he is now, restructuring the connections he had long let disintegrate.

The only reason he was in the position he was now in—struggling to right the crown on his head—was because shortly after Kathryn had been taken it became pristinely apparent that if he sat stagnant in his manor one more night without her joyous laughter, quick wit, or flagrant nagging, he would have met the sun the very next morning.

It was difficult to turn from its rise now. *How easy it would be to end all this.* The thought crossed his mind over the last few months too easily, and each time he tried to replace it with another, more inspiring one. A less selfish one. But the longer he had gone without hearing word of Kathryn, the longer his hand rested upon the curtain in the morning. In those twinkling seconds of time, the determination to see this campaign done the right way—the warrior's way—would overtake and he would see himself to the righteous path once more.

But it has been a long time since I have taken such a path.

He was not a fool as to ignore the insight that this journey was and would continue to be a difficult one. War was on the horizon. But if anyone could put a stop to these foes it was him. It was his duty, his legacy, to lead the vampire nation to prosperity and contentment. *Something I have not done for a long time,* he thought, pushing away his guilt into an inner cage he seldom opened. He had to concentrate on the true endgame: put a stop to this madness overtaking one region after another and obtain *peace*—the peace they all deserved.

The war upon them was a new kind; a strange, modern war that maybe others had seen coming, but he had been blind to for a long time. Because of his ineptitude it was a war that he did not know how to navigate, which was both invigorating and discouraging. His centuries of leadership experience were being called to the fore and he felt the calling in his very marrow, but his time of inaction threatened to overbear. So much had changed in the past two centuries, so much that he had turned from, shirked from. The pain in his heart and the darkness that surrounded him after the loss of his wife had regrettably overwhelmed him for so long.

Too long. But I can only cast blame at myself, and there is no use in casting blame. Instead, he fixated on what he knew: war, both the politics and the bloodthirst of it. It was what he was born and bred to do, as his many years before being made into a vampire were spent as a marauding Pict. The ghost of his former self reminded him of that fact nightly, reinforcing the ideal that he now had to act for first the retribution of Kathryn and then the vampire nation. He would see her avenged above all else, as his soul pushed through the shattered shards of his icy heart in the face of what she had to endure. Yet the anguish he felt from her near-loss emitted doubt, like a rainstorm without an end; always there, always clouding, immersing him in drenching pain.

How can I stand to lose another? How do I turn the tide? How can I withstand being in her presence when I so disastrously failed her?

You are not one to vacillate, his conscience boomed. *You will not lose her. You are doing what you can. Trust in yourself, your love for your daughter.*

But how could he, knowing it was his own nonactions that landed him in this exact predicament? If only he had paid more attention to what she had to say, cared to learn and grow with his nation, been present in not just her life but so many others…maybe things would be different.

I cannot think like that, dwelling on what could have been.

Kathryn's face swirled to the forefront of his cognizance then, her slender smirk which prefaced her riotous laughter barely filling the void in his heart. He could recall in an instant the cadence of her voice, the feel of her embrace, the glittering of her cerulean eyes. He could almost hear her humming, usually done only while she was baking, or snorting in laughter at those romantic comedies she liked to watch.

Could he really do this? Could he unify a torn and fallen nation? With no one but his Guards of Nightfall and a makeshift army that had been pulled together in a matter of weeks? It felt futile. Unachievable. Laughable, even. Yet for Kathryn he would do anything. *Anything.* There was no choice; he would not *let himself* have a choice. He was going to turn the tide to his advantage. He had many lives to make amends for, many trusts yet to earn—both of which he had let falter in the first place. *His* choice to sit by and do nothing. *His* choice to let the vampire nation suffer and live in fear. It was something that he would live with for the rest of his days, however many of them were left.

He vowed to atone for every single disappointment he had caused. To avenge every life lost as if it were personal. Earn back those trusts he had squandered. He would not let his guilt eat at him and tear him down. He would rebuild the foundation of his empire, one that the vampires would be proud to uphold, and reign supreme over the wraiths. He knew many of his kind hated him, would hate him for the many months and years to come. He could live with that. He had to. He would take that hatred and let it fuel his fire. A fire that his daughter would be proud of, as she had not been in a very long time.

Unchecked, a fond memory of Kathryn washed over him...

June 1880
Warwick

"Athair!"
Talorc lifted his head from the book of strategies he had been perusing to meet a more enjoyable sight: his youthful daughter, her eyes alight with life, hopping and skipping toward him. He was sitting at the base of the steps in front of his home, a large farmhouse he had purchased with his deceased beloved some one hundred years ago. At his daughter's approach he put his book to the side, and Kathryn halted in front of him, out of breath but grinning enough to expose a pair of tiny fangs, clutching a trinket in her fist.

The most wonderous of summer nights was upon them. The velvet sky above was speckled with silver stars, each of varying sizes and vibrancy. Fireflies swirled in the air, the occasional warm breeze helping them along the way. The trees from the surrounding forest loomed from afar, watching steadfast over his land. The stables bustled with energy as the horses were brought out for their exercise, and the house behind Talorc filled with the raucous sounds of a meal being cleaned up and daily chores commencing. For Talorc, tonight was one of his better ones; the suffocating tightness of sorrow was not as hostile, allowing him to be present for his only youngling.

Most nights were not so kind. As much as he tried to relegate his mourning to the daytime hours, when there were fewer beings around to witness his sodden mood, he was still learning how to cope with the grief brought on by the loss of his beloved. His daughter remained the sole reason he woke every night to do so.

Kathryn settled against his knee and Talorc wrapped an arm around her shoulders. "I retrieved this for you!" She excitedly stuck her hand out over top of his own and unfurled her fingers to drop a smooth, sand-colored stone into his palm.

Talorc lifted an eyebrow and then his gaze to pin on his daughter, who was bouncing on the soles of her feet. "You brought me a rock."

His daughter adorably huffed and stomped a slippered foot, ruffling the folds of her green satin gown. "Not just any *rock; turn it over!"*

Talorc smiled and did as she asked, surprised to find etched on the back of the stone was a crude sword, one that he could tell she had tenaciously carved.

"Promise me you will keep this with you." Her youngling's voice was pleading, so earnest that it melted some of the ice that encased Talorc's heart. "Whenever you need strength, like when Mora scolds you or you get hurt when you practice with your sword, remember this rock and how hard it would be to break it. Like you, Athair.*"*

Talorc laughed gently, his eyes warm with tears that he would not let fall. What had he done in life to deserve the gift that was his daughter? He cherished her above all else, and it was moments like this that he was reminded of such. How was she so young but so kind? So brave? So astute? His only wish was that his dear Herja were here to see the fine young female she was becoming. Because he knew that if he were proud then she would be prouder.

He clasped the stone tightly in his hand and looked up at his Kathryn, her eyes shining with spirit. She was so innocent; she knew naught of the cruel world they lived in or what could possibly be plaguing him. And right then and there, Talorc made a silent promise that he would always protect her from truly knowing the world, the demons that lurked within, and anything that could take away the innocent wonder he saw in her.

"Thank you, Piseag Bheag. *I will keep it with me always." He used the nickname he and the others closest to him christened her with to reflect her goodness and curiosity: Little Kitten.*

"Promise?" she demanded, crossing her arms with a pointed look.

He pocketed the stone in the leather vest he had on, patting it into place. "I promise."

She squealed then, throwing her tiny self into his embrace. "Now you are more strong than you were before!"

"Stronger," he corrected her gently, and she stuck her tongue out at him before prancing away to twirl in the small dirt path before the manor.

"You sound like Mora. Always correcting me." Round and round she went, kicking her dress about her as she adopted a high, regal voice that sounded too much like his Herja's. "'Do not say that, Kathryn! Do not do that, Kathryn! Ladies do not act that way, Kathryn!'"

Talorc boomed with laughter. "You should hope she does not hear you lest she have you whipped."

"Let her," Kathryn goaded, twirling faster. "I do not care."

"You will care when your hide is sore."

"You will not let her do so."

"I may."

Kathryn stuck her tongue out at him again and then brashly kicked dirt at his clean attire. Talorc shot to his feet and began swiping the dust from his clothes, glowering at his rebellious daughter.

"You will clean these anon!"

"Nay!" Kathryn laughed, dancing away from him as Talorc lunged for her.

"Kathryn!"

"I will if you can catch me!" She took off then, and Talorc was quick on her tail.

Oh, to be as carefree as she.

He smiled then, so softly. For a while, I suppose it cannot hurt.

He let himself go, if only for a brief moment in his very long life, as they encroached on the tree line. Kathryn shrieked in delight, keeping a good distance ahead of him, as she dodged tall trunks and low-hanging branches.

But only because he allowed it.

The memory wisped away and Talorc opened his eyes, dropping his arm from where it cradled his head while pushing away the emotions that flanked the recollection. He swallowed the thick lump lodged in his throat and sat back in the chair, the leather creaking as he did so. He had failed his daughter. Failed to keep her safe, to keep her shielded from this world of hatred and darkness. He struggled to understand how she had been kidnapped but blamed himself for his lack of heed. His lack of foresight. His lack of disinterest in her everyday life.

No more.

He would not continue to fail her. He would become the leader she saw in him, the leader of legend. He would no longer let fear and sorrow obscure his world. He would strive to embolden the vampire nation and in turn keep them protected while staying true and strong to his legacy. He would cherish the moments he had shared with his daughter and endeavor to make new ones when this was over.

With otherworldly power and strident determination coursing through him, he only had one regret: that she could not see him now, the male he was becoming, an evolution of who he once was. The one she always believed he could be. How many times had she stormed into his den or his office, prodding him to spar with her, to walk with her, to eat with her? Some days it was only by her bidding that he did so. How many times had she brushed his shoulder after a witty joke, pulling his own laughter forth? How often did she bring him her latest baking concoction and a steaming mug of coffee when he wanted nothing more than the darkness to consume him? She was always there for him, and he would be there for her now.

He brought a hand to the blazer he was wearing and felt for the breast pocket, where he carried the stone she had given him all those years ago. He brought it with him always, as he promised her he would.

That promise meant more to him than any other he had ever made.

In another world removed from Earth, hidden from those who only knew of it from lore and far beyond the outer stretches of the universe, Oleander slashed a hand through the wavering orb before him, causing the scene he had been watching to disappear. Imra stood behind him, her hands clasped demurely in front of white robes which touched the mirroring glass floor. They stood in a vast open space of night air, circled by black columns and slender, flickering torches. The sky above glittered with silver stars, an indigo and violet expanse that both swallowed them whole and swept out before them in lengths that were unfathomable.

"They are all in turmoil," Imra said softly, her feathery wings lying in graceful arches behind her.

"I can see that." Oleander strode past Imra with his head bent while his ebony wings snapped open brusquely.

"They are on the wrong path. They need guidance."

"We have tried that route."

"Not truly. We could do better. Do more."

"We are limited." Oleander's pacing was severe, a terse staccato rhythm. "Without guidance of our own, it feels wrong to act."

"The others are restless," Imra hedged. "Hydra, Raham, Undulane… They want to know where we go from here."

Oleander whirled on the female watcher, his black robes swaying with his angry movements. "It is up to us then? You and I?" He huffed in annoyance. "How did we get fitted with such a task?"

"We were there," Imra replied, her tone haunting as her eyes grew distant. "At the beginning, we were there."

Oleander remained quiet, unsure that what he wanted to say next would not have him struck for blasphemy. As far removed as The Creator was…Oleander knew It was always watching.

"You know they look to us for resolution of all things," Imra continued, the antithesis to Oleander's restlessness in her pristine tranquility. "And we have not heard from The Creator for longer than either of us would like to admit. We know not what It desires, It heeds."

"You would have us tip the scales of the universe by our own hands?" Oleander fixed his sharp orange gaze on Imra's crystalline sapphire one. They clashed without animosity, but the turbulence within both sent waves throughout the cosmos.

"If it meant for the good of humankind…" Imra nodded her

head in a solemn gesture. "Yes."

Oleander huffed again, a guttural sound of frustration. Heat emanated from him in waves, expressing the volatility he was barely keeping at bay. "Why is this world so important to you? There are others. Others that are in much more disorder than this Earth."

Imra looked away then, her gaze carrying over the swells of night, to the sparkling waves of star clusters and nebulas beyond. A cool gust pushed her white, shoulder-length hair over her shoulders and away from her pointed face, so ethereal with its sloping lines and pearlescent hue. "We were created to care for them, for the betterment of humankind." Her melodious voice was so soft it barely carried over the currents of the breeze. "Humans...they are dear to me."

Oleander paused, eyes caught on the divine being before him, on the longing he captured in the lilt of her voice.

He blinked when she turned bright eyes to him, fervor burning within. "I know that if we do not act now, Earth will be destroyed."

Oleander felt himself yield under her regard, to the power she so inadvertently bore. He did not fear or condemn her for that; he respected her. He would always defer to her knowledge, her wisdom. She saw far more than he could; her sight went beyond the present, well into the future, and far into the past—far beyond what even he could recall.

"Our divergence... Tell me how it would not liken us to *him*." Oleander spoke maliciously of the single watcher who had dared defy The Creator; the same one who had absconded and abstained from righteousness since the dawn of time.

"We are acting for the good of humanity," Imra replied with conviction. "He acts only for himself."

"That is who is orchestrating this, then? Him? You know this for certain?"

Imra said nothing, but her ice blue eyes never strayed from Oleander's amber ones. She was not testing him—they both knew who was the more powerful being. Still, Oleander warred with his innate need to act with fire and to acquiesce to Imra. He was uneasy about diverting from his master, the one who had conceived them all. It was The Creator who had given him life. The Creator who made the places in which he inhabited. The Creator who produced humankind. The Creator who risked it all to pull away from what It knew to give life to Earth and everything beyond.

But The Creator had been silent for years. Generations. Centuries. *Millenia.* There were no new watchers being made. No communication with other realms, hardly between the watchers themselves. No counsel, no intervention, no signs of anything. There was nothing. Imra and Oleander had been living in a limbo of stark nothingness, doing naught, for longer than Oleander had ever been idle in his long, limitless life.

Although he did not have foresight like Imra, he knew what she said was true. And while he would go on to live beyond whatever happened to Earth, a life aligned with a malevolent reign was no life he wanted to abide. It would be worse than the one of monotony he was living now, for it would be rife with bedlam and desolation. Furthermore, he wanted justice. Oleander's frequent talks with Imra as of late opened his eyes to the place their nonaction had put them, which he knew was exactly where the dissenter wanted them to be to gain the upper hand.

It was time they, the watchers as a whole, took back that hand.

Oleander wanted *purpose,* and he was the kind of male who made his own.

"Then we shall act," he finally, after so long, concurred. "I will share your role in this, but I will look to you for direction."

Imra averted, her slippered feet starting a slow stroll as her eyes wandered to the beyond. "Ultimately, we seek his annihilation," she murmured, and the wind whipped past her in urgence at her utterance.

"His death would alter the very universe," Oleander said lowly, his voice rumbling like a volcano. "His evil is uncontainable; it would spurt from his ashes and raze the world."

"Can we live in such disequilibrium?" Imra mused, more to herself. "Are we not now?"

"The duality..."

"The balance has been tipped for some time."

"Then we would have to plan to contain his evil. Trap it so the balance remains but he cannot wield it."

"There is so much to account for." Imra stopped at the edge

of the floor, gazing off into the night as if searching for answers. Oleander knew better: she was trying to sort through her millions of memories, the yawning present, and the future of the entirety of life, space, and time.

She finally turned her gleaming eyes to Oleander. "We must involve the others. Alert them of our thoughts. Include them in this decision. This goes beyond just us two if it has the ability to redefine what they control. The dissenter's powers know no bounds, his cruelty no limits. We are forgetting what he is truly capable of. We will need all the support we can manage."

"He is but one being," Oleander reminded Imra.

"But he has been festering in his maliciousness for so long, amassing power that we know nothing of." Her icy eyes flashed; so brief was the malevolence within that Oleander thought he imagined it. "The vampires, Talorc and his ilk, are bearing the brunt of our procrastination and idleness. We must work with them to overcome this."

"First, though, we must talk with the others; you were right in that." His robes rustled about his feet as the wind whispered by, and if he did not know any better Oleander would think Xypher was prying.

"Then call them," Imra said firmly, her regard resolute. "Let us see this begun."

Chapter Six

T he summer night was a beautiful one, conflicting with the unrest Damian felt within. He was coming back to Warwick after being away for years, and while he was ready to reunite with his brethren, the prolonged distance made him nervous. Would they greet him with cheer? With hesitancy? What did he miss while he'd been away? He'd stayed in contact, but admittedly could've done better. For all Talorc had done for him, provided for him, and opened for him, Damian almost felt like he betrayed the male for being so removed. After all, it was Talorc who took Damian under his wing, promising him a life of acceptance, security, and wealth in exchange for his valor against their most dire enemies.

What choice did I have but to leave? I had to do what was right for myself.

When Talorc and his beloved had talked about settling in North America and starting a family, Damian knew a drastic decline in fighting and warmongering would follow, and it wasn't in his nature to be idle or dormant. He was a soldier through and through, living fully and robustly by the blade. Talorc, understanding this of him, had given Damian a leave of absence from The Guards of Nightfall, as long as he continued to defer to Talorc when Talorc needed him. So for the last two hundred and some years Damian had been a mercenary soldier for both humans and vampires, jumping from conflict to conflict to appease his need for bloodshed. What started out as his involvement in the Quasi-

65

War for pirating fun led to his participation in The War of 1812, carried him through the Civil War, the world wars, and the Vietnam War. As it became harder and harder to blend into a society that was so advanced, Damian finally retired from mercenary work.

And there are no wars left to be had, at least not on a large scale, *he thought to himself, running a hand through his hair, his elbow propped on the open window of his rented Audi.* And honestly, I'm tired of the endless revolving door. Creating a new persona every time. Finding someone to forge new documents and all that bullshit. Finding new places to live. It's exhausting.

In the beginning of his journey to find himself, Damian visited Talorc and Herja often. Their home had always been a gathering place for The Guards of Nightfall, as they each found a sense of comfort in the manor. However when Herja passed, everything changed. Talorc grew sheltered. The manor fell into shadow, and for a time Talorc forbade anyone from coming or going. In return, Damian's visits to Warwick grew less and less. His time while there was restless, filled with growing resentment and uncertainty. Ashamedly, he hadn't been to Talorc's home for a good eighty-some years.

Even I can admit that's too long. Especially when I promised myself to Talorc and the vampires' cause all those years ago, *Damian thought, steering his sedan off the freeway and toward Talorc's manor outside the city. The last time he'd been down this road he'd been on a horse, and the path itself had neither been an asphalt one nor dirt. It had simply been a forest. That's what converged on him now in towering pines, their bristles bright this time of year. There were telephone poles, electrical transformers, single-family homes, and streetlights to line his way, and he used a global positioning system on his phone to guide him to the address Ryder had provided.* What a time to be alive, *he mused with a slow smile.* And I've lived to see a lot of them.

So much had changed. Civilization had exploded, burgeoning technologies and wonders that fascinated as much as vexed him. Cars replaced horses and people looked at their phones more than the sky up above. Clocks were no longer analog, traded solely for digital. Buildings replaced trees and smog filled the air. Battles no longer consisted of swords, spears, and bludgeons, but technical devices and automatic weapons. There were computers and cameras and TVs and stores and all sorts of modernities; the world was constantly at everyone's fingertips, information and access a click away. One hundred years ago, Damian could never picture such a life.

There were a few things that hadn't changed: the wraiths were still a nuisance, but thankfully not devastatingly so. Talorc remained liege of the vampire nation despite his withdrawal into solitude. The vampire population remained steady and loyal to him. Combined with what Damian heard about what life was like for the other Guardsmales, who lived in or around Warwick, being a Guard seemed easy. What they relayed sounded perfect: continue to serve Talorc in his needs and slaughter wraiths at every opportunity, but largely lead a life of leisure.

Damian knew he needed a change. He wanted respite and camaraderie with his kin. Companionship and ease. He was looking forward to this new—dare he say laidback?—and contemporary battle of wits and strategy the vampire world had become. Because of Talorc's years of dedication and Damian's own loyalty, along with the rest of The Guard, the world was a safe and stable place, and he was ready to bask in the peace brought on by his years of hard work.

What continued to unnerve him, however, were the rumors of Talorc becoming more distant. There were even whisperings of an abdication. Maybe I can get him to engage again. It would be good to spar with him. Teach him what I learned being in all these wars. *Yet in the back of Damian's mind, his conscience warned him that it might be too little, too late. Ryder and the others shared their inner thoughts with him easily, and none of them sounded promising where it concerned Talorc's readiness and willingness to continue to be a leader.*

Damian's contacts in various covens confirmed such talk. With his being involved in various conflicts, he had connections that spanned borders and seas. Many coven leaders wondered why Talorc didn't speak with them, meet with them, interact with them. Even more murmured of his mental state, musing if he would ever break from the darkened depression that hovered over him after losing Herja. Maybe it isn't as bad as they make it seem, *Damian thought as he guided the Audi over the smooth roadway.* Maybe Talorc just needs to be reminded of everything he's accomplished.

Damian would be lying to himself if he didn't admit that he wondered the same thing a time or two, but he knew deep inside that Talorc would never let the vampire nation fall to their demise. He'd staunchly protected human- and vampire-kind through countless wars against the wraiths. He'd started many of the covens, helping them cultivate the unique resources of the land, navigate their respective territories, build homes, and construct markets and governments. Once he'd gotten them on their feet, he'd pushed to proliferate the North American covens and was the sole reason they'd spread and held so quickly. He was a leader through and through, and was the most cunning, resourceful, and vehement male Damian had ever known.

Creator, *but he couldn't wait to see his brethren. He couldn't wait to see Cyrus's latest weaponry and swap stories about times present and past. He couldn't wait to take Vadin out for a drink so he could show him the best spots to pick up females. While he talked to Ryder the most, he couldn't wait to actually see the male, who would fill him in on other various gaps throughout the years. He couldn't wait to explore the city with Noir, who would know every nook and cranny, and could find him a spot to rent.* Put that on the to-do list. *He'd lived all over the world during his travels and never settled down, but decided here and now it was time to.*

And then there was Talorc. Creator, we have so much to catch up on. Six months is too long without contact. *The male had been there since the beginning, had supported his being made at the behest of Ryder. Talorc helped mold him from the firebrand he'd been on the battlefield into the general that led armies across the globe. He helped teach him restraint, poise, and delicacy. He shaped him from the murderous Byzantian-Greek soldier he'd been into the astute and morally competent male he was today. Easily, though without saying, Talorc had become the father Damian lost before birth, and Damian looked up to him now as he so faithfully did back then.*

Enough about that. More importantly is the fact I'll finally be free to find some females. All the females. Every night. *Damian adopted a wide grin, fantasizing about all the legs he could be between in the very near future. That was the downside to war: not a lot of mingling with the other sex.*

Something else I need to add to the to-do list.

Damian knew The Guard waited for him at Talorc's, and along with the reunion he was looking forward to a Mora-made dinner. Creator, but he missed that female too. No one could cook like Mora. No one ran a house like Mora, either. She'd been with Talorc as long as he could remember, and always brought with her a sense of warm relief and comfort, much like a summer breeze.

After several more minutes of pondering, he pulled up to the gate that separated Talorc's land from the surrounding forest. He dialed the number Ryder shared with him to open the gate and traversed from the public road to a private one. He turned down the stereo blaring Metallica to listen to the world around him, thankful he'd made it this far in life to finally know peace.

Maybe I am getting old. *The call of the night carried over the wind as he slowed the Audi to a crawl. Leaves varying in color from spring to sage trilled a jovial tune, as if heralding him back to where he belonged. Twinkling stars winked from gold to silver in an ebony swath of sky, so clear he thought he could see into the depths of the universe. The air, carried by Xypher himself, was crisp and smelled sweetly of fireflies and fresh earth. For so long Damian could only recall the scent of blood, metal, and melting flesh, so this...this was wondrous. And while there would always be a part of him that wanted blood and fighting and war, there was another new, growing part of him that could appreciate serenity and simple prosperity.*

The trees split suddenly to reveal Talorc's mansion. Damian lowly whistled at the sight: a three-story stone monstrosity spread left and right to form wings, cast with turrets, balconies, and sprawling windows. Candles flickered in each of the panes, while golden light shimmered from sconces on either side of the towering oak front doors. A fountain boasting statues from Greek mythology almost as big as the Trevi and lit to show off sprouting water lay before the home, the concrete driveway curling around it. Lush greenery lined the house, bushes in full bloom boasting bright shades of pink, scarlet, and violet.

The last time Damian had been here the house hadn't been this big, but what else was one supposed to do with twenty thousand acres of land? Expand, obviously. *The perfectly maintained drive rounded a separate guest house, stables to the left, and a pond down a small hill to the right. It was evident Talorc had been adding* to the home over the years, though Damian wondered if he kept it updated in modernity inside as well as he did out. It was never like Talorc to get lost in the details of the contemporary world; he'd always been a simple man of simpler means.

I guess I'll find out shortly. *Damian pulled his borrowed Audi around to just in front of the entryway.* Though how you could keep up in a structure like this is beyond me.

He wasn't entirely out of the car when one of the front doors swung open and Mora appeared. She clasped her hands to her heart and then her mouth as Damian shut the car door in his wake, grinning from ear to ear. Ryder, ever the mountain, emerged behind her, before Mora raced down the concrete stairs and into Damian's open arms.

"Mora," he said with a chuckle as she buried her face into his shoulder, her arms curled around his neck. "You don't know how good it is to see you."

Mora pulled back to look at him, her long, gray braid slipping over her shoulder to fall down her back. Her brown eyes were bright, sparkling with unshed tears as she smiled up at him, her dainty fangs peeking out from her mouth. "Damianos," she breathed, shaking her head from side to side as if in disbelief. "Do my eyes deceive me?"

Damian was still grinning as he ran his hands over her slight shoulders, which were sheathed in a white linen shirt covered by a beige apron that led to a pair of matching khakis. "Only if you claim to be old." He leaned forward and kissed her cheek affectionately, squeezing her shoulders at the same time. "And it's Damian now."

Mora swatted at him for the affront. "I may be old, but I will still tan your hide."

Damian laughed. "No one says that anymore, Mora. Doesn't Talorc let you out?"

"Oh!" Mora swatted at him again, stepping back as she wiped at her eyes, which despite her words, still glimmered with mirth. "Here I thought you would have changed. You are still the rascal I know you to be."

"Damian," Ryder interjected as Mora stepped back, and the two males clasped hands before pulling into a brief embrace. "I'm glad you made it here safely."

"And on such short notice! One night is all you could spare?" Mora chastised him as a holler sounded from the front doors. A quick glance told Damian that Vadin appeared, and his grin widened. "Do you know what I had to do to get the house together for you?"

"Damian!" Vadin barreled into him like a battering ram, almost knocking them both back into the shining black Audi. Vadin whooped again as he slapped Damian on the back and then held him at arm's length, his smile all fang. "It's good to see you brother."

"Likewise," Damian rumbled as Vadin let go of him to let Cyrus through their now bustling, chittering crew.

"Damian." Cyrus clapped him on the back with a heavy hand. "It's been too long."

"I know it," Damian said as Noir appeared, seemingly out of thin air. "I won't let so much time pass again."

"Here to stay?" Noir asked, flicking away a cigarette. The gesture had Mora narrowing her eyes on the male, who noticed and quickly retrieved the discarded butt, wiping it on his jeans and then pocketing it for waste later, mumbling a hasty, "Sorry."

Noir and Damian repeated the same greeting as the others as Damian replied, "Here to stay. I'll need your help scouting a new place."

"Done. You owe me tequila anyway."

"You still remember that?"

Noir huffed a laugh, shuffling restlessly from one Converse to another. "Forget tequila? Never."

"Come on!" Vadin slung a hefty arm across Damian's shoulders and patted him on the chest with his other hand. "Let's get you inside. Mora and Kate have been cooking all day. Place has been in an uproar. We can show you around after they get dinner on the table."

As their group headed inside, Damian recalled fleetingly that Kate was the name of Talorc's daughter. Mora led the way, calling out to who Damian guessed were other servants before disappearing down a hall, while Damian halted swiftly in the foyer.

"Creator be." He whistled low as he looked around the entryway, Noir shutting the doors behind him as the others piled in. "Is the whole house like this?"

The foyer was huge, a circular room open to the three stories of the home, decorated in hues of taupe. A domed glass ceiling swooped above while stairs flanked either side of the large space, sweeping in curves up to the second and then third levels. The glass of the dome was patterned in a mosaic, made with enough dark panes that the piercing rays of daylight wouldn't offend the vampires within. Arched openings on the first floor to the left, right, and center of the foyer led to different spaces within the massive structure, and from what Damian could see, the home was impeccably and tastefully decorated.

"Yup," Noir supplied, rocking back and forth on his feet. "Kate does a lot of it."

Damian craned his head to appreciate the marble balustrades separating the second and third floors above. A crystal chandelier bigger than a Prius dangled from the center of the ceiling, sparkling low light throughout. Ancient busts from different eras flanked both sets of stairs and there was a starburst pattern breaking up the swirling, beige marble floor in the center. In the middle of the starburst was a circular pine table boasting a summer floral display, one that Damian knew Mora fussed over every day to make sure it was appropriately hydrated and pruned.

"Disgusting isn't it?" Vadin chirped, his grin revealing he spoke in jest. "Between the chef's kitchen, two indoor pools and one outdoor, the enormous underground gym, training area complete with small infirmary, fully stocked and functioning sauna, observatory, solarium, wine cellar, two separate wings complete up to three stories that house innumerable bedrooms and bathrooms, and the movie theater, there's barely enough to keep you occupied for the day."

Damian laughed out loud as Cyrus shook his head. "Poor Mora."

"Poor Mora is right."

Damian looked up and to the right, and his grin returned as his eyes landed on Talorc descending the stairs from the second level.

"Talorc." Damian broke away from Vadin and crossed the floor to meet the male, stopping just a step away to place his hand over his heart and bow at the waist.

"There is no need for that." Talorc dismissed his gesture

and instead reached forward to grasp Damian's forearm in warm welcome. "It is so good to see you, Damianos."

"Damian," Damian corrected him as he slapped Talorc on the back with a wink. "It's Damian now."

Talorc stepped back with a nod of regard. "It will take some getting used to. You will have to excuse me for a time."

Damian took his first, full look at Talorc after the years they'd spent apart. His initial thought was that Talorc looked old, much older than he remembered. And he looked tired. His greying blonde hair was loosely pulled back in a low ponytail, and his black dress shirt was untucked from his black pants. His boots weren't shining, as Damian always remembered them being, and the gold cuff he wore on his exposed forearm was dim. His beard was long and unkempt, more grey than not, and his brown eyes, though crinkled with a smile, were shadowed. His tanned skin was more wrinkled than Damian remembered, and not from laughing or smiling; he looked burdened, as if the weight of the world were bearing down on him.

To dissuade himself from thinking of how ill Talorc looked, Damian replied cheekily, "Four hundred years of repetition is hard to break."

"And eighty is too long not to see you," Talorc countered. "You are staying this time?"

Damian felt guilt ping him sharply before he replied, "Staying."

Talorc lifted a hand to clasp his shoulder, guiding him toward the center hallway. "Then come. We have much to speak about."

The peaked arch led them into a wide hall, and if Damian remembered correctly this was part of the original house. Exposed stone on either side confirmed his thoughts, and Damian wondered idly what secrets the walls would expose. They passed a small den to the right and a powder room that had been converted from the previous study on the left. The décor lining the hall was immaculately kept, and Damian marveled at the paintings, floral displays, and furniture as he walked, the others trailing behind him and still talking amongst themselves.

"You've done a lot to this place," Damian said to Talorc, peeking into rooms here and there: a small office, a mud room, and

a tiny room where herbs were growing on the walls and on shallow tables, while others hung from the ceiling to dry.

Talorc glanced over his shoulder. "Kathryn has. She keeps the manor spritely."

The second time he'd heard that name, and he was only vaguely familiar. "Your daughter?"

"Yes. You will meet her shortly. She is finishing up in the kitchen."

Damian had left before she was born, and when he'd visited in the past it was short-lived. He'd rarely stayed at the manor, either; it was too melancholy. The abbreviated times he was around he never saw her, assuming she was elsewhere doing female things and couldn't be bothered with another wayward soldier just as he couldn't be bothered with a youngling. He supposed he'd heard her over the phone a time or two, but again, younglings were not his forte and so it had never been a priority to meet her.

"How old is she now?" he wondered aloud as the two walked into what had to be the main dining room of the house.

"She just turned two-hundred and seventeen," Talorc replied, moving to the head of the table. He mumbled more to himself than anyone else, "Though it is the equivalent of her being twenty-seven years old in human years, she acts as if she is thirteen."

Damn. I have been gone a long time. She isn't a youngling anymore.

The dining room had been converted from the main part of the house, as told by the original stone floor, towering wooden hearth on the far side of the room, and exposed-beam ceiling. A large taxidermied hen harrier soared above the fireplace, its mouth poised in a cry that spanned nearly a millennium. The walls of the room had been partially redone with plaster and painted oyster gray, while the bottom remained the original wood paneling. From the ceiling hung the original chandelier, a three-tiered wood and iron eyesore that boasted countless flickering candles. The dining room table was made of dark walnut and sprawled to feature twenty-five high-backed chairs with red velvet insets. The décor matched the room in its antiquity, where woodsmen met garden maiden in various antlered animal heads and expansive floral arrangements.

Damian took the seat that Talorc offered him, to his left. The table had already been made with black china and matching utensils, and as Damian took off the crimson napkin to place in his lap, the others took their seats as well.

"In the big dining room?" Vadin reached for the pitcher of water on the table. "Must be something special going on." He winked at Damian, who took the pitcher when he was finished filling his crystal glass.

"Where are you coming from?" Talorc asked, placing his own napkin in his lap as Mora bustled in with two pitchers of beer.

"Just finished in Cyprus," Damian replied.

"Secret spy bullshit?" Vadin quipped.

"Keeping an eye on the peace in the Middle East," Damian responded. "There's a defense site there. We were contracted to help the U.S. military."

"See anyone you know?" Cyrus asked as Mora hurried back into the kitchen, calling out to the others as she went.

"I went to the coven there a lot," Damian said, looking up as the swinging door to the kitchen opened, then shortly fell shut. He pushed back his chair to stand, crossing the floor to hold open the door for Mora who was clearly struggling with all she had to bring out. "Yiorgos is a good male. He always made a place for me at their table."

"You are finished then?" Talorc asked.

"There's probably some bullshit I have to do, but I don't owe the contractors anymore of my time," Damian replied, sliding his hand along the door to prop it open as he looked back at Talorc to continue talking. "My focus will be—"

"'Scuse me!"

Lavender. I smell lavender. *The thought startled him into looking down at the figure housing the voice that certainly didn't belong to Mora.*

His breath stalled in his lungs.

The female who hovered just below his arm looked up at him with a slender set of carmine lips poised in a wide smile, revealing petite fangs. Glittering blue irises set in almond-shaped eyes rested in an unblemished, oval face, parted by a slightly upturned nose. Long lashes fanned out, framed by eyebrows impeccably arched, their hue the same as her raven-colored hair currently pulled haphazardly out of her face in a bun high on her head. Her skin was the color of champagne and just as luminescent, streaked here and there with flour. In her perfectly manicured hands tipped with bright pink claws was a tray of rolls, and beneath her red apron which read 'Kiss the Crook' was a white tank-top and the smallest pair of black shorts Damian had ever seen.

"I don't have much to open the door with if my hands are busy." The female winked at him and whizzed into the dining room on bare feet that sported matching polish on her toes. Damian distantly grasped she was poking fun about her lack of curves, and he had to bite his tongue to stop himself from correcting her. "So thanks for getting the door."

He faintly heard Talorc call in a warning tone, "Where are your shoes?"

Damian held open the door long after the female passed through it, mesmerized by her slim-legged gait before she draped herself over the table between Cyrus and Ryder to place the tray of rolls near the middle. Damian's mouth went dry as her shorts rode up, baring even more decadent flesh.

A new servant? *Talorc had a handful, and the same lot of them had been with him for years.* I've never seen her before.

Servants at Talorc's don't wear that gear, you imbecile, *his conscience chided harshly.*

"My shoes should be the least of your worries," she replied sassily to Talorc, turning back toward Damian and wiping her hands on her apron. She walked directly up to him and beamed brightly, holding out a hand. "I'm Kate. It's nice to meet you. Damianos, right?"

Damian merely stared. He could do little else.

By all the Creator possesses...she is magnificent.

His balls shriveled and then swelled as he continued to mutely gape at the female. Talorc's daughter. This is Talorc's daughter. *Shrivel. Swell. Shrivel. Swell.*

When he didn't place his hand in her own after a full ten seconds, Kate widened her eyes and looked back at the table filled with his comrades. "Something wrong with this one?"

Vadin replied around a mouthful of bread, "He's usually charming around females. Something must be wrong with you. But we knew that already."

Realizing she still held out her hand, Kate dropped it to her side and tipped her head in a gesture that clearly said, 'oooookaaaayyyy' before heading back into the kitchen and mumbling, "Weirdo."

Damian dropped his hand to his side to allow the door to swing shut so he didn't look like a complete wacko. He forced himself to turn back to the table to sit down as his head swirled with suddenly riotous thoughts. That's Talorc's daughter? I was ogling Talorc's daughter? I have a semi because of Talorc's daughter? Fuck. Fuck fuck fuck. No. No way. There is no way.

"You will have to excuse my daughter," Talorc passed him the tray of rolls, just as oblivious to Damian's physical reaction to Kate as he was of the fact that Damian's stomach bottomed out as his king confirmed his inner thoughts. "Kathryn, despite my best efforts, marches to the beat of her own drum."

"And is terrible at it," Vadin interposed. "Do you remember her rockstar phase? You dropped a fortune on all those instruments."

A hint of a smile found its way to Talorc's face, but Damian was too busy still reeling with his damnable thoughts to notice.

"I remember it well."

"I don't think our eardrums will ever recover," Cyrus said with a laugh.

Mora and Kate bustled back into the room with serving trays laden with food Damian suddenly didn't care about. His eyes pulled back to Kate as if she were a flame and he was a moth, and her power was as strong as the sun. She was saying something to Mora about where to place the dishes and what to move so the males could easily reach the utensils, but the commotion of the room faded so all Damian sensed was her.

Wisps of lavender trailed after her as if the sprigs were in her hair. She glowed under the light from the chandelier, her lips shining, her teeth pristinely white in complement to her skin and hair. Already her radiance and positivity were infectious, as Damian couldn't drag his regard from her slender form. He'd never seen, felt moved by, been around, or heard anyone quite like...her.

And it had been all of five minutes.

Creator take me...but what would a lifetime be like?

He physically shook himself and busied his hands with

gathering food for his plate. The others fell into an easy banter around him while he piled his platter high, only belatedly realizing the seat across from him had remained unoccupied until now.

Irrepressibly, his eyes trailed back to her, and he wavered in his movements. He watched as, with a heavy sigh that was more relieving than exhaustive, Kate reached for the pitcher of beer and her mug.

"Kathryn."

"What?" Kate responded innocently as she looked at her father but continued to fill her stein.

Talorc looked pointedly at her mug, which Kate filled to the very top without spilling. She continued to lock eyes with her father as she put the pitcher down, lifted her glass, sipped from the top, and then let out a satisfied breath.

Talorc sighed. "Could you behave for just five minutes? Hence Damian does not get the wrong impression of you?"

The wrong impression? *Damian couldn't fathom what impression he was getting, but it was far from wrong, and he wanted more of it.*

"He's the one who didn't shake my hand," Kate said as she sipped her beer again. "Talk about rude.*"*

"It could be because you called him by the wrong name," Ryder said playfully, and Kate gawked first at him and then at Damian.

"Yeah, it's Damian," *Vadin crooned with a toothy grin.*

Damian knew he was poking fun at him, but he suddenly didn't have the wherewithal to care.

"I'm so sorry," Kate told him earnestly, brushing a stray hair from her face after she put down her mug. "They told me your name was Damianos."

"It was." His voice cracked at the end, and he cleared it to continue, "That's the name I was born with, but I changed it. I've changed it a lot."

"Really? Why?"

Wine. She has a voice like wine. *Damian blinked twice to disperse the thought before he replied, "I've been in a lot of wars."*

She frowned. "Yeah, that's what they told me about you; that you were off fighting all those wars because you were bored here."

"Kathryn," Talorc intoned with firmness.

"*What?*" *Kate huffed in annoyance.* "*That's what Vadin said.*"

Vadin snickered from his seat, earning him a stern look from Ryder. "*You couldn't have waited a day before starting your antics?*"

"*What's the fun in that?*" *Vadin winked at Kate before resuming his meal.*

"*You know you're a jerk, right?*" *Kate snapped at Vadin, who laughed around a chicken thigh.*

As the banter from the others picked up, Damian's focus tapered solely to Kate. Already he noted that she laughed freely and teased mercilessly in a voice that held the sweetest swells. He wished with everything in him that he'd taken her hand in his own to see if her skin were as soft as it looked, because he suddenly couldn't think of anything else. Except her legs. Creator take him, but she had the legs of a goddess. As she tilted her head to address Noir, he noticed one of her ears was daintily pierced all the way around the rim while the other was only three times, and her mascara was smudged under one eye.

She was glorious.

"*Well then you tell me* Damian," *Kate stressed his name while making a face at Vadin, and Damian was suddenly thrown into a fantasy where she said it a hundred different ways and it never got old.* "*Why did you leave? Why are you back?*"

Silence fell over the room, only broken up by the faint scratching of utensils on plates.

"*Damian.*"

Damian whipped his head from Kate to Ryder, who looked at him with raised brows.

"*Why did you leave?*"

Why did I leave?

Damian was rarely lost for words, but as he glanced back at Kate, he could only think that the reason he'd returned was as clear as the shining night sky.

"*You always saw opportunity and never hesitated to take it,*" *Talorc said, tapping the edge of his stein before lifting it to his lips.* "*We appreciated that in you from the very beginning.*"

"*How did you two meet?*" *Kate asked her father, before looking back at Damian.*

"The Siege of Thessalonica," Ryder said, snagging Kate's attention. "We'd been watching Damian for a long time, even fought against him a time or two. He always gave us a run for our money."

"But could never out-drink us." Vadin raised his own glass to Damian.

"So you were made then, not borne?" Kate asked him.

"Yes," was all Damian could manage to utter.

"Who made you? Do you have any abilities?"

He shook his head, busying himself with taking a drink. The more he looked at her the more words became an enigma.

"Come now," Talorc said with a soft smile. "You always have so much to say."

Damian looked at Talorc, then Kate, but forced himself to look away. Noir sat beside her, so he asked him, "You all are close?"

"They're like brothers to me. Been there through it all." Kate waved her hand nonchalantly at the four ferocious males seated around her at the massive table. She spoke to The Guards of Nightfall as if they were no more than civilians—certainly not the males of legend they were.

"We were there when she was borne," Ryder said.

"And haven't left her side since," Vadin finished.

"You've all stayed in Warwick?" Damian asked.

"More or less," Cyrus replied.

Damian looked from one face to another and abruptly developed the sinking feeling he'd missed out on so much—maybe too much. He suddenly didn't want to miss a single moment more. At the same time, he knew being around Kate would be incredibly dangerous to his morals, his will, and his commitment to Talorc.

How the fuck did I get into this predicament?

"Okay so," Kate waved around her fork, pulling a stern look from Talorc. "If you left because you were looking for new opportunities, why are you back?"

Damian swallowed the mouthful of food he'd forced himself to eat as his thoughts twisted, turned, and catapulted through his mind. He was pulled back to Kate as if he couldn't resist her, and as he captured her gleaming gaze once more, his heart slowed to a thunderous roll within the confines of his chest.

He thought he'd seen the universe before?
He was looking at it now.
It was her.
Subsequently, what he thought lay before him as his future became violently upended.
Which horrified him.

No. I didn't come here for this. This—she is off limits. *He couldn't think this way about Talorc's daughter, not to mention the only link he had left to his dead beloved. But there was no way he could leave again; he owed too much to Talorc. He had to find a middle ground. He had to avoid her. He had to keep himself from her. He would busy himself with his friends, new hobbies, and other females. Once the realization settled that she was Talorc's daughter, it would be averting enough.*

Avoid. Avoid avoid avoid.

"When are we going out?" he asked loudly and abruptly, tearing his eyes to Vadin.

"Uh…" Vadin looked at him blankly. "You just got here?"

Damian shoveled food into his mouth to keep his body occupied, because if he didn't, his gaze would lock back on Kate and not let up. And to look at her was to want her. But I can't. I have to avoid her. If I remain loyal to Talorc, I have to figure out how to be around her and not—

Creator, how can I want her so badly? I don't even know her.

"Who am I staying with?" Damian reached for his beer and took a long drink. And then another. And then one more.

Avoid.

"Mora has arranged a room for you," Talorc said, raising a brow at Damian's gluttonous behavior. "You can stay here as long as you need to get settled on your own."

"I could show you around the place," Kate offered enthusiastically. "I know you have a lot to catch up on with the boys, but if you're staying here—"

"You have room, right?" Damian continued to look at Vadin.

Avoid.

"Sure," Vadin said slowly, looking at Talorc and then back at Damian. "But it's cooler here. The movie theater has a new

projector that—"

"I'll stay with you." Realizing that he was being disastrously rude to his liege and his host, Damian looked hastily at Talorc. "I—It would be easier for me to settle in somewhere small. I wouldn't want to get used to the luxuries here." He grappled onto the only thing he could think of as an excuse, even though it was a glaringly stupid one.

Avoid.

"Whatever suits you," Talorc said. "But I would ask that you come here often so we may reacquaint ourselves."

"Of course, Talorc," Damian tried to sound thankful and respectful as he continued to eat the meal that had been specially prepared for his arrival in the house that had been arranged specifically for his welcome surrounded by the people who had gathered to honor his homecoming.

When all he really felt was a seismic change in who and what he was to become.

Chapter Seven

Damian stormed down the stairs from Kate's room, having been denied entry yet again. It was another night he would go without hearing her voice, another night he would go without seeing her face, another night he wasted hours trying to convince her to *leave her damn room*. The only reason he knew she still lived was the gentle thrumming of her heartbeat and the soft wisps of breath he heard through the tall cherry doors. But it wasn't enough. It hadn't *been* enough, and he was over it. He needed to see her, hear her, *feel* her.

I don't understand. He clambered down the second set of curling marble treads with all the grace of a buffalo. Kate occupied an entire wing on the third floor to herself, but she hadn't breached the confines of any of her other spaces. *I know she wants to go to her solarium to check on her plants.* He'd kept the winter blooms under control for her while she recovered, not even letting Asha help, but he was clumsy with pruners and found himself easily frustrated. It had been a lot easier when he'd simply been Kate's helper, holding the small trashcan as she trimmed leaves and browned branches.

She hasn't been to see Rook. He jumped the last step into the hall that connected the wings of the second floor. Despite that ugly horse hating his absolute guts, Damian took the Friesian out every night for exercise in hopes Kate would notice and be tempted to leave her room. It took him hours to corral the beast, and the effort left Damian sweating and stinking, but he had to at least try for Kate.

To no avail.

She hasn't been to the kitchen to bake, she hasn't been swimming, she hasn't gone to the gym, the TV hasn't been turned on, she hasn't gone exploring. He knew these were all things she loved to do, as he'd joined her on so many occasions. He couldn't understand why she just wouldn't *try* to get back into something. He knew if she would just give it a shot, she would enjoy herself and break out of this depression she was in. It would be that easy. He tried to be tolerant and understanding. He truly did. But as the weeks dragged on, he became more impatient with her refusal to socialize. More and more he thought about forcing open the door and dragging her out of there because *he knew* that's what she needed.

I have bigger problems at the moment, he thought to himself as he whisked down the hall to Talorc's office. Talorc had a mind to leave Warwick tonight, to continue his trek through Canada, and The Guard was gathering to put a stop to it. Talorc had barely prepared for such a journey, and now that they knew for sure Santiago was targeting him and him alone, they needed a better plan of offense and defense.

But for some reason he can't wait to get out of this house. He tasted acid in his mouth as he counted on one hand the number of times Talorc tried to see Kate. It churned, turning molten, as the resentment he'd been harboring for months bubbled to a head.

The door to Talorc's office was already ajar, and Damian burst through it without preamble. The slight had Talorc raising his head from where he stood behind his desk rifling through papers, his frown stern. Damian ignored the look and instead stopped in a wide-legged stance and crossed his lean arms over his chest. The others were already there: Vadin and Noir slouched in the chairs in front of Talorc's desk while Ryder lingered by the open doorway. Cyrus was seated across the room in another chair, speculating on the scene with aloof perturbance.

"You don't even know where you're going." Ryder drew the attention of the others as he spoke to Talorc, his voice full of frustration. "If you could at least give us a map of your projected route, we would feel better."

"It is as I told you." Talorc didn't bother to look up from whatever paper he had in his hand. "I need to backtrack to Prince Edward Island, but then I am heading west through the other provinces before journeying back into the United States."

"Yes, but *where?*"

"You know where the covens are. The rest I will figure out as I go."

"Talorc, you can't go alone," Vadin said, both elbows propped on the arms of his chair while one hand traced the lines of his mouth and the other flopped open in a gesture that said *obviously*. "Santiago made it clear that you're his target."

"I move faster alone."

"It doesn't matter. It's not safe."

"I can defend myself."

Vadin lifted a brow that had Talorc blasting an icy wave of irritation at him. His innate ability to control the temperature in the surrounding area was a tactic he used to intimidate lesser beings, but The Guard was used to it by now and Vadin merely stared at Talorc, brow still raised.

"There's more to it than where you're going to go," Cyrus said from across the room. "We need to know who you're meeting with, at what time, where you'll be during the day, where you'll be eating. The list goes on."

"I can provide you with all of that as I know it."

"Not good enough Talorc," Ryder growled. "You are underestimating our enemy, something we've been doing for weeks and have learned greatly from. Understand that the mistakes we made, we won't let you make, too. Santiago has proved time and time again that while his endgame is your seat of power, he will use any means necessary to torture you along the way."

"Whatever we need to be doing is not in Warwick anymore." Talorc cast his gaze back to the papers on his desk. "All of your reports have come back that this is no longer an area of interest. The port revealed nothing when we finally got into it. Santiago is operating out of many different places, and the drugs, prostitution, and the port are just an elaborate, distracting cover that we need not occupy ourselves with any longer. Until you find out more information, which I will remind you is *your job*, I am taking to the road."

"There's too many unknowns." Vadin flopped his arms back into his lap, lacing his fingers. "For example: we now know that there are more vampires who can disappear and reappear at will, which means they are being created by the same watcher. But how many of them are out there? Who is the watcher?"

"We also don't know the limitations of that ability, if there are any," Ryder said earnestly. "Can they appear in places they've never been, or only to places they've been before? Is there a threshold for how many times a night they can use that ability? Can they just appear partially somewhere, making the daylight hours accessible to them?"

"And don't forget that cloaking spell on the country house or whatever the fuck it was," Cyrus grumbled.

"There are things, beings, Creator, even *powers* that we are just starting to comprehend," Ryder said. "Now is not the time to tread boldly. We have to proceed with caution."

"Then you come with me," Talorc said stubbornly, deliberately.

Ryder's face darkened in disdain. "You know I can't."

Talorc's jaw swiveled from one side to the other. They all knew Ryder had Taryn to think about now; she was newly made, and Ryder wouldn't readily put himself in danger when she needed him most. He was also Talorc's second-in-command and had to stay back in case something *did* happen to Talorc, and he had to take over. With Kate in her current state, she was unfit to oversee a position of authority; the decision was one they all had agreed on throughout their deliberations over the past weeks.

"Then send someone else," Talorc said, his eyes traveling around the room to the various males. The obvious choice was Damian for his personal connections that stretched the globe, but Talorc looked over him as if he were a pile of dirt that had been forgotten to be swept up.

That's it. Damin felt the red-hot fury within him implode.

"You're so ready to leave when there's still things that need to be put in order here," he said sharply, "You keep forgetting Kate."

"I am not *forgetting* her," Talorc said, that frosty wind swirling from him once more.

"Then tell me what you *are* doing for her," Damian replied, his voice rising with each word. "Because you haven't been to talk to her this week. You haven't brought her favorite meal to her. You haven't offered to listen to her. You haven't encouraged her to come out of her room. You haven't pushed her to drink. Tell me Talorc: what are you doing for her?"

Talorc slammed his hands down on his desk and levelled Damian with a look that would have felled any other male. "I am trying to make things right."

"By running away?" Damian asked with fiery incredulity.

"By changing something I have the power to control," Talorc snarled, his fingers curling into the papers on his desk.

"You can help change Kate!" Damian shouted, throwing an arm out in a gesture of frustration. "You can help change the way she is thinking by *being there for her*."

Talorc didn't move, went still as stone. His voice was low, oppressive, as he said, "I alone have the power to change this world. To protect her as I should have been protecting her this whole time. The goal of this campaign for unification is not just for the safety of the nation but for the safety of Kathryn. I will see the end of this wraith filth for *her*."

"More are involved. It's not just the wraiths. It's vampires now too."

"I know this."

Damian plowed on without regard. "The answer isn't to turn your back."

"You have all the answers now, is it?"

"At least *show her* that you care."

"Do not," Talorc growled. "Lay that accusation at my feet. I care for her more than any other being on this planet."

Damian laughed without joy. "So you run."

Talorc rounded the desk with fire at his heels, but Damian stood strong. "*How dare you accuse me of running*? Need I remind you of the *two hundred years* you spent abroad, running, chasing who you thought you were, trying to remind yourself why you were, at one point, important?" Talorc raked Damian with an indignant glare, their faces barely a handsbreadth apart. "What good did it do you? What did you discover?"

"It's your fault!" Damian yelled, brazen with contempt. "If it weren't for your decades of inaction we wouldn't be where we are now."

"I am done with that blame. I am making amends with that part of my life and will hear no more about it."

"You can't just pick and choose what to remember, Talorc," Damian fired back hotly. "If you learned anything from before, you would know that ignorance will set you back even more. Look at where it's getting you now: Kate is…she's dying."

Verity burned the length of his throat. It was a truth he himself hadn't acknowledged, and when he tried to swallow the confession, the burning only grew worse. It spread from his throat to his chest, down his limbs and through his blood, before sweeping back up to intensify in his core, beyond the shuddering organ at his center. He wasn't the only one physically aggrieved by his words: Noir restlessly twined a half-smoked cigarette between his fingers, Vadin switched the legs he had crossed and cleared his throat as he looked at the floor, Cyrus turned his head toward the fire, and Ryder's face changed from aggravated engagement to blatant startlement. Even the snapping fire dimmed and receded.

Talorc's eyes widened and then narrowed as a gust of arctic air hit Damian so hard his breath froze in his lungs. "*She will not die.* I refuse to let that happen."

"Are you blind and deaf?" Damian asked rhetorically as his lungs re-expanded. "She has not eaten in days, fed in weeks; the blood Mora brings her goes untouched. She sits in her window, night after night, staring at nothing. How many times has she tried to walk into the morning light, Talorc? *How many*? You don't know."

Talorc's teeth ground so hard that Damian could hear the cracking from where he stood. His eyes flashed as he ate his retort, the earthen color lightening to a frenzied bronze.

"The longer you look away and pretend there is no problem, the larger the problem will become," Damian heeded Talorc, the burning in his chest swelling with animosity, which thankfully incinerated the veracity.

"I will not take observations from someone who does not have the wisdom and experience I do," Talorc responded with venom in his tone. "Your opinion means nothing to me."

Damian's eyes flared at the open hostility Talorc threw at him. He opened his mouth to respond, but Talorc continued.

"My reasons for continuing this journey I have clarified time and time again, but you—you *all*—forget that I answer to *no one*. I am Talorc: king of the vampires and your superior in every way. I do not have to explain myself to you or anyone in this household and I will do as I wish.

"Now," he lowered his voice and swung to address Ryder, who was stoically staring at Talorc, his face now masked in neutrality. "You have two weeks to get together a schedule for me, acquire the information you need, dredge up security, and formulate a plan. After a fortnight has passed, I am leaving for the Canadian provinces and *none of you* will stop me."

Talorc went back to his desk and sat down heavily in the chair, lifting his gaze to meet every single male in the room—except for Damian. "Leave me and see it done."

"Are you out of your mind?"

Damian swirled his drink in his glass, closing his eyes against Vadin's loud, incredulous tone.

"I wasn't saying anything that anyone hasn't been thinking," Damian grumbled before tipping his head back to take a swig of his double-vodka-cranberry.

They were holed up at their favorite dive bar *Jeffers*, and as the hour crawled toward five in the morning, Damian sullenly realized they only had an hour left to drink. He wasn't nearly drunk enough to stop now and threw back the contents of his glass before motioning to the less-than-enthusiastic bartender for another.

"Yeahhhh, but Talorc isn't in a state to hear all that." Vadin leaned back on the wooden barstool that had definitely seen better days. It creaked under the ex-Viking's weight, the spindles of the posterior portion bending under his musculature. "Think about it. He's still trying to figure out the best play in this wraith mess while dealing with his daughter who is on the verge of a mental break."

"Don't talk about Kate like that. She's not. She can pull through. She just needs help. All the help she can get." Throwing away the reminder that he'd just accused Talorc of worse, Damian cut Vadin an accusing glare as he said irritably, "Have you been to see her?"

"Most nights." Vadin cut Damian a sidelong glance, reaching forward to roll the bottom of his glass of whisky in a circle on the bar top. "You know we all have."

Damian leaned back in his chair as the bartender delivered his drink. *Fuck. He's right. I'm being an asshole.* He skimmed the single drunken patron slumped at the other end of the bar, who no longer pretended to watch the television propped in the corner of the room, before flicking his gaze back to the bartender. She yawned heartily, bracing herself against the bar with half-open eyes, less than interested in anything Damian or Vadin had to say.

"I'm tired of all the excuses. If Talorc wants to be a leader, he has to be able to tackle all these problems at once or appoint people who can." Damian played with the coaster on the bar as he spoke in a tone that bubbled with acid. "I don't know why all of a sudden we're being cautious around him. Talorc chose us as his Guard because we spoke up when it was needed and never hid from confrontation. He used to be able to handle a lot more than he is now."

"Things are different," Vadin mused, sighing heavily. "We can't just think about ourselves and our own paths anymore. Ryder has Taryn. Kate is more fragile than ever. Talorc has never been put in a position where he has to think beyond what to buy to appease her. And it's clear that Santiago is going to use any weakness against us to get to what he wants, which is an additional worry. We have to consider every possibility from every angle. We have to work together. Your arguing with Talorc is getting us nowhere."

Damian took a drink of his cocktail and said on a hiss, "I know that."

"And now Ryder is stuck back there trying to undo what you did." Vadin finished the whisky in his glass and when the bartender sleepily looked over to see if he wanted another, he shook his head. "You're making it harder by only thinking about you and your main concern, which we really can't ding you for because it is Kate's welfare. But you're three paces behind when we're all moving forward. Talorc also chose us because we pushed headfirst into any and everything; we wanted to be the best at what we did."

How can I move forward without her? Damian ran a hand through his hair. *Knowing she is suffering?*

"My brother," Vadin softened his tone. "What's the issue? This isn't you. At least, not a side that I know. And I know many of them."

Damian cradled his head in a hand and stared at the bar as his drink soured in his stomach.

"If there's anyone you can talk to," Vadin continued to roll the empty glass, and Damian flipped his vacant gaze to the monotonous movement. "It's me."

While Ryder was like a brother to him and the others just as tight, he and Vadin were the closest. The one he spent the most time with and consequently got into the most trouble with. From racing stolen horses to dragging cars down late-night freeways, from drinking every tavern dry to knowing the surrounding strip clubs like the back of their hands, Vadin had done it all with him. He was the one who always had his back: when Damian got in trouble with Talorc, or pestered the other Guards a little too much, or got into a tussle with a wife's violent husband...the former of whom Damian just happened to be sleeping with. Vadin liked to laugh and never took things too seriously, but was a straight shooter like Damian, and that's why they clicked the best.

But was Damian really ready to share what he had secretly been holding onto for...for years?

"I... Kate..." he started and then stopped, curling his fingers against the weathered bar top. The stench of sour beer filled his nostrils as he took a deep breath, his boot bouncing against the lower rung of the stool in edginess.

I can't do this.

"Damian," Vadin said dully, drawing Damian's eyes up to him. The charming smirk that got them both waiting rosters of females taunted him, and Damian suddenly despised it. "Do you think I'm stupid?"

Damian felt his throat constrict and a lump form as he stared at Vadin, hoping and wishing that he wouldn't continue. He'd been playing the 'what he didn't admit wouldn't hurt him' game long enough to convince himself what he truly felt didn't matter. But if Vadin continued it would be too close to an admittance from Damian.

Even though it wasn't. It couldn't be. Damian had long ago convinced himself that his *friend*ship with Kate was enough, leading him to believe he wouldn't live a life of bleakness and unfulfillment. That feeble convincing—that painfully plagued every single second of his life—was the only thing that kept him from being swallowed by all the things he couldn't have, and all the ways his life would be complete if he just…

It was that exact mindset that got him where he was now, four years later, sitting next to Vadin, feeling bleak and unfulfilled.

He'd been denying all of it for too long. He'd been denying *her* for too long. But acceptance…acceptance was something he couldn't do. Not in this. There was too much damage done. *He* had done too much damage. Not to himself. But to her.

To Kate.

The guilt constantly ate at him, yet over the last couple of weeks it was more vicious, more demanding. Almost losing her had put into perspective the years he'd wasted being a complete and utter jackass.

And now…

Now she might not ever be who she was before.

Which meant they…couldn't…

"Talorc and the others might be thick," Vadin leaned back in his chair as he spoke, crossing his arms over his broad chest. "But you also have to admit they have a lot on their respective plates. But I see you, brother. I see you and I know you. I can put two and two together.

"You were explosive when Kate was taken. I thought it was just because you were worried about her like the rest of us and expressing yourself in the only way you knew how. But it didn't stop, and you started to act more rashly than usual. You changed during that time, in the early days of her abduction. You spoke less of war and strategy, things you have lived for your entire life, to focus on her. Your only focus was her, and sometimes it obscured other things that were more important—like thinking before acting. You also stopped coming out with me, which, let's be honest, you've been shit at for a couple years now anyway. You started concentrating on sparring and training and hunting and researching. Nothing else was as important to you as getting Kate back."

Damian tried to swallow the thick lump in his throat but couldn't, so he looked back to his drink for moral support.

"I couldn't figure out why. I mean, yes, it's Kate, but there was only so much we could do with what we had, which in the beginning wasn't a lot. There were a lot of hurdles to jump over but you kept trying to jump the same one—get Kate at all costs. And you couldn't see past that hurdle to the bigger picture that Talorc's been trying to get us to see. Had you always been like this, so single-minded? I thought back to when you first came home, because maybe that's when you changed, but the more I did the more I realized that I couldn't think of a single time you weren't without Kate. You haven't left her side since you came back four years ago. Why is that?"

"She's my friend," Damian croaked, picking at a chip on his glass. "Just my friend."

"My brother, we have never spent that much time together and I've known you for over six hundred years." Vadin raised his brows. "Who are you trying to convince?"

Fuck. Damian continued to pick at the chip on his glass.

That first night...when I came home... Damian stared at the burgundy concoction in his glass. *Did I even see anything else besides her?*

His stomach began to churn. *No. Whenever I look at anything, anyone, all I see is her. All the time. Everywhere.*

Fuck.

"Look," Vadin stared knowingly at Damian, and Damian diligently ignored it. "I can't help you if you don't want help. But avoiding and denying what you feel for Kate isn't benefiting you or her. It hasn't for a long time. You've slapped a bandage on something that isn't a wound. You're trying to suppress something that needs to breathe. If you act constructively, this could be the push she needs to break through.

"You've probably seen more war than all of us, and you know it's an endless pit of despair. It's dark. It's depressing. That depression is consuming. You know that what Kate is feeling right now is consuming her. She can't help it. That darkness is pulling and pulling and pulling on her and she's drowning."

"Why don't you help her?" Damian said, only interjecting with such a baseless comment because what Vadin was saying was too real, too right, and he still wasn't drunk enough to listen to all of this.

"Because I'm not what she needs," Vadin told him frankly. "*Who* she needs."

Damian shot him an irritated slice of a glare. "Fuck you, Oh Wise One."

Vadin chuckled, but the sound was without its usual touch of humor. "What I'm saying is, there are things in motion now that can't be undone. Talorc is ready and eager to move forward. Santiago is pushing us to act. The wraiths are circling. The vampire nation is indecisive. And there's nothing, no amount of time, care, or sympathy, that will change what happened to Kate. She's experienced something substantially transformative." Vadin's lips curled into a shit-eating grin. "But then again, so have you, haven't you?"

Fuck.

Fuuuuuuck.

Damian lifted his glass to take a hefty swallow. "She doesn't need more stress right now."

"Then I'll ask you this—how long can *you* keep this up?" Vadin rocked back and forth in his chair, the legs creaking. "How long can you let your life be meaningless? How long can you string her along? You think she doesn't wonder about you, too? You're kidding yourself if you don't think you're part of her depression."

Bastard. Damian shot Vadin another glare, but the male only shrugged.

"What is it that you told Talorc? 'Further ignorance will set you back even more'?" Vadin eyed him knowingly, his lips pursed. "'The longer you look away and pretend there is no problem, the larger the problem will become'?"

Damian snarled lowly, "I get it."

"You should tell her how you feel," Vadin said as if it were the easiest thing in the world. He plopped his chair back on four feet and reached into his back pocket for his wallet. "It may change things for the both of you, for the better."

"I don't *feel* anything."

Vadin huffed a laugh through his nose, throwing some bills on the bar top.

"At any rate," Damian said. "Talorc would never let it happen."

"You would be surprised, I think, if you tried to look at the situation from a different point of view."

Damian upended his glass, emptying the contents into his mouth. He slammed the tumbler down a little more forcefully than he meant to and then reached into his jacket pocket to draw out his own wallet to throw some bills on the bar top.

He's wrong. What I'm doing is working. I don't need to change.

When he stood, he swayed gently, and Vadin clapped a burley hand onto his shoulder to steady him and said, "Come on, I'll give you a ride home."

Chapter Eight

S antiago was given little preamble as he materialized in the depths of where he'd been summoned, a particularly negative characteristic of the ability he'd been gifted. Water dripped slowly from somewhere far away, its echo an indication of how cavernous the space was, yet Santiago didn't know the true bounds of this place. He didn't know where it was located or if it even existed in Earth's realm. There were no windows, no doors, no hidden entries or exits. Just walls of dark, jagged, wet stone for as high as the eye could see, with only a handful of torches lighting the circular space that was no wider than thirty feet in any direction. Santiago believed the space was cut from a mountain, though if that were true, it was one that was stagnant and untouched by human hands.

"They think to act against me."

"They're too disjointed and uninformed." Santiago bowed before his overlord. "Greetings, by the way."

The other being, marred by shadow, waved away Santiago's words with a disinterested hand in a gesture he couldn't see.

"They gather." His hissing voice caused a wind to cut by, mirroring the creature's disdain.

Santiago suppressed a shiver. When he met him it was always here, in this desolate place. *I hate it here.* The cavern chilled Santiago's bones, and not just because the temperature within was always cool.

It was being in *his* vicinity.

Adhamh.

Even though Adhamh was his sire and Santiago had been serving him for years, his vile omnipresence always threatened to suffocate him immediately upon their meeting. Abruptly, Santiago realized he didn't actually know what the male looked like, but almost just as quickly noted it was probably for the better. Santiago had heard rumors that no one could stand to be in Adhamh's true presence because it would drive them instantaneously to madness. *Sometimes I wonder...*

Santiago narrowed his eyes to the space where Adhamh was sitting. The only thing he could make out was an egregiously large seat made of stone, crumbled at the base and surrounded by smaller stones that had fallen over time. The seat was in the middle of the floor so far away from any torchlight that the low, orange luminescence wouldn't reach. The shadows that manifested, that clung to Adhamh and swirled around the mockful throne, were a physical representation of the evil that was fundamental in the male. Perhaps they shielded Santiago from Adhamh's true malevolence as they writhed at the base of the seat, curling up to blacken the area where the male sat, veiling his visage.

"Let them gather," Santiago said dismissively, interrupting his own musings. "They won't act without The Creator's blessing."

Adhamh fell silent, and Santiago knew he was thinking. The male was always thinking. He was always planning, navigating, strategizing. Most of the time he shared with Santiago his views, but like any diabolical organism hiding secrets, he kept some things to himself.

As did Santiago.

"We cannot count on that fact," Adhamh finally responded. "We need more information. But their boundaries are impenetrable, have been to me for years." Santiago heard a subtle shifting of fabric and deduced that Adhamh changed his position, perhaps restlessly, though such an act was unusual for him. *But what do I know of the male?*

Other than the fact that he is my sire? I know he is the notorious Adhamh, the first and only watcher to descend from grace after falling in love with a human. He is the sole being capable of and responsible for the proliferation of the wraiths. Santiago paused briefly in thought as he watched the shadows warp. *He promised me a life of infinite ability and prolongation in exchange for fealty to his cause. He also promised me supreme power over the vampire nation. He rarely shows emotion. I don't know what he looks like, how he truly feels, if he is stuck here in this abysmal place, or who else he cavorts with. He could be having similar conversations with countless vampires.*

But I know I've proven to him I'm invaluable, a staunch supporter in whatever he wants to accomplish. And that's why he has chosen me for this.

"Why don't you use your spheros?" Santiago asked.

"I seem to have misplaced it," Adhamh replied, and though his tone didn't betray sentiment, Santiago was inclined to believe he was lying. Continuing, he asked, "What news do you have of Talorc?"

Ignoring the abrupt change of subject, Santiago curbed his sneer of irritation. "Wherever he lives he hasn't breached for weeks. We lost track of him after the situation in Ursuline and haven't caught wind of him since."

"It has been almost a month," was the answering growl. "Why have you not relocated him?"

"It's difficult to say," Santiago, undeterred by the growl, continued. "Some of my contacts within the covens have redacted their support, making it challenging to gain new insight. The only thing I can think of is that he has improved his security and could be using magic."

"That skill is arbitrary at best, difficult to pinpoint and pursue, and holds little sustainability on Earth. It worked well for you when it was needed, but it was demolished when the house imploded and thus is unreliable. Besides, Talorc has no knowledge of it. Few do."

Santiago knew it had been a one-time thing, but he already was operating under the table to get his hands on such an ability again.

"Not one of your contacts ever told you where Talorc lived?"

"I get the impression that it was never common knowledge, and as the *Elden Edicts* waned, so did everyone's concern with Talorc."

"Your contact up north? She did not know through her own connections?"

"She vacillates still because of them. But I can convince her. Especially since we both have an idea where Talorc is headed next."

"But you think he lives in Warwick?"

"I think he lives in many places. He wouldn't be so stupid as to let his daughter roam the area in which he lived unattended. Her activity within the city was so random and infrequent it leads me to believe they may have a domicile there, but it's not their home."

"And you have canvassed the city completely?"

Santiago lowered his eyes in a look that bled only the slightest bit of annoyance. "I need more bodies. Warwick has a population of over five hundred thousand."

"Is that not something you can accomplish?"

"Only on the vampire front, and the more Talorc reaches out to the covens the less support I get. On that same hand, every time we meet an opposing force, we lose great numbers. The vampires haven't lost their skill at decimating wraiths."

"Appoint someone to scout areas to access bodies and I will make more wraiths," Adhamh said with an indifference that would alarm a more empathetic being; Santiago, however, was unfazed.

"I'll see to it." Santiago shifted on his booted feet to slide his bejeweled hands into his black jean pockets. "What's the plan going forward?"

"What it has always been." Santiago felt the tension in the room thicken, and he had the strong suspicion that Adhamh was eyeing him as he would the slime from a snail. "I think you need not focus on being so personal and instead remember the bigger picture of what we are after."

Of what you are after, Santiago thought. *I seek to gain more. I have a plan. And to enact that plan we have to be patient. I can be patient. There are covens yet untouched and if we could get our hands on them...*

"The Guard are more impermeable than you think," he countered aloud. They were upping their game, especially now that Kate was back in their hands.

I miss crushing her beneath my fist. Knowing that every ounce of torture I brought on her would get me closer to succeeding the throne of the vampire was the invigorating burst of power I didn't know I'd been missing.

Should I have killed her to hurry this along? Santiago lifted an eyebrow to his internal thoughts, but quickly sheathed his face with neutrality. *No. I don't think we're ready to push to the top just yet. We need more time. Besides, I enjoyed prolonging her useless, baseless life. She got what she deserved for thinking she could pull one over on me.*

He continued to Adhamh, "We'll be successful if we stay this course. Obliterate them piece by piece. Once Kate dies from her psychosis, Talorc will shortly follow, and The Guard will be dismantled. While most covens have created their own councils, they are tenuous ventures and will crumble with the slightest pressure. And just like that we'll gain control of the vampires."

"The goal is not to take over the vampire nation." Adhamh hissed like a snake, and an unavoidable chill gripped Santiago's spine. "It is to eradicate humankind."

"But if you eradicate humankind, there will be no humans left to make wraiths," Santiago pointed out, and not for the first time. "Then what are you going to be king of?"

"Let me worry about that. You focus on pressing forward."

"To our joint goal, yes," Santiago tempered himself slightly. "But you said—"

"I said I do not care what you do with the vampires as long as you help me succeed. However, you are forgetting that, and in turn, losing sight of the end goal," Adhamh retorted sharply. "I have the power to remove you from this world, Santiago, just as I brought you into it."

Wisely, albeit with some anger, Santiago did not reply.

"Besides, you do not have the leverage you think you do. Only one Guard is tethered. The rest remain rogue bachelors without extended family. If you insist on this path, you need to utilize your allies and hit all the covens at once. Doing so will decimate their specific leaders, leaving you to replace them with who you trust. But you must do so quickly. We do not have the luxury of time or privacy; the watchers will notice our movements and this human world...it is vibrant and vulgar and knows no bounds."

You're wrong, Santiago thought traitorously. *They have family. They have desires. They have whims. And I can play on them. I am playing on them.*

He could prove Adhamh wrong. Santiago could be patient whereas he knew Adhamh couldn't. *I don't know why,* Santiago thought unenthusiastically. *It seems that all he has is time locked away down here.*

While Santiago disagreed on how to specifically proceed, he knew what Adhamh wanted and could align it with his own ideals. *I can do both,* he thought, ravenous at the thought. *I know I can. I just need to show Adhamh. To make him understand that there is more to be had, and if we work to achieve both goals simultaneously, the outcome will be extraordinary.*

Imagine, Santiago thought, suddenly alive with conviction. *Me, the new vampire king, leading them through this world with confidence and competence, working alongside Adhamh, the watcher who's given us a new purpose. It will be a new night, a righteous night, the night we all have been waiting for.*

He hedged whether or not to continue, ultimately deciding reserve wouldn't help him advance. "You are not out there on the streets, fighting, working, talking with those who have insight. I am your vessel. I know what is best in this and working from the inside out is how we will be successful. Let me show you, Adhamh. I can do this. I can win on both fronts."

Shadows lashed out before Santiago could defend himself, wrapping themselves around him both physically and mentally. His thoughts conceded to nightmares, creatures and torment and blackness and pain spiraling out from his gaping mouth, while his throat tensed as if corporeal hands wrapped around it. He drew in a breath only to choke, and he felt icy bindings lock his arms and legs in place as his sight went black.

"You forget to whom you speak," Adhamh warned, his low voice hissing with scorn. "I am your sire, your creator, *your master.* I pull your strings. You dance to *my* hands. Whatever bond you have to Talorc—sever it. Our goal is to start a new world. Do not lose sight of that. I will provide you what you need, but *you will heed me.*"

Santiago was forced back to his previous destination abruptly. The bindings that had hindered him disappeared, and he fell to his knees in his home with a hand to his neck as he choked on precious air. His sight returned slowly, and his mind felt the pressure of asphyxiating darkness lift, but it was still a full minute before he could realign his thoughts.

He knew what he was doing was right. He knew where to focus. Adhamh was wrong and he would prove him so, and in the end the watcher would thank him for it.

Hangovers rarely, if ever, plagued vampires, however Damian was to be the exception this night.

He awoke with a groan and a hand on his head, and when he sat up his stomach simultaneously rolled with sour nausea and growled in dissatisfaction at being empty. Something clinked and then fell to the floor beside him, and as he leaned forward enough to rest an elbow on his thigh, he peeked open a single eye to see a bottle of Yuengling clanging against another. There were four more, making the total number of empty beer bottles six. Coupled with the four double-vodka-cranberries he had at *Jeffers*, he was hurting.

I'm too old for this, he thought as he shifted his legs over the side of his sectional to place his feet on the floor. He squeezed his eyes shut and then inhaled a breath to stave off the worst of the nausea before he looked out the window of his penthouse's living room.

The curtains were mostly drawn, but a slender crack revealed the last light of day in its golden glow. The city sprawled out for miles beyond the panes, tall skyscrapers and homely brick storefronts lining a labyrinth of roadways. Lights from said buildings were flickering to life as the sun made its descent, and the vociferous sounds of rush-hour traffic began to assault his sensitive ears. If he went to his bedroom, a view of the port and river would dominate, while the other end of the house would boast a view of the expansive park situated in the center of the city. When Noir had told him about this place, Damian had fallen in love with it and the amenities he was allotted, like the twenty-four-seven secured front door, extensive gym, and cleaning service.

Distantly he remembered turning away said cleaning service this morning, and as he kicked away the Yuengling bottles he was thankful, because a bottle of vodka lay half-empty next to them...and a pizza box, a bag of tortilla chips, and an open container of Chipotle. His boots lay haphazardly where he supposed he'd kicked them off, but he'd tracked enough road salt and mud into the space that the rug would need to be shampooed. *I had a night last night.* As he straightened on the sectional, his vertebrae cracking with the movement, he was even more thankful that he'd turned away the cleaning service because he realized he could smell himself—and it was not pleasant.

He rose to unsteady feet and turned toward his bedroom. *A night I do* not *want to remember.* But Damian had always been one to recall his less than stellar actions no matter how much he drank. As he trudged miserably over the cold concrete floors into his wood and steel bathroom, his conversation with Vadin reeled back to smash him heavily with recollection. He leaned one elbow on the wall outside of the shower and placed his head in the crook as he turned on the water and tempered it to something tolerable before stripping out of his stinking clothes and sliding underneath the stream.

I have to get to Talorc's. He sighed as he ran both hands through his hair. *I'll pick up some pho on the way from that Vietnamese place for Kate. I'll take that stupid horse out for a run then head out with Cyrus to meet that weapons dealer. I'll catch up with Ryder at some point to see how the discussion with Talorc went. Then maybe I'll have time for a workout.*

Begrudgingly, Damian thought, *and I should stop and see Talorc to apologize.* The argument he had with him weighed heavily on Damian's conscience. While they were both stubborn, hot-headed males, they'd never had an argument like that. For all their faults they were also virtuous and valorous, and in all their long years as brethren, things had never culminated so disastrously. So…personally. Damian distantly realized the dispute was part of the reason he drank so heavily last night; he'd wanted to forget that conversation too.

Vadin is right about one thing, he thought as he reached for his washcloth and soap. *I need to focus on moving forward. Get a plan going for myself, for Kate, and what's next in this war against the wraiths.*

Those thoughts enveloped him as he showered, changed into a dark gray Henley shirt and blue jeans, stowed a few weapons on his person, and set out for the night.

The pho place had been packed and Damian spent more time in there waiting than he wanted to, thus when he pulled into Talorc's driveway it was well after eight o'clock in the evening. He grabbed the paper bag that held their food and the two Vietnamese iced coffees before taking the stairs two at a time to the front door. It would've been easier to park in the garage, but he was already anxious about potentially seeing Kate and couldn't waste the time navigating the tight spot and then balancing the food and drinks.

Should I warm the food up before I go up to her? He placed the bag on top of his hand, deduced the temperature would suffice, and stopped in front of the door. He turned his face up to the security camera and impatiently waited for someone from the remote security site to notice and unlock the door for him, which took entirely too long. When he heard the door unlatch, he placed the handles of the paper bag in his mouth to push the lever to open the door, and it was in the next breath that he was halfway up the stairs to the second level.

He didn't have any new tactics to try and get Kate to talk to him tonight, but he was approaching the situation with a clarity he hadn't possessed before. *New angles, or whatever the fuck Vadin was saying,* he thought to himself as he topped the stairs to Kate's wing of the manor. He wasn't going to have a come-to-Creator moment with her; he didn't need to. While Vadin was right about moving forward, his relationship with Kate was going to remain the same. There was no need to change anything. They were friends. *And things are working just fine that way.*

Kate just needs to move on. He knew her mind needed to heal before she would become herself again. And to do that she had to believe she could. If he expected Talorc to acknowledge and grow from his past, he needed to apply the same sentiment to Kate. *Simple.* He could empower her to believe she could grow from what happened, and she would. *Just like that.* All of that could be accomplished as her friend. Because that's what friends did.

Damian decided when he met up with Cyrus later, he would ask if he knew anyone that could help Kate along. *I think he's been in contact with Lilith, and maybe she knows someone.* The Guard's unofficial medical liaison could be pivotal, but as he jostled to a stop outside Kate's bedroom door the thought disappeared.

"Hey." He knocked twice to let her know he was there and stooped to place the bag and one of the coffees on the floor. The other he sipped for himself before he crouched to rustle through his offerings. "I got pho from that place with the little tiger statue out front." He popped open one of the containers and reached in for a snack. "I also got you rice rolls, those mini pancakes you like, and some pork buns." He hadn't eaten since whenever he'd gotten home, and compared to the motley of things he'd run through this morning the Vietnamese food was decadent.

"Oh, and there's spring rolls too," he called to her as he sat down with his back propped against the door intricately carved with large moonflowers. He stretched his legs out before him while he took another swig of his coffee and reached into the bag for his own bowl of pho. While he got himself comfortable to have another conversation with just himself and the door, he hoped what he was going to say would begin to turn the tide.

"Look, I know you've been through a lot." Damian popped the lid off his bowl, cursing when the broth sloshed toward the rim. "And that's putting it lightly. Everyone wants you to snap out of it. I know it's not really that easy but Kate it *is*. You need to make like a phoenix and rise from the ashes.

"I've been taking care of things for you." Damian searched for a spoon in the bag before taking his first bite of pho. "I've been exercising Rook, even though you know he fucking hates me. And your garden is a lot of work and I'm sorry if I've jacked something up, but it's in okay shape for now. Asha's mad. She hates it when I go in there. She says she can't wait for you to come back and get things in order. She misses you. A lot.

"The kitchen's not the same without you in it, and Noir is really missing your brownies. He's started smoking again, and you're the only one who can get him to quit. Mora can't wait to get into your room and snag your laundry. I think she misses you more than Asha. Vadin has been complaining nonstop because he doesn't have anyone to watch *Below Deck* with. And you missed it—Cyrus got bit by one of the security dogs yesterday. *Cyrus*! He was so fucking mad."

He chewed for a few minutes, thinking about what to say next. "Taryn and Ryder are doing good. They're starting to look at houses together. It's weird: they fight a lot, but it seems to work for them. She puts him in his place like no one I've ever seen. I know I've told you all this before, but I feel... I just...

"We miss you, Kate. That's all," he finished lamely, scooping up some more pho before choosing his next words. "I know you're not ready, but when you are...we'll all be here. I'll be the one to open the door for you."

He finished his pho in silence, not knowing what else to say. Words he felt needed saying wouldn't form in his mind let alone traipse his tongue, and instead of further sounding like an idiot, he abstained.

"I'm going to help you, Kate." He cleaned up his mess before delicately laying her food in a spot where opening the door, if it so ailed her, wouldn't upset anything. "I'm going to help you through this. I have an idea, okay? Just...I have an idea."

He stood slowly, his stomach finally settling with what he had put in there. He took his trash with him as he turned and, with one last look over his shoulder at her impenetrable door, headed back down the hall. He knew the food would go cold and untouched, but there was a part of him that had to look out for her, even if she didn't want to look out for herself.

Tossing his trash in a bin in a vacant room, he bolted back down the stairs while checking his watch. Cyrus would be here in a half an hour, and Damian chastised himself for not having enough time to properly exercise Rook. *I can get him started, but Isaac will have to finish,* he thought of Talorc's stablemaster. That's exactly what he did, and after a cursory stop in a powder room to wash his hands, he was just walking back into the foyer when Cyrus appeared from the garage.

"You ready?" Damian asked by way of greeting. "We can take my car."

"I figured," Cyrus rumbled his reply, his long, black beard swaying with the movement. "How's Kate tonight?"

Damian glanced at Cyrus as he grabbed his jacket out of the closet, so quickly thrown there on his way in that it was barely on the hanger. The male was dressed in black from head to toe as usual, his bald head gleaming under the light from the chandelier. He wore a brown canvas jacket with what Damian knew was countless knives stowed in the folds, while a Desert Eagle was tucked into the waistband of his jeans at his back. Damian detected a hint of hope in his chestnut regard, which stoked his own as he folded himself into his leather jacket.

"The same." Damian grabbed his keys out of a pocket to remotely start his car from inside. "Brought her some pho tonight."

"From that tiger place?"

"Yeah."

Together they walked back into the night, and the cold February air whistled by them in earnest. There was a blanket of snow on the ground that was fresh from the day before, and as Damian looked out over the hills and trees surrounding the property, he couldn't help but think that Kate would unquestionably love to be out here stuffing the BMW's tailpipe with ice to irritate the absolute hell out of him.

Any time now, Kate.

Reminded of his earlier motives, he looked across the roof of the car after opening his door. The movement stopped Cyrus, who met his gaze. "You have Lilith's number, right?"

Cyrus frowned at him. "Yes. As do you."

"I need her personal one."

Cyrus's frown deepened as he continued in his task of getting in the car. However, by the time he was seated and strapping himself in, the frown had slipped from his face. "What do you need it for?"

"I want to see if she can talk to Kate," Damian said as he fully started the Beemer. "I know the physical stuff is more her specialty, but maybe she knows someone who could talk to Kate if she can't. Like a psychiatrist or something."

"Psychologist." Cyrus attempted to settle into the leather seat, but his massive, six-plus frame rarely fit well in normal places. "You're talking about a psychologist."

"Whatever." Damian navigated the car down the driveway with a flippant gesture of his hand. "Just send me the number so I can give her a call."

"It's not the worst idea you've ever had," Cyrus admitted after a few heartbeats of silence. "Lilith might actually be able to help."

At the gentler tone Cyrus took with the latter statement, Damian glanced at him. The male had his gaze fixed out the window, watching the gaunt frames of the trees whisk by. The only telltale sign that something was on his mind was the curl of his fist against his jeans. Usually completely open to how he felt, Cyrus's face was now impassive, as if he were forcing himself to reveal nothing about his inner thoughts.

He's just worried about Kate. Damian smoothly navigated the car from the property, reaching for the hope that burned just out of reach. *But hopefully not for much longer if this all pans out the way I want.*

Chapter Nine

Not much changed over the next few days except the space Kate occupied, because it took too much energy when she needed to conserve it for breathing. She was currently on the floor of her room staring at the ceiling, but she saw neither the fabric strung along her bedframe in elegant slopes nor the mural on her ceiling. The ticking of the grandfather clock at the end of the hall was her constant companion, but she didn't hear it. The rug beneath her was cool, the wood planks under that hard and rigid, but Kate didn't feel either. The food Asha brought her this morning still sat outside the door, now cold and tasteless. If Kate cared to be concerned by the stench her festering body propagated, she would maybe open a window, but her senses were slowly dying.

She was wasting away, but not quick enough. The small amount of blood she'd drank a few weeks ago barely sustained her anymore, and she knew it wouldn't be long before her father or Mora or one of the boys came and forced her to drink. To eat. To do anything other than what she was. *I can't live like that anymore.* For too long she'd lived by the whims of others. This state, this way of being, was the only thing she could control. She knew she was pushing a month of utter desolation, but the pit to where she'd descended was dark and consumed every ounce of her soul.

At least it was quiet there. There was something gentle about the blackness. Comforting, in a way. Oddly enough, she yearned for its soothing, tranquil rapture.

Every waking moment she wondered why she wouldn't succumb to it.

She felt in her marrow that she neared death once more. She'd been on the reaper's doorstep enough and so frequently over the last few months that she knew the signs: the weakness in her bones, the irregularity of her breath, not remembering certain aspects of the day or night as unconsciousness took over. Every so often her heart would palpitate so rapidly that her breath would still and her mind would whisper *yes*. But she always came back.

It seems I don't have that much control after all.

She hated herself for it. She hated her mind for rousing her body to survive. She hated her body for listening. She hated the small part of her that cried with victory each time she woke to consciousness once more.

Because of... she thought distantly, her eyes closing against the darkness of the room. *I can't... I won't... Something won't let me part from...from...*

She rolled onto her side and curled tightly into a ball, her elbows pressing into her hips. The bones bit through her skin, reminding her how thin she'd become, and the movement itself was painful. Her hair, barely long enough to touch her ears, rubbed against the indigo rug embroidered with emerald flora and was no deterrent against the short, brittle fibers. She lifted a curled hand to place as a barrier between the two, the position so familiar to her. How many times had she laid like this on floors that were less forgiving? Countless. How many times had she danced on the precipice of sanity, wishing for psychosis to take her? Too many. She vaguely wondered why Fate was being so cruel as to give her no reprieve, then shucked the thought. *I am nothing to everyone.*

No matter how far she descended into the pit of her agony or how often she thought death was near, there was no abatement from the memories. Over the past weeks Kate relived every single thing they'd done to her. *Every single one.* She couldn't stop the recollections. She didn't know how. They were so overwhelming, oftentimes they catapulted her into a stifling storm of despair, laden with panic and hopelessness. Sometimes the panic came first. Sometimes suffocating fear or a drowning sense of sorrow precluded the memories. But it was the crushing mental pain that ensued afterward which sent her deeper into the hole vying to claim her to oblivion.

The only thing that stopped her from falling entirely was a small piece of her conscience which had enough of her blithering feebleness. It was yet a part of her that urged her to realize she was bigger than her past and present.

She ignored it and wished for death instead.

She felt the gripping swells of panic lance through her now, clutching onto her limbs before staking through her chest. The pain of it was breathtaking, and it felt like there was an icepick stuck in her sternum. She tried to take in a breath but couldn't, and she began to shake as memories assaulted her...

"—be careful not to sever her spine. I want her to feel every ounce of pain..."

"—one eye. Blur the other. Bleach will do. Acid if she heals too quickly. Make her fear the sound of feet on the floor but be unable to see to get away..."

"—with metal chains in a way that she cannot lift her head to see. Then strike..."

"—blood. Then beat her until she vomits. And then feed her the expectorations..."

The worst of the memories she buried. But they were always there, haunting her...

She squeezed her eyes shut tightly. The mysterious voice within her, born from the small part of her hellbent on survival, said forcefully, *think about something else. Anything else.*

He arose in her darkened mind like a beacon in the night, dashing and charming with his wayward grin and curling black hair. Her chest relaxed somewhat as his copper eyes, bright with laughter, blazed to break away the abyss that consumed her. Though most of her memories before her imprisonment were hazy at best, the ones with him were as prominent as if he stood beside her, as if her mind knew he would always be the pillar she needed to anchor her desolately chaotic world.

It's okay, the mysterious voice murmured softly. *Let yourself focus on him. He is your center. Your core. Your strength. And you need strength. You need to pull through this. This is not your end.*

Kate curled in tighter to herself as the panic receded, only to constrict her chest with her next breath and whip out to assault her with the force of a hurricane. She felt it pressing down on her, pushing her into the floor, and she whimpered through vocal cords that hadn't been struck for weeks.

Your center. Your core. Your strength.

She took a deep, shaking breath and held it before releasing slowly. Then another, and another, and another...

September 2019
Warwick

The speaker on the kitchen counter blared Eminem while the double oven beeped to signify that it was preheated. Kate sashayed her way over to the waiting baking sheets while mouthing the words to Cleaning Out My Closet, *her black block-heeled boots gliding across the white stone floor peppered with ingredients she'd dropped and yet to clean up. She snatched her pumpkin-shaped oven mitt and began putting the prepared trays in the ovens, her scarlet apron hanging around slim hips. Autumn was briskly upon the manor, and she couldn't wait to have the boys sample her latest cookie concoctions while she opened her newest shipment of fall candles.*

She rose as she shut both doors, flipping her waist-length hair over her shoulder. As she slowly slipped the oven mitt off her hand, her eyes snagged on Damian and her heart stuttered in its path, causing her gait to falter. It was the same reaction she had every time she laid eyes on him for the past two years, and she reveled in it as much as she kicked herself for it.

Creator, but he is gorgeous. *She kept her sigh at bay. He was taller than her five-eleven stature and lean, his muscles cutting through his skin in their definition. He had the sleeves of his maroon shirt rolled up as he washed the mountain of dishes she'd created from her baking, and her eyes travelled the tanned skin of his forearms to his broad shoulders, slender waist, and delicious backside. He wore black jeans which thankfully highlighted every curve, and Kate let her head fall to one side as her eyes trailed back up his body to his sharp features. His hooded eyes were focused on his task, though his shadowed, square jaw and long, dark brows were relaxed. His nose gave him a profile befit of the Greek soldier he used to be, with the planes of his cheeks sloping to a set of sumptuous lips. They were lips Kate had dreamed about kissing since the moment she saw him, and even now she got lost in fantasy as she continued to stare.*

Her reverie was only broken when Damian glanced at her

and said in a voice that coated her insides like a fine glass of red wine, *"You can start drying, you know. This is your mess."*

She narrowed her eyes and tossed her mitt to the countertop. With a smirk she replied, *"You're just mad because you couldn't keep up earlier."*

They'd returned about an hour ago from a jaunt to her favorite spot on the property, a small mountain with a crest that overlooked the manor. It had taken most of the night because it was quite a hike to get to in the first place, but Kate had been begging Damian to go with her for days now to appreciate the turn of foliage. Her father couldn't be swayed to accompany her, and Asha hated hiking, so Kate pressed Damian hard enough to agree. He always bent under her, and while she wished it were because he cared for her more than he wanted to admit, he'd never once gone beyond friendly gestures.

Can't forget the fact that he's always picking up different females—sometimes right in front of my face. *Kate pulled her stool over and stepped up on it to open the forest-green cabinet above the microwave to put away her spices, sloughing the glare she wanted to cut at Damian.* If he had any thought that went beyond friends, he wouldn't do that.

Asha thinks I've been playing lovesick schoolgirl for too long. *Kate pushed back the sleeves of her black cropped sweatshirt that had an open coffin and the words 'Wake Me When It's October' on the front.* But maybe he just needs a little more pushing...

She was infinitely hopeful Damian would one day realize he was deeply in love with her as much as she fancied herself to be with him. I mean, why else does he spend so much time here? *She placed her spices back in the cabinet one by one but found herself drawn to him, her regard filled with longing. He worked diligently to pile the pots and bowls on the other side of the sink to be dried, and her heart stuttered once more.* I know Father is here and all that, but he has other friends, his own place...

Thoughts like these ones plagued her daily, and somewhere deep inside Kate knew them to be silly. But that didn't stop her from incessantly flirting with him or pushing his buttons to see how far she could get. Regardless of her tangled feelings, the male had become close to her over the past few years in a way that surpassed the bonds she'd made with the other Guards of Nightfall—who she playfully nicknamed 'the boys'. She and Damian were similar in their likes and dislikes, had the same viewpoints on important matters, and understood each other in ways that transcended a normal friendship.

Or so Kate liked to think, anyway.

"You can blend, Kate." Damian cast a dull look over his shoulder that Kate almost didn't see. Her eyes had slipped down to his callused hands as they slid over the large mixing bowl he was washing, and she momentarily got lost for the thousandth time in what it would be like to have those hands caressing her skin.

"It's not fair to race you," Damian continued, pulling Kate from her wicked illusion. "I don't have any abilities."

"It's not my fault your watcher sucks." Kate closed the cabinet and hopped down to snag a rag from the sink, brushing against Damian as she went. The soothing scent of saltwater enveloped her, slowing her thoughts, her mind. Damian settled her in a way that only he could, and he didn't even know it.

"But you have to admit I am faster than you. More agile. Limber-er. With you being so…" She looked him up and down, both to emphasize her point and sate her hunger for him. "Big and bulky."

Damian cut her a look with narrowed eyes, and he opened his mouth to respond before thinking better of it and handing her a set of measuring spoons to dry. The glint of his ivory fangs made Kate's mind wander into decadently dangerous territory, and she felt the answering heat of her wanton fantasy coil low in her belly.

"What?" Kate snapped her towel at him to derail her wicked musings. "What were you going to say?"

"Nothing," Damian said gruffly, but Kate was so used to his bite by now that she merely laughed.

"Come on! You know you can say anything to me." She tapped him with her hip, pressing their shoulders together briefly to get another rush. When the ensuing flash of a flame coursed through her, she hardly suppressed the answering shudder. "We're friends."

But if you would just give me a chance… *She watched as Damian's eyes lingered on her before turning back to his task, not saying anything in reply. Her heart wilted ever so slightly, and she turned to the pile of dishes she had yet to dry to shield her disappointment.*

"What do you have me doing after this?" Damian asked, changing the subject.

"I have to get the rest of my fall stuff down from the attic. I don't think we'll have time to put them up tonight, but if you stay over, we can get a jumpstart on the inside stuff." And I can watch you walk around in gray sweatpants.

"Vadin's coming here to pick me up so we can go target shooting," Damian said, and Kate withered, unable to hide a pout. "Don't you have a sparring session with Ryder in the morning anyway?"

Kate waved an unconcerned hand. "He'll reschedule if I ask him to."

"Weren't you the one that pushed for the lessons?"

Kate glared at him impishly. "Yeah, but on my own time."

Damian fought a grin and instead raised a brow. "You won't get any better if you prioritize fall décor over working out."

"What do I need to work out for?" Kate shrugged. "I already have the body of a goddess thanks to my impeccable genes."

Damian rumbled a laugh, shaking his head. "You said you wanted to learn how to fight because you wanted to get more involved, and to be able to defend yourself."

"Yeah, but is Father really going to let me?" She levelled Damian with a look that said 'when the Pope sprouts horns'. "I don't leave the property by myself...ever."

"Don't you want to change that? Maybe if you prove to Talorc that you can handle your own..."

Kate shrugged again. "It won't happen."

"You never know."

She smiled, brushing away the topic because, unlike Damian, she knew it would truly never happen. "I can slack a little; I've been pretty consistent with my training. Fall decorating takes precedence, anyway. I got my hands on these twelve-foot skeletons that apparently aren't supposed to be out until next year. I ordered five of them, one for each of you guys. I'm going to put little things on them so I know which is which. Ryder's is getting a sword, because his weapon's collection is weirdly mesmerizing. Vadin's is getting a bottle of whisky, obviously. For Cyrus's I was thinking of ordering a skeleton dog to sit next to him. Noir's I was going to make a big cigarette and make some long hair out of fabric or something." She eyed him mischievously with a twinkle to her eye, her smile widening. "Some flippers because you like to swim."

"Kate," Damian barely held back his laughter as he turned off the water and reached for the towel in her hand. "Who are you even decorating for?"

"Myself!" Kate let Damian take the towel, unsure of what he needed it for when there was another nearby. He stepped nearer to her, and it took Kate a full three heartbeats to realize he was going to take over her job so she didn't have to dry anymore. Creator save me. *His proximity to her rendered her so momentarily mindless that she looked like a fool in front of him more times than not.*

His hand brushed hers as he took the towel, and whether it was inadvertent or not, they both paused in their banter to look at one another. Kate's heart began to gallop, and she knew that if he cared to he would see the answering flicker at her throat. Their gazes collided, burnt orange to sparkling celadon, and Kate's smile, ever there, grew as Damian's look of teasing faded to neutrality.

If you would just give us the chance... *She continued her musing from earlier, allowing herself to be swallowed by his regard and the dreams she thought she saw rippling within.* I know we would be absolutely perfect.

Damian cleared his throat and took the towel entirely, turning to face the pile of dishes Kate had forgone. Kate watched him for a moment more before suppressing a gentle sigh and moving to the other side of the pile, hoisting herself onto the counter. She crossed her legs and began kicking out the higher one in restlessness, placing her palms on the surface to lean back and ogle Damian shamelessly.

"I keep telling Father that we should set up the manor like a haunted mansion." Kate tilted her head to one side, not caring that she was leaving all the work to Damian. He never complained anyway, and a small part of her liked to think that he enjoyed facilitating her pampered lifestyle. "Can you imagine how much we could make?"

Damian fought another smile as he continued to dry the

dishes. *"What did you say-not-say earlier? When the Pope sprouts horns?"*

She internally swooned because he knew her so well, but she rolled her eyes to hide it. *"I know, I know. But wouldn't it be fun? Oh, speaking of! Think I can convince you to go to Killgrew's Asylum this year with me?"*

Damian looked at her with a raised brow.

"Damian," Kate laughed, tipping back her head. *"You're a* vampire. *Things that go 'boo' in the night shouldn't scare you."*

"Jump scares are different," Damian said grumpily.

"Not for a six-hundred-and-nineteen-year-old vampire!"

"I have a fragile heart," Damian countered begrudgingly. *"One wrong move and I could keel over."*

"You would never be able to part with me," Kate teased, leaning over the pile of now dry dishes to beam sassily at him. That small part of her again wished he would make his move and finally agree.

"If it meant not listening to your choice in music I could," Damian ragged right back, causing Kate to gasp as if affronted. Which she was.

"What's wrong with Eminem?"

"This song is almost twenty years old, Kate."

"It's a classic!"

"No, AC/DC is a classic. Alexa," Damian called, causing Kate to smack him playfully on the shoulder. *"Play Thunderstruck."*

"Early two-thousands will always *be the best choice of music."* Kate continued to lean toward him and narrowed her eyes as she pursed her lips. She focused on his own before trailing back to his eyes—eyes that would always pull her in and then under, drowning her...

"You're delusional," Damian said lowly with that charming smirk she dreamt about as often sleep took her, while the song blared in the background.

"You like me this way," Kate said, her own grin never faltering.

Damian's gaze skimmed over her face, trickling from her eyes to her nose, to her cheeks, to settle on her lips. He opened his mouth to retort but hesitated, his eyes fixated on the plush seam.

"What's wrong?" Kate tantalized mercilessly, unable to stop herself from pushing to see how far he would bend. "Kate got your tongue?"

If freaking only.

"Admit it," she murmured to him, possibly a little more sensually than she meant to be. "You wouldn't change a thing about me."

She uncrossed her legs and leaned further into his space, tilting her head so her hair fell over her shoulder and inhibited his work. However, Damian had stopped his efforts long ago, and Kate imagined it was because she was so incredibly mesmerizing. Let me show you all the ways I can be. She bit her lower lip with a tempting fang, barely a hairsbreadth from his face.

"If you had the chance," Her voice dropped an octave to adopt a sultry tone she reserved for her wildest fantasies. "You would eat me up." The last three words were said with increasing emphasis, and Kate watched as a muscle jumped in Damian's jaw.

Want me, she thought unabashedly. Just say it.

How she wished in her core, in her soul, he would just say it.

"Am I interrupting something?"

They both jolted as if zapped, and Damian hopped back a full foot as they simultaneously looked over the kitchen island and to the door that led into the main dining room. Vadin was standing in the doorway, jangling his keys in one hand while his eyes went back and forth between the two of them accusingly.

"Just finishing up the dishes," Damian said in a rush, throwing the towel onto the counter as Kate leaned back.

"Did you forget about target practice?" Vadin asked with a frown at Damian's stuttering body language, while Kate remained relaxed, although admittedly a little perturbed at being interrupted.

"No, I was just helping Kate clean up her mess." Damian turned away from Kate, moving to the opposite side of the kitchen, causing her to glare at his back.

So easily dismissed. As always. She hopped down from the counter and moved to lean across the island, placing her chin in her hand as she watched Damian slide on his discarded jacket from earlier.

"You guys are lucky that place opens early," she said,

continuing to stare at Damian as if Vadin weren't there.

"It's an old cop that runs the place," Vadin supplied, his eyes lingering on Kate, though she couldn't be bothered to notice. "Opens early in case the morning shift wants some practice before going on the beat."

Kate sighed as Damian busied himself with tasks that were monotonous and mundane; she counted as he checked the same pocket three times, and then inspected his shoes as if wanting to make sure they were still on his feet.

"Your cell phone is plugged in by the Alexa," she told him with a small smirk, chin still cradled in her hand. "And Mora is going to kill you for wearing your shoes in the kitchen. You know how weird she is about that stuff."

Damian shot her a glare, and the sting of it sliced Kate. His voice was harsh, almost childish, as he replied, "You had your boots on."

Yeah, because they make my butt look great and I was hoping you would notice, *Kate thought, tossing him a sneer that made her heart hurt. This was the cycle they tread most days: have fun together, bicker and banter, laugh, but when someone else comes around start treating Kate like a snail trail.*

"At any rate," She pushed herself up slowly from the counter and stretched her arms high above her head. Even though he treated her poorly sometimes, she was confident enough to not be deterred. She knew it was only a matter of time before he bent so much that he broke.

And that day would be glorious.

"Mora won't yell at me." Kate tossed her hair over one shoulder, her sparkling, black-polished claws catching the light from the dangling fixtures above the island.

Damian could barely contain his curling lip before turning his attention to Vadin and asking, "Do we have time to stop at Tolber's?"

Kate's stomach dropped and her mouth went dry. She knew the place; the posh taproom was a favorite of both Damian's and Vadin's to pick up females. An upscale establishment that was frequented by vampires, more times than not Kate watched from a shadowed table as Damian charmed his way into someone else's bed, leaving her to catch a ride home with another Guardsmale or

Asha.

She hated that place.

Damian continued, "I could use a drink."

"Maybe," Vadin responded with a thoughtful shrug. "If you don't mind cutting our time at the range short."

"Nope," Damian said sharply, stomping across the kitchen to snatch his cell phone from the charger. He pulled so hard the cord came dislodged from the wall. "Could use more than a drink, actually."

A knife pierced her heart, and Kate had to catch the clearing of her throat she knew sounded more like a noise of pain, which would upset the careless visage she was trying to display.

"It still burns, you know, even if vampires can't get STDs. All that chafing." The way her voice rang with contemptuous jealousy made her cringe, and she turned toward the counter to grab the towel to look busy...and hide her embarrassment for acting like the youngling they all thought she was.

"Worth it," Damian snapped as he rounded the island and pushed through the door closest to the exit without a look back.

"Bye!" Kate called cheerily after him, the complete antithesis to the shriveled way she felt inside.

Damian was already gone.

Vadin smiled gently at Kate, catching the door before it closed. Kate refused to let him see her despondent, so she chucked a joyful, "Have fun!" at him as she turned to scrub the counter with all the resentment and jealousy and rejection she felt by being replaced so easily, so quickly.

Don't cry. He's not worth it. Don't you dare cry.

"What's in the oven?"

Kate paused, looking at Vadin over her shoulder, trying and failing to smile. She knew he was trying to make her feel better about being left out, as Vadin had a big, carefree heart. He was the most lovable male Kate had ever met and was always thinking of others above himself. On the rare occasions he wasn't bouncing from one friend to another—so busy he never didn't have anything to do—he could be found at Talorc's with his feet propped up on the nearest table, the latest reality show on the tube, a bowl of popcorn in his lap as he sat next to Kate. He treated her like the sister he'd lost so many years ago, while he was the closest thing she had to a brother.

But he's not Damian, *Kate thought, stilling the sigh that wanted to escape her lips.*

"I have four different types of cookies," she answered, moving to the Alexa to turn it off; she didn't feel like listening to music anymore. "You'll have to try some later, tell me what you think."

"New recipes?"

"Vadin!"

Vadin glanced over his shoulder while Kate rolled her eyes at Damian's cutting yell from halfway across the house.

"I'd better go. Chin up, Little Kitten." He gave her a wink and that handsome smile that melted the stoutest of feminine hearts. "Can't wait to try those cookies."

Kate gave him a small wave as he disappeared, leaning against the corner of two counters. She dropped her head between her shoulders and looked at her boots. Can't believe I risked the wrath of Mora for him. *Petulantly, she reached down and unzipped both boots, kicking them off and away from her.*

As she stared at the heap of discarded leather on the floor, she felt resolve replace the disheartenment that threatened to overtake her. He can pretend that he doesn't like spending time with me, be mean to me when other people are around, and think that he can kick me to the curb.

Kate turned back to the Alexa, swiped to her favorite station, and cranked up the volume. But one day he won't be able to. One day he'll realize what he's been missing. And if I keep prodding him, it'll come sooner rather than later. *Kate did a twirl with the towel in her hand and began singing along with Brett Scallions as* Hemorrhage *played on the device.*

I just have to keep up the confidence, the fire, the desire, *she thought roguishly, moving back to finish her task of drying the dishes.* And one day he won't be able to resist me.

Kate took another deep breath in and released it as the memory faded to nothingness. She stayed grounded to the present, which she wasn't sure if she was appreciative of or frustrated by.

The less you capitulate on the negative, the less of the upper hand they have over you, the voice inside her told her boldly, firmly.

Santiago wants you to fall. He wants you to suffer. He wants to see you live steps from death waiting for insanity to take you, because it means he wins. He wins and takes away everything you have ever known and loved. His goal is to destroy. And you are not to be destroyed.

Kate felt the panic in her receding to a level that was tolerable, but she couldn't…she faltered still. She didn't care if they won. *I can't… I'm not… I'm…* She clenched her eyes shut and tried to swallow the despair that choked her. *I will never be that female again. I will never be that confident, that bold, that brash. They took that from me.*

They broke me.

The single thought shattered what she'd been trying to build to block the horrors, the fears, the anxiety she lived with day in and day out.

Worthless. Pathetic. Useless. Disgraceful.
Hopeless. Dark. Morbid. Plaguing.
Defiled. Hateful. Disgusting. Woeful.
She gasped, inhaling a sorrowful sob.
They broke me.

The immediate weight of failure collapsed on her, and Kate opened her mouth to scream. It was the first time she ever admitted the reality of the situation—and its repercussions—to herself. Rather, it was the first time she had *the ability to admit it to herself.* The clarity. The perception.

I will never be that female again. They stole my light. My joy. My fight. My fire. My lightheartedness, my love, my passion… They took it from me. And I will never get it back.

That faraway voice whispered forcibly to her, *only because you believe it to be so! Take it back! It is* yours *to take!*

How could she? She'd become so distant from reality that anything other than how she was living was an illusion. She was damaged beyond repair. Her mind and her body had been abused in ways that no person could comprehend. What could she offer anyone with her presence as it was? It was clear no one wanted to take the time to care for her the way she needed to be cared for. Her father couldn't wait to leave. *He*—the center of her every waking thought—had proved time and time again she was not worth his time. The Guard were going to be busier than ever before. She would continue to be swept under the rug, brushed to the side, and treated like a youngling like she'd been her whole life. Just like before. The Guard, Mora, her father, Asha…they all only cared so much now because—

Stop this madness, the voice, still not her own, ordered her severely. In times like these, so bleak and despairing, she thought it was the specter of her mother coming forth to try and invigorate her. But why would she? The female could be nothing but ashamed of everything Kate had become. Conversely, Kate *liked* to think that she would be joining her soon as this life fell from her grasp, her mindfulness, or any sort of cognition. Falling, falling, falling…

I'm sorry mother, she thought hopelessly. She closed her mouth and bit her lip hard enough to puncture the flesh, choking on the scream that hovered beneath the surface.

I never knew you. I've hardly ever spoken your name. But it feels like I've failed you. Like I've failed everyone else. Like I've failed myself.

Did she fail herself? Would the female she was before pity the female now, or resent her? She certainly wouldn't be proud of her. Did Kate even know herself anymore? Could she remember who she once was? If she looked in the mirror, would she comprehend who she had become, both physically and mentally?

It doesn't matter.

Kate allowed the bitter blackness to ensnare her once more. It was much easier than having such raw conversations with herself, those of which brought feelings and memories to the surface she didn't want to acknowledge.

I will never be that female again.

Chapter Ten

Damian plopped down heavily onto the sectional in his apartment, digging his phone out of his pocket as he settled. He thumbed to his message list and pulled up the thread he had with Cyrus, tapping on the icon that would lead him to Lilith's personal number. He leaned forward with his elbows on his knees, the phone held to one ear, and his other hand pinching his lower lip as the line began ringing. He stared across his dark apartment, seeing nothing, hoping against hope Lilith would answer the phone and he wouldn't have to leave a message.

But after three rings the line dropped into her voicemail, and with a muttered curse Damian pulled his phone down to hang up but stopped short. *She won't call back a number she's unfamiliar with.* He placed his phone back up to his ear just as the beep sounded for him to leave a message.

"Hey, Lilith, it's Damian." He ran a hand through his hair as he leaned back on the couch. "I need a favor. A big one. I know I should be calling your work line, but this is…it's personal." He paused, unsure of how to proceed and feeling slightly foolish. *Fuck it,* he thought, clearing his throat. *This is for Kate.*

"I wanted to know if—"

The phone beeped to let him know he had a call on the other line, and he pulled it away to look at his screen. His eyes flared slightly, and he ended the call he had been in the middle of placing to answer the other.

"Hey Lilith."

"*Damian,*" the female responded, her voice smooth like the flowing notes of a piano. "*Is everything okay?*"

"How did you know it was me?"

"*Cyrus gave me The Guard's personal numbers in case of emergencies,*" she replied. "*Sorry I didn't pick up when you answered. I just walked in the door.*"

"Everything's okay," Damian went back to answer her first question. "I just...I have a favor to ask. A personal one."

Damian heard her putting her keys down and some shuffling, as if she were removing a coat. "*Okay, go on.*"

"I need you to come and talk to Kate," Damian said abruptly, his impatience in the matter getting the better of him. "She's—it's been a month since she's been home and she's still not okay. I've tried everything. I don't know what else to do. I think she needs to talk to someone. She's not processing what happened to her and I'm worried that...that it will..." He couldn't bring himself to continue the sentence; one utterance had been enough. "She won't talk to me or anyone else she knows. We've all tried. We've *been* trying. And I thought because you're a doctor you could help her. Or you might know someone that can help her. I know you do physical stuff, but if you could just maybe think about it..." He trailed off after realizing he was rambling.

Lilith was quiet for a few heartbeats, and then asked, "*Did Cyrus tell you I could help?*"

"No," Damian said quickly. "I asked him for your number though. Sorry if that's not how to go about things or if I crossed some sort of boundary." He wasn't sorry, but it felt like the right thing to say.

"*You're not sorry, but it's fine,*" Lilith retorted dryly, and Damian huffed out a laugh. She was a remarkably astute female, and he learned almost immediately upon meeting her that little got by her.

"I'll pay you for your time," Damian tacked on hurriedly. Money was of no consequence to him—he'd been a mercenary soldier for more than six hundred years, after all. "Whatever your rate is I'll double it. Triple it. Just...please. She needs *someone.*"

"*Does she want help?*"

Damian felt irritation ripple through him. "It doesn't matter if she *wants* it; she *needs* it."

"*It does matter,*" Lilith replied, and his irritation blazed to anger. "*She won't listen to me if she's not ready to hear.*"

"You don't understand." Damian jumped up from the couch

and began to pace. "She's rotting away in there. I know what's going through her mind: the depression, the darkness, the loss of self. I've been there. I've seen other men and males go through it. It's a horrible black pit that'll swallow you whole if you allow it, and she's on the edge looking over. She's *never* experienced anything but being indulged and pampered and I think…" His voice trailed off to gentle as he faltered in his pacing. "I think this might have broken her.

"She needs help, and I can't help her," Damian finished as he ran his hand through his hair again. The admittance doused the fiery wrath wrapped around him, incensing him to near recklessness while simultaneously quelling the inferno. It also had him feeling as though he lost the most important battle of his life. Acknowledging that he couldn't help her…

I failed her again. Like all those times before.

He shook himself out of that thought. Throwing his own pity party would get him nowhere. Looking back on the past wouldn't change where they were now. He needed to… *Fuck if I know.* He was figuring that part out still. But he wanted to try. He had to. *For Kate.*

"Just please come and talk to her." Damian walked restlessly over to the unlit fireplace and ran a hand over the smooth stone hearth. "Just *try*. Please. I know it's a long drive. I know you have better things to do. But I need help. *Kate* needs help."

Lilith was silent for longer than Damian liked, and his heart pounded when he finally heard her sigh.

"*I can't.*"

Damian closed his eyes and dropped his head.

"*At least not tonight. But Saturdays are my days off and I can come down then. I can have Fiona rearrange my schedule in case I need to stay longer.*"

Damian's eyes flashed open, and he flung his head up, clenching his fist in a gesture of triumph. A rush overtook him, reinvigorating him with purpose. He opened his mouth to declare his thanks, but Lilith continued.

"*You need to organize things with Talorc.*"

Damian bit back his groan of annoyance. He'd been avoiding Talorc and didn't relish the idea of an apology so soon.

For Kate. "I can do that," Damian replied through clenched teeth. He forced his jaw to loosen before saying, "Thank you, Lilith."

"*This may not work.*" Damian ignored the flip his stomach did. "*But I will try.*"

"Thank you," Damian repeated. "I'll call Talorc and then send you the details."

"*Sounds good,*" Lilith said, and Damian prepared to end the call before she added, "*And Damian?*"

"Yeah?"

"*You don't owe me anything for this.*"

They parted ways thereafter, Damian feeling both hopeful and apprehensive. He stared down at his phone as the screen went dim, then blank, thinking, *oh for fuck's sake, just get it over with.*

He dialed Talorc's number and walked around the fireplace into the kitchen to grab a beer, more than half convinced he would need it for what he was about to do. He almost anticipated the male not to answer, admittedly projecting his own dissuasion through the phone. However, the call went through on the second ring, and Damian took a deep breath and held it.

"*Damian.*"

"Talorc." Damian rummaged through his junk drawer for a bottle opener. He was rewarded for his juvenile courage with a crisp *shhhh* and *clink* as the bottlecap fell to the counter. "Thanks for picking up."

"*I am not a youngling, Damian,*" Talorc responded dully as Damian took a swig of his beer.

"Yeah, but I've kinda been acting like one, which is why I called," Damian replied, deciding to get straight to the point. "I'm sorry about the other night. I'm just worried about Kate. And what I said came out harsher than how I meant it."

"*I understand.*" Damian heard the telltale squeaking of his office chair as he leaned back. "*As did what I said. I did not mean to be so retaliatory in tone and in words. I respect you more than that.*"

"And I, you." Damian rested against the kitchen counter as he took another swig of his beer. "We're all under an extreme amount of pressure and more reactive than usual."

"*I concur. But I have a feeling this is not the only reason you called. It usually takes you more than a week to apologize.*"

Damian laughed, his lips quirking up on one side. "Old dogs can learn new tricks." He swirled his beer in his bottle before continuing, "You probably know what I'm about to say concerns Kate."

"*I assumed such.*"

"I asked Lilith to come and talk with her. I figured she might know how to handle these situations in a different way than we do. Kate's not talking to any of us, but maybe someone from a medical background will have better luck."

Talorc was silent for a small span of time. "*It is a good idea. I had not thought Lilith could be beneficial beyond anything physical.*"

"You have a lot on your plate." Damian pushed away from the counter to wander aimlessly. "This is something I can handle."

"*I know you have been persistent when it comes to this, and I thank you for that,*" Talorc said, his tone soft. "*I... It is...*" He trailed off, and Damian suddenly didn't want to know what he was going to say.

"I won't stop until she's herself again."

"*Good. See it done.*" There was more squeaking as Damian pictured Talorc shifting his weight in his seat. "*What of your international connections? Anything?*"

"Waiting to hear back from half; I'm guessing they're conversing amongst themselves. The other half are ready to convene. I think it will be a month or more until I can set an in-person meeting in stone."

"*Too long,*" Talorc murmured, more to himself than to Damian. "*I may need you to go over there and meet with them on my behalf to hasten things.*"

Damian's stomach dropped to his feet, and the beer he had been drinking immediately soured. *Kate. I can't leave Kate.* He scrambled for something to say, and the words came out jumbled as he said, "I—I have a lot to do here. I've been helping Cyrus get better weapons. And Vadin...Vadin asked me to help pin down Santiago's homes. Ryder needs—"

"*Not as of yet, Damian,*" Talorc cut him off. "*I know you have your hands in many pots. It is just something I want to put on your radar.*"

"Don't you think it would be better if you went?"

"*No. Time is of the essence in this matter. You know it has gone on for too long.*"

Fuck. Damian took a long drink from his beer. *Maybe if I'm more diligent about conversing remotely I can stay here?*

"I'll see where I'm at today. I'll go through my emails and make some phone calls. Push a little harder."

"*Good, that will be good,*" Talorc replied. "*What am I to expect of this venture with Lilith?*"

"She's making plans to come Saturday, could be staying. I said I would coordinate with you first."

"*I will let Mora know.*" There was another long pause. "*Should we tell Kathryn?*"

"I don't think it will change anything if we do. Kate is going to make of this what she will."

Talorc sighed heavily. "*She always has been that way, has she not?*"

"One of her more endearing qualities."

"*I will see you then,*" Talorc finished. "*Thank you for calling, Damian. We have been at odds more frequently than not lately and I thought the damage I had done was irrefutable.*"

Damian blinked back his surprise at the admonition from Talorc; it was extremely rare the male ever spoke in such a manner.

"I owe you too much Talorc." He did. And maybe he had forgotten that over the last few weeks, but it was a thought that he had several times since their last acidic conversation. "You're like family to me."

"*You have always been loyal to me, and I am grateful for that. I might need redirection here and there, but I will never forget what you have sacrificed to stay by my side.*"

Damian swallowed a heavy pour of his beer, as much to relax as to dislodge the thick knot that suddenly formed in his throat and was settling in his chest.

"I could've been better," Damian confessed, wondering what in the actual world of the Creator possessed him to extrapolate such. "I was gone for a long time."

"*You visited as much as you could, and ultimately came back. Besides, what is two hundred years in the span of our lifetime?*" Talorc asked rhetorically. "*You took that time for yourself. It was necessary. It made you who you are today: a male of worth, of value, of prominence, and of utmost value. I am lucky you have chosen to live your life in service to mine, as well as the cause of the vampires."*

Unsure of what to say, seared by emotions he couldn't name, Damian simply replied, "I'll see you in a few days."

The night started like any other, but Kate sensed something shifting beneath the surface. The sky was muddled with clouds, making the luminescence of the moon muted and the grounds bordering the forest darker than they truly were. Her bedroom faced west, and if she cared to look far enough, she would see the glow of the city in the distance. The pond on the property was murky and still, so much like her internal thoughts that she envisioned herself within the depths.

While Kate found the wherewithal to be vertical, curled in her window seat, there was not much else she was interested in. She failed to concern herself with the shifting she felt within the manor, within her bones, within her core. She ignored the added weight she felt within the home, and the fact that the residence seemed to be in a little more upheaval tonight compared to others. She disregarded the additional bodies she felt moving two stories below. She neglected to react to the tantalizing scent of blood that wafted through her door. She certainly wasn't about to answer the knock that sounded.

However, she did note one thing: it wasn't *he* who called on her this night. No, *his* knock was quick and loud, a rapping of only two bursts. It wasn't her father's heavy hand, who steadily knocked three times. It wasn't Ryder or Vadin or Cyrus or Noir. It wasn't Mora or Asha or any of the other servants. This knock was gentle, soft, almost soundless in its tender plea.

"Kate? It's Lilith."

Kate closed her eyes, pulling her knees tighter to her chest.

"You may not remember or even know of me, but I'm a

physician from the New York City coven. I oversaw your care when you came home, and I've been working with The Guard for a couple of months. Damian asked me to come and speak with you tonight."

Meddling, Kate thought sourly. *Sticking his nose where it doesn't belong.*

"I know you might not want to listen, and that's okay," Lilith continued. "But I would ask that you open the door so I may come in, as what I have to say is…it's personal. And I would ask that you show respect for my own confidentiality in granting me privacy."

I owe you nothing, Kate wanted to snap, her eyes flashing open, and for the first time in weeks she felt the swell of what she remembered anger to feel like rise in her chest.

"I know you probably feel like you don't owe me anything." The frankness with which the female spoke gave Kate pause in her caustic thoughts. "But I need you to know a lot of people care about you. A lot of people are waiting for you to make the next move. And while emotions and mental health aren't my strong suit, I want to tell them I at least tried to help you. All I ask is that you let me in and listen to what I have to say."

Kate looked toward the door. She knew, though her sight was dull, that resentment smoldered within her gaze. Resentment and ire and annoyance and pain. Did she want to show all that? Was she ready to share with someone who she had become? It didn't feel like it, but then again, would she ever? Admittedly, there was something about the female's voice that was…comforting, in a way. Maybe it was the firmness in which she spoke, or the candor of her words. Maybe it was the lilting hum of music that undulated below her speech, or the subtle scent of wildflowers that wisped beneath the door. Perhaps it was the comprehension that Kate sensed no ill will when it came to Lilith, leading her to feel inexplicably inclined to oblige the female in her request.

The first time in weeks I will have seen another being…

Do I have the strength?

Find out, the ethereal voice within her breathed. *It's time to find out.*

When Kate remained silent, Lilith didn't push her. She didn't speak further. She neither discouraged nor encouraged Kate to perform in a certain way. But she didn't leave, either. Kate knew she remained on the other side of the enormous doors to her bedroom the entire five minutes it took her to cross the floor because the scent of wildflowers never wavered.

Kate paused just a step away from the door. She stared at the intricate carvings of moonflowers that crept the length, one hand on the deadbolt. The other was lost to the sleeves of the oversized, black sweatshirt she had been wearing for...Creator, countless days. She brought that hand up to place on the long handle, as if to open the door, but it was truly to steady her quivering stance. Her heart, so strained as it was, beat erratically within the confines of her chest, and Kate closed her eyes as her hands began to tremble.

It's time, that voice she didn't recognize within her whispered.

Before she lost her nerve, she pushed the deadbolt to unlock.

Lilith didn't barge in, or even move right away. Kate stepped back and tipped her head up, opening her eyes, taking a deep breath. It was only when she released it that the door opened ever so slightly and in slipped Lilith, who shut and then locked it behind her.

The females looked at one another for a moment. Kate assessed Lilith bluntly: her long, platinum blonde hair was pulled back in a strict ponytail, contouring her face in sharp lines. She was tall and thin, dressed plainly in a black turtleneck sweater and overflowing black slacks. Her sage eyes looked almost grey in the darkness of the room and betrayed nothing about what she might be feeling or thinking. In her slender hands was a mug of blood, and she asked Kate where she could put it as she moved into the room.

Kate motioned toward a small sitting area by the door. The space consisted of a sprawling stone fireplace which had a long, elegant couch and throne-like chair perched before it, with a TV that hung above the hearth. There was a small table between the couch and the chair that housed an art deco table lamp, to which Lilith gestured. "May I turn on a light?"

Kate nodded once, pausing by the edge of the couch. She knew the room was cold, but she made no move to turn on the fireplace or increase the thermostat. Instead, Kate wrapped her arms around her middle and watched as Lilith placed the mug of blood on a coaster, then turned toward Kate once more.

"May I sit down?"

Kate nodded again and, coupled with the closeness of the blood and her weakness, the gesture made her dizzy. She watched through bleary eyes Lilith note how she clutched the back of the couch with a frail hand, her bones biting through her skin.

Lilith's eyes moved up to Kate's face, but she didn't come toward her. "Do you need help?"

Kate didn't reply, but she did use the couch to guide herself to sit on the plush, indigo upholstery. Her breath rushed out of her as her back fell against the tufted velvet fabric, and she closed her eyes to stave off the nausea that came with the dizziness. *I can't do this. I'm not ready for this.*

Yes you can, and you will, the voice within her insisted, and in that moment time began to warp, taking with it memory, perspective, and reality.

She forced herself to open her eyes again when she knew Lilith was done settling in the chair. The female was sitting stiffly with her legs rigidly parallel, hands clasped in her lap, and a nondescript gaze on her face. Kate couldn't discern much from her other than a faint aura of sadness that enveloped her in a low hue of starry blue.

"I won't sit here and say that I know what you went through. I won't sit here and say I understand how you're feeling, or that it will get easier with time," Lilith started, and although her tone was firm, it wasn't harsh. "I know those words would feel empty coming from someone you barely know. But I will tell you that I'm sorry. I'm sorry you went through what you did. No matter what you believe, you didn't deserve that. Not for a second. If anyone had the power to change what happened to you—including the six males that I know are waiting with bated breath to hear about how tonight turns out—they would have in a heartbeat. But unfortunately, nothing and no one will ever change your experience."

Kate continued to stare at Lilith, and the shifting throughout the manor swelled to incorporate time and the universe, warping sentiment even more. Intrinsically, she knew something was happening on a scale much larger than she could comprehend. She suddenly felt the slithering sensation of restlessness undulate over her spine, and she ignored the exultation that started to brighten from a place long dead and buried within her.

"I think, and correct me if I'm wrong, I know the space you're in now is a black one. It's hopeless, and it feels never-ending. It's suffocating. And you want to get lost in the spiral because it's easier than facing reality. I know you want to walk toward the morning light. I know your thoughts have been grave and endless and so very dark."

How does she know? Kate thought to herself, staring at Lilith vacantly. *How could she know?*

Lilith's gaze didn't waver. "I also know there's no way to compare the individual horrors we all personally experience, but I've been in a similar place. I'll share my past with you if you'll hear it. It's not something I do casually; in fact, fewer than a handful of people know my story. But I think it would help you if I were to share. To know that you are not alone. To know that good can come from so much evil. To know there is a place beyond the pain and the darkness."

Kate didn't know how to respond. And although there might have been a small part of her that wanted to, she was devastatingly afraid of what would follow.

Worthless. Pathetic. Useless. Disgraceful.
Hopeless. Dark. Morbid. Plaguing.
Defiled. Hateful. Disgusting. Woeful.

She sat silently, willing the more brazen part of her to react, to answer for her. But it too, was silent. As if it knew she needed to take this moment for herself.

Lilith allowed an entire minute to pass before: "I'm going to stand up now and bring the cup of blood to you."

Chapter Eleven

K ate only looked up when Lilith's body blocked her view, and mechanically she reached for the mug that was offered. *Warmth.* A foreign feeling, a forgotten concept, one she didn't deserve. Her fingers were like a skeleton's as they wrapped around the ceramic, and it was with a will stronger than her instinct that she denied the temptation of blood. She didn't deserve to drink it, to indulge.

Worthless. Pathetic. Useless. Disgraceful.

Hopeless. Dark. Morbid. Plaguing.

Defiled. Hateful. Disgusting. Woeful.

But Creator, she was *starved.* The feral survivalist in her, the side of her that had been browbeaten and dormant for so long, wanted to throw back her head and yell. She wanted to imbibe in this cup, and then another, and another…

We must get revenge, something whispered to her, from so far away in her consciousness that the notion fell away easily into the recesses of her mind.

Lilith sat back down in the chair, which was a perfect complement to the couch. Much of the décor in Kate's room was in hues of indigo, violet, and emerald, with the dark wood of walnut making up her four-poster bed, vanity, and other miscellaneous furniture. Kate remembered remodeling the room just two years ago, telling Asha she was looking to meld *sex nymph* and *Victorian garden;* "like cottagecore, but naughty".

What a fool I was, Kate thought, closing her eyes to shun the memory. *There were always bigger things to think about, but I was too stupid, too oblivious to care.*

"Whatever you're thinking—don't." Lilith settled back into her previous position, no less uncomfortable than she was before.

If Kate could bring herself to care, she would think that Lilith was dreading this conversation as much as she. "Don't think for a time. You've done too much of that. Allow yourself to rest. Just listen."

Kate opened her eyes and focused back on Lilith, though her sight was hazy. She was exhausted, truly didn't have the energy to fight this situation, so she sat with the mug in her hands and did what Lilith bade her do. With a slight nod, she encouraged the female to speak.

"I was born in Turkey in eighteen-twenty-three. I had no siblings, so when my mother died it was just my father and I. He was a physician. A sharp man; brilliant, ahead of his time. He was always busy, always going places, tending to this person or that. I went with him everywhere, his little personal attendant, and so my love for medicine was born. But Turkey during the early eighteen-hundreds was a challenging time for a woman, as it was for women everywhere. Especially women who spoke up, or were smart, or wanted to make a difference. Unfortunately, or maybe fortunately, I was one of those women."

Lilith paused then, glancing down at her hands in her lap. Kate's eyes followed the movement and saw Lilith rearranging her fingers so they weren't crushing in her grasp. Kate's eyes trickled away, to her own fingers, which still held onto the mug. *The closest I've been to blood in weeks...* The ebbing crimson within smelled delicious, and the longer she stared the harder it was to refute how truly hungry she was.

Suddenly, everything—her senses, her thoughts, her will—was overpowered by Kate's need to drink. Yet she was brought back to her self-inflicted reality by—

Worthless. Pathetic. Useless. Disgraceful.

Hopeless. Dark. Morbid. Plaguing.

Defiled. Hateful. Disgusting. Woeful.

"The Crimean War started in eighteen fifty-three. My father was a physician on the frontlines." Drawn back to the present by her voice, Kate watched as Lilith's fingers tightened around themselves once more. "It was a bloody war, but aren't they all? This one seemed more wretched than anything I'd seen; every night I woke with terrors. The things I experienced..."

Lilith paused to swallow thickly, as if the words lodged in her throat and doing so would displace them. Her sage eyes remained impassive, though she now stared past Kate instead of at her, and her fingers were locked together so tightly and so deeply in her lap that it would take a crowbar to break them apart.

Her next words were forced, as if pulled from her physically. Kate listened as the story unfolded, obviously a crushing, painful recanting of a time best left in memory.

As Lilith continued to speak, Kate felt an abrupt jolt, as the shifting within her and around her surged. It was no longer subtle; it was untamed, and the fire in the darkest place within her flared brightly, urging her to *burn*. She looked down at her mug of blood once more and for the first time in months…

Kate wanted to drink.

She lifted the mug slowly, as if she were still unsure of herself. She listened to Lilith intently, noting the pain, the determination, the brutal rawness in which she spoke. As she absorbed the words, almost distracted by the story, the cup got closer to her, and the more difficult it was to reject. The more difficult it was to remind herself why she wanted to refuse. The more difficult it was to remember she was punishing herself. The more difficult it was to remember she didn't deserve to live…

The cool ceramic met her lips, and she paused. She took a slow breath in through her nose and the metallic odor of the blood called to a part of her soul that had been beaten and had hidden because of it. It was the wild side of her, the vicious side of her, the *vampire* side of her. It couldn't be denied, *wouldn't* be denied—not any longer.

She tipped the mug back and swallowed a small amount of blood. Her stomach rolled and threatened to regurgitate the sustenance. But that wild part of her—the part that wanted to *survive* with rage and retribution—forced her physical body to keep it down. That wild part took hold of her mentation and coerced her not to think about what this might mean going forward. It was in charge in this moment. Kate let the reins go to that part of her and swallowed another mouthful, this one a little bigger than the last. Her eyes trailed to Lilith's, and she found them unfocused and distant.

"Know the path you tread, I've been down too. I've lived through things I thought would bring me to an end. Done things I thought I would never be able to come back from." Shame flashed for a moment, so quickly Kate thought she imagined it. "I didn't suffer as long as you did by any means, but for two weeks I laid in mud, wishing for nothing but death to take me. Every second I was awake I begged for some sort of deliverance. Instead I died cold and alone, with nothing but rage in my heart.

"Unbeknownst to me there was a watcher who heard my pleas. I don't remember much about him, but it was through him I was made. The night I awoke as a vampire on earth I found those who betrayed me and slaughtered every single one. And I would do it over, and over, and over again, for a hundred—a thousand—years if I could."

Kate paused after her fifth sip of blood and licked her lips slowly as she placed her mug in her lap. Lilith's eyes were intensely fixed on her, and it was with a clarity that Kate didn't have moments ago that she saw wrath like she'd never seen before in the swirling, stormy depths of Lilith's eyes. *That's how she knows. She's been there. Where I am.*

"The things I experienced," Lilith continued, continuing to speak as if the words were pulled from her. "Were horrendous. They altered who I was and changed the trajectory of my life forever. For the better? I still wonder. But I've learned lingering in memory is a futile venture."

Kate stared at Lilith as she emptied the contents of her mug. *And look at her now.* She lowered the mug to her lap as she continued to gaze at Lilith, who met her eyes with confidence sparkling underneath the storm within. *She came out on the other side. She's better for it. She is learned and appreciated and worthy.*

Maybe...maybe I can be too.

The ensuing strength that came with the satiety of blood started slowly, unfurling along Kate's limbs to meet the fire that smoldered within her core. Her sight cleared gradually, bringing with it brightening hues and sharper images. Her heart rate increased, no longer irregular, and she felt the breath in her lungs move in and out with ease instead of pain.

And finally, after weeks of self-inflicted torture upon herself, Kate began to have thoughts other than those which kept her drowning in her pit of despair.

The first? *Survive.*

The second? *Wrath.*

The third? *Revenge.*

"You've taken the time you needed to grieve, but now it's time to realize your renewed purpose. You made it through your ordeal to *be able* to make a difference. Fate gave you a second chance. It's time to make of it what you need to endure," Lilith continued boldly, with not a single waver to her voice. "Cast those empty thoughts of anguish away and use your *anger* as fuel to carry on. Rise with it. Use it to your advantage. Because it's *okay* to be angry. You *deserve* to be angry. What you went through was horrifying, and a lesser female would have succumbed a long time ago. *But you didn't* because you are a formidable, resilient, resourceful female. And you *will* make a difference."

Make a difference, Kate thought, her chest rising and falling quickly as invigoration blazed bright within her, overpowering everything else.

"I remember every *second* of what happened to me like it was yesterday, and I don't ever want to forget what I went through because it made me who I am today. I caution you to do the same, because you will lose sight of how far you've come and what it means to come out on the other side. But it's time to move past the despair and onto a different stage of the healing process."

Healing. It was something Kate didn't think she would ever be capable of. But the way Lilith spoke to her, empowered her…

Kate began to believe she could.

"Don't ever discount the courage it took for you to find your way back here. You needed that journey through the blackness, the sorrow, and the agony. It's a testament to your psyche and your core that you made it—and it shows that you *know* you have more to do. That you want to be here for a new reason, a different reason."

Make a difference.

Vengeance crashed in her clear, crystal blue depths as Kate said with an astoundingly steady voice, "I want to kill them all for what they did to me."

Talorc drummed his fingers along the top of his desk, his eyes blank as he stared at the door to his office. Lilith had been with Kathryn most of the night; in fact, the sun was to rise soon. He would admit to only few that he wished he knew the depth of their exchange, but he was too old to eavesdrop. If there was even a conversation happening at all. Kathryn was unpredictable, enchanting at her best but aggressively defiant at her worst.

That was before, Talorc thought to himself as he sighed deeply, his fingers still tapping along the shining cherry top, his work long forgotten. *Before everything that happened.* He was not a fool to think the situation had not drastically changed his daughter. He knew what happened in battle. He knew what happened to enemies across the line. He knew what happened to *females* who were taken prisoner. Furthermore, he knew what a broken individual looked like.

He had pushed that thought away countless times. Refused to give it strength, to believe it could happen to Kathryn. He put all his energy into hoping she would pull through. Beseeched anyone who would listen to make this all a bitter dream. But when Kathryn did not come around after a week, then another, and then yet another, his rational side forced him to face the truth of the matter.

Kathryn had been broken.

He was beyond afraid his wish for Kathryn to split the veil of her despair would lie forever unfulfilled. Endless weeks went by in which he told himself she would resurface the next day, and if not that one then the next. Weeks he kept telling himself she was strong enough to do so. She had access to all the resources. All she had to do was ask. She even had the bonus attributes of the confidence and resilience of her mother, who had been the Queen of the Valkyries if there ever was one.

Herja. Talorc let her name whisper through his mind, and for a moment in time he got lost in the memory of her cobalt gaze, her mirthful laugh, and her entrancing smile.

My Herja...

He closed his eyes, barring the memory in the cage he kept within him, where he locked away emotions, thoughts, and feelings he did not want to or could not face. He had built the cage not long after her death, knowing he needed a space to put things he could not handle. Yet despite the cage, for a time it had been easier to let the shadows reign and desolation lead his life. Easier, after he fell, to never get up. To lie there. Because no one knew the hidden wounds he bore, no one knew how difficult it was to see beyond the darkness, no one knew the emptiness he felt. Even with Kathryn—his light, his purpose—the days were long.

You are not that male anymore, he thought boldly. *You are standing now.*

Although the start of the campaign to mend his battered relationships was going well, he knew almost half of the coven leaders were massively displeased with him. They criticized him for continuing to collect their taxes, amassing astronomical wealth, without doing anything to support them—among so many other things a leader should be held accountable for. They and their kin lived in fear of their enemies night in and night out. The wraiths were becoming uncontrollable. There were also humans to be leery of, driven by a vengeance rooted in lore. He sensed the watchers lurked from above, scrutinizing his inaction and now reactions. He wouldn't be surprised if they delivered his end unto him as he so deserved, and truth be told he had been avoiding contact as of late.

Talorc knew Herja would ridicule him for his behavior if she could; she had never been one of inaction or dereliction. He knew he was failing *her* in not being there fully for Kathryn. Their daughter had been everything to Herja since the moment she knew she was carrying. She loved being pregnant and talked of little else other than what their youngling would be like the entire nine months.

In this very moment of vulnerability, memories from times of old came upon him, as fresh as if they had been created yesterday...

—and as she runs from me, her hair flowing on the night wind, her laughter pulls the pieces of my fractured soul together, making me believe there is more to this world than death and destruction...

—eyes, so piercing, so enrapturing, halt my breath in my lungs, and as she runs her calloused hands over my bared skin in the flickering firelight of our war tent, I cannot help but burn with passion in response...

—atop her noble steed her cry of battle, so resplendent, will

echo within me for all of eternity, as often as her siren's song when she breathes my name as if she would a prayer...

He slammed the door of his inner cage and locked it tight. No one would ever fully understand the constant turmoil he was in, but that did not mean he would let the pain grip and constrain him now. He was not that male anymore. He *could not be* that male anymore. He had a nation that needed him, a contingent of males who looked to him for guidance, and a daughter who had become his sole reason for being—a beacon out of the darkness.

Talorc needed to regain control. He had to lock the recollections away for another time, another place, far off in the distance, perhaps after all of this was settled. Maybe by then he would be another male, one who could look back fondly on the memories and not be distracted by them. He had to remain cognizant of the fact that giving up now would tear his family, both immediate and extended, apart, and would result in turmoil for everyone he was inadvertently tied to.

He knew every step he took had a rippling effect that went well beyond him, could carry repercussions that would change the course of the world. He turned over the thought a thousand different ways in his mind. It haunted him in sleep. Crept into his dreams, twisting them into nightmares. It followed him as he meandered between his office, his den, and his room, spending countless nights doing nothing but staring into various fireplaces, his lucidity temporarily lost to the abyss that was his mind. It was why he detested the idea of sitting in his manor longer than he had to—he needed an outlet, a distraction.

Shamefully, that thought was not the only one that kept him from his daughter.

Some nights he wondered how close he was to losing his mind in its entirety. *No.* He shook his head forcefully. He had over a thousand years of life under his belt—he refused to accept this was the coming of the end. It could not and would not end like this. Not with him alone, bitter, and more than halfway to madness.

My Herja...

He severed the trailing thought. Forced himself to focus on Kathryn. She was his purpose. He had to push forward for her. Something he had been unable to do...until now.

Guilt pushed against the bars of the cage he kept within

himself. Lately, the guilt had gotten stronger, more vociferous, more vulgar. Too many times it asked him why he was so removed from her recovery. Kathryn had been part of him from the moment she was borne. Yet here he was, behaving as if he were in the same place he had been years ago, drowning in depression.

How can I even begin to atone for my negligence? He thought, slipping a hand down his face to deter his darkening thoughts.

The guilt, the guilt... It bayed unmercifully, rattling the bars. Talorc had *so much* guilt that it was nearly asphyxiating. *Why did I never go for her myself?* He knew the answer, was ashamed of it, ran away from its plaguing daily. *Why did I not listen to her sooner when she asked to learn how to defend herself? When she asked for small freedoms?* He knew the answer to that too, and resented himself severely as the next thought assailed him: *Why did I never let her do anything outside of what I thought was best for her?*

Look where my control has gotten her. Where my rules have gotten her. Where my severity has gotten her.

The guilt reached between the bars to swipe at him, snarling its rage. Talorc closed his eyes and attempted to take a deep breath to quell it, but the beast would not be assuaged.

Talorc feared, if it got out, that it would eat him alive.

The crackling of the fire across the room drew his attention, and as he stared at the flames, one last musing of his beautiful Herja danced within. *She is everywhere, all the time,* Talorc thought, but again forced the remembrance away, and this time her memories were dissuaded for good.

Distantly, he heard the creaking of Kathryn's door, followed closely by its gentle shutting. He snapped his eyes away from the fire to the door to his office and stood hastily from his seat. The enormous picture behind the desk loomed mightily, an ancient field of battle sprawling with foes and creatures alike. High in the painted gray sky a hen harrier flew above it all, crying heathenistic contempt in her own lust for blood. The painting fell into shadow as Talorc's boots plunged heavily across the floor. He opened the door to the office with more force than was necessary before barreling down the hall to the foyer. He heard the light footsteps of a single being walking the length of the hall above him, and he accelerated his pace to beat them to the foyer.

Though in his heart he knew it was not Kathryn.

Talorc glanced up when he met the balustrade of the rotunda and saw Lilith descending the stairs from the third wing. Her face was impassive, her gait and posture stiff, and if she noticed that he was there she gave no inclination. Talorc hurried down the opposite stairs to meet her in the foyer and waited impatiently while she took the last few steps, finally looking up as her flats touched the swirling, beige marble.

"How did it go?" Talorc asked without preamble, walking past the large decorative winter arrangement that Mora would soon be changing to reflect the oncoming spring.

"I've come to bring her food," Lilith said softly, her green eyes shadowed. Talorc assumed it was because of the burden that had been put on her shoulders, but he could not be encumbered by that now. Instead, his eyes flared at her revelation.

"She eats?" His gaze darted to the empty mug she had in her hand, and then quickly back up to her face. "Drinks?"

"Yes," Lilith replied tonelessly.

"Thank you," Talorc breathed in relief, and the weight on his chest gave way to bliss. "I cannot thank you enough."

"There's still a road to cross, and it's a wide one." Her eyes shadowed further, though she did not look away nor balk from the veracity of the situation. "There's still a lot of work to be done. A lot to make amends for." A sudden sharpness edged her form. "She's not the same, Talorc. She'll never be the daughter you once knew. You'll have to abide by this new being. The answers you seek might not be forthcoming and you have to be okay with that. She still needs time, understanding, and patience, but most of all healing."

Slightly taken aback at her firm tone and stance, Talorc nodded once. "I assumed as such."

"It's one thing to anticipate it, another to say it out loud, and yet another to live it," Lilith said, her voice harboring a dangerous warning. "This situation changes not just Kate, but everyone around her as well. Remember that. Give yourself grace but save the most for her. This has been a metamorphosis for her and in time you will come to realize that it's for the better."

Lilith turned to embark into the kitchen, leaving Talorc

144

readily stunned. She disappeared down the hall and he heard Mora titter excitedly as Lilith asked her to arrange a plate of food for Kathryn. Talorc, however, could no more move than he could easily breathe.

Time. Understanding. Patience. Talorc felt as though he was capable of those things. But what stilled him, even frightened him slightly, was the thought of *healing.*

It was the healing that would be the most arduous, the hardest to obtain. *For how does one heal? I, myself, have not an idea. How can I help Kathryn heal?*

Talorc's eyes wandered to the stairs, past the second floor to the third, and then to the wing that Kate occupied in singularity. The heaviness that so easily lifted from his chest returned, and his thoughts turned dismal once more.

It is my fault she was put in this position. How can I ever forgive myself for all I have done to her? My promise to be strong, be courageous, has fallen woefully short. Not in all the eons to follow this one could I atone for how badly I have failed her.

Chapter Twelve

August 2021
Warwick

Kate tossed the towel to the counter, calling a quick farewell to Mora and Asha as she left the kitchen. Asha returned the sendoff, but Kate didn't hear it, her steps hurried, her thoughts elsewhere. She had plans to meet Ryder in the gym for training, and she didn't realize how close she'd been cutting it by bending Asha's ear for so long with her trivial ruminations while they'd cooked dinner. Asha had done everything she could to divert Kate from reflecting on what a complete douchebag Damian was while Mora listened quietly from the other side of the kitchen. Kate secretly feared her friend—and Mora for that matter—saw deeper than her bitter demeanor to the hurt beneath, no matter how badly she tried to hide it with caustic snark and confident retorts.

Ditched. Again.

Kate and Damian had plans to go to the observatory tonight—it was the perfect time of year to point out Cygnus, Hercules, and Sagittarius—but Vadin had come a'callin', flaunting a plan to go into the city to pick up females. Before she could even think to stop him, Damian was galloping after him. Demoralized and disheartened, Kate had gloomily curled up alone in the movie theater to watch serial killer documentaries, her forgotten popcorn cold and stale. Mora had come to retrieve her after two morbid hours, briskly demanding help in the kitchen, and Kate only admitted to herself that the distraction had been a welcome necessity. Now she was eager for the upcoming physical outlet, her

146

sullenness turned to livid poison in her veins.

Yet she was still unable to shake the discomforting
vulnerability she felt constricting her mood, and she hated herself
for it. She made quick work of the stairs, chanting stupid stupid
stupid, *hoping she could make herself more angry than miserable*
to fuel her practice. Always going after other females. Right in
front of me. Without a care in the world.

Douchebag is putting it mildly.

Kate pushed open the door to her room and headed for her
massive walk-in closet, stripping out of her sullied T-shirt as she
went. As she moved across the white faux-fur rug, recessed lights
flared to life, but all Kate could see was the haze of rage. She
dispelled the sudden rise of pure, tortuous longing that enveloped
her by viciously tossing her clothing to the floor in front of her
hamper.

Why does he always push me away? Why can't he see what
I see?

Because he's not yours, *her conscience told her dully.* And
you're not his. You're not in a relationship, and frankly, you never
will be. Stop pining after someone who clearly does not pine for
you.

Kate swallowed hard past the lump of sour disappointment
that lodged in her throat as she shimmied out of her pants. She dug
through her closet drawers until she found a sports bra and
spandex biker shorts, both royal blue in color. She stripped down
naked and then redressed, kicking off her slippers in favor of a pair
of matching sneakers. Anger made her eyes feel hot, and she
preoccupied herself by tying her shoes and then stopping to
appreciate the enormous closet she called her own. Each wall
boasted a different season's worth of clothing, which she readily
updated as styles changed. In the center of the floor was a large
tower of shoes, showcasing footwear to match the seasons. There
was also an oversized, ivory chaise next to a large marble island
which housed all her jewelry, and a backlit floor-length mirror
broke up the wall on the far side of the room.

Usually, her closet made her beyond happy, but today she
turned away and headed for the door with aggravation gnawing at
her. Her melancholy was readily replaced with bitterness as she
attempted to give herself the peptalk she needed to push past yet

another instance where Damian had brushed her to the side.
He's not worth your tears, *she thought to herself, sweeping her hair back as she strode toward her ensuite bathroom. Lights winked awake and the floor immediately started heating, but she didn't pay any mind to those comforts as she looked at herself in the mirror.* Get yourself together. *She picked up her brush and began vigorously combing her hair.* You're beautiful. Brave. Sassy. Funny. Independent. Clever. Quick. Smart. A hundred males would fall at your feet. Don't get caught up on the one that won't. *Resolute, she reminded herself she'd never cried over a male and wasn't about to start now.*
He doesn't let you affect him as such.
Get. It. Together.
She'd always been a strong, (non-admittedly barely) level-headed female who stood composed and calm in the worst of situations (not really). She hardly sweat the little things (untrue). She could rise from this. Move on from this. Maybe it was time to consider moving on altogether. It's been four years since I've been running after him, *she thought with only a small amount of self-pity.*
Decisively, she stared harshly at herself in the mirror as she tied her hair back with a scrunchie. You're better than how he treats you. *Her movements were jagged, rough, and she narrowed her eyes on her reflection.* No one should have the power to make me so upset.
Never mind the fact that Damian turned her inside-out, upside-down, and backward with emotions she couldn't explain. She also ignored the small detail that she'd felt drawn to him since the moment she laid eyes on him. Surely both could be overlooked in the face of such repeated, adamant dismissals on his part. Ugh. Her long, straight hair swayed as she walked out of the bathroom, the lights turning off by the time she'd crossed the floor to exit her room.
It will never be what I want it to be. *Kate headed back down the stairs, her gait noticeably slower.*
More time, just give it more time, *the optimistic part of her whispered slyly as she crossed the foyer.* If you just keep at it—
No. *Kate ripped open the door to the basement with more force than was warranted.* He's...he's not worth it.
She kept telling herself that as she jogged past the wine

room, past the old root cellar, down the hall, and into the sprawling gym space. The size of three basketball courts with said court to the far left, there was an area with various gym equipment to the right, and a space with mats where Ryder was setting up some sparring gear in between. There was a door that led to a locker room, another door to an infirmary, and between the two stood a kitchenette. In a last-ditch effort to forget the first few hours of the night, Kate went to the counter and connected her phone to a Bose speaker, smiling coyly at Ryder as Taylor Swift began to play.

"Start warming up," Ryder said, ignoring her choice of music, which she selected solely to annoy him.

"I don't need to warm up." Kate crossed the mat with a confident swish of her hips. "I'm good."

"You always need to warm up."

"Not me."

"Stretching. Ten minutes," Ryder prompted her, and Kate stuck her tongue out at him as she sat heavily down on the mat and did as he bade.

"What are we doing today?"

Ryder walked to the wall and grabbed two jump ropes, dressed in a pair of gym shorts and a black T-shirt to match. "The basics."

Kate groaned, dropping her head against her outstretched leg. "We've been *doing the basics. When are we going to get to something cool like sword-fighting? I want to use a gun."*

"You know how to use a gun and a blade. Besides, guns are rarely good for killing our kind. Wraiths, sure. But you should learn to use guns as more of a distraction and rely on your own inherent strengths when it comes to fighting."

"Okay so we'll start with swords?"

Ryder eyed her shrewdly. "When you get down the basics."

"You're so mean."

"And you're inconsistent and sloppy."

Kate huffed, switching one outstretched leg for the other, coiling her relaxed foot inward. "I only missed a week."

"When are you going to start taking this seriously? It's been almost five years Kate, and you still don't know how to execute certain moves."

I am taking this seriously. I'll show you I can make a

difference. *She turned her face from Ryder to not give her inner thoughts away, reaching down her extended leg with the arm of the same side. Ever one to have the last word, she opened her mouth to retort mockingly,* "When are you going to—"

"You can do the stair climber for thirty minutes if you finish that sentence," Ryder warned.

Puffing out an exasperated breath, Kate stayed silent as Ryder finished grabbing the equipment necessary for their session. Kate knew he wasn't going to be easy on her, and she spent the remaining time warming up trying to curb her more opinionated side in favor of one that was acquiescent. I did ask for this, after all.

Kate hadn't grown up a warrior. She had to beg to be trained in combat, and even that had taken months of nagging and being on her best behavior. She knew she would never be as steadfast as Ryder, as strong as Cyrus, as intelligent as Noir, as confident as Vadin, as cunning as Damian, or as brave as her father, but she was fast, and she could think on her feet. She could be stealthy enough thanks to her ability to blend, a rare vampiric ability that allowed her to camouflage in with her surroundings. She could even be smart enough in the right moment. Let me show him how far I've come, *she thought for the hundredth time.* Then they'll all see. It's time to put my plan into action. The boys are bound to my father's whims and my father's whims are mute...

But I'm not.

She popped to her feet the moment ten minutes passed, and Ryder crossed the mat to face her, about six feet between them. "Show me your ready stance."

Kate's face dropped into one of disbelief. "Seriously? We're going that basic?"

Ryder arched a brow and Kate sighed, easily falling into a posture with her feet shoulder-width apart and her hands open and raised before her face.

"Stagger your legs," Ryder told her, and Kate amended. "Good. Bend your knees a bit. Heel up in the back." Ryder mirrored what he wanted her to do, and Kate corrected her stance perfectly. She threw a confident smile at him, all fang, which Ryder promptly disregarded.

"Good. But that was easy. Let's try the—"

The door to the gym creaked open, and both Ryder and Kate looked over at the sound.

Creator take me.

Damian swaggered over the threshold dressed in an outfit similar to Ryder's, his curling dark hair framing his face and laying just above his shoulders. Kate could see the shining copper of his eyes from where she stood over a hundred feet away, and the smirk he had on his dusky lips made her falter and drop her arms to her sides. He looked absolutely mouthwatering—as he usually did—and Kate cursed herself over and over again, hating that she yearned to see those hips move in a different way and with much less clothing.

"Just getting started?" Damian stopped a few feet from them, his gaze jumping between the two before settling on Ryder. "I can cut in. You can guide."

No. *Kate's eyes flared briefly, and she said with unchecked hostility aggravated by dread, "This is a one-on-one session. Ryder was helping me."* AKA, if you're here I'm not going to be able to concentrate.

Damian ignored her. "It would be easier for you to watch and make pointers."

Ryder looked from Damian to Kate, who was glaring at Damian with no small amount of fire.

"Fine," Ryder said, taking a step back.

Kate whipped her head to him and nearly shouted, "Ryder!"

Damian stepped into Ryder's place, grinning at Kate wide enough to expose his fangs.

Kate wasn't one to curse—the habit heavily penalized by her father from an early age , but the ensuing thoughts she couldn't help: damn you Damian and damn everything you've ever made me feel. Damn that smile and swagger. Damn the way those clothes fit you. Damn you for pushing me away. Damn damn damn.

Damian's eyes flicked from her clothes to her hair before lifting his eyes to meet her gaze. "Show me everything those lessons have taught you."

Fleetingly stunned by the rolling timbre of his masculine voice, Kate could only stare. A heartbeat later the intensely fierce part of her took over, urging, kick his ass and show him exactly what he's missing.

She fell effortlessly into her ready stance. "You asked for it."

Damian hurried to the gym where he knew Kate would be, hoping that he'd left the bar in enough time to catch her before she started training. Although he and Vadin were successful in their ploy to pick up women, Damian had quickly grown bored and restless and left Vadin with the three humans to come back to Talorc's. He'd speedily changed from his clothing to some workout gear in one of the bedrooms that had been allotted to him, before checking his phone for the umpteenth time to see if Kate texted him like she usually did.

She hadn't.

Which irked him.

She must've been busy. *He was eager in his steps as he almost jogged, ignoring the inevitable guilt that came with how dismissively he'd treated Kate. He distracted himself by thinking,* they had to have just started, so I couldn't have missed much.

Their earlier time together had been set to be a night in, where he made them popcorn and she chose what documentaries to watch. They were his favorite types of nights, and as he'd gazed at her sitting on the couch, chatting to him and scrolling through Netflix, he'd felt incredibly happy and at ease. Like this was the exact space he needed to be in for the rest of his life.

Those feelings...the nearness of Kate... He'd suddenly felt overwhelmed and needed an out. Retrospectively he knew he'd left abruptly, but being close with her in dark quarters was dangerous to what willpower and morals he had left. She was becoming harder to keep at arm's length while it simultaneously became more difficult for him to remember why he should avoid her in the first place.

Who am I kidding? *He* couldn't *avoid her. He'd been coming to Talorc's every night for four years just to see* her. *And it was getting more and more cumbersome to overlook that.*

He broke the threshold into the gym and stumbled to a stop. The universe always came to a crashing halt whenever she was near. Even as her eyes blazed at him from across the gym with pure revulsion, she would always have that effect on him. He could sense her lividity from where she was, yet despite it, she seized his breath, his thoughts, and his heart in his chest.

Keep moving. Don't let her see how she affects you. *Damian continued his trek across the gym floor, stepping onto the black mats. He barely threw a greeting at Ryder as he looked Kate from head to toe, noticing how the contours of her body pressed against the spandex material of her outfit, leaving nothing to the imagination. His mouth subsequently went dry, and he could no more stop picturing how her breasts would bounce when she began to move as he could stop picturing himself peeling her shorts off in the locker room to reveal her alabaster skin to his covetous gaze.*

She looks better in leather. *Her wardrobe was heavy in the material, which was completely detrimental to his every waking thought. He got further distracted in the moment as he pictured her wearing leather that covered less than the outfit she was wearing now.*

He said something out loud to divert himself and his cock from his yearning, but he didn't know what. When he saw Kate's eyes flare in irritation, he knew it was something she didn't like.

"Ryder was helping me," she said hotly.

Barely able to think over the notion that her bountiful cleavage pushed against her top solely to tempt his lustful gaze, Damian said to Ryder, "It would be easier for you to watch and make pointers."

When Ryder didn't disagree, Kate made her disdain known. Creator, but I love her fire, *Damian thought, shifting from one foot to another to deter his hard-on from growing any more. It was a futile gesture, as he couldn't stop thinking that the blue color of her workout clothing brought beautiful contrast to her black hair and creamy skin. Skin he wanted to touch, to taste, to feel beneath his own...*

Lost in a fantasy he knew better than to entertain, Damian realized he must've said something inciting because Kate narrowed those paralyzing blue eyes on him and snarled, "You asked for it."

The left hook came out of nowhere, especially since Damian knew Kate was dominant with her right hand. He stumbled to avoid it but didn't lose his footing and quickly squared up against her. Kate smirked and raised her fists to block her face as Ryder chastised her for being impulsive. Damian suddenly knew this match was going to be less about Kate practicing and more about her getting revenge on his behavior toward her, yet he still looked forward to every single jab.

"That was a cheap shot," he said to goad her.

"I have to take what I can get."

"This is just practice." Damian tipped his head to the right, then to the left, and the vertebrae within gave a crunch as he matched her defensive stance.

Kate's eyes narrowed to slits. "Scared I might actually get one over on you?"

Damian's mind solely focused on the words over *and* you *as he pictured her naked doing just that.*

He cast away the errant illusion and forced himself to be mocking, his lips curving into a wolfish smile. "As if you ever could."

Kate threw a strike compelling him to block his face in defense. "You might choke on that arrogance before we even start. Don't underestimate me."

Damian raised a provoking brow. "Given the fact that you're a third of my size and have less than half the muscle I do, forgive me if I don't tremble in fear."

*"You might not tremble," Kate replied, her eyes roving his body—*for weak points, *he assured himself. "But I'll be sure to make you piss blood for a week."*

She's definitely mad. Cursing? *"Who's arrogant—"*

Kate feinted right but Damian knew what she was about; he followed her to the left and she was forced to draw back. She struck again quick as lightning with a swipe of her claws to his face, but Damian blocked it. He wasn't ready for the leg she smashed into the side of his knee however, and the move made him grit his teeth and buckle.

"Good move with the claws," Ryder called from his perch on the edge of the mat; Damian had forgotten he was there. "Use any advantage over him you have."

Kate smirked and danced away from Damian on agile feet, keeping her face well-guarded with raised fists. She began to bounce from foot to foot as a boxer might do, and to prevent himself from staring at her chest Damian leapt at her, using the speed graced to him by his kind. He feinted left, then right, swooped past her, and smacked the back of her knees with his forearm to bring her to the mat. From her knees she blindly lashed out with her right arm with a wide reverse-haymaker, but Damian was already past her, and he spun to face her as she jumped to her feet and did the same to him.

Just a little longer, *Damian thought of Kate being on her knees.* What I wouldn't give—

"You're being brash. Don't be a hero. Think before you strike," Ryder said to Kate from the sidelines.

"Don't hurt yourself doing it though," Damian told Kate with another fang-filled grin, and she snapped her teeth at him before lashing out again.

She was radiant. She moved effortlessly, and though her movements were easily anticipated by a warrior like him, she was graceful and nimble. Damian caught himself getting mesmerized by the gleam of her raven hair and the calculating way her azure eyes tapered in their musings. She was focused on proving a point and retaliating against him for abandoning her earlier, and if her motivation wasn't the sexiest thing he'd seen in his entire six hundred years of living, then he didn't know what he was doing with his life.

The wide space didn't allow her to blend into her surroundings as her inherent vampiric trait allowed, and she was admittedly mismatched against her experienced partner. But that didn't stop her, and her conviction and determination were absolutely enthralling. They lent her a glow that wouldn't be dimmed, and Damian was drawn to it. She had so many captivating facets to her and Damian admired them all, but he especially liked her confidence. It set her afire and stoked the core of him in response. Creator save her, but she was so sure of herself even though she was losing. While she was quick, Damian was quicker. When she struck, he had an evasive move already in place. Whenever she tried to be cheap and aim for his balls, he blocked.

"Regretting being lazy now, aren't you," Damian prodded.

He knew she would never admit such, and in true Kate fashion she responded, "Just needed a little warm-up." And with fire on her heels, she sprang at him once more.

Five minutes passed. Ten. Fifteen. Ryder chastised her movements here and there, but otherwise let them spar instead of whatever he'd planned. Kate had begun sweating while Damian didn't so much as have a sheen on his face, and he tried not to get distracted at the way small droplets clung to her breasts. Instead, he thought about how he'd surprisingly only been able to pull her to the mat twice. She refused to back down from him and wasn't letting herself be intimidated. She would run to the grave before she ever conceded defeat. And honestly, she was giving him a slight run for his money.

She struck out with a right hook to his face, but Damian grabbed her wrist, spun her around, and locked a thick arm around her throat as his chest crushed her back. She tried to stomp his foot, but he kneed the back of hers and she went down, her delicate hands wrapping around his forearm as she went. He went to the ground with her, his body tight against her own, with a leg between hers.

Which was the wrong position to be in. Her ass fit perfectly against his thigh, and her heaving chest pushed her breasts against his forearm. The heat from her body, from the most intimate part of her, sparked out to enflame him, and his body answered hers by roiling. He pressed into her, wanting—needing—to get as close as possible, and placed his mouth by her ear. "You've tried to hit me like that four times already. Change it up."

With a growl she tried to thrust her body back to make a counterattack, putting all her weight into bringing him down to the mat, but he was simply too big. He had her in a very uncompromising position by being so close, and Ryder called to her as such, but neither heard him.

"What's wrong?" Kate jostled to try and alleviate his arm around her throat. Damian felt the fluttering of her pulse, and he turned his lips to press against her ear. "Stuck?"

Kate bent an elbow to strike him in the ribs, but he moved away, keeping his offensive position. Her breathing increased and she became very still, and Damian knew she was thinking about her next move. Conversely, rational thought was leaving him the longer he held her. It feels too good. Too right.

"Try to remember to wear something with pockets so you can call me to save your pretty little neck. What you have on is lacking." In all the right places.

Damian had to let go then, or she would've felt his erection press for attention. Kate hissed as she jumped to her feet, spinning to face him, flushed and panting.

"I don't need you," she seethed, *and Damian thought maybe she meant it before she sprung directly into her next attack. It was an arcing leg kick, one that was meant for his femur. Instead, Damian grabbed her ankle and easily sent Kate to her back.*

"That was stupid," Ryder chided. *"You have to think, Kate."*

"Not in a fight," she panted, *rising to her feet once more. Damian's eyes dipped to her chest and then back up quickly as she began a slow circle around him.*

"A lot can happen in the span of a few seconds. One of your defenses can be taking your time, which can be interpreted as putting pressure on your foe. Your enemy could surrender, make a hasty move out of desperation, or turn and run in the other direction."

"Which always makes for a fun chase," Damian added with a grin.

Kate glared at him. "I'd rather smash their face and be done with it."

Damian barked out a laugh. Fire. Pure fire. *"You're doing a shitty job of it."*

They continued, and seeming as though she listened for once, Kate changed her combos. She spun. She ducked. She retreated. She slid. But Damian matched it all. She was getting angrier and angrier, her moves quicker and sloppier, and finally out of sheer exasperation, she threw all her weight and momentum into one last punch at his jaw with a shriek to shatter the lights. The move actually clipped Damian in the chin and his face jerked to one side, catching him so genuinely off guard that he stumbled. Accepting her limits, Kate withdrew, panting heavy breaths.

Damian tipped his face toward her, lifting a hand to graze his bearded chin. "That was pretty good."

Kate circled him, her narrowed eyes roving his body.

Taking this seriously then, *Damian thought.* She has more

than a point to prove. Maybe she really does want to learn.

"Don't focus so heavily on one target," Ryder *called from the sidelines. "There could be one in front of you, but ten in the shadows. Remember, you're fighting wraiths, not some punk who wants your purse. They're bent on blood."*

He could tell she was nearly out of energy, yet Damian still had to brace himself as Kate used what lingered of her fury to come at him again. And again and again and again. The more she fought, the more she grew visibly tired and physically slowed, but she wouldn't be deterred. No, that fire that burned within her blazed, making her cerulean eyes sparkle. And Damian's admiration of her grew exponentially. He knew she had drive. He knew she had determination and zeal and fervor. But he'd never seen it like this, and Creator take him, but he was so immensely proud of her.

Yet after about thirty more minutes of her getting completely annihilated, Ryder called it. Kate swiped beads of sweat from her forehead and, amazingly without any sort of rebuttal, went to the nearby fridge and grabbed a bottle of water to guzzle and a towel to blot her hair and face. She kept her back to the males, and as Ryder began putting away the supplies he'd gathered, Damian meandered over to Kate, unable to stay away.

"You did well," he said, and she barely turned to flash him with an ireful stare.

"We're mismatched."

"You're not used to this style of fighting." He came to rest with his back against the counter of the kitchenette after grabbing his own bottle of water from the fridge. *"You'll get better with time."*

"What's the point?" Kate pushed, irritated. *"It's not like I'm ever allowed past the property line without a GPS tracker and someone to watch my every move."*

In that moment Damian's countenance changed from lighthearted to doused, and pity began gnawing at the center of his chest. He knew Kate was independent, and much wilder than what was allowed of her. She'd been born into her life of secrecy and confinement, and without a doubt there was an untamed part of her that yearned for more. She talked often about traveling, exploring new places, meeting new people; it pained him to think she would never get to experience any of that.

His eyes softened as he watched her sip her water, his gaze swirling with a turbulence that was made of wanting to provide her with everything she could ever desire and knowing he had to keep himself from her at all costs. The line between the two, however, had grown increasingly faded—had been fading since he had haphazardly drawn it after meeting her all those years ago.

"We have to make sure you can protect yourself first. That's why you have to take this seriously."

"I can, I am," she insisted firmly, taking a few steps from the kitchenette. "Maybe not up to your standards, but I'm doing just fine."

"Kate..." Damian started, but she turned on him fully with that fire that he so adored, and her words burned with the flames she'd been harboring.

"I don't need you, or Ryder, or anyone else. When will someone realize that I'm an adult? That I am capable of taking care of myself? Why will no one give me the chance? Why do I have to prove it to you, to him, to my father?"

"It's not—"

"I owe you nothing," Kate spat, and Damian knew she was projecting her earlier feelings of bitterness at him, as well as her irritation at being sequestered. "I don't have to show anyone anything. I'll do it to prove it to myself. And then I'll show all of you that I can do this on my own. You're too busy dredging up the depths of the dating pool to even give a shit about me anyway."

There it is. What he knew was truly bothering her. Her words, so caustic, said with such vehemence, seared his flesh.

And piqued his ire.

"It's not like that, Kate."

"Then how is it, Damian?" She crushed her water bottle in her hand, thankfully with the lid in place. "You easily ditched me to go hang out with Vadin. Pretty shitty if you ask me."

The number of times she was cursing told him exactly how frustrated she was with him. He felt remorse for abandoning her as quickly as he had, but nothing had come of his outing so what did it matter?

"Okay. It's done. Over with. So?"

His response made him cringe, and he watched as her eyes flared with contempt.

"So? So what? My feelings don't matter?"

"You know that's not what I meant—"

"No. I don't. Tell me what you meant."

He knew he sounded as stupid as he felt as he sputtered, "Well...I mean...I'm friends with Vadin, and you and I are just friends too—"

"So what if we're just friends!" Kate cut him off sharply. "We had plans, Damian, and you still left me to go hang out with Vadin! What kind of friend does that?"

Damian knew the implication that he'd spent time with other females rang loudly, clearly, between them. Unwanted. Unsaid. But there.

"Kate, you have to—"

"I don't want to hear it." Kate turned from him and began to storm from the gym with all the grace of an elephant. "It's obvious your priorities are elsewhere. Maybe stay away from here for a while."

Just the thought turned his stomach. "You don't mean that."

She said nothing as she crossed the mat.

"Don't forget your post-workout stretches," Ryder called after her.

Kate turned while still walking, her feet taking her backward, and lifted both middle fingers in the air.

Damian watched her go, discomfited by her show of anger. She'd never been so volatile toward him. I didn't deserve that. Did I? As Ryder came to settle next to him, he was again lost to his torturous thoughts.

"That didn't seem to go well." Ryder placed the cap back on his own bottle after he took a drink.

Damian found he couldn't utter a single word in response to Ryder, preoccupied still. Did I deserve that? He frowned slightly, fighting the urge to rub the knot he suddenly felt forming in his chest. She doesn't know...why I have to... He flinched when Kate slammed the door shut behind her, and the shame for his selfish actions suddenly grew larger than his retaliatory wrath.

I can't stay away from her. If I do, then I crave her. If I don't, I get closer and closer to giving in. But I have to keep her at arm's length. She's Talorc's daughter, for Creator's sake. And of the few ways he knew how to do that, making her think he was seeing other *females was the most successful.*

If I let her think I don't want to be around her, that she means nothing to me… If I let her continue think I'm with others… Maybe she's finally starting to realize we can't work…

No matter how much I might want us to.

Fighting with himself never proved resourceful, and he closed his eyes to dispel his thoughts. The tarry taste of rejection still coated his throat, and before he could dissuade it completely, he dimly realized he would rather face a horde of wraiths than make her feel the way he was right now.

Distraught, vulnerable, and angry, Damian pushed himself away from the kitchenette but paused, unsure of what to do now. This is bullshit. Confusing, infuriating, and a worthless waste of time, *he thought miserably.* If I want to further myself from her then I seriously have to start staying away and doing more of what will drive us apart. It's the only way that I can detach myself from her.

It's the best thing for us.

Yet Damian couldn't extinguish the warm pinpricks of her lingering fire that swept his body, tempering the raging waters he kept within. The memory of her pressed against him rushed to overcome him once more, and Damian opened his eyes to focus on something else, anything else—

"You good?" Ryder asked him, still steady beside him.

No, *Damian thought crossly.*

Creator save him, but he wanted to follow her. To slam into her room, pin her to the bed, and ravish her fully as he'd been imagining since the day he laid eyes on her. Fuck denying it. Fuck the line he'd drawn between them. He wanted to stop with the lies and the falsehoods and pretenses and just—

He wanted Kate.

He took a deep breath to control himself, but only succeeded in inhaling the last of her lavender scent on his skin, his clothing. His body radiated pure, unadulterated lust for her in response. Creator take him, but he was beginning to think he would never be able to explain how Kate made him feel, made him think, or why her control over him superseded every logical thought he had. She consumed him, not just metaphorically but physically. The hole in his chest, the fluttering in his stomach, was proof.

It can never be.

"Fine." Damian turned to face his friend. Ever stoic, the look on Ryder's face revealed not a single thought, but his golden eyes held volumes that Damian didn't want to read. *"I could use another go-round."*

Ryder nodded, placing his water bottle on the counter and moving toward the mats once more.

Using combat as a distraction, Damian repeated his last thought over and over and over again until it was all he saw, all he felt, all he knew.

Chapter Thirteen

D amian pulled himself from reverie with a strong shake of his head, refocusing on the movement of the treadmill. *Was that really just seven months ago?* he thought to himself, pushing harder on the machine. *Creator, we've been on this merry-go-round for too fucking long.*

His face turned sour, reflecting his whirling thoughts. *She showed us signs back then. Signs that she was restless, angry, and unfulfilled. Signs that we all ignored. Maybe if we'd paid attention to them, we wouldn't be where we are right now.*

He glanced down at the timer on the treadmill, which told him he had been on it for well over an hour. Another glance, one of many, at the large clock on the wall above the locker room door told him that night was quickly approaching. As restless as he was, he would go through his routine like he always did: eat a hasty dinner, check on Kate, exercise Rook, then set out for the night on whatever his task was to be. His rigorous workout had earned him a shower too, but he could easily add that without setting his evening back. Which he especially couldn't afford tonight.

Because Damian was convinced that things would be different. Lilith had been successful in talking with Kate, and while she had yet to emerge, he knew the tide was changing. He knew things were going to get back on the right path. He could feel it. *They have to.*

Though he only slept four hours, Damian felt as though he'd had a full day's worth and drank a mug's worth of blood on top of it. *Should do that soon,* he thought passively; it'd been some time since he drank, what with his thoughts constantly on Kate's recovery. But he would make it a priority tonight. He wanted to keep up his momentum. *Things can only go up.* He felt energized.

Ready to go. More confident and motivated than he had in weeks.

Utilizing his newfound dynamism, he hopped from the treadmill and headed into the locker room, rushing through a shower before changing into a pair of dark jeans and a long-sleeved grey shirt. With his hair still wet, he charged up the path from the basement, through the foyer, and into the smallest of the three dining rooms where breakfast was being served by Asha. Talorc and Lilith were sitting at the table, talking in muted tones, and paused as Damian breezed through with a quick, "I'll be right back."

He plucked a cinnamon roll from the tray Asha was carrying and winked at her, causing her to scowl. *Hates my guts, just like that stupid horse.* Uncaring, he pushed his way through the swinging door and into the kitchen, where Mora was instructing various servants in different tasks. He slipped past her and headed for the mammoth fridge, peeking through the glass door before opening the other solid, stainless steel one. When he found his target, he took the glass pitcher from the fridge and moved to a nearby cabinet to retrieve a ceramic mug.

He pushed the entire roll into his mouth and chewed as he filled his mug with blood, sloshing a bit on the counter in his haste. When he moved back to the fridge to replace the pitcher, Mora swept in to wipe his mess, to which Damian tossed her a cursory, "Thanks," before moving to the microwave to warm his sustenance.

He impatiently pulled the mug from the microwave before the timer went off, and with a swift sip that had him hissing at the temperature, he moved to a drawer to retrieve a spoon and began stirring the contents of his mug as he walked back into the dining room.

"Okay I'm here," he announced as he sat down heavily to Talorc's left. He reached to the center of the table for the eggs benedict to begin loading his plate, though no one else had. "How is she?" he asked Lilith, moving to the fruit next.

"As expected," Lilith answered, little to no inflection in her tone.

"What does that mean?"

"It means that she has taken what I've said in stride and will do with it what is necessary."

"She's coming out then?" Damian made quick work of his

eggs after helping himself to some sausage links.

"I don't know," Lilith reached for her water to sip, unperturbed by Damian's sharp demeanor.

Damian frowned. "Then you're staying to make sure she does, right?"

"My work here is done."

Damian paused, his fork poised above his plate. The manner in which he delivered his next words were icy: "I called you here to fix her."

"Kate doesn't need fixed. She needs healing. Transcendence."

Transformative. Transcendence. Damian thought back to his conversation with Vadin before bringing himself back to the present with a shake of his head.

"Fixed, healing, whatever," Damian barked, earning himself a stern look from Talorc. "Just stay until she's better."

Lilith looked away from him, focusing on helping herself to the breakfast that had been prepared. "I have others to tend to."

"You're not done here until she's better."

"Damian," Talorc warned.

"No." Damian took a large swig of his blood. "I asked her to come here to see Kate better. That means seeing it through."

"There's nothing else I can do. Kate's betterment is in her own hands."

Fuming, his restless energy swirling, Damian snapped, "This is some *bullshit—*"

"Damian, I would caution you further," Talorc interjected. "Lilith is the professional. She has insight we do not. You must take her word and let the rest fall to Kathryn. Tell me instead: did you reach out to any of the overseas covens?"

His jaw sliding from one side of his face to the other in his barely controlled disapproval, Damian replied, "Still working on it."

"Mayhap that would be a good distraction for you." Talorc began filling his own plate as he met Damian's eyes purposefully. "I am thinking that should take priority rather than the recuperation of Kathryn at this point, seeing as how it is underway."

Fuck that. Damian thought, and tried to sound less biting as he said, "I can handle both."

"Mayhap it is time to reconsider."

"Aren't you leaving soon?"

Damian instantly curtailed his aggression when Talorc leveled him with a look that said he disagreed with the trajectory of the conversation and the angst with which Damian spoke.

"In less than a week." To mirror his disdain, the temperature in the room dipped slightly. "Everything is being accounted for. Ryder has made the appropriate arrangements."

Should know more about that, Damian thought of his lack of participation. *Maybe I'll try to catch up with Ryder tonight, too.*

Damian ate the rest of his meal in silence, as did Talorc and Lilith. *Take the high road. No reason to be the bug in the ear.*

As he was standing to leave the table, Cyrus appeared, and the stare between him and Lilith lingered—not that Damian cared. He quickly pushed his chair back from the table and grabbed a nearby plate, loading it up with the eggs benedict and some choice pieces of fruit for Kate, forgoing the sausage he knew she didn't like. He threw a hasty greeting at his friend, and with one last look at Lilith and Talorc, he hurried from the cherrywood and green-décored dining room and up the stairs to Kate's room.

"Hey." A quick one-two rap preceded his greeting to Kate, and he bent to sit on the other side of the door as he had every day for a month. "I brought you some breakfast. Mora's eggs benedict. One of your favorites."

"I know Lilith came and talked to you. She said it went well." *In not so many words,* Damian thought acidly. "I have some time before I have to go exercise Rook. I need to meet up with Ryder tonight, too. Your father is leaving soon to continue on with his campaign. He wants me to go overseas to start talking to the other covens, but I just…" He faltered, unsure of how to continue. "I'm not ready to leave yet."

To leave you.

He took a deep breath in and held it before releasing it forcefully. *Avoid. There's nothing else to say. That's it. You're friends. Just friends.*

"Besides, I think you still need me here," he redirected, putting his head against the door. "Who's going to sneak you out when you want pho? To get your nails done? Who's going to let you be the most obnoxious passenger princess just so we can ride through the city blasting hip-hop? Who are you going to people-watch with at Smitty's? I'm the best workout buddy you've got, too. Vadin isn't shit for hiking, and Asha hates it. I'm the only one that can make it to the top of Mount Olympus with you. Who's going to binge crime documentaries with you? We have yet to find one with Cyrus in it. Because you know he's definitely featured. And let's be honest Kate, no one is helping you cart in all your Amazon boxes. Your shopping is out of control. But I promise if you pull yourself out of this, I'll bring them all inside, help you put whatever it is you bought away, *and* break them all down.

"If you want, I can go grab a tablet now and we could put on *Project Runway*. You missed most of the last season," Damian continued his rambling, staring at the sconce across the hall as it glowed yellow. "You don't even have to open the door, Kate. Just…come around. You've got to come around. Lilith is leaving. She said she's done enough. But you're still not here. You haven't come out. And I don't know what else to do."

I'll do anything to see you again.

"You're missing too much." Damian changed the course of his words so as not to reflect his innermost, fathomless thoughts. "You don't like to be left out of anything. And I'm trying to include you. But you need to do some work now. You need to come out. You've had your time. It's time to move on and come out."

He stopped, for his breath began to rush out of him as quickly as his words, and he was dangerously on the verge of getting ahead of himself. He steeled himself; his expression, his countenance, his words became hardened as he finished, "Just do *something.*"

He almost didn't recognize the voice that responded through the thick paneling of the door when Kate uttered, "No."

His heart jumped into his throat. Damian swallowed it, but it jumped again, and he scrambled to face the door, pulling himself clumsily to his feet. He placed a hand on the wood to push, but it didn't give, just like the female within.

"*Kate.*"

Her name was whispered like a prayer, and the faintest whisp of lavender unfurled from beyond to tease him. He balled his hand into a fist as to not let his tremble show, but the smile that curled his lips was unavoidable…until he realized what she'd said.

"No?" he asked incredulously, his eyes widening in shock.

Anger took over. Anger from months of pent-up frustrations. Anger from his continual rift with Talorc, and the knowledge he would have to bend to him soon. Anger against the wraiths. Anger against Lilith. Anger at himself, for so many reasons he couldn't begin to name them all.

"What do you mean *no?*" he thundered through the door, striking the carving of a moonflower with his fist before he stepped back to stare at the wood that separated them. "I've done *nothing* but see to your wellbeing for the last *month.* I've taken care of your belongings. Urged Talorc to see to your health. I was the *only* one that appealed for him to stay, to make sure that *you* were cared for! And before that I made sure you even *got* home. I helped arrange special transportation for you. I made sure Cyrus carried you safely from that fucking house. *I gave you my blood.*" His chest was rising and falling rapidly, his copper eyes fierce in their fury. "I've been doing everything in my power to get you back and you say *no*?

"You know what Kate? Go ahead. Stay in there." He pushed back again, turning from the door before whirling back to point an accusatory finger in her direction. "I'm done."

His tumultuous feelings roving within, Damian turned in the direction from which he came and began his trek back downstairs. *Fuck this.* Her singular reply played over and over in his head as he took the stairs, galloping into the foyer as if he couldn't get away fast enough. But as if chained, he halted abruptly, turning his face up to the glass mosaic above, the glittering pattern reflecting the starlight beyond.

She owes me.

She owes all of us.

I should go back there and force her to come out.

He closed his eyes.

Yet all he saw was her face, and by all that was holy it hurt like hell.

Avoid.

Ignore.

Run.

Damian looked toward the front doors to do just that. He could hear the riotous commotion of the house behind him, and inadvertently, as he supposed it always would, his gaze was pulled up the two flights of stairs, to the west wing of the house, toward *her*. He took one step, and then another, before he caught himself and turned his path toward the doors once more.

Fuck. This.

The glass floor mirrored those who deigned it their prerogative to congregate. The night air was thick with the individuals' swirling auras, each omnipotent, each devastating, colliding with each other's to assert dominance. The black columns which lined the space stood solemn, while the amber torches flickered spritely with unease. The sky above glittered with silver stars, a billowing navy expanse that stood watch over the strengths that assembled, wary of what their collective powers could wield.

This was The Ether, the cosmically immense home of the watchers.

And those who gathered, albeit grudgingly so, were those whom others bowed to, looked to for guidance, and would defer their leadership to for all things. For they were there at the start of it all: The First Arc.

"Thank you all for coming," Imra began. Her white robes undulated in swirling diaphanous wisps of ivory, and her feathery wings spread wide before tucking against her back once more. "I know it has been ages since we have last gathered, and the feat is not done nor taken lightly."

"Where are the others?" Hydra asked, her rippling gown reflecting the starlight above as the tide would the sun. The Creator relinquished control of the seas to her, and to reflect such she wore hues of blue and green in a gossamer cascade of fabric, which collected in a dipping neckline to reveal slender cleavage. The robing bared her arms and fell around pale legs, opposite-sided slits exposing skin shimmering with a pearlescent tone. Long hair the color of seafoam lay in tight curls to her waist and collected wildly in her lap as she sat back in the seat that had been procured for her.

Her feet were bare, though adorned with bands of rare seashells, as were her neck, ears, and upper arms. The wings that arched beyond her shoulders were the color of the palest sand, though some cerulean feathers could be discerned sporadically. Sharp brown eyes met Imra's own ashen ones, and her face was no less wary than her tone as she continued, "Bara Khan, Xypher, and Raham are absent."

"I am here," A strong voice replied, preamble to the watcher named Raham. A massive set of ivory wings tipped in gold unfurled widely, lowering the watcher to one of the empty seats. His broad shoulders and chest were bare, as he wore nothing but a slim, brown covering about his muscular hips. His skin, bronze in color, absorbed the light that surrounded him only to reflect it back in a subtle glow. The embodiment and master of sun and light, his chair was slightly removed from the others because to be near him was fatal; his beaming form radiated unimaginable heat. His dark hair was shorn to his scalp, his face clean-shaven, and he settled in his chair with his arms upon the rests, back straight, face impassive.

"The others did not deem it important to reply to the invitation," Oleander said in his volcanic rumble of a voice from beside Imra, their contrasting forms almighty above the others.

"Fetching," was Hydra's hissing reply.

"Let us not preoccupy ourselves with minute details, and instead focus on why I have asked you here," Imra redirected precisely, her melodious voice firm as she clasped her bejeweled hands before her. "There is unrest. Adhamh is rising."

More than one set of wings unfurled and rescinded, and several sets of eyes exchanged guarded looks.

"You know it to be true," Imra continued, while Oleander assessed the beings who sat in a wide semi-circle around the two. "You have ignored it just as we."

"It is not up to us to control peace and discord," Hydra intoned, her voice accusatory in her defense. "That is for you to delve. Are you not in keeping with your added task, Oleander?"

"Caution yourself," Oleander warned, his low voice thick with wrath.

"It is not beyond us to recognize that Earth is special to you, Imra," Undulane said, her voice rolling like the plains of the land which she controlled. Straight black hair slid from muscular shoulders as she tilted her head back, and her bright green eyes glowed from beneath the mightily antlered elk skull she wore to cover her face. Brown straps of linen fell down from her shoulders to cover her body, interspersed with vines of greenery. "You are more involved with its success than any of us. Have recently made a new vampire for its protection."

"It is within Earth that lies our future." Imra's tone relayed that she would never deter her whims and desires in favor of the powerful beings around her. She was, after all, the first to be made by The Creator; she held sway over them all. "It is the largest, the most prosperous of all the realms. Humankind has proved to be the most efficient and successful."

"And the most volatile," Hydra muttered.

"I would argue not more than others," Imra countered. "The Realm of the Beast is in constant turmoil. The Crimson Realm is rife with conflict. The Realm of Enchantment's inhabitants are nefarious at best, malicious at worst. Countless others know no peace."

"Why do you believe our fate is linked to Earth?" Raham asked, his wings spreading out to drape behind him, eliciting a wave of heat.

"We were created for humankind. While we all reflect various facets of The Creator, it was through us Earth flourished. The other realms…they have been around just as long as we have. They will go on."

"What does Adhamh have to do with this?" Undulane asked, and her voice held no little contempt for the watcher in question.

"He is pushing for superiority," Imra said. "He is trying to bend the vampires on Earth to his will in order to dominate."

"And after that he will target humans, and then us." Oleander's eyes darted around the watchers, surmising their responses. "His power surmounts with every victory over human- and vampire-kind."

"He has been dormant for too long." Undulane brushed away the notion easily, sweeping a tanned hand to show her distaste. "He is under my control."

"We made sure he could not rise," Raham supplied further. "The Creator did."

"We have been lenient in our sentry."

"Who is to blame for that?" Hydra asked, her tone poisonous despite the fact she directed it toward Imra. "Dare you besmirch The Creator? Accuse Undulane of negligence?"

Both Imra and Oleander leveled Hydra with a look that saw her quiet, though her eyes reflected her disdain plainly enough.

"The Creator has been reticent," Imra continued. "It has not spoken for quite some time. Even Oleander and I are ignorant of why It continues to remain silent despite our pleas for guidance."

Hush fell over those that were present and no one dared to meet the eyes of another, for the words were blasphemous.

"How do you know all this?" Undulane's wings shifted as she rearranged herself restlessly.

"We have been watching," Oleander responded. "Using a spheros."

"An all-seeing orb," Hydra mumbled. "Instead of getting your hands dirty."

A reverberation began under their feet, and Hydra looked quickly to Oleander as roiling embers encased his frame, begetting his volcanic power. In rebuttal she hissed, her skin flashing blue as her hair rose around her, as if alive. Imra sent a murmur of cessation to them both, and after a moment of challenge the two began to settle. But there would always be discord between fire and water, the greatest of opposing forces.

"You risk much by using one," Undulane said sternly. "They are all connected. To see through one is the portal to see through another."

"We know this," Oleander retorted gruffly. "We are only using it when obligatory."

"We must be careful not to tip the balance of things; all we are is based in duality. Our involvement has to be calculated. Dissected from all angles." Imra glanced at Oleander to further quell his fury. The fire receded at her gesture, but Oleander continued to stare at Hydra in barely restrained warning. "It has been difficult to know the right path without direction from The Creator. We do not use the spheros carelessly."

"Is that not what you are asking us to do?" Undulane asked, doing well to keep her tone level, though distrust shimmered in her emerald gaze. "Tip the balance? Challenge duality?"

"If we do not intervene," Imra said heavily. "We will fall."

Raham asked softly then, "You have seen it?"

Pale eyes clashed with brown, and Imra's reply was full of peril. "Yes."

Hush descended once more, and it was a long while before someone spoke.

"Adhamh cannot be eradicated. He is part of the balance."

Imra looked to Undulane. "There is evil that will prevail in his stead; there always is, for there must be balance. Unfortunately, that balance is already being tried, and can very well be swayed in the wrong direction. That is why I have asked you here. To seek your opinion on how to proceed."

"To get involved..." Raham started, and then stopped, uncertain on how to finish.

"Is a large endeavor to consider, I am aware," Imra said, and the wind on the plane they inhabited whipped her robes to a frenzy. "I ask that you do not take this lightly."

"What of the others?" Raham asked. "Xypher and Bara Khan are not present. We cannot make decisions without them. And there are others in the hierarchy to consider."

"We will continue to reach out," Imra said, hedging a look to Oleander. "We understand we are bound to wait."

"What would you have us do?" Undulane's voice was wary, her gaze shadowing with caution. "What is your plan?"

"Join forces with the vampires."

The only movement was the wind as it whipped and swirled. The torches jumped at its beckon, their low tones howling in response.

"Physically? In person? *On Earth?*" Hydra's tone was low in whisper. She had settled in her chair, but her hair rose again around her, rippling with agitation, and her wings snapped open abruptly.

"It is time we take matters into our own hands," Imra replied firmly. "We were meant to be the overseers of man-, vampire-, and watcher-kind. That has never changed. What will change is the superiority we have over this matter. I know that is an ideal that does not sit well with each of you, but it is the truth of the matter. The longer we do not act and wait for The Creator to declare Its desires, the more we all suffer. It will not be long until Adhamh comes to power as he did all those years ago.

"The fate of the Earth rests in our hands," Imra finished. "It is our duty to protect it and those who dwell there. It was given to us to see prosper. Let us not fail it, and its inhabitants, now."

"So says Fate herself," Hydra muttered, and more than one set of ireful eyes fixated on her.

"It is clear you have restraints," Imra said, mostly to Hydra, but her eyes roved them all. "Which is why I ask you to take the time necessary to decipher the information I have given you. I will advise you not to take long, because things are happening on Earth in a rapid manner. Talorc means to journey soon in his quest to unite the vampire nation. After that we will hold little sway over what happens. His support is feeble, fragile, and can crumble at any minute."

"You bring much to the table, Imra."

Imra met each set of eyes and said without hesitation, "I know."

Undulane was the first to depart once it was clear that the discussion had concluded. Her wings, an ombre of brown to forest green, fluttered open before taking the watcher into the vast beyond. Hydra lingered in her contemptuous stare of Imra before leaving, Oleander's growl protracted in her wake. Lastly there was Raham, who paused to stare knowingly at Imra.

"Much rests on your shoulders," he said, his brown eyes softening with empathy. "I do not envy you the burden. Do not let Hydra bother you. You know it is her nature to be so unruly."

Fluttering wings extended and then lifted the watcher into the air, the radiating essence of heat lingering until fading on the wind.

Sighing softly, Imra turned to Oleander, and pale sapphire clashed with amber as their gazes met.

"That went as well as I expected."

Oleander couldn't stop the snarl. "Hydra should know her boundaries better. She treads them boldly."

"As she should." Imra peered at the sky in the direction the watcher in question had flown to. "They all must ask questions to make informed decisions. I would anticipate nothing less."

"She needs to practice respect."

"As the celestial overseer of water," Imra countered, almost

174

wryly. "She is not known for her tranquil side. I do not know respect to be one of her strong suits."

Oleander blinked at Imra. "And that does not bother you?"

Imra smiled, turning her stunning, gold-rimmed blue eyes back to Oleander. "Why should it? She knows I am the supreme being."

Oleander grumbled stubbornly, "Still."

Imra spread her wings then, a beautiful ombre of the palest of grays to shining whites. "Ready the warriors," she said to Oleander. "We may need to make an appearance on Earth sooner than we like."

Chapter Fourteen

K ate sat silently on the velvet divan in her room, her hands wrapped around a warm mug of blood. She was freshly showered, though barely made it through the undertaking as it was the first time she'd taken care to do so in months. After being deprived of it for so long she still felt unworthy. *How will I ever not?* She'd sobbed for a half hour, curled into herself as she sat on the bathroom floor, before finally pulling herself under the running water. Only when she had no tears left did she leave the warm stream. Now she watched Mora move about her room, the female straightening the newly changed bed linen before fluffing the fabric cascading over her bed. By the way she moved, constantly glancing at her and stumbling over her tasks, Kate could tell Mora had another reason for being here other than tidying, and she watched her guardedly.

Another barrier I have to break, Kate thought of her momentous day; she'd eaten, showered, and opened her door to yet another being. She'd done so hesitantly, knowing the conversation to come would be, if not as significant as the one she had with Lilith, altering in some way.

Kate shifted so her feet were gathered beneath her bottom, and she settled back against the plush tufted pillow as she watched Mora open the curtains to her room, exposing the night beyond. Kate was clad in a pair of black leggings and a matching sweatshirt, though no humorous pun was displayed across the front as was her usual. Out of all her clothing she'd picked the plainest, because although she was feeling lighter and somewhat liberated, she still didn't feel like herself. The feelings that plagued her for months continued to linger, though every once in a while, rage swirled to the surface. She grasped onto it tightly when it did, using it as a buoy in the sea of drowning emotions, feelings, auras, and colors she was trying to endure.

"I will come back and give the bathroom a good cleaning," Mora called from said room, appearing with Kate's hamper of dirty clothing and linen. She padded across the floor with the basket tucked against one hip, her khakis and white linen shirt rustling as she moved. "Is your blood warm enough?"

Kate nodded once. "Thank you."

Mora smiled gently and stopped near the couch. Brown eyes trailed Kate from her head down, before moving back to the half-eaten plate of food on the end table. "Will you not eat further?"

Kate shook her head. "I've had enough for now." The food churned, her stomach still unused to nourishment, but Kate didn't want to worry Mora more by admitting such.

Mora shifted restlessly from one beige flat to another, though the movement was subtle. The worry reflected in her eyes, however, was strong, and Kate knew her vampiric gift of perception was picking up on every single one of Kate's feelings. Nothing ever slipped by Mora, and she learned things easily.

"You are sure?"

Kate nodded, unused to having to speak, her voice hoarse from doing it so much in the past day. Unable to bear the scrutiny of Mora's discerning gaze, she looked down at her mug. The assessment was enough to make her want to recede into the pit she'd called home for months, which lay behind the wall she was building to keep things at bay, but Kate forced herself to remain present. *I have to start somewhere.* She watched the blood ebb from one side of the mug to the other as she shifted her hands, focusing on the curvature, the way it flowed. The crimson was thick, and smelled delicious to the feral side of her that was pushing for survival.

Yet Kate couldn't help but think it tasted like bitter defeat.

I couldn't make a difference. I don't deserve to—

Stop this, that feral side of her snarled, the one that spoke confidence into her in the darkest of times. It drowned out the desolate parts of her, forcing them to be quiet as the fiercest depths of her soul bayed for retribution, to take back everything she'd lost. *That is quite enough.*

Mora transferred the basket from one hip to another and

gave Kate a last lingering look before moving to the door. Kate glanced up, her gaze snagging on Mora's long gray braid as it swept from side to side. Her slender form moved with an ease that didn't reveal her age, which Kate knew was close to her father's, or the tumultuous way Kate knew she felt inside. It was obvious; the disquiet emanated from her in murky wisps of gray, seeming to hold several millennia's worth of unrest.

In that moment Kate knew she couldn't hold onto the entirety of her pain any longer because it was doing nothing but holding her back. And not just her. But beings like Mora, Asha, her father, and the boys too. *Just like Lilith said.* Her continued angst would only drag her further toward the pit she was barely beginning to pull herself out of—and would happily take her family and friends with it.

"Mora?"

The female stopped, frozen in place. She peered over a slim shoulder but dared not speak.

Kate was unsure of how to even begin. But with her feelings so riotous, so overwhelming, she needed an outlet. She felt her voice tremble as she asked, "How can I move forward?"

The females stared at one another, neither daring to breathe.

Without a doubt in her heart Kate suddenly realized Mora was dearer to her than most everyone, and had always been the comforting, listening ear for some of her deepest thoughts and feelings. *That shouldn't change now.* She'd always been there for Kate; from the moment she was borne and through it all ever since. She readily took on the role of mother and was all Kate knew as such. She helped teach Kate to walk, to talk, her numbers and letters, the *Elden Edicts*, and about being a female and a vampire and all the hardships she would go through as she got older. She taught her how to apply cosmetics, bake, and to play the piano. The list went on, and the memories that followed were innumerable.

They cascaded over Kate as Mora turned to face her fully, gently placing the basket on the floor. She clasped her hands before her and stepped toward the couch once, then twice, before pausing.

"If I may?" she asked cautiously, and Kate nodded.

Mora closed the distance between them slowly and sat on the other end of the divan. She studied Kate meticulously, her gaze soft, her voice even softer. "To rise, even from the most suffocating of ashes, is an evolution worth undertaking. Do not look at the change as the end of who or what you used to be, but a progression of character."

Kate sat silently, absorbing the words. Mora allowed her to, but watched her closely, ensuring the verses did not detrimentally affect the young female.

"But I won't be..." Kate's fingers tightened around her mug. "I'm afraid I've lost...myself. What makes me, me."

"You have not," Mora whispered, and Kate looked up to meet her earthen eyes. "The pieces of your soul are not gone. Who you think you lost still resides in you. But you have transcended that place in your life. She is beyond you. You are beyond *her*. You have endured a revolutionarily atrocious situation and now stand on the other side a new female. You must give yourself credit for being courageous and staunch in your perseverance."

"I gave up," Kate admitted weakly, her low voice cracking as her eyes fell once more. "I wished for death more times than I can count."

Mora reached forward, gently placing a hand on her forearm. Kate looked up, feeling so pitiful, and the darkness that would forever lurk sensed this and reached out from the pit that Kate dangled precariously over.

"But you did not give up." Mora squeezed Kate's arm. Warmth seeped from the gesture, bright and glowing, chasing away the darkness. "You may think you did, but you would not be here if you had."

"The side that pushed me to survive..." Kate trailed off, unsure of what to say or how to say it. She stumbled to say, "I didn't recognize it. I still don't. I have this voice in me that forces me to be brave. Strong."

"That side of you has always been there; it is a part of you. It is what prompted you to act in the first place," Mora squeezed again before letting go. "The untamed part of you. The warrior part of you. The resilient part of you. They have combined to give you strength when you need it most."

"It doesn't feel like they were always in me," Kate murmured, torment trailing every syllable. "And I'm scared I'll get stuck in this limbo where I feel like I don't deserve to move on, want to move on, but don't know how to move on."

How she put into words what she was feeling was beyond Kate, but as soon as she finished speaking, the weight that had been sitting on her chest began to lift.

"You are feeling something other than pain and sorrow," Mora said with the softest of smiles. "Do you know how important that is? The grief is moving through you so you can focus on other things. Even if those other things are fear and uncertainty, at least they are not the suffocation of despair.

"Beyond the desolation, Kathryn," Mora continued. "You must forgive yourself. Whatever they did to you, whatever happened to you, whatever you thought or felt and or begged for, you must forgive yourself. You had no control in those moments. Realizing that, forgiving yourself, is how you will move on."

"But I let them—"

"No," Mora cut her off, almost sharply. "You did not. They took control. And now you will take it back."

"I want to," Kate admitted, and it felt good to do so. "But I feel angry, Mora. I'm angry at them. I'm angry at Father. I'm angry at the boys. I'm angry at myself. And I'm worried that anger will get in the way of my healing."

"It is okay to be angry. It is part of what you have to go through. Just like you went through the depression and the denial and the grief."

"The anger... It grows. Every day. Every hour. I want to do something about it. I want to harness it. Use it to make a difference."

"Then do so."

Kate rubbed her chafed fingers against her mug of blood and took a pensive sip before looking up to meet Mora's eyes. "That's what I was trying to do. Before all this happened."

Mora's features softened. "I suspected as much."

Kate looked down once more, and the shame she barely kept at bay started to creep over the wall where she had started forcing things she didn't want to feel. "Father had become so removed and the boys were letting everything they had all worked so hard for just fall by the wayside. I couldn't let that happen. I was so frustrated with everything. If it was clear to me that the tides were changing, then why wasn't it for him? Why did he sit in his den, night after night, doing nothing? Doesn't he realize now that it's probably too little too late?" Kate paused, the irritation that had long been dormant rushing to the surface so swiftly she didn't know how to articulate it. "The covens, other vampires, the watchers… We need to unite. We need to fight these wraiths. They want to overtake us. They want to kill everyone and everything. We can't let that happen."

A pause as long as a heartbeat transpired and then Mora said quietly, "You are more like your mother than you know."

Kate looked up at Mora quickly. It was few and far between that her mother was ever spoken of, especially by Mora. She always believed Mora knew her mother, but never asked for fear of her father's wrath. For some reason, now she had no such qualms. *Maybe it's the fact that I almost died, and nothing is really much more important than that.* She parted her lips to reply, yet the tears that burned in Mora's eyes, their sharp briny scent acrid to Kate's nose, halted her in doing so.

"And you so look like her," Mora whispered, the tears she couldn't hold trailing down her cheeks. "If only you knew how much you resemble her, in spirit and in likeness."

"Will you tell me?" Kate pleaded in a hushed tone, desperate for something she couldn't name. "Just a little bit?"

Mora's smile was one made of the fondest of recollections, the warmest of sentiments, and the aura that surrounded her glowed golden. Kate thought this is what a sunrise would feel like: enriching, soothing, tepid, and inspiring.

"Your mother was a Valkyrie come to life," Mora said, her tone full of admiration. "She grew up in a village off the coast of what is now Norway in the tenth century. She was one of seven children: the youngest, the most unruly. She was loved by every one of her siblings, more so by her mother and father. Radiant and bold, she was constantly getting into trouble and charming her way out of it. She never took no for an answer. She learned to read and write runes just as well as she learned to wield a blade and ride a horse. She was uncontrollable, so much so that she left home as soon as she was able to pursue her one true love: battle.

"For years she led a contingent of Viking men and women in raids that saw her profits beyond the wildest of dreams. She was no one of importance, but they followed her because she saw them to prosperity and notoriety. Beyond that, she could part the heavens with her laughter, con Loki himself, and beguile her way into the homes of the most malicious of chieftains. She knew how to coax others to do her bidding with just the tilt of her head and a tip of her lips. That is not to say she did not have her dark side. She did not come to be known for her benevolence. She could be shrewd, volatile, and was nefarious at worst. She did not show mercy, but that was the way of it back then.

"Regardless," Mora continued. "She was a natural on the field of battle. What she won she sent home, to her village and the family she left behind. She loved them more than anything, but it was the fondness for war and pilfering that kept her steadfast on a battlefield. The times she did come home, her parting words were always: 'The land and the sea beyond call me more strongly than any longhouse ever will.'"

"How did she become a vampire?" Kate asked in breathless awe.

Mora's smile became pained. "It was that love for battle that would be her downfall, as it always is with the greatest of warriors. When she was barely thirty she died just where she wanted to, and her name went down in history as one of the fiercest women in Viking lore. Her very name would come to mean 'she who devastates'. She was written in time as Herja the Harrier; she would be on you before you knew it and could decimate the entirety of your life in the blink of an eye."

Kate's eyes flared. *The harrier in the painting behind Father's desk. The statue in the library. The taxidermy in the dining room…*

How could I have never known?

Why…how could Father keep this from me?

I deserved to know. She was my mother.

Anger curtailed the devotion she felt in the wake of Mora's veracity. Crisp, raw anger. *Just another thing he kept from me. On purpose. For himself.*

"But others were observing," Mora continued with her saga. "The prowess of your mother did not go unnoticed by the watchers. They made her an ancient deal: accept fate as a vampire and continue her legacy, though her service would have to pivot to the betterment of humankind. She agreed, and thus was made into a vampire and began to devour her newest enemies: the wraiths. That is how she met your father."

Kate turned to face Mora, enraptured by the story, her anger simmering to a tolerable level.

"He had already been made a vampire and was a fierce warlord that conquered every battlefield he came across...except when it came to your mother. I will never forget the night they met." Mora's eyes misted and it appeared as though she got lost in time for a moment, her gaze clouding. "She could not wait to be rid of him, but he spent the next ten years galivanting after her, following her from field to field, trying to gain her attentions. I lost count of how many times we had to change course, backtrack, or take a contract for battle simply to get away from him. He did everything in his power to be nearer your mother, who was so set on her own course that she could not be bogged down with what I recall her saying was 'monotonous monotony'.

"Later your mother would tell me that she got just as much entertainment out of avoiding Talorc as she did when she was around him, and it had given her a sense of juvenile joy to keep him on the run. However, when they finally came together..." Mora's gaze softened as cherished memories filtered through her reverie. "Fate had blessed them immensely."

Realization crept slowly upon Kate. "You were there?"

Another tear slipped from Mora's eye. And then another. Endlessly, they began to fall. Kate felt a rush of grief before the swelling tide of fondness took her form. "Herja was my sister."

Shock gripped Kate so abruptly that her jaw fell open. "*What?*" Disbelief, anger, and betrayal all clamored at once, so loudly that anything else she had been feeling drowned in the sentiments.

"How... Why..." She gaped at Mora, almost unable to comprehend what she'd said. The treachery was sharp, and it stung Kate's very heart. "You never told me! How could you never tell me?"

"Would it have changed anything?" Mora asked, wiping the tears from her weathered face.

The sharp sting twisted in Kate's chest before abruptly alleviating. "No, but..." She faltered, flabbergasted to silence.

"It was not my place to say. I... It... It was decided that it would've complicated things for everyone."

"Why?" Kate's tone bordered ire. "How? What does that mean?"

"Any mention of your mother…left your father bereft."

Suddenly, everything made sense. Everything Mora had ever done for her, how she had guided her, taught her, so readily taking the role of mother…

Father, Kate thought bitterly. *Getting in the way of things. Controlling things he has no business controlling.*

This is my *life*, Kate thought as her anger swirled and swirled. *How dare he.*

"I made a promise to your mother, long before the night of her death," Mora murmured with such emotion that it evaporated any negative feelings Kate had. "That I would care for you as if you were my own; how could I not when we were family? It was never beyond me nor beneath me to do so, and I never envisioned myself doing anything else. Yet when I made that promise I never accounted for your mother not being here. When she died, the vow became more of a reality than I wanted to acknowledge, but I would not fail you nor your mother in not taking it seriously.

"Nevertheless, it was agonizing to assume the matronly position when I knew that was all your mother wanted after her love of battle became subdued. It is rare for a vampire to be borne so when she got pregnant with you her life swiftly filled with new purpose. She was so incredibly happy. She dreamt of you day and night, wondering what you would look like, how you would act, what you would grow to achieve. She secretly hoped she carried a daughter so she could teach her everything she knew. It grieves me endlessly to know she will never know the extraordinary female you have become. She would be *so proud* of you now, Kathryn. Know that. No matter what, she would be proud of you."

The doubt that constantly plagued her pulled through all the other sensations and forced Kate to say through trembling lips, "How could she be proud of what I have become?"

Worthless. Pathetic. Useless. Disgraceful.

Hopeless. Dark. Morbid. Plaguing.

Defiled—

"Oh Kathryn," Mora said on a breathless whisper. "You are so much more than what happened to you. I know it is hard to see now. This faceless stage of grief, the forgiveness, is the hardest to overcome." Mora sidled closer to her, taking the mug to place it on the end table, and then clasped her hands in her own. "And everyone achieves it differently in their own amount of time. Sometimes it takes weeks. Sometimes it takes years. Just know that whatever you may need, whenever you need to talk or if you simply need someone to sit by you in silence, know that I will be there for you. I will never ask more. I know what it is like to grieve, for both oneself and others."

Kate felt tears prick along her lashes as emotion, so shining but so dark, enveloped her. "I don't know if I can forgive myself."

"I promise you will." Mora reached to wipe the tears from Kate's face before they fell. "Your desire to make a difference, to avenge yourself, to seek retribution for the horrible wrongs taken against you will overcome anything that holds you back. You will learn to love again, to feel things other than pain and suffering. You will rise a new female, though there will always be a part of you that will harbor that darker self. But, as I have promised you other things, I promise you will learn to rein that darker part and use it to your advantage."

Those words struck a chord, and another sparkling revelation cascaded over Kate. "*You were there*. With my mother. All those times, you were there."

Mora nodded, and that soft smile turned shadowed with haunting memories. "Retaliatory carnage took me and my own family when I was nearly forty years old; your mother had her enemies, and they knew no bounds. Your mother petitioned for my being made, for her own making had barely been a year prior, and I took to the calling of a vampire with ease. Though I was never a staunch warrior like your mother—truly, few were—I know the tales of retribution and warmongering well."

"Will you tell me what happened to my mother?" Kate asked after a ponderous moment of silence. "Here, in Warwick?"

The shadows deepened in Mora's face before dissipating altogether. "It is not my story to tell."

Kate's eyes became distant as she sorted through everything Mora had told her: about her mother, the shocking revelation of kinship between them, and how so many missing pieces within her life now fell together. *So much...* Kate thought, reaching for her mug of blood to sip once more.

Maybe I can *move on.* Kate's eyes drifted to the sparking fire in the hearth to her left. *If others can overcome so much, then I can too.* The boys and their feats, Mora and her life, Lilith, Father...

Kate drank her blood quietly. She knew there was another path to tread, one she would have to cross on her voyage of acceptance.

It is time, that voice inside of her—her *mother's voice*—said.

Kate looked back at Mora. "Everything still seems so unobtainable."

"It will come to you in time," Mora said, her empathy soothing with its gentle purple hue. "The acceptance of yourself will bring the acceptance of others. And whatever you need to do to achieve that is understandable. Though we all appreciate it in different ways, we have sympathized with your journey thus far, because every one of us has been in a variation of your shoes. We understand that healing takes time. Continue to take the time you need, Kathryn. We will all be here for you, as we always have been."

Tears gathered in Kate's eyes again, so close to spilling. Her voice wavered as she said, "Thank you, Mora." She felt her lips try to tilt in a smile. "Do I call you Aunt Mora now?"

Mora laughed softly. "You may call me whatever you like."

Mora reached for her, and Kate let her pull her into an earnest hug. Kate closed her eyes, pulling strongly of Mora's warmth and her honeysuckle scent.

I have family, Kate thought. *I've had family all along...*

If Asha knew about this, I'm going to kill her.

Mora pulled back and then stood, reaching forward to take the plate of food that Kate was finished with. Kate watched the movements, feeling lighter than she had since even before her abduction, which allowed her sense of fervor to flourish.

Mora moved to the door, balancing the plate in one hand and picking up the hamper with the other. She paused, turning to face Kate one last time. "Though I will admit, I do like the ring of *Aunt Mora.*"

With one last shared smile, Mora exited Kate's room.

Kate finished the blood in her mug and then placed it on the end table, getting up from the divan to go into the bathroom. *I won't be that female again, the one from before all of this,* she thought as she walked into the sage and blush space, overrun with weeping succulents and tender peonies. *I've learned too much. Seen too much. Experienced too much.* The white hexagon-tiled floor immediately began to heat beneath her feet as Kate pulled herself to stand in front of the mirror. She forced herself to take in the female reflected back at her, glowing with the light from the golden sconces on either side of the mirror.

In the two weeks since she last cared to notice, her hair had grown only slightly, though she was sure the more she nourished herself the faster it would grow. Vampires' hair naturally grew quickly, and Kate used to regularly maintain her flowing locks with monthly cuts. However, with her lack of nutrients in the past weeks, not only had her physical healing been inhibited but the growth and luster of her hair as well. It barely reached her ears now and gathered there in a stunted, uneven bob. Distantly, she thought her long hair reflected who she used to be: beautiful, wild, carefree.

Will I ever grow it long again? she thought to herself, tilting her head to the right, then to the left. As the lights from the sconces caught the angles of her face, she noticed they looked sharper, more gaunt than she remembered. Her eyes didn't hold the gleam of sapphire she was so used to seeing, and the stormy blue that gazed back at her was unfamiliar. Her skin was pale, so pale she looked ill, but she knew the more she revitalized herself, the more she would mend.

I will never be the female I once was.
I'm not who I used to be.
And that's...that's okay.

Kate turned on the gold tap of the raised sink and splashed cold water on her face. She grabbed the nearby towel and dried off, looking at her reflection with a new sense of self. Tiny droplets of water clung to the hair nearest her face, and Kate lifted a battered hand, rife with scars and puncture wounds, to push it so it flopped to one side, revealing the ear that had been cut off and had yet to fully rejuvenate.

I will be someone better, she thought, placing the towel back on its hook. *I can move on. I will move on.*

I deserve to move on.

I need to move on.

She suddenly knew what she had to do.

Kate strode from the bathroom and moved to her closet, heading for her tower of shoes. She found a pair of black combat boots and laced them tightly before taking one last look at herself in the mirror and embarking from her room. As she approached the enormous door with the swirling carvings of moonflowers, she knew she was about to transcend a time in her life that she would look back on fondly, if not cautiously. She would always be wary of the darkness that lurked, of the pit that held the feelings and memories of the past, both of which would forever call to her. She would use them as a reminder to tread strongly, surely, and only look back when remembrance was necessary to push forward. Instead, she would use the wall she found relief in building to give her reprieve and fortitude.

She placed her hand on the handle and pushed open the door. Her boots falling heavily, her core ruminative of the pivotal moment that was about to ensue, she crossed the threshold into the hallway.

Surprisingly, she didn't hesitate at all.

She was resolute in her startling need to see certain aspects of her life closed. She knew in doing so, other doors would open that would further lead her along her journey of acceptance and healing.

And I can open my own doors. I am strong enough. Brave enough. I am resilient. I am untamed. I will show them who I've become.

And I will learn to forgive myself along the way.

She pulled the door shut behind her and made her way down the hall, the sconces flickering in their low gleams as she went. Her boots ate up the beige oriental runner hungrily, and she scaled down the stairs smoothly before routing to her destination. Kate had to focus solely on her new goal if she was going to pick up where she left off before the abduction, which she abruptly had the clarity, drive, and wherewithal to do.

Down another hall she tread, and it was with a new, burgeoning confidence that she tipped her chin high and threw her shoulders back. She felt the bones of her blades scrape against the fabric of her sweatshirt, and her stomach still churned with a slight nausea, but she tamped down both sentiments as she placed a hand on the door to her objective and pushed it open without preamble.

Talorc was already up out of his chair as Kate crossed over the entryway, and his wide eyes were disbelieving in their stare. Kate paused in the doorway, glowingly resplendent in her conviction. Her piercing, tempestuous eyes latched onto her father after snagging on the harrier that soared in the painting beyond him, and it was with renewed resolution that she uttered assertively, "Hello *Athair.*"

Chapter Fifteen

Santiago placed his cell phone down on the desk after ending the conversation with his second-in-command, a vampire by the name of Naseer. He'd given instructions for Naseer to begin to accumulate any and all available associates in favor of turning their focus to North America, for Santiago just learned Talorc was leaving in four days for his next destination. His source told him she'd personally been reached out to by Talorc within the last few months and was certain an in-person reconciliation was coming. They both knew Talorc had already been to covens in Newfoundland and Labrador, Quebec, and Ontario, and assumed geographically the Manitoban covens would be next.

A perpetually wintry, mountainous expanse littered with lakes, Santiago thought as he pulled up a map on his laptop. There were three covens in Manitoba: the largest was in Winnipeg, a smaller one in Snow Lake, and finally the smallest near Ruskill. The climate in Manitoba was cold at best, frigid at worst, and this time of year would pose to be of the worse category. Santiago didn't look forward to packing his parka, but the open land of Manitoba would serve as the perfect grounds for a large battle.

Santiago thought as he clicked through pictures of the subarctic landscape, *and who am I to not host a good slaughter?*

While his source was hesitant to shed light as to where Talorc lived—which Santiago found to be extremely frustrating because with one single attack half of their problem would be solved—she'd told Santiago when Talorc headed north she suspected he planned to bring The Guard. How many they couldn't speculate, but Santiago was putting things in order for the confrontation to be a large one. *A complete decimation for Talorc.*

I won't be caught unexpectedly by them again. I know what they can bring and what they're capable of.

Santiago leaned back in his leather office chair, eyes flicking to the locked door to his den. Beyond the panels he heard his younglings shrieking, and with annoyance he turned his gaze back to his laptop. He couldn't wait to leave his townhome and not return, abandoning the family he thought he'd wanted until Adhamh had come into his life and changed everything. He could feel it in his bones: the tide was shifting in his favor, and he wouldn't be returning to Warwick once he left for Manitoba. He had bigger, better things to attain for. More to achieve. His life was more meaningful than younglings and a nagging partner.

Slow and steady to win the race, he thought, scrolling over the map. *Strategy and planning will see this through thoroughly and without a way for Talorc to undo it. He will fall. I will rise.*

A particularly loud screech had him pausing to growl his disdain, and it was in a guttural snap that he yelled, "Shut those heathens up or it'll be your throat I mutilate!"

The townhome rang quiet, and Santiago rubbed his hand around his beard and mustache before kneading his eyes. He needed to feed and would have to detain his partner to do so before leaving, and the thought of doing so invigorated him. She feared him tremendously, and he always liked cornering her and inhaling her strong scent of fear before striking and leaving her dry. It was the only reason he kept her around; he relished the fight. He always won, and the feeling of accomplishment afterwards kept him high for days.

He knew she fancied herself in love with him, gloomily pining for him when he was gone, but they weren't beloveds, and thus he couldn't bring himself to care much about anything to do with her. Santiago couldn't be deterred with such an asinine notion as love anyway. He only tolerated the spawn she'd insisted on producing because it intercepted her concern of him and his business, leaving him all the time and space he needed to navigate his human and vampire dealings.

Even if Talorc doesn't bring the entirety of The Guard, Santiago redirected his thoughts back to his plans. *I can arrange to have the others annihilated in the aftermath. And if I can continue to sway the covens to my side...*

The opportunities are endless.

A smirk curled his lips, and Santiago raised a bejeweled hand to twist one end of his mustache in contemplation. *A month of dormancy is enough. The time is now. We need to act.*

And, I think, Santiago closed his laptop, *another meeting with Adhamh is necessary.* He hadn't heard from the watcher as of late, and thus had no idea if he'd been successful in making more wraiths. The thought of being in close quarters with the male caused an inadvertent shiver to race down his spine, but he shook it off as he stood. He turned off the nearby lamp and moved around his desk, but paused, his smirk curving into a perverse grin.

But not before I feed.

"*Piseag Bheag...*"

Kate didn't let any emotion cross her face, though the sound of her father's hoarse voice, coupled with her childhood nickname, made her heart stutter.

"We need to talk," Kate said frankly, forcing her voice to be firm.

Talorc stared disbelievingly at her while Kate refused to back down from the regard, yet neither being moved. An exceptionally loud *crack* from the fireplace finally broke their reverie, and Talorc moved from behind the large cherry desk to the chairs before it.

"Yes. Please. Sit." He pulled one of the seats back to make space for her.

Kate said nothing as she moved into the room, closing the door behind her. As she took her station the fire crackled again, and a log shifted in the steel grate. Embers popped and flared, sparking against the stone before the hearth. Kate could feel the warmth of it from where she sat and as she settled against the shining leather of the chair, she centered herself on the tangible heat of the flames. Reality, to her, was still fluid, changing, but could become consumingly stifling in less than a minute. Wary of this, she took a measured, deep breath and used the familiarity of the room to focus her thoughts.

Her eyes roved the office, from the wood-paneled walls, the dark coffered ceiling, the navy oriental rug, before settling on the painting behind her father, who was slowly taking his own seat. The depiction of battle, so large that it took up the entirety of the wall, sprawled in neutral tones, with an ornate golden frame that glinted in the lamplight. The most detailed section of the painting was the hen harrier, magnificent in her ombre of tanned feathers and a face ringed with a black and white pattern. Chillingly piercing amber eyes seemed to gaze back at Kate in corporality, and the resounding echo of the open-mouthed cry urged her to seek the resolution she needed.

It's time.

Kate drew her eyes from the bird of prey to hone on her father, who swallowed the enormous chair he sat in with an equally large frame. His graying blonde hair was slicked back from his weathered face, and the like beard was groomed to perfection. He wore a grey sweater, the sleeves rolled back to reveal the golden cuff he wore on his right arm, and a pair of beige slacks paired with similarly colored boots. Although he appeared well put together, his visage and the sentiments that poured from him were deeply rife with pain.

Kate decided on the short walk here she would not tread lightly; she was tired of doing so. Feebleness and carelessness had not gotten her anywhere in life. The feral side of her that pushed for retribution wanted answers and wasn't moving forward without them; it dug its heels in the ground steadfastly while simultaneously thrusting her forward. Kate knew it was the same side of her that needed forgiveness, which would ultimately lead to healing, and it wouldn't let go until it got what it wanted.

It was with that feral countenance that she spoke, and her equally savage voice was biting as it crossed her lips. "Why did you never come for me?"

Talorc didn't respond immediately. His brown eyes were clouded by his heavy brow, yet the emotions that drifted from him were as distinct as if he named them: the ashen, obscuring clout of uncertainty; the sting of rust-colored fear; and a deep-seated sadness, so blue that it was virtually colorless and almost swallowed Kate whole. She steeled herself against the onslaught, refusing to balk, internally reinforcing her wall to separate her from the intense emotions forming. They ebbed from Talorc in pulsating waves, but after a moment he reined them enough to prepare a reply.

"I…" he started, then paused, his frown deepening. He shifted restlessly in his chair, both boots planted firmly on the floor, and the emotions continued to pour from him as if a dam had been released.

The most potent of all was *regret*. Bitter, acidic green, the aura festered at her, but Kate was in no mood to acquiesce to the nuance.

"You owe me," Kate murmured softly, and her voice wavered only slightly. "I deserve *at least* this. To know why *you* didn't come for me. You: the only person I thought I could count on to do so. You: my own *father*."

Kate's nostrils flared as Talorc shifted his position once more, his fingers curling then uncurling against the arms of his chair. The gnawing, undulating wave of regret from her father grew, creeping from her feet up her legs, but Kate would not be deterred.

She continued, growing in her rage, "Tell me why you left me in the darkness for nights on end. Tell me why you let me endure countless episodes of beatings, starvation, and torture. Tell me why you were not leading the hunt. Tell me why you did not raze the city to the ground. Tell. Me. Why."

"Kathryn—"

"Why spend all that time protecting me, shielding me, controlling me, if just to let me rot?" Her tone increased. "Why shelter me for so long—from everyone—just to leave me for dead? Because I *was dying, Athair.* Does that mean *anything* to you? Do you even have any idea what they did to me? Do you know what I had to suffer? *Do you?*"

Talorc's eyes softened with harrowing grief. "Please, Kathryn—"

"No!" Kate stood from her chair. "You're going to sit and listen to what I have to say. I've had enough of being browbeaten by everyone.

"I must mean so little to you," Kate's voice lowered to a

dangerous level, her anger so black that she knew the aura shadowed her frame. "*So little* for you to turn your back on me, to continue to do so even when I was home. Do you know how many times you called to check on me, *Father*?" She spit his name as though it were poison. "I'll remind you: *twice*. For an entire month you could be bothered to bring yourself to the third floor *twice*."

She was shaking where she stood, and she clenched her jaw so her teeth wouldn't rattle. "What I was doing…I was doing *for you*. You'll never know the lengths I went to *for you*. When you were too blind and too idle to remember how you got to this seat in the first place, *I* wanted to be the one to remind you. To prove to you that I *could* have a purpose, that I *am* meaningful. I was naïve enough to think I could sway you. And I was naïve enough to think that if I could sway you, then you would realize that I have *actual* potential to do something. Anything other than being the no-name daughter of Talorc, who most people don't even know exist.

"All I ever wanted was for *you* to realize that I could *be someone*. More than a pretty face, a spoiled princess that sits in her mansion watching TV and shopping, wondering when she was going to get her nails done next. I wanted you to see that I took all those lessons in self-defense and gun safety seriously because I was desperate to be a part of something bigger, something that could change the course of the world. *Because I am more than what you made of me.* Yet you stopped me whenever and however you could. And *every* time you suppressed me, I wanted to show you harder. But you were never going to give me the chance to be who I wanted to be. And look what it did. Look where it got us."

The snarl that came out of her was brutal. "*I* was the blind one to think that you would ever see me as more than the precious little youngling who needed to be cosseted and pampered. But look at me now. Defiled. Beaten. Broken. A shell of the female, a shell of the daughter you once knew. I would say this is your fault, but I'm beyond that. It would be easy to blame you, but I made the choice to be proactive. I have to live with that. However, *you* have to live with the crushing remorse that you failed me when I needed you most.

"All I wanted was you, *Athair*," Kate finished, and finally her voice broke. Tears, born from both anger and sadness, rimmed her eyes. "All I *needed* was you. You were always there for me. The

195

shoulder I cried on. The listening ear. The patient guide. The steady hand. Through everything. Except in this…you weren't. And I will never, for as long as I live, understand why you abandoned me."

"I would never—" Talorc's voice caught, and the firelight danced in his eyes as he slowly stood from his chair. He splayed a trembling hand across his desk as he did so, and he swallowed thickly before continuing. "I would *never* abandon you."

"Then what is it that you did?" Kate thrust her hands wide, her voice provoking. "Because I would call it desertion after neglect and indifference."

"*I did not want to fail you like I failed her!*" Talorc bellowed, a blast of arctic air sluicing from his form. He placed both his hands on the top of the desk, as if to steady himself. "I could not…I could not live with myself if I failed you too."

"*You did fail me!* Can't you see that? You turned your back on me." The tears fell, so hot they scalded, and Kate let them burn. "Tell me why you left, *Athair*. Tell me why you didn't just come for me. I don't understand why you didn't just *come for me*. How was it so easy for you to turn your back?"

"I left because I could not stand to be here, in this house, without you," Talorc said, his voice like gravel. "The memories we created together, the only recollections of joy and vibrancy and love that I have left, would have driven me to meet the blaze of morning light. And that would be after I set fire to this dwelling, incinerating everything and everyone to the ground. Because here, in this house, in this world, without you…" His voice, once at a crescendo, became a whisper as he said, "I am nothing."

Kate's lips trembled, and she wanted to be angry. She *needed* to be angry. Anger would carry her through this. Anger would push her to the other side, where she could continue to heal without acquiring more intrinsic wounds. But suddenly she felt vulnerable and raw, which was too much like how she felt when she was in captivity. In reprisal, she built her internal wall a little higher, a little sturdier, and stared at her father with what antipathy she could muster.

"*Piseag Bheag…*" Talorc rounded his desk, but when Kate took a step back from him, he stopped. "I am not a warrior anymore; I have not been for some time. I do not have the stamina nor the strength. Whether that is due to my age or my leniency… I think I know, and it pains me to admit that it is more the latter. But you must understand..." He paused as if physically aggrieved, and Kate saw the cobalt stain of agony warp his form before dissipating. "I have been living in darkness since your mother passed. Do you know how often I want to succumb to the madness of grief? It bays, always it bays, echoing in my mind, keeping me from sleep, sometimes from rational thought. The ache of her not being a part of my soul... It is a difficult reality to abide.

"But I abide it *for you*," Talorc continued. "Just like you, everything *I* do is for *you*. Because in the never-ending darkness that is my life you are my only light; the beacon that calls me, that guides me. Your radiance, your abundance for life and love and happiness... I covet it myself, and that is why I wanted to preserve it. That is why I cosseted you and pampered you and shielded you. And *that* is why I could not jeopardize you. I refused to. What you mean to me goes beyond logic.

"When you were taken, I did not know how to pull myself from the darkness. I feared that, because I lost you, that when the sun called to me, I would heed it. I reverted to doing the only thing I could: utilizing anything and everything for a distraction. I distanced myself from our home to divert my ominously melancholy thoughts, endeavoring to busy myself with far easier problems to solve than how I could have let harm come to you. Because this is a world, a time, a place that I no longer understand. And without you, my guide...I was lost."

The tears that fell singed her cheeks, her throat, and continued to fall in hot rivulets as she stared at her father's dim form. "But when I came home..."

"I did not know how to move forward. I was afraid to face the wounds you bore, the reality of what you went through. It brought back too many memories. Memories of the last time I knew true suffering. True loss. The *greatest* loss.

"How *selfish* of me," Talorc intoned gruffly, taking a step further around the desk. "How humiliating, how pitiful, that a male such as I could not be there for his own daughter? How pathetic that I could not even offer you an ounce of solace? How despicable to think that you were the one who endured the strife and yet I was the one who cowered?"

Kate found that she couldn't move, and as Talorc came to

stand before the desk, she belatedly realized he was only about two feet from her. They faced each other, she molten with explosive feelings and he glacially numb from his admissions.

"Forgive me," Talorc whispered, lifting a hand to brush Kate's cheek. She closed her eyes as his thumb swiped away some of her tears, and when she opened them again the wall within her had been built a little higher. "Forgive me for being wretched. Forgive me for being obstinate. Forgive me for not being the father you truly needed. I am not trying to mollify the situation in any way, for I know I have grievously wronged you, but if only you knew how the pain has eaten at me these last months, maybe you would understand, if only just a diminutive amount.

"Please understand..." He swiped again, and Kate was not strong enough at the moment to pull away from the tenderness he shared. So few and far between was Talorc ever gentle with her, and the words they now shared were the deepest they'd ever disclosed. "If I were as resilient as you, I would have been there for you. Alas, that is a trait you get from your mother."

"That isn't good enough," Kate said flatly, stepping back and removing her face from his grasp. Talorc dropped his hand down to his side, the dejection he felt so heavily expressed through his features and movements.

"Kathryn, it was not just these past months, but for years and years and years that I lived with unsurmountable pain—"

"This isn't about you! This is about me and what I went through. Don't you think you've had enough time to be selfish? Enough time to brood and be useless? To let others do your bidding for you while you mope in the dark?"

Talorc flinched as if struck.

"I don't need you anymore, *Athair,*" Kate spat, wiping away her own tears with aggression. "I will take care of myself."

"The pain is what hindered me," Talorc snapped, his own irritability getting the best of him. "I admit to you that I was wrong, that I was weak. Do you not think it grieves me to know that, to live with that? That I will have to live with that for the rest of my days?"

"And didn't you hear me?" Kate swiped a hand between them in a cutting motion. "*This isn't about you.*"

"I know it is not about me!" Talorc roared, stepping closer to her. Kate stepped back, closer to the fire that she used to ground her to the present; she needed it, because she was slowly losing her grip on reality.

"What I *am* trying to tell you is that since the moment you were borne, it has *always* been about you. Through everything that we have surmounted together, I always acted with you in mind. This time was no different. I just...handled it in a way that I realize has jeopardized our relationship, though hopefully not beyond repair."

Kate bit the inside of her cheek so hard it hurt. The wall was high enough now that she almost couldn't see her father, and if she could just withstand this conversation a little more it would be high enough that she could sever it.

"There are no words for how badly I have failed you—I know I have, as much as I aspired not to. For a time I let the darkness win. I let fear and sorrow and trepidation win. But I am taking control back. I endeavor to be a stronger male in the future. In this moment as I bare myself to you, know that I have only been so vulnerable and visceral once before, and I do not do so lightly. I hope it is enough that you understand the depth of my despair. I am so very sorry, *Piseag Bheag.*"

The only movement in the room was the popping fire, yet in the wake of the discourse even the flames seemed subdued. Talorc stared at Kate with emotion so intense that it scalded worse than her tears, and she used the idle moment to build her wall as high as she could with the flailing sentiments she had left. There were so many she didn't want to name, more she didn't recognize, others she ignored completely.

Because above it all, Kate didn't want to concede that she *did* understand. After everything that happened, she knew the pain and longing and regret her father spoke of. She'd *lived it.* And the sentiments brought her back to every single sordid moment she experienced, and every dismal consequence she felt in between.

Still, she was furious. *And I deserve to be furious.*

At least for a little longer.

She swept away from Talorc, brushing past him forcefully. "I hope you rot from your grief."

She pushed open his office door with both hands, so hard that it ricocheted off the adjacent wall, its echoing crack traveling down through the rotunda. She didn't meet the several stunned visages of those who'd gathered in the hallway in the wake of their argument, though she recognized their various scents: Mora's sweet honeysuckle, Asha's morning dew, Ryder's faint gunsmoke, Dami—

"Kathryn!"

It was her father who called her, and Kate disregarded his heeding as she shoved past the bodies congregated in the hall. Servants and Guard alike, even a female she didn't recognize, watched her tromp heavily, refusing to stop or look back. She knew they regarded her in shock, some with their mouths open, others more muted, but she didn't care. She needed out. She needed to *get out*. She was suffocating. Behind her wall, under the intense anguish, and through the shadows of what she'd overcome, she couldn't breathe.

"Kate, wait!"

His voice almost stilled her, but Kate stormed down the curving stairs into the foyer harder, faster. Her breath sawed in and out of her so forcefully that it hurt, and her vision swam as she rounded the end of the stairs and crossed the foyer to the front doors.

Can't drive, she thought, noticing how her body still trembled. The passcode to the garage was changed monthly, and she had a feeling someone would stop her before she even got her hands on a set of keys.

Need to get out. She barreled through the front doors, ignoring the distraught voices that called after her. Rain slashed from the night sky, thick and freezing, almost like snow. It was enough to steal her breath from her lungs, but only momentarily, and Kate used the hesitation to turn her gaze upward. Clouds obscured the sky, swirling chaotically before the moon and stars, mirroring Kate's inner musings. Barren trees on the outskirts of the property bent this way and that as the wind whipped, while the stables and the guesthouse loomed like specters in the distance. The concrete driveway curled around the dormant fountain, the landscaping subdued this time of year. Light spilled out from the manor behind her, warm and golden and welcoming, unlike the turbulent night that sprawled before her.

She huffed her breaths as the rain poured down, soaking her hair, her clothing, in a matter of seconds. Her body didn't respond to the drenching; there was no gooseflesh, no shivering, no rush of chill to sweep her form. She was immune to the frigid temperature of the February night and the cut of the wind. What she felt inside was colder, heavier, and more disturbing than anything she would meet in the darkness beyond.

A whinny cut the air, and Kate's eyes diverted to the right, down a hill and across a plane of grass. It pulled her from her stagnation in enough time to realize that there were bodies piling up behind her, eager to intercept her unpredictable ambling. To avert, she leapt the stairs in a single bound, running as fast as she could across the driveway.

"Kate, *stop!*"

She couldn't. She wouldn't. The further she got from the manor the easier it was to breathe. She needed air. She needed space. She needed time to sort through her thoughts and the disaster of a conversation she'd just had with her father. She was unused to anything else besides space and quiet, because for weeks she only had her own thoughts. The sudden onslaught of feelings, presences, and words was nearly devastating.

"Kate!"

She sprinted down the small hill to approach the forest. The wind carried her, and the moon glanced from behind a cloud only momentarily; she used the illumination to guide her into the bowels of the woods that surrounded the manor. She crashed into the underbrush without slowing and darted between skeletal trees and over fallen earth. She didn't know where she was going. Had no sense of direction. But she knew the further she got from her home, the better she felt.

The persistent tears that scorched trails down her face, lost to the deluge in the next heartbeat, said otherwise.

Chapter Sixteen

Damian's face fell from hopeful anticipation to blackened rage as he watched Kate sprint down the sloping lawn, disappearing with the torrential downpour.

She came out.

She finally came out of her room.

But she didn't come see me.

Ryder, Mora, Taryn, Talorc, and Asha crowded around him from behind, their bodies shielded from the rain by the arch of the doors. No one said a word, but Damian could feel the bitter arctic bite of Talorc's sorrowful fury. Overwhelming was Damian's own ire, the involuntary curl and release of his fists telltale enough, while his nostrils flared and his body churned with violent waves he could barely contain.

After everything I've done. Everything I've said. Everything I've been through. Every moment I've sacrificed, he thought, copper eyes narrowing on the tree line a half a mile away.

The anger roiled, whipped, flashed, though it wasn't the only sentiment he suffered. He was extremely apprehensive, bewilderingly confounded, and terrifyingly concerned. Each emotion warred with the wrath that singed his skin, flared in his chest, and constricted his throat, gnawing, clawing, baying to be let out.

He knew what was coming.

He knew, could feel in his very bones, the simmering confrontation that was going to burst into flame between him and Kate. *It's been long coming,* his conscience cautiously said, but Damian flipped away the ideal as he took a step forward, into the rain.

It's been a long time coming that she reckoned with the destruction she's left in her path, he thought, sliding his tongue along one of his fangs. *She has to own up to her past, what she's created for her present, and how the future is going to go. She can't hide from any of it. And she owes everyone—most of all me—for everything she's put us through.*

You have your own acceptance to attain for, his conscience warned. Again, Damian dismissed the concept. He didn't have to accept or apologize for anything. He'd spent a goddamn month of his time pitying after Kate who clearly didn't need nor want it. *She ignored everything I did for her. It all meant nothing.* He suddenly felt the frustrations of the entire month grip his chest so tightly that his breaths turned shallow, angry in their release.

Yet while he so relished the idea of holding Kate accountable, he simultaneously wanted to shirk from the conflict to come. An entire month of nonactivity and resistance was about to culminate into chaos. Because with Kate it wouldn't be anything less than a flaming rollercoaster ride into Hell. In the state she was currently in, Damian knew coaxing her back to reality was going to be anything but simple. But there was more to it than that, and that's what he feared the most.

I would give anything to change what happened—and before that do everything differently—if it meant that we wouldn't be here.

The thought took him by surprise. Something changed in that moment, both intrinsically and ex. It started from within to ripple beyond, encapsulating everything he was currently feeling and that which he continued to deny. The change was profound; it left him breathless, numb, yet startlingly clear.

I can't do this any longer.

I can't live this dichotomous life.

I don't deserve it. Kate doesn't deserve it.

And maybe, he yielded in the most intimate recesses of his mind, *maybe if I accept my feelings of her, it will help her move on.*

We both need transcendence.

Fear clutched him coldly, and he had to swallow the dread that threatened to dull the scintillating electricity coursing through him.

I can't. I shouldn't. Too much would change.

Deep in the darkness of his mind, he knew if he went after Kate now there would be no going back to the way things were. His conversation with Vadin surged forward from memory, clipped pieces resounding from within:

"—haven't left her side since you came back four years ago. Why is that?"

"—denying what you feel for Kate isn't benefiting you or her… You're trying to suppress something that needs to breathe."

"—she has experienced something substantially transformative. But then again, so have you, haven't you?"

At first, denying her had simply been about her being Talorc's daughter. That swiftly changed into a staunch fear that he would lose himself in accepting another being into his life. He didn't want to change who he was or what he wanted to accomplish. He didn't want to bend to someone else's whims. Certainly no female would ever hold such sway over him. He did what he wanted, when he wanted, how he wanted, with whom he wanted.

Until he met Kate.

It dawned on him that it never mattered how many females he took to bed. How many he drank from. It never mattered if he avoided her—how long he stayed away, how hard he trained, or how much distance he put between them. He always came back. He was always drawn to her. He always had been, from the very first moment he laid eyes on her.

Fuck. He wasn't ready. But then he reasoned, *will I ever be?*

His conscience whispered that thought might be the first reasonable one he's had in a while, but he internally swatted away the inkling with a thundering growl to follow as his irritation resurfaced.

Let's fucking go.

Wasting not a moment more he vaulted off the stairs and dashed across the driveway. Several voices called after him, but their cadences were lost to the downpour brought by an unusually unseasonable February night. He immediately got soaked, the rain saturating his blue jeans and long-sleeved black crewneck, and his boots skidded across the concrete and through puddles before he met the grass.

Fuck it all, Kate. Why do you have to be so damn dramatic?

His boots trudged heavily through wet grass and mud that

felt like sludge as he used his enhanced senses to lock on Kate's distancing body. He physically slipped a time or two, causing him to nearly lose focus, but he flew past the large guest house and outdoor pool in no time. He crashed into the woods, leaves and branches crunching underneath him, and began the race through the forest, thinking only about *getting* to Kate. What he did when he got ahold of her…he was still working on. He just had to get to her. Slow her down. Reorient her to reality. And finally admit to her that he—

No. This isn't about that. It's about corralling her, bringing her in, and putting her back on track with what's happening. She has key information about our enemy that she's been harboring for weeks, and we need it to push forward. Talorc is planning to leave, Ryder is going to take charge, and we need to see this through once and for all. She's been selfishly holding onto pivotal information as we struggled to stay afloat.

His conscience, ever the grounding voice, chided softly from within, *what you have planned for Kate is never on track with what Kate has planned for anyone or anything else. Tread lightly in this, or you may not be able to reach her.*

Damian bit back another curse as the wind whipped across his sodden clothes and rain pelted his face. His clothing and boots were plastered to him, making for an uncomfortable surge through the woods, but he had a good idea where Kate was headed and could hold out against the nuisances. If she could even make it that far. Her current physical circumstances were…emaciated, at best. However if the rumors were true, she'd eaten and drank, which would bolster her enough…

It wouldn't be the first time she went to the falls to distance herself, Damian thought of the waterfall where Kate visited to collect her thoughts. She named the space 'Forbidden Falls' because Talorc prohibited her from going there, as she liked to jump from the top repeatedly until the sun threatened its rise. She never listened, and Damian was her self-admitted unbegrudging coconspirator any time she wanted to go. Over the years it had become one of her favorite places, as the clearing lent a tranquility that its expanse maintained.

But, on a perfect day, the area was roughly five miles from the manor. In the wind and the rain on a day that bordered on frigid?

Damian wasn't sure Kate would make it. In the swift glance he got of her, she appeared to be barely any different from the last time he saw her.

He clenched his jaw and quickened his pace, trying to focus on her dissipating presence and not the gaunt and ghostly form that haunted his dreams. Creator take him, but he didn't think he would *ever* forget the way she looked when he first saw her after all those weeks. Even then she'd been shrouded in coldly acerbic death. Mercifully, she now raged with fire, and he could sense her almost easily, her lavender scent pulling pulling *pulling*. He didn't know how, but she was keeping quite the void between them, following the path she'd meandered for years. The uphill trail was made slippery by the rain, and Damian forced himself to concentrate on the draw she had on him—that she would always have on him—to keep him steady.

Not. Now.

Seconds turned into minutes and minutes quickly compiled into a half an hour. The rain never once let up and the wind continued to brutally beat him. Determination saw him rigid, and with his enhanced vampiric abilities of heightened smell, agility, and pace, he pushed on. Every so often he noticed that the gap between them grew shorter: her scent grew stronger, her fire brighter, her presence warmer. When the time pushed close to an hour, he focused on his surroundings to note they were in fact nearing Forbidden Falls. The trickling of the creek that led from the cascade was nearby, and the trees began to thin in their groupings. In a rare moment of clarity, the waxing gibbous moon peeked through the clouds to reveal the boulder Kate notched each time she came here, but Damian passed it without regard. Any minute now he would—

He leapt into the clearing completely out of breath and vibrating with fervor. Not just because of the awesome expanse before him: water surged from falls two-stories high, dumping into a shallow pool that narrowed into a stream that sluiced across Talorc's massive property. Bordering the pool were boulders of various sizes, which also made up the backdrop of the expanse of the waterfall. Browned rockface bordered both sides of the waterscape, leveling off to grass before meeting the trees once more. Vividly, he recalled in the summer, particularly on the nights of the full moon, Kate could be found here basking in the glow or trying different tricks from the top of the falls.

Tonight, what light the full moon could shed found her still. Damian heaved heavy breaths from his position about twenty feet away, his gaze fixated on her slender form.

Ire was easily replaced with reverence as he beheld her. She had her back to him, yet he felt as drawn to her as if she were in his arms. Her once luxuriously long hair was cropped short, and her previously toned legs looked thin and shook from her exertion. Her shoulders, so slight, surged up and down, up and down, while her hands splayed at her sides to reveal short, broken nails. Her clothing hung on her from the drenching rain, highlighting the fact that she was less than half of the size she used to be, which had been lean to begin with.

"Kate…" Damian heard himself whisper, yet the flinch the sound elicited from her surprised him to silence.

"Leave me alone." Her rasping voice was almost lost to the rain and the waterfall as it poured.

Now it was Damian's turn to flinch, and he did so as if struck. "*Leave you alone?*" He compulsively took a step toward her. The anger within him surged once more, and he grappled onto it with a roughened hand and used it to continue, "How can you say that? After everything I've done?"

Kate remained quiet.

"Do you have any idea the amount of effort I've put in to see you better?" Damian chuffed without humor at the remembrance. "I've pushed a lot of friendships, and other arguably more important things have taken a backseat. You should be grateful I was one of the only people who didn't give up on you."

Kate still didn't speak. Wouldn't even turn to look at him. She continued to stare at the falls, rushing water mingling with crystal ice, her boots steady upon the stones that bordered the pool.

"Look at me," Damian snarled, taking another step. "I deserve for you to at least acknowledge my presence."

I need to see you. To finally see you. To know that you're okay. That this isn't the tip of the iceberg, the straw that will break the camel's back, and you aren't going to run until you meet the sun.

I need… I need…

Damian dug his heels into the sopping ground, grinding his

teeth together. *Fuck.*

Kate didn't move, nor did she speak.

"I've centered my entire life around you for the last month," Damian snapped, and a particularly sharp gust of wind took his breath for a moment. *More than. More than that.* He inhaled deeply before bursting to continue, "I've visited you every night, twice a night, for weeks. I've taken care of your things. Rook. I calmed Asha and Mora as they worried for you. I made sure there were fresh eggs in the fridge. I recorded every reality TV show I could think of. I brought you your favorite foods. Heated cups of blood for you. *My* blood. The least you can do is *look at me.*"

"No," Kate retorted, her voice quaking but resounding.

Damian's eyes flared, their copper color bright with fury. "You owe me—"

She spun then, and the sapphire of her eyes cut through him as piercingly as any sword. His breath stalled again, and he felt his insides collapse and then swell as he stared at her in awe.

As it always did when he looked at her, he saw the universe in her eyes.

Kate was *radiant.*

She shone with the light of a thousand moons, and the allure she captivated him with excelled his wildest fantasies. Though she looked far from the female she used to exude, the boldened vibrancy that gleamed from her was born of something new, something vivid, something dangerous—and it caressed a side of him he didn't know needed consideration, awakening in him something he'd never felt before. Even in this weakened state she was glorious, in a way that resonated down to the marrow of his bones, calling to a primal part of him he couldn't name, rendering him utterly mute.

"*Nothing,*" she seethed, and the sound of her voice eviscerated the lingering logic he had. "I owe you *nothing*. I owe my father nothing. I owe The Guard nothing. I owe Mora nothing. I owe my friends nothing. I am only beholden to myself, and from here on out I will be doing what suits my needs and my agenda. I will *never* be at the mercy of another *again*. Do you understand me?"

In astonishment of her vigor, the candor and intensity of her words, Damian couldn't respond.

"No one ever listened to me. Took me seriously. No one ever wanted to believe that I could be more than a pretty face. That I could do something worthwhile. That I could make a difference. And even though I stand here to prove you all wrong, look at me," The words fell out of her, and her voice cracked on the last sentence as she gestured haphazardly at her drenched form. Her tone changed from enraged to defeated. "I'm not pretty now. I've been reduced to near nothing. How could I owe anyone anything when there is nothing left to give? From now on I push forward for *myself,* and only to forget…to…to ignore…this worthless. Pathetic. Useless. Disgraceful form." Her words punctuated from her with force, though her voice quivered through her clenched teeth.

"Don't say that," Damian warned, and his chest began to burn.

"Hopeless. Dark. Morbid. Plaguing," Kate continued, and the fresh scent of salted water joined the mix of other perceptions that plagued him.

"Stop," Damian growled, closing the distance between them to ten feet.

"Defiled," Kate snarled, her fangs snapping as she continued. "*Hateful.* Disgusting. Woeful."

"*Enough,*" Damian said roughly, his own voice threatening to break.

"You think I want to be these things? That I'm proud of what I went through?" Kate narrowed her eyes at him. "They are what *I am* now. Reflective of the creature that stands before you, marred in the face of whatever the future holds. You have no *idea* what they did to me, do you? Or is it that you don't want to think about it?"

Damian's world halted suddenly; his mind went blank.

No. He had gone weeks pushing the vile images from his mind. The nightmares they brought forth. He had woken countless nights soaked in sweat, her screams ringing in his ears as his mind whirled with the horrors she had been forced to face. He'd been a prisoner of war once or twice but had also been on the operating end of things when enemies were captured. He knew…but he didn't want to. Not when it came to Kate.

"I can tell you." The words tumbled out of her with all the pain she would forever hold onto. "Because I remember every single second of it like it happened yesterday. Even though I lost track of time, I can recall every moment in the greatest of detail, and every day I relive the horrors over and over and *over again*."

Damian swallowed thickly, forcing himself to breathe, to think. He stepped forward, and she must've been lost to the moment because she didn't react to his closeness. "You aren't those things," was all he could manage, and the words fell short of what she needed to hear because she continued voraciously.

"Early on, they didn't bother me much. They left me alone for long periods of time in small spaces." Her blue eyes dulled as the memories came forth from wherever she'd barricaded them. "I think they thought I would be rescued. Or maybe they forgot me. I'll never know. I don't want or need to know. I held onto the belief that I was going to be saved, but when that day came and went, I knew the tide was going to change. I was *so stupid* thinking the early days were the worst. Mourning things like TV, my books, or shopping. *None of that mattered.* It never did." The dimness in her eyes grew so bleak that it turned her gaze completely vacant. Quickly, she reverted to the pristine precision that she'd met Damian's regard with before, focusing clearly on him as she persisted.

"I was never offered food or water. In the beginning I thought that's what would drive me crazy; the hallucinations were incredible. Coupled with the small closets or corners they bound me in, I really did start to feel insane. And forget about hygiene. They purposefully left me in places filled with trash, ridden with bugs, or that were poorly maintained. When they first gave me blood, I was so hungry I didn't realize there were too many people watching me, waiting for me to finish. Because when I did, they made me throw it all up. I'll never forget the metallic sting bilious blood left in my nose, in my throat. I contemplated licking it off the floor, the filthy, dusty floor, but someone began to clean it up while the others beat me until I passed out. I woke up still able to smell the blood, but my eyes were too swollen to see the stain where it had been. And then they did it again the next day. And the next."

Damian winced, lifted an arm toward her, but she pulled back, snarling in contempt.

"They began with little tortures. Pulled my nails off with plyers, cut my hair with a blade. I cried so hard when they cut my hair. My beautiful, flowing hair. They burned my eyelashes and eyebrows. I remember screaming and flailing, but then thinking they were going to slip and burn my eyes, I held still. I was so afraid of not being able to see. I sobbed while they did it. Do you know how hard that is? To lay still while someone burns your face? Little did I know that would be the least of my concerns; they took my eyes anyway at one point. That was the worst: not being able to see. They started asking me questions, but I didn't know anything. Kept in the dark for so long, thanks to my father and all of you, I didn't know anything. That's when the torment really began.

"They peeled my skin from my hands. My face. My feet. I was whipped, like it was the fucking fourteen-hundreds. I don't know if the blows left scars; I know borne vampires technically don't scar, but after weeks of malnourishment I'm sure there are some marks. I can barely bring myself to look in the mirror; it hurts just as much as when the leather was on me.

"They crushed my bones. Slowly. By hand. They would press rebar along the lengths until they snapped. It was always the bones in my legs so I couldn't fight back or run. And my hands were always tied. My head strapped to whatever surface was nearby. Did I mention they used barbed wire to hold me in place? Chicken wire? Rope was too easy for me to get out of. The zipties, although tight, never caused enough pain to satisfy them. I was forced into submission with only the most *authentic* of materials.

"Do you know what the sound of a breaking bone is like? What burning flesh smells like? Especially when it's your own?" Her eyes brightened to a frightening degree as she bared her fangs in a crazed smile that bore no humor. "It does something with your mind. Fucks you up. *I am fucked up*, Damian. More than anyone can comprehend."

Damian.

It was the first time she'd said his name in...Creator, he didn't remember. And even though this wasn't the time or place or situation to realize such, Damian couldn't help but be cognizant of the fact lightning cracked in response to her voice. It left the same thundering reverence within him as it always had.

Forcing him to the present, his stomach flipped with nausea as his chest seized in its smoldering. He opened his mouth to stop her; he didn't know how much more he could stand to listen to. He saw, he smelled, he tasted, he *felt* every ounce of pain that she went through, as it all coalesced from her and into him. The sentiments threatened to overturn him, to unravel him, and not just because the thought of anything remotely unsatisfying happening to Kate made him susceptible to a vulnerability he wasn't ready to commit to. Kate had never known a turned hand in her entire life. To withstand the distress she had been put through...he knew few warriors who could.

"They drowned me. Over. And over. And over. How, you ask?" That crazed smile returned as she shrugged, as if speaking about the atrocities wasn't whittling away at what sanity she had left. "They took me to a house once. A house with a pool. The water was fetid, dark, and frigid. They threw me in after binding me with barbed wire. The more I struggled the worse it hurt, until I passed out. They would always fish me out, leave me on the ground for however long it took me to recuperate, then throw my frozen body in the water again. They did this for days. Then someone suggested fire. *To warm me up.*

"They stopped asking me questions at that point. They would hold me down and put fire against my skin, only to watch it melt and regrow. Over time it took longer because I was so starved. When they got bored of watching my skin melt, they strapped me to a table and began cutting me open. I felt every incision, though thankfully the pain took me to unconsciousness swiftly. Every once in a while I would wake up to their laughter...their laughter..." Her eyes threatened to haze over once more, but she notched her head back and finished, "Santiago oversaw it all. He ordered every single cruelty to be done to me. He watched, from near or far, but he was always there. All because he thought I knew something. Anything that would get him closer to Father. He's the one that's after Father's seat of power, as I'm sure you already know."

"We know," Damian croaked. "But Kate—"

"I may want to forget or ignore what I've become, but I will not rest until I see them all dead. Especially *him.* Santiago. That's the only thing I am living for now," Kate cut Damian off sharply. Her voice dropped to an almost inaudible level as she ended her tirade with, "To see this through."

Damian felt like he couldn't breathe as the distance between them shortened to not even five feet. He stepped closer still, his eyes boring into Kate's. The heat from her body mingled with the tendrils of coolness that swirled from his, creating a density between them that pressurized to bring them closer. He took in every inch of Kate as he moved: from the way her dark hair was plastered to her forehead, to the way her parted lips produced curling vapors, from the staggering pain in her consuming eyes, to the way her chest heaved with her frantic breaths. The staccato of her heartbeat drummed over the sound of the rain, the falls, his own, as he stared at her as if seeing her for the first time.

In that very moment, the world shifted on its axis.

"You are..." Damian whispered, the space between them closing to a mere foot. Their breaths mixed as he peered at her lips, before pulling his eyes to hers once more. "You are so much more... You think you're useless? Your smile lights up every room, invigorating every soul you encounter. Disgraceful? Far from it. Maybe your sense of humor sometimes. Pathetic? Would someone wallowing in pathetic pity be standing here, blazing in front of me like a phoenix come to life? You know Talorc, The Guard, Mora, and Asha are so proud of you. *I* am so proud of you, Kate. Getting to this point... *You're on the other side.*"

The world shifted again, and Damian felt the ground tremble beneath his feet. He thought he saw genuine lightning in the sky and not just flashing in the chaotic whirlwind of his mind, but then again reality as he knew it was disintegrating. He didn't know what was overcoming him, but he suddenly couldn't stop speaking.

"Hopelessness didn't get you out of Santiago's clutches, and it certainly doesn't define you now. Neither does darkness. You are *light* Kate. We look to *you* to guide us, to push us forward."

"Stop," she whispered, her lips trembling. Damian dared to lift a hand, to touch the flesh, and Kate's eyes fluttered in response.

He persisted. He didn't know how or why—or maybe he did. His throat burned as he said, "Morbid will never be a word to describe you. You are vigor. Vivacity. *Life.* Your very being here describes your willingness and eagerness to *live.* A plague you will never be. Except a plague on the manor. On Talorc. On everyone. On *me.*"

"Please stop," Kate begged, her voice an echo of a murmur. Her eyes were bright, and Damian shifted his thumb from where it

213

had rested on her chin to below one eye, and then the next. "You were defiled to expose the female you've become. You call yourself hateful? I call it resourceful. Use hate and woe to your advantage to see yourself from this time in your life; only the strongest warriors know how to harness wrath and hate to overcome their demons." Damian stepped closer to her, so close that his body aligned with hers. He took her face in both of his hands. "Disgusting? Not even a word in my vocabulary when it comes to you. You are far from it. Kate you are...*magnificent.*"

He drew in a steadying breath, watching as the cosmos swirled in eyes that he would forever get lost in. Her eyes. *Kate's* eyes.

There's no going back now.

"And worthless?" He tipped her head back, thumbs on her sunken cheeks as, again, the world seemed to rock beneath them, hauling their spirits closer. "I can think of no greater treasure within the entire universe than you."

"*Stop it!*" Kate shoved away from Damian so hard he stumbled back. She lurched away from him, sputtering against the rain as it drenched her face. "Stop saying those things."

"You need to hear them!" Damian took a step forward. She reciprocated by taking another back. "I... You..."

"What? You're going to profess your *undying love* for me?" Her voice was full of cynicism as she gestured wildly around her, to the torrential rain, half-frozen falls, and black sky above. The clouds parted briefly to reveal a stricken female, barely more than a ghost, filled with crazed sorrow. The trees wailed their own disdain, bending to and fro as Damian and Kate stared at each other with something only slightly less than malice. This female was so unlike the Kate that Damian knew, but the fire was the same; it glowed from her, threatening to corrode him to his core, revealing something he wasn't ready to accept.

"I'm not professing my love." The words sounded heavy, insincere to his own ears.

"Don't worry Damian," Kate spat, adopting a stance that told him she was going to take off once more. "I know."

"Don't run!" He moved toward her, suddenly panicked at the thought of her fleeing. "Please... Just... *Stay.*"

Kate stared at him, her form obscured by rain, and although

he had been sedentary for the last couple of moments his body continued to heave as though he was mid-sprint. He swore the ground beneath him continued to rock, but he knew he was the only one affected by it. Because the unsettling was *within him.* Intrinsically, and brought on by Kate.

No going back.

He'd never seen her like this. *Creator be,* but she took his absolute breath away. *The universe. My own—*

She moved to dash, but Damian called out, his frustrations deep, "Why do you keep running?" *Why can't you just stay with me?*

No going back, his conscience whispered.

Kate sagged slightly, her shoulders falling as her eyes dimmed. Her voice was haunting, almost lost to the cacophony around them, as she replied, "Because there's so much…too much I don't want to feel." The fire in her waned, and with it the tidal wave she roused within him quelled. She surprised him with the truth: "It's easier to run. Right now, it's easier than facing all…*this.*"

He knew of what she spoke.

Not only her memories, but the future.

Them.

No. Going. Back.

"Kate…" he started feebly, perhaps the only time he was so in his entire, long life. "You might have lost track of time…but I…I knew and lived and *felt* every second you were gone."

Chapter Seventeen

T he fire in her eyes flared, then went out completely. "Don't you dare," she seethed, balling shaking hands into fists. "Don't you *dare* do this. Because of what happened? After all this time? Don't you *dare*."

"Do what?" Damian barked, feeling confounded, embarrassed, and irate all at once. "Why won't you let me—"

"Because you're making it about you!" Kate shrieked, and the fire blazed to life as she gestured toward him. "This might feel like the right time to speak up—for *you*. Once again, you are completely oblivious to how I'm feeling."

"I know how you're feeling!" Damian stepped toward her once more. "I've been in your shoes. I've been around males who have been in your shoes. I know what it takes to pull yourself from the dredges of despair. I get it." He hated that he said the next words, hated that he felt as though he had to keep dancing around what he really wanted and needed to say: "But it's time for you to stop the pity party and come out of it already. We need you. You have information that could help us take Santiago down."

He knew he'd spoken ill when Kate laughed wildly, throwing her head back to face the rain. She then leveled him with a look that confirmed he had fucked up. "So that's what this is about? You want information? You want Vadin to do a dive into my mind and see what he can gather *for your benefit* before wiping me clean? Fuck you, Damian. *Fuck. You.*"

"That's not all this is about—"

"There's nothing in there but rot and the carcass of who I once was," Kate hissed, snapping her fangs at him. "I'll forever be useless. No one needs me."

"*I need you!*" Damian roared, closing the distance between

216

them once more with long strides. He stopped less than a foot from her, and almost reached out to grab her to him. He was gasping as he said, "I need you, okay? Just…fucking hell Kate, I need *you.*"

The mantra continued, urging him forward: *No going back.*

Damian stared at Kate, expecting some sort of acquiescence. *But it's Kate.* She glared at him with revulsion.

No going back.

"Kate…*you* drown me. I would take it all back if—"

"Don't finish that sentence," Kate interrupted bluntly. "It's a pathetic attempt at reneging and it's too late now. You've had years to come to terms with whatever you needed to come to terms with in regard to our relationship. But you refused. Or didn't want to. I don't care which. Because again—you're only thinking about yourself. And in this moment, the last thing this is, is about *you.* About us. Because, as you've always reminded me, there never was and never will be an us. But you'll always work toward your own end, so I'm sure you'll keep talking."

"I thought I was doing what was best for you." Damian admitted, and the shame that shadowed his words darkened his countenance. He stepped forward again and reached out to her. Kate dodged his hold, turning a shoulder to him and flinging an arm across her upper body. "By pushing away what I felt, I thought I was doing what was best for you. You didn't need a vagrant, indecisive, bullheaded male like me. Plus, you're Talorc's *daughter.* What kind of betrayal would that be to him if I pursued you?"

The truth of what he couldn't admit to Vadin so many nights ago tumbled out of him so easily that he almost wished he could take it back.

"So fuck me, right?" Kate asked rhetorically, fully facing him to snarl her angry retort. "Fuck my feelings, my wants, my desires, my future? Because you thought you *knew what was best?* There you go, proving my point. You'll always work toward your own end." She laughed, and there was a hint of genuine humor in her tone, which proved how dismissive she was of this conversation.

Spiraling. We're spiraling. Not going good. Fuck. How do I get back on track?

The truth hit him square in the chest: *put all thoughts of*

Kate first. See from her eyes. Live from her mind. Think with her thoughts, her memories, her feelings.

Immediately he resisted with the notion: *I have been. Hasn't it been enough?* His mind swirled and churned, and he almost got lost in the tempest until Kate continued.

"But this isn't about us, or what we could have been."

She dissipated all of Damian's thoughts to a single, shockingly singular one: *Could have?*

The world tilted again, and he felt himself slipping from the surface.

"It's about *my* revenge. What I want. What I need." Her eyes brightened as she glared at him, and her chest began to rise and fall rapidly. "Everyone, my entire life, has tried to control me. They all thought they knew what was best for me. No one ever *asked me* what *I* wanted. For once, I want control over my life. And I am going to take it."

Irresistibly drawn to her vigor, Damian closed the distance between them to less than a handsbreadth. Kate didn't move; perhaps she couldn't. They stayed like that as their heartbeats intertwined and the rain poured down around them, pattering against the ground, the rocks, the pool, with an intensity they themselves exuded.

"Tell me," Damian whispered, his voice urgent. "Tell me what you want."

Kate, startled to silence, stared first into his eyes before briefly dropping her regard to his lips. She looked back up hurriedly, but Damian was so sharpened on her every move that he didn't miss the fine flick of her gaze. His heart swelled so enormously that it filled his chest, as every fiber of his being began to slowly burn from the fire she emanated.

"Tell me." His own eyes dipped to her burgundy lips.

"I…" Kate stopped, her voice barely a murmur. She attempted to clear her throat. He didn't know if she realized it, but she stepped closer to him, so near that if he didn't know it before, he knew they were connected—someway, somehow—now.

"What do you want Kate?" Damian asked, and subconsciously he was pleading with her for permission. Permission to move forward. To forget the past. To push past the last months, his mistakes, the years he'd wasted…

Kate first. Put Kate first.
As it should have been and should always be.
"I want…"

He could see she was warring with herself. What she wanted to say and what resided in the deepest confines of her soul. Who she was now and who she'd been. He saw her pain as she stared into his eyes, as if begging him not to push her.

But Damian would never be that good of a male.

"Say it."

Her eyes closed as she whispered, "*You.*"

Damian captured that single breath and everything it meant in a euphorically chaotic kiss.

He reached a weathered hand to her cheek while wrapping his other around her waist, pulling her to him as she gasped into his mouth. She tried to pull away and in contrast he pulled her closer, and in the next moment she kissed him back with as much passion as he ensnared her with. She wrapped her arms around his neck, clinging to him as if he were both the blood and the breath in her body, almost crawling his lean frame to get closer. Understanding and evoking the same need, Damian crushed Kate to him, slamming his tongue into her mouth in an ardent desire to tame her.

At that same moment the world tilted fully, upending everything Damian knew and taking both of them with it.

No going back.

Kate began to pull at his shirt, her short nails dragging along his neck before dropping to the hem. In an enthusiastically mindless response, Damian pulled their bodies apart but kept their mouths together to help her remove his clothing. As if desperate to remain joined, Kate reached forward with both hands and dragged him back to her, her shaking fingers tightening on the front of his shirt. She twined a leg between his own as she shoved her own tongue into his mouth, pulling herself up so their lips slid against one another's. Damian knew nothing but pure bliss in this moment, and wrapped his arms around Kate once more, clasping her to him as she began to tear his shirt from his back.

Creator be—

"Kate…" Damian pulled back to plead mercy, knowing she was only sharing with him a hint of her aggression, but Kate would have none of it. She pulled him back to her once more, colliding their lips almost painfully. She bit his lower one, drawing blood before sucking it into her mouth, and the greed and selfishness in which she acted made Damian's cock swell. He groaned as she dragged her nails down either side of his neck, and bunched his own fists in the material of her sweatshirt as she dug her fingers into either of his shoulders and kissed him with all the fire with which she burned. He pressed into her once more, letting her know what she did to him; the reaction was always one he had to her, she just never knew it.

The leg she put between them brushed against his heavy erection, and Kate suddenly jolted and stopped her caresses. She sprang away from him, jumping back several feet. Sweet color resided in her cheeks and her Bordeaux-colored lips were bruised. Her hair remained matted to her head from the rain, which chose that very moment to increase in force. Damian stared at her in wonder, with desire so thick in his veins he could focus on nothing else save stripping her naked and fucking her on the forest floor, in the pool of the falls, against the rocks that bordered it...

Yet the look on her face, a mix of shame and hate, had him faltering.

"You still don't get it."

She backed up one step, then another. Damian felt terror grip him once more, and he stepped toward her while reaching out a hand. Kate looked at the appendage, then to him, and it was with sadness in her voice that she said, "Don't come for me until you do."

She fled then, without another word.

Time suddenly started slipping through Kate's fingers like water, whereas for the past month it seemed to fall like sludge. Bound to the perception was a sense of urgency no one in the manor—especially Kate—had felt for a very long time. The urgency surged forth with purpose, and it was with that fervent purpose that Kate strode to her father's office the next night.

Primed on a fresh mug of blood and her first full meal in weeks, with her hair freshly brushed, a familiar pair of leather pants adorning her legs, and a scarlet sweater on her torso, she walked down the hall with confidence and determination. The combat boots from last night she'd thrown in the trash—*don't think about him don't think about him don't think about him*—and instead a modest pair of black platform boots encased her feet. She wore no makeup, was certainly nothing like the picture of her past self, yet the blazing resolve that sharpened her features was enough to stop her father from packing a thin briefcase. His brown eyes widened as she took a resoundingly firm stance in the doorway, his own frame rigid with trepidation.

"As much as I deserve to be angry and linger in my resentment of you, it's not going to help me achieve my goal," Kate said. "We can talk about the forgiveness you want and how to achieve it, but first you will tell me about my mother."

She shut the door behind her and walked to one of the chairs at her father's desk, pulling herself around it to have a seat. She crossed her arms as she settled back, twining one leg overtop another. She stared at Talorc while he shut the lid to the briefcase slowly, clicking the locks into place, and then sat in the tall-backed chair behind the desk, suddenly looking more wary and weathered than he had in the last one hundred years.

"What do you want to know?" he asked softly, adopting a similar position to his daughter's.

Kate swallowed her own wariness. She had so many questions, and though she spent the entire day smoldering in her aggression, she still hadn't aligned her thoughts into starting a prosperous discussion. Sleep had eluded her, as her mind cast about all she had gone through in the last seventy-two hours: the conversation with Lilith, which subsequently ignited her rage and need for retaliation; the exchange with Mora, which turned the rage to hurt; the argument with her father which begat pain and deep sorrow; and finally the discussion with Damian, which she abruptly replaced with other thoughts. Though, in truth, her body would never let her forget...

Stop. Refocus. Don't go there. Not thinking about him.

Why not? Why can't I? I finally admitted it. It's not a secret anymore, the wantonly rebellious part of her wondered.

She ground her teeth together, flicking her tongue against the backs as she cleared her throat to reorient herself to the present and absolutely not to what had transpired at Forbidden Falls. Or the way she'd burned throughout the day. Or the way she constantly wondered about what Damian was doing. What he was thinking. How he was feeling. How he had made *her* feel. No length of the coldest shower could subside the lingering trail his hands left on her skin, and the dreams that flitted through what little sleep she'd got had been intensely intimate. *Doesn't change the fact that he still thinks this is about him. He's not seeing* me. *He's not thinking about* my needs. *And until he does…*

Refocus, Kate thought roughly, casting away the distraction. *I'm here to try and convince Father to let me ride with him to Canada so I can annihilate Santiago. That's all that matters now. My revenge.*

And then maybe I'll sort out the rest of my life.

"Why you forced everyone not to speak about mother for years is evident; the pain is easy to see," Kate started. "But why didn't you tell me the truth about Mora?"

"It was a joint decision, one that got lost with time," Talorc said, and it was with no small amount of shame that his words came forth. "In truth, it pained us both to speak of her. Mora and Herja were extremely close, especially after Herja petitioned Mora to be made. Neither of us thought she would ever need to take a motherly role in regard to you, so when the notion came to fruition it was easier not to speak of it and just assume it."

"Because she'd already been a mother," Kate replied softly, almost as if speaking to herself. "Twice over." *I now know.*

Talorc nodded. "The slaughter of her first family was almost a complete deterrent to building another, but when her beloved came into her life…" He stumbled to a halt, his eyes dipping to his desk briefly. "The pull is undeniable."

Kate knew all creatures The Creator produced were born with only half a soul; the other half rested in what was the perfect complement to that particular being, no matter the species. The two halves, when joined, were referred to as *beloveds*. Vampires gained much from the revelation: senses increased exponentially; strength, speed, and agility grew; a tangible bond formed; and auras could be detected. The only way for a vampire to confirm they'd met their beloved was through the covenant of sharing blood, but before that happened the pull between the two was usually intensely irrefutable. For anyone to revoke the formed bond—whether through death or refusal—meant intense heartache, longing, and darkness. The possibility was too wondrous a thing to lose, to jeopardize. True joy, true love, true yearning...

"So Asha is my cousin." Kate had put that piece of the puzzle together the night before but needed to hear the truth of it from her father.

"Yes. My niece."

"Everyone knew?" Kate asked of those that worked in the manor, The Guard.

Talorc nodded in a clipped motion. "Most, yes."

Ire simmered just below her skin, causing her to shift restlessly in her seat. "I just don't understand..." Kate pulled back on the frustrations threatening to overtake her rational mindset. "Why no one ever said anything."

"Would it have mattered?" Talor unknowingly echoed Mora's question from the night before. "Would it have changed anything?"

"No, but it still feels like a betrayal," Kate responded bitterly, and Talorc bowed his head in a show of regret.

"I've gone my entire life thinking my only family was you," Kate continued, and Talorc looked up slowly from his short bow. "My entire life thinking that the sole connection I had to my mother would forever be lost to me because you refused to talk about her and made everyone else afraid to do so. Do you understand how selfish that is?" Kate's eyes narrowed, and she relentlessly plowed on. "Do you know how many times I laid awake at night thinking about her? Do you know how many times I dreamt about what she looked like? Do you know how many times I scoured the library thinking I would find something with her handwriting in it? Do you have any care or thought about how I wished someone would slip just once and say something about her to me?"

Humbled, Talorc delayed in his response.

"I'm sure you thought you were doing it in my best interest," Kate said tartly. "In all honesty I can't say that the omission of the information had a negative impact on me; my relationships with Mora and Asha are close regardless of the fact that we're related. I also don't think it will change anything going forward. But it was cruel. Deceitful. And the farce ends here."

Talorc nodded once more. "There are many things to which I must atone. I should have known better than to keep such a large part of your life beyond a veil. All I ask now is that you understand my ideals in doing so."

"Pain, longing, fear," Kate named them easily, and met her father's gaze just as so. "It ends here, *Athair*. If we are to move on, it has to end here."

Talorc settled back in his chair, intertwining his fingers and staring at Kate with guarded eyes. His voice was heavy as he said, "Ask of her what you will."

So much rose to the surface and then receded, like a tsunami crashing to shore. The remnants of the wave—the rushing sweep of cool invigoration—centered Kate, and she took a long, deep breath before releasing it with the words, "Tell me about the night you met."

The valiant Pict warrior of legend and vampire king Talorc 'The Sword' softened in a way Kate had never seen. His shoulders relaxed, his eyes turned honey-brown, and the most subtle of smiles turned the corners of his rough features. His voice turned hoarse, but not in a way that radiated sadness; it was with warmth and fondness, and his aura emanated a soft golden glow.

"It was a sodden night, much like last. The rain fell in slants across a rocky field encumbered by night. There were mountains in the distance, and if I listened hard enough, in the distance was the sea. My contingent of warriors had been paid to join forces with another to overcome a larger force of wraiths that had been ravaging churches on the mainland of modern-day Norway. I did not know who I was meeting, only that the pay from the heads of the churches was good and vengeance would be easily obtained once our forces combined. I was sitting on my horse, Warhorse—"

"You named your horse *Warhorse*?" Kate raised a brow.

Talorc shrugged. "I was never a male of creativity."

Kate shook her head curtly, then gestured for her father to go on.

"I was annoyed that my freshly oiled leather armor was getting soaked when thundering took to the sky. Thinking it was the weather I paid no mind, until a Valkyrie from Valhalla rode up on a horse bigger than mine, in scarlet armor finer than mine, looked me from head to toe, and sneered, '*you* are who I am to fight alongside? The Creator has cursed me, surely'."

The smile that Kate thought she saw bloomed into a chuckle, one that startled her into adopting wide eyes for a moment. She couldn't remember the last time her father laughed. "I was immediately and immensely struck dumb with infatuation. Her long black hair streamed from under a helmet that hid most of her features, but her striking blue eyes seared me through and through. I remember the way her skin shone, as if it held the full light of the moon. Her voice was sharp, commanding, stern for a female, but lilted with the smoothest of honey, both waking and quelling my soul.

"I had naught to say, muted by her presence, and with another sneer she began directing *my* soldiers into formation. Perturbed but intrigued, they obeyed. I watched in awe: she was beauty, the night sky come to life. How could a being so small, so fragile-appearing, command so mightily? I traipsed after her like a bard would a tune for years yearning for the answer, and each moment I spent doing so I found myself more enraptured with her. *My Herja.*

"It wasn't until a comparable night had me saving her from a band of vampires-turned-traitors that she finally would acquiesce to my hand. I learned of their treachery from an inside source and intervened as they were tying her to a pagan alter in sacrifice to an ancient sun deity. I slaughtered them all, of course, and after I untied the last bit of rope from her wrists, she looked me straight in the eye and said, 'so I am to be cursed, then'. I grinned at her, as any victorious rogue would, and the temper that followed would cloud her for days. I could not be so deterred, as I finally had the other half to my soul. I did not know it for sure then, but I felt it."

Talorc lifted a booted foot and placed it on the opposite knee, resting his bearded chin against a fist. His eyes were not on Kate as he continued, "The rest... It matters naught. Our lives entwined, and that is all I could ever ask for."

Warmth from a love that Kate longed to know bloomed from her father, cloaking him in an aura that turned radiantly crimson. Kate asked softly, "Will you tell me what she was like?"

The aura surrounding her father changed from scarlet to

gold, before the two mixed like lengths of diaphanous fabric. *Love. Happiness.*

"She could just as easily bite with cynicism as she could lure with charm. She practiced her sword-fighting as steadfastly as she did her languages; she spoke six fluently. She read books as avidly as she trained her horses, for she would let no other get her hands on them. 'No one can do it like I can', she would say. And she was right. She had a way with animals, and at any given time we had no less than five dogs on the property. She taught them all by her own hand, and Creator take me, but she let them all sleep in our bed.

"She laughed as easily as she sang, though she could not carry a tune to save her soul. Or dance. She hated dancing. And she hated dresses. The minute we solidified our bond in front of our friends and families she changed from the gown Mora had sewn diligently for weeks into a tunic and leathers. When we argued she always got her way, because she was just as obstinate as the fiercest warlord. She knew compromise with everyone but me, but perhaps that is my own fault. I forever knelt before her, for any and everything."

Tears gathered in Kate's eyes as Talorc spoke, and her heart melted within the confines of her chest.

"A better sailor I never knew, and a less mischievous creature I would never meet. Her harrowing battle skills and conniving warmongering turned more playful as age carried her through the years, off the field and into the home. She would play little pranks on me throughout the manor: putting rocks in my boots or tying an impossible knot to tether my steed. Her ability to blend lent her stealth, and she utilized it readily. One night while I was trying to untie the rope to said steed, she dumped a bucket of honeyed feathers on me from the rafters of the stables. I found them wherever I went for weeks, and they stuck to everything. She laughed whenever she plucked one from my form, and I will admit I found them as slowly as I could to savor the sound."

Kate knew her next words were going to bring forth agony. She almost didn't want to know. But the truth had been held from her so long…

"What happened to her?" she whispered, and the warmth in her chest began to seep away.

Talorc's jaw shifted one way, then another, as he lifted his head from his fist. It was the only sign, if it was a subtle one, that what he was to say next was not easily forthcoming.

"Two months after you were borne, I was called into town," he started, his voice deepening with an emotion he wouldn't show. "A fire had been set to the largest store of grain in our community, and it was starting to blaze across the adjoining fields. Herja begged of me to go and help the humans that ran the small settlement just outside of where we lived; we were more friend than foe, though they did not know our true nature. I was hesitant to leave you both, but I knew she would be safe under the watchful eye of her sister. I took The Guard with me and set off into town.

"In hindsight I should have known better, for the night was eerily similar to the others that had been pivotal in my life: suddenly saturated with tumultuous rain. But I had experienced so many like nights throughout my life that this one did not stand out in the moment. Perhaps I am being overly melancholy. Overly precise. Overly exhaustive. But it is a night that lives in my mind more frequently than all the others, in a detailed manner so shattering that every night like it has me sleepless for several afterward."

Talorc stopped speaking then and swallowed hard. His eyes narrowed on a point beyond Kate, and she shifted uneasily in her seat, wondering again if she should redact her request.

No. I need this. I deserve this. She was a part of my life too. She is *a part of* me.

"The rain doused most of the fires. I was not gone long. But it was long enough."

He stopped again, and it was with cold malice that he looked at Kate, arctic ebbs swirling in his eyes.

"Have you heard of The Hangmen?"

Kate frowned slightly. "Yes. Well, vaguely. I don't know much about them."

"They are a self-righteous group of humans who have decided to hunt vampires and eradicate us, unbelieving, unknowing, and untrusting of our true purpose, sometimes even confusing us with wraiths. In times past they were known for stealing into vampire homes, kidnapping them by any means possible, and hanging them. As you should know, a hanging will not kill a vampire; rather they will rejuvenate over and over and over again, after suffering through suffocation or snapped spinal cords. Because of this, well-lit places were chosen so when the sun rose, it would finally kill them. Some Hangmen choose places where the sun would rise later for extended torture." The temperature in the room fell to an almost unbearable level. "In this day and age it does not matter how they kill us, so long as the job gets done."

Kate picked up quickly on her father's words. "You speak in the present tense."

"They still survive. Their numbers are few, but they are out there."

Realization was slow, and it crept from the shadows as though looking for prey. Kate's stomach turned with nausea as she stared at her father. "What does this have to do with my mother?"

A rush of icy air swirled around the room, curbing the fire that jumped in the hearth. Talorc's voice was full of hatred as he said, "The Hangmen captured your mother and stole away with her. They ripped her from our bed, beat her unconscious, and left a trail of blood from our home into the woods. Our bond was strong, the pull faint but there, however they had at least three hours' worth of time to hide her from me. And on horseback... Even with the help of The Guard, I could not locate her.

"Ryder pulled me from the rays of the sun into the manor as morning broke, else I would be nothing but ash. In my soul I heard her shriek as the sun took to the sky, and at that same moment my world turned black."

Horrified, Kate couldn't bring herself to speak.

Talorc continued, the temperature in the room remaining chilled. "Whether by the hand of Fate or not, they spared you and the others in the house. Maybe The Hangmen thought there was no one else. Maybe they did not want to waste time. Maybe they only had one agenda. I will never know the answer. I do not want to."

"How did you know it was them?" Kate murmured, her voice choked with grief.

"Their crest," Talorc's words were clipped as he planted both feet on the ground, his hands on the arms of his chair gripping tightly. "A noose made from a serpent had been crudely etched on the framing of the front door. By the streaks of soot that remained near the entryway I think they meant to burn our house down as well, but those within thwarted the endeavor."

"Why didn't anyone stop them?" Kate breathed, her eyes widened in terror. "Follow them? Fight back? Anything!"

"Who was there to? I took all the warriors with me. Mora was no longer a crusader. Her own Asha was a mere child. The males that resided here were no more soldiers than The Guard are laymen. As it was, their numbers were few, and no one wanted to risk losing more that night."

Dread settled within Kate like a heavy brick. The temperature in the room gradually dissipated back into warmth, but a shroud hung, casting shadows brought by memories best left forgotten.

"You well know what transpired after. Everything I did not do in the wake of losing my beloved has brought us here. I will not douse you in any more pity or misery, but I hope you will continue to attempt to understand the depths of my sorrow and how difficult it has been for me to push forward. I have you, yes, but…one half of my soul has been brutally ripped from me. I felt fractured and incapable for a very long time. All I wanted was for death to be dealt to me, and that is how I lived my days. It caused me to lose the sight that is now just coming back to me."

"Why did they do it? The Hangmen?"

Talorc clasped his hands together as if to steady the chaotic emotions that he so desperately tried to keep from her. "After The Guard eventually tracked them down, we learned the attack had been random. There was some word within the town we were different, and they acted on their suspicions accordingly. The fire in the grain barn and the fields had been planned as a diversion to get me from the house. We never did find out why they did not ambush and kill us while we were out that night. Malicious intent, I would assume, to cause the most pain. Though they never came for us again."

"Were they killed?"

Talorc didn't answer. Kate knew the *Elden Edicts* indicated an unprovoked act that brought about death of a human was considered a violation of a vampire's oath and resulted in capital punishment from the watchers. Kate also knew that her father would never utter the truth for that same reason.

But someone knows, Kate thought, and her musings caused

her eyes to flicker skyward. They *have to know. So why are they silent? Even then, were they so far removed?*

"This is all the more reason to continue to push forward," Kate urged, standing from her chair. "Mother deserves justice. The Hangmen have to be stopped, just like Santiago and his henchmen have to be stopped. There are so many who would see us fall, Father, and we have to act. As a team." Kate's hands curled into fists that shook. "And I deserve to be part of that team."

Talorc's eyes skimmed over Kate before fixing on the snapping fire.

"Father, listen to me," Kate said, capturing his attention once more. "*This* is how you earn my forgiveness—by letting me go on this journey. I might not be the best fighter, the fastest, the smartest, the most courageous. But I can blend. I can withstand all manners of torture. But most of all I *know* Santiago. Where he lives. Where he hides. His safehouses. They talked around me like I didn't matter. Like I wouldn't pull through to be standing before you now as a crucial resource. I know things that can help. Let me share with you what I know. I want to help. I need to—I *deserve* to.

"You can imagine what they did to me," Kate lowered her voice, her brows falling harshly over her eyes. "Revenge is something you know well, so you understand the need I have to grasp my own. *Santiago needs to die*. For what he did to me, commanded happen to me..." Her voice turned into a growl. "I don't care what it takes, but it'll be by my hand that I see him fall. You will *not* take that right from me."

Talorc stared up at Kate for several heartbeats, the fire crackling wildly from across the room. She wouldn't let her father's gaze go, and she didn't know she'd been holding a breath until he said, "See it done."

Chapter Eighteen

Within the hour Talorc's office was filled with all the members of The Guard: Ryder and his mountainous frame took a stance by the fireplace, Vadin and Cyrus had taken seats in the chairs before Talorc's enormous desk, Noir stood between two windows, and Damian had already begun pacing a trail across the oriental rug. Kate perched on the edge of her father's desk, avoiding Damian with everything in her. He'd drilled holes into her with his eyes as he stormed into the room, even opened his mouth to say something to her, but Kate cut him off with a biting hiss that even had Talorc lifting a brow. The exchange was easily forgotten, and now Talorc clicked on his computer before the printer beneath the desk chugged out a detailed map of Manitoba.

"Where I left off." Talorc circled a point just out of range of the province. He passed the paper to Ryder, whose forehead creased as he looked it over. "But plans have changed."

"We need to focus on Santiago," Kate started, bouncing the leg that was crossed over the other. As six pairs of fierce eyes turned to her, Kate refused to writhe under the pressure. "He's driving all of this. He's made it clear several times that he's after only one thing: Father. He wants his seat of power. He thinks he can capitalize on Father's lack of action and the coven leaders will easily fall to his feet, desperate for a leader. He was planning on vying for their support after targeting The Guard one by one to bring them down, which is why he went after Taryn." Kate felt as though she was amassing the pieces of an intricate puzzle. "Santiago wants to control the vampire nation while using the wraiths as pawns to get to the top."

"That doesn't make sense. If Santiago prioritizes vampires,

humankind will fall and he'll have no wraiths to do his bidding," Cyrus rumbled.

"Because wraiths are made from humans, and then need to survive off their blood," Vadin filled in with an inquisitive tone, as if speaking out loud would help organize the conversation in a manageable way. "We all know the way wraiths are made is corrupt—a nasty transformation from dead to deader— and that's why they're mindless and murderous."

"And don't survive for very long," Cyrus finished.

"But lately they have been," Kate disputed. "Hundreds of years ago they didn't live for long, but their genetics have changed. You yourselves have seen a difference in their behavior. They're smarter, more organized. They talk. Which makes me believe their maker is getting better at what he does."

"Which means there are more wraiths out there, doing Creator only knows what," Vadin supplied.

"Wraiths are still being made, humans are still being preyed on, the vampire population is dwindling…" Cyrus started. "Why would anyone want control of a dying breed?"

"We are not dying," Talorc rumbled, anger edged in his tone. "I will not allow it. *We* will not allow it. This is our home, our country, our world. We belong here."

"There's a deeper motive," Kate replied, knowing the puzzle was far from completed. "It goes beyond ruling the vampires."

"And it's not coming from Santiago," Vadin muttered, his eyes lifting to Kate. "It has to be from above him."

"Adhamh," Noir uttered, rubbing a hand along his smooth chin. The sharp angles of his features caught the light of the fire as he looked at Kate. "It has to be Adhamh."

"It can't be."

"Why not?" Vadin hedged, and none too happily. "Things are out of control. That's his definition. Chaos. War. Unrest."

"So you're saying he can make vampires too?" Kate asked, the theory burning like acid in her mouth.

"What other watcher would be making vampires for the sake of evil? He's the only one with the means to orchestrate all this." Vadin scuffed his fingers through his strawberry-blonde beard, green eyes shrouded with a frown.

"But why? What's the end goal for Adhamh?"

No one responded.

"From what I know of Santiago, the drug and prostitution thing is a deterrent. Something he can hide under while he schemes below the surface with things that have to do with the vampires and wraiths. He's constantly traveling, moving, strategizing. He's well-known to humans but rarely shows face; he makes other humans or vampires do his bidding. He has a lot of people that work for him—and I mean a lot. All over the world. His hands are everywhere. His connections are endless. Claudia was running his prostitution ring in the city, and she was the one in charge of my imprisonment initially, but we know how that ended. Someone else ran the drugs. There was always someone else. Always. I rarely saw the same face twice." Kate's eyes flashed from bright sapphire to the darkest hues of blue. "But I remember their names."

"Still," Vadin said, glancing up at Kate from his leisurely seat in front of Talorc's desk. "What's the goal?"

"Does it matter? Santiago wants domination," Kate said vehemently, uncrossing her legs as she pinned each and every one of the males—except Damian—with a pointed look. "He wants eternal life and complete domination. And I believe he has the means to achieve it."

"He wants to rule the vampires and bend them to his will," Cyrus added. "He's not looking for acquiescence. He's looking for control. Power."

"Exactly. He's preoccupied with power and using Father's lineage to get it. He sees a new future, a new world: one of only wraiths and vampires."

"Adhamh's one of the only beings that we know of who would coordinate a largescale movement like this in a bid for power. He must be using Santiago for his connections," Vadin said, glancing at Kate and then Ryder.

"He's bound," Ryder answered with a look of clouded consternation. "He has no power anymore."

"That's what we were made to believe," Cyrus tested, ever the one to dispute.

"You think there's someone else?" Noir hedged, and more than one set of eyes shifted uneasily away from him. "Someone like Adhamh?"

233

"Watchers are the only ones capable of making vampires. Adhamh is the only one we know of who can make wraiths. If he passed that ability to someone else..." Ryder didn't want to continue, the thought morbidly demoralizing.

"Could there be another watcher?"

"For evil?" Talorc's tone was disbelieving. "Never in all of history has there been another watcher to deflect from The Creator."

"Do we even know them? The full extent of their capabilities?" Noir asked, running his fingers along the unlit cigarette behind his ear.

"No. And they've been little to no help." Ryder said, disappointment heavy in his words. "Their silence speaks volumes. But I like to believe they would get involved if they thought Adhamh was involved."

"They have their own rules to follow," Talorc supplied, his eyes sharp on Ryder. "Ones even I hardly understand. Not so easily are they motivated; their movements are severely calculated. With that motivation would come great change, not just for us, but for the entire world."

"During my time I never heard Santiago speak about Adhamh." Kate said, refusing to let her tone reveal her inner discord.

Ryder pushed, "And he's been dormant for years."

"Has he though?" Cyrus challenged. "After his binding his existence became a mystery. We wrote him off, thinking that if he was contained, he wasn't a threat. But if he is influencing Santiago, he must have some autonomy. He's making wraiths, after all. And now apparently vampires. Think about it: planes going missing, uprisings all over the globe, epidemics, mass shootings... It could all be him. We just don't know. His capabilities may be hindered, but from what I remember they are vilely limitless."

"We need the watchers' help, their insight," Vadin urged, looking at Talorc.

"They have given no indication that they are ready to communicate," Talorc replied. "But I can try and reach out in the next day or two."

"The world will fall into chaos if Adhamh takes power," Ryder uttered deeply, his face heavy with a frown. "It will be like it once was…except so much more…"

"Horrendous," Cyrus finished.

"We can stop this," Kate said fervently; in this very moment, she almost felt like herself again. Anticipation, joyous anticipation, flowed through her veins, warming her from her head down to her toes. "I can show you where Santiago lives. He has a family, though using them for any intel or insight won't be useful; he's hateful toward them and shares nothing about his life. I can show you his safehouses. I know most. I can write down the names of the people he associated with. I can take you to where I know his prostitutes work and where he peddles his drugs. You guys could take it from there."

"How do you know all this?" Ryder asked Kate, looking up from the map he still had in his hand.

"At the end of last summer I started infiltrating his circles," Kate said, and more than one set of eyes widened. "I tried starting with the junkies, but they were useless; they only cared about getting high. I started asking around and learned from Mike, that bouncer from The Tomb, that Santiago pushed a lot of his girls and drugs through there. So I moved onto the prostitutes. They were nice enough, although the smarter ones were apprehensive about me. I hung around almost every night, pretending to be interested in prostituting until I could get a meeting with Santiago, where I thought I would try to persuade him to be a confidant of mine. I planned to feed him useless and misleading information about Father to string him along, and then return what I learned to you guys. I figured not a lot of people know who I am, and I could make up this mysterious persona.

"I followed the street mules when I wasn't with the prostitutes. I was finally able to find out where Santiago lives. I know he gets his drugs from Colombia. I know he meets with the heads of his rings every Monday night. I know the drug routes, could walk them with you guys if you want. Of course, my being able to blend helped; I was never caught. But somehow Santiago knew who I was and used the same tactics on me as I was him."

Kate swallowed away the terror the memory of the night she was captured wrought within her. She refused to go back to that place of fear and danger, and she curled her hands into fists to stave off the crippling sense of trepidation that slithered up her spine and wanted to coil in her chest.

The males stared at her like they had never seen her before. Kate merely stared back, meeting their looks with impassivity.

"Four *months* you were doing this?" Ryder asked, the dubious way he felt plainly etched on his usually inexpressive face.

"Give or take."

"But you were here?" Vadin asked in disbelief.

"I snuck out a lot. I caught ride services into town." She shrugged. "No one was paying attention to me. Or if any of you were, it wasn't for very long. None of you truly thought I could be capable of such a thing, so I took advantage of your nearsightedness. I know your haunts, your routes, your plans, so I avoided wherever and whenever I could. I lied. A lot. To everyone."

Guilt bit harshly at her, and Kate glanced at her father almost sheepishly. "Sorry, *Athair.* But I had my own agenda."

Surprisingly, Talorc bowed his head slightly. "It is the fault of my own for not putting my trust in you or including you when it was obvious that you should have been."

Damian's jaw fell open as he stumbled to a halt. "Talorc! You can't be serious." He swung his incredulous look to Kate. "We still hung out most nights," he said, as if there was a bluff to be called. "We watched movies. Baked. Hiked. Sparred."

"You always had somewhere to be half the night, so I utilized my time elsewhere," Kate said with another shrug, and only a little twinge of ice in her tone. "You were getting busier with The Guard as things started to ramp up."

Damian let his jaw fall open again, and then closed it in a rage. "I can't believe—"

"It doesn't matter now," Ryder cut him off sharply. "What's done is done. We have to move forward." His eyes narrowed on Kate. "Do you think you were ever followed here? Do you know if Santiago knows where the rest of us live?"

"I don't think I was ever followed here, but I don't know for sure. Santiago was starting to keep tabs on The Guard, and could have leads, yes."

Distressed grumbling filled the room, and Kate quickly jumped down from the desk to divert them. "But listen. I have a plan."

Damian stumbled again, slowing his pacing to look at her.

His tone was foul as he said, "No."

Kate leveled Damian with a stare that would've made Medusa harden to stone. "No. What?"

Forgetting the others in the room, Damian snapped, "Consider your involvement in this complete. Tell us what you know and be done with it. It's too dangerous for you going forward."

Kate sputtered, striding between Vadin and Cyrus to confront Damian. Vadin swiveled in his chair and grinned as if waiting for the main act to start while Cyrus closed his eyes and tried unsuccessfully to bite back a groan. "Too dangerous? *Too dangerous*? Did you not hear anything I just said? Did you forget everything I told you last night?"

"What is this now?" Talorc asked with a sudden stern frown, but his words were forgotten as Kate continued.

"What you think and feel and want is moot, Damian." Kate balled her fists at her sides as she glared at him, feeling like the youngling she suddenly wanted to be again when everything wasn't so confusing or exasperating. "In fact, this matter doesn't concern *you*. Didn't you say that you would be leaving soon to go overseas?" She threw that bit of information in his face, recalling the one-sided conversation from a few days ago.

Damian opened his mouth to retort, managed an annoyed grunt, but couldn't continue. Vadin practically vibrated with glee from his chair as they faced off.

"*This is what I mean*," Kate hissed at him like the serpent she felt like being. Poisonous was her tone as she continued, "Until you realize this is bigger than you, than me, than all of us, you will *never* find your way past the wall I've made."

Damian reared as if struck and Kate pulled back slowly, tipping her head back to look at him in disdain. It didn't last, however, for the pain that cut from Damian was so ripe, so rife with sadness, that her own aura faded from black to blue. The copper shade of his firelight eyes waned to rusted orange, dimming as his shoulders slumped in what Kate would never believe was defeat.

Because you're too stubborn to ever be defeated.

But so am I. And you won't win this battle against me.

I'm in control. Of myself, my vengeance.

"If we are going to take on Santiago," Ryder intervened

loudly to douse the fire between the two, while Vadin cut him an unamused glare. "We'll need all the hands we can get. Kate, what's your plan?"

Kate continued to stare at Damian, refusing to back down from his now veiled regard. He stared back, also refusing to bow out, opening his mouth, but closing it just as readily. He did this two more times while Kate watched him, widening her eyes as if inviting him to say something else stupid. *Arrogant asshat.* He turned away after a moment to resume his pacing, more vigorous than before.

Kate turned to address Ryder. "Santiago's downfall is he likes to move slowly. Think things through. Coupled with the fact that he always seemed preoccupied by getting Father's throne, I think if we let him continue to think Father is going on a tour to Canada, we can use his fixation to his disadvantage. We can use Father as a trap. Bait." More than one body shifted uncomfortably. "We can put word out that he is going to stay at one of the Canadian covens, and then watch the movement into that area. Once we know that Santiago is there we can strike."

"We can turn the tables," Vadin said excitedly.

"No," Ryder said flatly but Kate continued as if she didn't hear him.

"Yes, exactly. Remember Santiago likes to take his time. He's meticulous. If they are planning an attack half of the work is already done. We have to stay one step ahead, and they won't be expecting an offensive move, especially if they think Father isn't well guarded."

"But they'll have to expect that he is, especially after everything that happened." Cyrus refuted.

"But if we can get more covens on board to meet us in Canada and if Father reaches out to the watchers…"

"We could take them by surprise," Noir finished.

"We just have to make him believe that Talorc is traveling with scarce resources. Maybe even ham it up a bit and say that he's more distressed and removed than ever and this might be his last stop before he quits the tour all together. That would really light the fire under Santiago. We'll put the word out, get the rumor mill going," Vadin said, straightening in his chair.

"We will only employ who we know we can trust

explicitly," Talorc warned, earning a nod from Cyrus. "Although I am beginning to suspect that no one can be fully trusted. I am hearing rumors Santiago has infiltrated our population to an unnerving degree."

"Noir could go up before we do and scout the area, meet with at least the leader of the Winnipeg coven, maybe reach out to the Ruskill leader to gauge which way they lean and where the best place would be for our offense," Kate gestured toward the male. "Winnipeg is too populated for a big attack. The Snow Lake coven is smaller, but Ruskill, being on the water, could be our best bet."

"Lots of wilderness up there." Vadin snatched the map from Ryder. "There's even a national park nearby."

"I don't like this," Ryder said, his voice a thunderous roll.

"We can stop at the Winnipeg coven first, and then send one of The Guard to Snow Lake to ask for reinforcements while the rest of us go to Ruskill," Kate said, powering over Ryder once more with her enthusiasm, her drive. "But we need to strike quickly. Who knows what else Santiago has up his sleeve."

"There isn't much time to accomplish this," Talorc said.

"So let's start now. Tonight. We can start making calls to the covens you've already been to and branch out from there. I know Jean-Luc and Robertha will stand behind you." Kate gestured toward his desk.

"This isn't going to work. We haven't thought it all the way through. We need more time," Ryder interjected. "And I don't like the idea of using Talorc for bait. Something could go wrong. What if we are attacked along the way?"

"We can plan for that. Have other covens follow us, or prep ahead," Kate said. *I'll have a reason to go against everything I knew you would say Ryder, so let's do this.*

"What if Winnipeg isn't welcoming?" Ryder countered.

"The friendship between Paavak and I has never waned," Talorc murmured, taking his eyes from Kate to Ryder. "We have kept in close contact over the years. I doubt he will turn his back on me."

"There's still Snow Lake and Ruskill to consider," Ryder fired back. "For all we know Santiago could have infiltrated them already."

"He hasn't," Kate said firmly. "He never spoke of them."

"We'll need places to stay," Ryder argued, though his words were weakening the more he spoke.

"I can have that covered," Talorc responded. "And I believe there is a cabin near Ruskill at the very edge of that park that I can use to draw Santiago to me. It belongs to Paavak. He would stay there while he was hunting caribou."

"The travel alone," Ryder tread his final hill, his amber eyes smoldering with fire. "Will take days. To get to Ruskill…the rail is unreliable. We'll have to fly. That will bring its own worries and problems."

"Yeah, and with PETA around dogsledding is probably cancelled. Which sucks. Loved doing that," Vadin said flippantly, earning a small chortle from Noir.

"I know someone who can fly us up to Ruskill," Cyrus said.

Noir added, "If I leave tomorrow, I'll have at least twenty-four hours to solidify our plans with Paavak."

Silence waned for a moment until Ryder said, "I guess I'm outvoted."

"We," Damian mumbled from his pacing pattern across the carpet. "We're outvoted."

"Sorry boss, but I'm with Kate on this one," Vadin said, tipping his head over his shoulder to look at Ryder. Kate swallowed the gasp that almost passed her lips as her eyes darted to him in surprise. "I think we have to act now."

"The plan isn't horrible," Cyrus admitted, and Kate's heart started to pound.

"And Santiago has been silent and still for over a month," Kate said. "It won't last much longer." She turned toward her father, and he met her eyes with his chin cradled in his hand and a finger pressed against his lips, deep in thought. "We need to act."

Talorc lingered in his stare of Kate, and in the wake of their private conversation Kate knew he was thinking only of Herja in this moment; the subtle softening of his eyes was telltale enough. Kate now knew without a doubt she looked like her mother, and the voice in which Kate was now speaking, although her own, was bolstered by a specter she would only hear of in tales. She knew she was encouraged by the spirit of her mother in this moment— and in the moments that led to it—and she straightened her shoulders, wanting to make the female proud from wherever she was looking down with what Kate now believed was nothing but pride and love.

"How many covens do you think we could get to our side and to act with us, and how many bodies could they bring?" Kate asked her father.

"Back up here," Ryder said, and his tone bordered on hostile as he narrowed his eyes on Kate. "Don't you think, if they've been tracking us, they'll know, or at least suspect, we'll be with Talorc?"

"Probably. And they'll probably figure Father will be keeping me close as well. Which will take the attention away from the manor," Kate said easily. "But I'm telling you he doesn't expect more than The Guard. He doesn't think Father has the support."

"You said you were going back to Prince Edward Island," Ryder continued to counter.

Talorc waved his free hand, the other still cradling his chin. "Easily redirected to another time."

"No, I mean, what if we *say* we're going there but we go to Winnipeg first? It would give us more time and allow for us to watch the influx to Manitoba."

Kate's stomach flipped as Ryder changed his trajectory. She swallowed back a *whoop!* of victory before saying, "It could work."

"But you're supposed to leave in three days," Damian barked from the path he paced.

"Then we best get to work," Vadin said, slapping his hands on his chair as he stood. "I can see what I can hack into if you give me everything you know about Santiago and his associates, Kate."

"I'll reach out to my pilot contact and start getting supplies together," Cyrus said, looking from Kate to Talorc. "I can get Lilith on board too."

"Think you can get me in touch with that pilot you know?" Noir asked Cyrus, who nodded. "I'll need a way up to Winnipeg."

"I will start making the phone calls necessary to garner support," Talorc said, removing his hand from his chin.

Ryder sighed heavily. "I can get started mapping out the details of the plan." His ember eyes flashed to Talorc as he said, "I will have a private word with you."

Talorc nodded once. To his comrades he said, "See it done."

With their fists over their hearts, The Guard bowed to Talorc and then strode from the room. Kate moved to follow but stopped on the opposite side of the desk from where her father was seated.

"Thank you," she murmured gently. With her eyes she said, *for your honesty, your strength, your support, and your trust.*

"This will not be easy, Kathryn," Talorc said, and though he respected her enough to listen and included her in the conversation, his words were hesitant as he continued, "You have never left the manor, and rarely congregate with those outside of it. The world and the beings that inhabit it are harsh."

Kate met his eyes with a soft, sad smile, one that barely turned her lips. "I know."

"Beyond that," Talorc continued. "In my absence, others will look to you for guidance. As my daughter, you are considered the heir to the vampire throne. They will respect you for your heritage, but it will be up to you to show them that you transcend your ancestry."

Somewhat stunned, Kate mused, *didn't think about that.*

"Prove to them as you have proved to me your worth."

With too many thoughts swirling about her head, Kate could only nod once in response. Talorc bowed his head and Kate left the office, pulling the door to snick shut in her wake.

Chapter Nineteen

Hey."

She wasn't going to get far, and he certainly wasn't going to let her get any peace. *She owes me a decent conversation.*

"*Hey!*"

Kate kept walking down the long hall, her steps muffled by the runner. Damian kept her pace even when she quickened it.

"Kate, stop!"

Anger bit at his heels, and he watched with burning eyes as she swiped to the right, disappearing around the bend. Damian jogged after her, rounding that same bend, only to catch her leaping up the far stairs to the third floor.

Don't let her go, his mind whispered, and he broke into a jog after her.

"*Kate!*"

She didn't slow. Never once looked back.

The sconces gleamed low, flickering with mirth, seeming to mock his ill attempts at catching her. His heart pounded, louder than his footfalls, and his breath slipped out of him in short huffs as he jogged the length of the pale hall after her. Kate had broken into her own jog, which became more of a run, and the doors breezed by them in flashes as he called after her once more.

"Kate, stop running goddamnit!"

She didn't. She flew by countless rooms he'd forgotten the purpose of, the doors to her own room, and neared the end of the hall. *A library. Smaller than the main one.* It was one of Kate's favorite spots; the circular room overlooked the forest in a swath of floor-to-ceiling windows. Her collection of first-edition books resided on arcing handmade bookshelves within, alongside other trinkets she'd carried through time: a candlestick phone, a Victorian-era lamp, a set of hand-painted Russian nesting dolls. Damian couldn't recall how many times he'd carried her from the room as she slept, long before the sun's murderous rays could claim her.

She was always so careless, he thought as she approached the doors with her arms outstretched, pushing through them mightily.

She will never be again, his conscience keened. *Not with her life, her mind, her heart. You would do well to learn that.*

Damian blasted over the threshold to the library and came to a panting stop, a light sheen of sweat coating the back of his neck. He couldn't say that it was entirely from his plight as nervousness crept into his chest to twine with the fury that simmered beneath his skin. *Why am I nervous?* he thought with admonishment. *I... She... It doesn't...* He flinched slightly as the doors crashed closed behind him, heavily barring the rest of the world from them.

Kate stood with her back to him, staring out the windows into the night beyond. This night was the opposite the last, shining crystal clear after the torrential rain. The waxing moon above glittered resplendently while the stars twinkled merriment all around; they lent the only light to the library, which smelled of old paper and balsam. The frames of the trees three stories below held still, the complete antithesis to the raging of Damian's blood, the turbulent waves he felt in response to his irrational convictions.

"You have to stop running," he said to her, and even to his own ears his voice sounded breathless.

Kate whirled on him in all her ferocious glory, a beautiful harpy exposing sharpened talons ready to fight. "*You* have to stop thinking you can control me."

"I'm not trying to control you Kate," Damian said, taking a step forward. "But you have to know this plan you've half concocted by extorting your father for your forgiveness is far beyond your expertise. Not to mention morally wrong."

Kate barked a humorless laugh. "You telling me what's *morally wrong* is the darkest pot calling the kettle black."

Damian glowered at her. "You're extorting your father for your own gains. Didn't you remind me that this isn't *just about me?*

Yet here you are," he gestured at her erratically. "Just thinking about yourself."

A muscle beneath her eye twitched, but Kate remained unmoved. "I deserve to think about myself. To put *myself* first. Even though I'm not. I'm doing this for the good of the vampire nation." She scoffed then, her hands curling into fists so tight her knuckles turned white, before releasing slowly. "I don't owe you an explanation about anything."

"I'm not asking for an explanation."

"Then why are you here? I've asked you not to follow me. Not to come for me." She hesitated before saying with venom, "I want you to leave me alone, Damian. For good."

The words stabbed, but with his bleeding wound, Damian continued. "I want to make you understand that this situation is beyond your proficiency level, Kate."

He closed the distance between them, noting a writing desk catty-corner to the right, while aforementioned bookshelves lined the wall to the left. They were so tall a ladder stood in one corner, with wheels that would take the wielder to one side and then the other with ease. A nook had been carved of arcing wood in the center of the windows, with pillows and blankets arranged neatly for comfortable reading. A massive, rounded chandelier hung in the center of the room over a white carpet inlaid with a gray pattern. Next to the writing desk was a long chaise, colored to match the oval carpet. There were no other exits or entrances, and so with nowhere to go, Kate didn't move back, but she also didn't shed the look of malice on her features or retract her harpy's claws.

"I'm not telling you this in an effort to control you." Damian lowered his voice slightly. "I'm telling you this because I'm worried about you. You're just mending. Your body is still healing. Your mind—"

"Nothing about me is okay for you to comment on," Kate snapped heatedly, her removed façade cracking. "I thought I made that clear last night."

Starkly reminded of everything but their discussion, Damian's body rolled with the thundering of rapids brought on by their moment of passion.

Her hair, her eyes, her lips, her skin... He stared at her as desire threatened to consume him, drown him. *They call to me again...*

You have to think from her point of view, the small, rational part of him suddenly intervened. *Wear her woes and worries. See life through her lens; everything she has experienced, been through, both new and old. Appreciate the absolute evisceration her life has suffered before thinking of yourself, or anything else for that matter. What you've been doing has not and will never be enough to erase that part of her life. She needs support. Be her support.*

Startled into silence by the abrupt thought, Damian didn't reply.

"Whatever you think I need, or can handle, or should consider, you can keep to yourself." Kate returned to the conversation with ferocity. "I don't need your antiquated, oppressive, and misogynistic opinions clouding my judgement."

"*Misogynistic?*" Damian snapped in response, disbelief sparking his eyes wide. "When have I acted that way toward you?"

"If you continue to think you have a say because you are a *small* part of my life, that's on you. You're only holding yourself back." Kate ignored the question as she crossed her arms. She sneered then, her upper lip curling as her anger turned to acid. "Your thoughts, your opinions, your words mean nothing to me."

"What is *wrong* with you?" Damian asked breathlessly, stretching his arms open toward her in inquiry. "Why are you so angry with me?"

The truth flickered to the surface in her eyes, but she shoved it away behind the wall she had admitted to building to keep him out. But still he knew...

You are her easiest target because in her heart, her soul, she knows you are the only one who can take her anger and not be burned from it.

Kate looked away from him, toward the writing desk in the corner of the dark room. On its surface was a single notebook with a lonely pen, accompanied by a statue of a harrier hen. The austerely noble bird was poised in widespread descent, its hooked talons unfurled toward prey, its mouth agape in a cry that had seen centuries pass. Kate stared at the statue with her jaw set in a way that Damian knew she wouldn't answer, so he pressed on.

"Harness that anger and use it elsewhere," Damian

encouraged her, though his tone was flat. "Your anger is wasted on me. I don't give a shit if you're mad at me; I'm going to be around no matter what. I just want to see you *move on.*

"Kate, listen to me. You don't know your limits right now. You are riding high on adrenaline and a determination that's born from rage. You need to think about what you're saying, what you're doing, and how it's affecting others. This isn't just about *you.* There's so much more at stake. Talorc, the manor, life as we know it... It could all come crashing down."

"Don't do that. Don't throw my words at me." Kate threw her arms into the air as she whirled to face him. "I'm trying to prevent exactly that from happening. But you keep getting in my way with your barbaric opinions. *This isn't just about you,*" she mimicked hotly. "What I do with my anger, how I utilize it to shape my behavior, is none of your concern. But you still think you have an opinion on my life and how I should go about living it, so here we are, wasting time arguing when I could be helping father and Ryder plan for the trip ahead."

You're not going to reach her; her mind is set, his mind warned him cautiously. *Meet her. Match her in this. Be her comrade instead of her barricade.*

"Just tell me why you're so angry with me." Damian's eyes softened even though his body stood rigid. "Tell me why you're so angry so we can get past this point in our lives."

"Because I deserve to be!" Kate yelled, eyes flaring, arms shaking. "I have been everything *but* my entire life."

"Okay so get your aggression out and move on!" Damian shouted back. "You're going to burn from it if you don't release it Kate, and it will feed from you until you're nothing but ash.

"You need to move on," he finished. And with a final gust of breath he said, "And if you need to use me to get to the finish line, then do it. Because I can't live like this anymore. With you... I can't..." He faltered for the right words, and with a great release of the pressure in his chest he concluded, "I can't live without *you.* I miss you, Kate. I miss you."

The look of ire that twisted Kate's features with spite fell, and the sparkling calamity that held her frame unyielding left her in the next heartbeat.

Damian paused, unsure of where his thoughts, his most

inner feelings, would take him next. It was on a rush of breath that he said, "What I'm saying is…I've stayed this long. I know you need me. As much as I need you, you need me. I'm not going to leave you." The truth flowed from him easily, but he hardened his tone as he continued, "You can yell and run and cry all you want. But I'm not going anywhere."

Unadulterated, crystal realization crashed over him, and he faltered. The world trembled, causing the universe to catapult—

I'm not going anywhere. Staring at her now, dumbfounded and abruptly mute, he knew it to be true. *I'm never going anywhere. Putting Kate first, being a part of her life, means more to me than anything else. That's why I've stayed so long. So I could figure that out.*

The ground shook beneath his feet. The cosmos beyond the windows swirled and twinkled like never before, illuminating her with an ethereal glow. All of this—because of her.

I won't go anywhere without her.

The moon, reflective of Fate herself, smiled.

Because my place is with her. It always has been.

Clarity rang like the tolling of a bell through his soul.

I am to be a part *of her. She is me. I am her.*

The world tilted again, for the umpteenth time since he'd met her. Yet finally the universe he saw in her paralleled with the way his world was shifting.

The trajectory he hadn't seen. The path overlooked. The journey he'd been afraid to take.

It had always been aligned *with her.*

In that moment, his mind reset with a sense of rightness that had him swelling with pride, fascination, and reverence. His breathing turned erratic, irregular, as emotions he didn't recognize swept him like a tranquil, lavender-scented summer breeze, undulating over the surface of the riotous waves that had readily ebbed within him only moments ago.

I need to be her sanctuary, not the storm, Damian thought. *Because she's worth it. And she needs it. By the Creator, she needs it.*

His mind whispered, *tell her.*

Taking a breath, it was all he could do not to. "I want to make you believe that I'm worth your anger, your spite, your devotion, your happiness. I want to be the place you go when you need shelter and comfort and warmth. Because I've done everything to try and show you otherwise. And it's been wrong. It felt *so wrong*." Damian said to her, closing the distance between them to three, then two, then one foot. He reached out to cup her cheek. "But being with you now, back by your side…it's where I need to be. So say what you need to. Do what you need to. Go where you need to. But let me go *with you*."

Her lips parted and her eyes widened, her breath halting on trembling lips. Her body thrummed, visibly rippling with emotion.

She was on him in the next instant.

Time came crashing to a halt as their bodies collided, Kate arcing above him as she twined one arm around his shoulders, her other hand splaying across his chest as her legs wrapped around his waist. Their lips met in a chaotic, fervent kiss, tongues thrashing, breath rushing out in heated pants. Damian clung to her, his fingers digging into one of her thighs and her back as he returned her kiss with every ounce of passion he'd ever held from her. The overwhelming awareness that *she was in his arms* was suffocating but at the same time invigorating, filling his lungs with new life, awakening his soul with new purpose.

Kate.

No, not new purpose.

The same. Just in a new light.

Her light.

His sweetened thoughts drifted away on waters churning with burgeoning desire, drowning who he used to be and how he used to think. In this moment he belonged to her. This moment was *theirs*. And he wanted every moment after to be just the same.

Too long… He thought, sliding the hand on her back up her spine to tug at the short tufts of her hair. *For too long I've denied her…*

Kate drew his lower lip into her mouth, which sent Damian's mind into a spiral, causing him to lose his balance. He staggered to the right, reaching out a hand to take the bite from the desk they went crashing into. The statue of the harrier hen teetered while the pen rolled to the floor and the notepad skittered across the polished top. Kate used the desk to propel herself into him harder, her thighs tightening around him as she ran her hands up both sides of his neck, his face, before tangling in the loose curls of his dark hair. Damian moaned as she licked his lower lip and then sucked on his tongue, holding his face in her hands as she curved over him, kissing him as desperately as he needed to be kissed.

Years of repressed lust soared to the surface of his skin, smothering him with desire only she could tame. *Why, when this— when she—was waiting for me, did I waste so much time?* Suddenly, every other female he'd ever been with burnt to ash, not even a memory, as his entire past, present, and future became everything *Kate.* He couldn't hold her tight enough, though her bones through her clothing reminded him how fragile she still was. He inhaled her delicate lavender scent; now it mixed with a saltwater tinge, his own desire potent. He drowned in the taste of her, a rich Bordeaux to match the color of her lips which he bruised again without a care.

Pressing her back against the desk, steadying her body with one hand and using the other to prop himself up, Damian pushed his thick erection into the center of her body. The resounding moan that released from Kate's throat was enough to have him pulsing, growing harder than he'd ever been. Kate raked her nails down his cheeks, through his beard, down his neck, leaving welts as she slid her body down to rest on the base of his shaft, before drawing up once more. With another twist of her lithe form, she sat fully on the desk, unhooking her legs from his waist but wrapping them back around his thighs, as if not wanting him to go far. Her hands found the collar of his shirt and to his great surprise and darkest pleasure she tore the material in two, baring him to her covetous gaze.

"Kate…"

Damian watched as she rested her hands on his heaving shoulders, gazing at the coiled tendons of his neck, the fine hair on his chest, his broad shoulders, before trickling down to his navel. He felt heat spring from somewhere low in his groin, and his erection pushed against the fly of his jeans, eager to show her what it had to offer. Kate's eyes dipped there briefly, and Damian's heart jumped into his throat as she dropped her hands to his belt.

A better male would have stopped her, but he wasn't that male tonight.

He never would be when it came to her.

Kate made quick work of the accessory, snapping it from

his waist and flinging it into the darkness. She pushed him back a step and he stumbled, his jaw falling slack as she fell to her knees before him and frantically began undoing the button on his jeans. Then went the zipper. Then her hands were at the top of his pants, curling around the material, tugging them down down down—

Commando, his erection sprang from the confines of his pants and Kate had him in her mouth before he could even think about saying anything. Damian threw his arms out behind him as if there were something that would catch him, and when nothing did, he faltered for a third time, more so with his jeans around his ankles. A laugh stole from Kate as he fell to the floor, but her laugh was quickly swallowed by the predator who took her place, watching him with eyes that were lit with a carnal calling. She sat back to pull her sweater over her head in one sweeping motion, and Damian watched in utter fascination as she released her breasts from the confines of her dark lingerie, leaving her in her leather pants and boots.

Creator. Fuck. It would be a vision that would be ingrained in his memory for the rest of his life. *The way those pants cling to her...*

She dropped to the floor at his feet, crawling up his legs to sit just above his knees. Her form was so slight he barely felt the weight of her, and he tried not to notice the way her ribs lined her skin or her collarbones pushed at the base of her neck. Fortunately it was easy, because she grabbed his cock in one of her hands and began to stroke him, looking down at him with a feral smirk he'd never seen. That look, coupled with the way her perfect hand wrapped around his aching cock, had him seeding slightly, his head thrown back against the rug in abandon.

"That's not fair," he breathed as she stroked slow, languid caresses up and down, up and down, up and down.

"I'm not trying to be," she told him in her wine-heady voice, her eyes hooded, her breasts bobbing with her movements. They were generous, pert, her nipples the same color as her lips. Lips that he looked at now, swollen from their kiss. Lips that smiled down at him, revealing the tips of her dainty fangs. Lips that called to him...

"Kiss me," he ordered of her, and she didn't hesitate to obey.

Kate arched her body so she could continue her ministrations as she kissed first his shoulders, then his neck, then nipped at his bearded chin. Damian groaned, eyes shut tight, and it was only then that Kate captured his lips in another erotic kiss. Her tongue danced along his lips before delving into his mouth, learning all the crevices within. When he tried to meet her, she snipped at him, reminding him that she was dominant in this situation.

The tang of his blood mixing in their mouths had his body rolling, sending his erection harder into her hand. Reminded that she still held him, Kate broke from his kiss and slithered back down his flesh, pressing her breasts against his chest as she went. Damian hissed, reaching for her to bring her back to his mouth, but she pulled at his cock almost recklessly before settling her mouth at the tip, licking a hot line around the rim. Damian groaned again, his back bowing, and had to bite the sound before it turned into a yell when she took his full member into her mouth. She swallowed him whole, her throat working hard, at the same time her fist moved along the base. Her other hand she held onto his hip with, digging her short nails into his skin.

Damian gripped the back of her head with both hands, trying desperately not to pump his cock deeper into her mouth. But he had no thoughts. Only whims and cravings, and she was matching every one. He cracked open his eyes and tilted his head to watch her, perched over his legs, bobbing her head in a frenzy he couldn't keep up with. Even now he felt the swirling of pulsing heat settle at the base of his groin, sending sharp shards of pleasure down his shaft with each pump of her fist.

He groaned as she stopped moving and instead worked her throat around his member, squeezing at the same time she moaned her own desire. Damian trembled, pulling at her hair and begging of her, "Don't stop. Keep going."

Kate pulled her head up with a slow lick, locking her eyes with his and smiling wickedly. Damian could barely breathe as he watched her lick her own lips before returning ravenously to his dick once more, her hand thrusting around him even more forcefully. He felt his toes curl into the floor as his hips moved of their own abandon. She sucked him harder, faster, and Damian had to close his eyes as his chest began to heave with the breaths he'd been trying to control.

Yet there was no control to be had.

Kate sucked his dick with a torturous pull that had him

biting his tongue as to not cry to the rafters his release. Her hand pumped frantically up and down his shaft, never slowing as he came into her mouth. His hands fell from her hair to her shoulders before landing on the floor, his body convulsing as she pulled every last bit of seed from his body. And Creator take him, but he got hard in a rush all over again thinking about how she swallowed every last drop.

After a time, she slowed her attentions, pulling her mouth away from his cock to lap at the head. Her slow licks had him begging for mercy, saying things that he would never recall and she didn't hear. Her hand around his dick finally slackened, and the other that had embedded into the skin of thigh released its grip. It was then and only then that Damian found the strength to open his eyes, staring at her in absolute wonder through the haze of his passion.

He found her fixated on his throat.

"Take." His voice was so hoarse he barely recognized it. "Take from me."

She didn't need to be told a third time.

Kate opened her mouth wide and struck his vein, pulling deeply of the fount that he offered. Damian immediately felt a second wave of pleasure take him, his body trembling as it slid from his chest, past his navel, directly into his groin. Kate groaned against his skin, her own hands shaking as she clung to his broad shoulders. Her back arched as she pressed her hands from his shoulders to his chest, curling her fingers into his pectoral muscles, through the sparse hair there. Damian's head swam as the heat from the core of her body penetrated his being, rupturing any thought he had left that would be purposeful. The only thing he could think was *more*.

Take more.

Take me.

As if she heard him, Kate swallowed greatly of his rich blood. Lost to her lavender scent and the way her nipples brushed his chest as she moved, Damian could only lay on the floor as his second release erupted all over her stomach and leather pants. His hands, which had been idle on her hips, fell to the floor in surrender. His cries were lost to the satisfied mewling Kate made as she swallowed mouthful after mouthful of his blood, rapt by the fervor.

In the next minute she pulled away, and Damian parted his eyes once more to look at her. He couldn't—would never—get enough of her, and as she rose above him in radiance, his sight suddenly sharpened. Her short hair was disheveled, her blue eyes brilliant, her skin shining in the light afforded from the moon. She was panting through her own mangled breaths, staring down at him in both shock and awe. Damian's eyes danced along her fine features, so beautifully etched, before honing on the small dribble of blood that rested on her lower lip.

Something in him resonated. Like rapids crashing over stone, the waters of desire that had been quelled by her tempering hands and mouth flowed once more.

Damian grabbed onto Kate's upper arms and rolled them so she laid on the floor beneath him. In another motion he kicked his shoes, jeans, and socks from his legs and feet. In the next he had Kate in his arms and was lifting her from the ground and onto the chaise. The small pillow fit perfectly against her back as she laid down on the piece, her head resting against the arm, her legs twining with his own. She stared up at him with eyes narrowed in lust, and Damian didn't look away once as he prowled overtop her, pressing his semi-hard dick between her clothed legs, rubbing along the seed he had spilled. He braced one hand on the back of the tufted chaise behind her head and the other against the soft material of the base as he lowered his lips to hover just above her own.

"My turn," he whispered, before capturing her lips in a decadently searing kiss.

Kate moaned into his mouth, grabbing onto his upper arms. Damian moved the hand from the back of the chaise to the waistband of her leather pants, slipping beneath the material. He found her wearing what he imagined were the matching pair of underwear to her bra, and he growled into her mouth as he glided his hand fully over her mound. Kate pressed herself into him, making him more than aware that she was soaking wet. He pushed the heel of his hand to the top of her mound and she moaned again, gripping his arms tighter than before.

"Damian," she gasped, breaking their kiss briefly. "Please..."

Damian didn't have to be asked; he already knew what he

was going to do. He retracted his hand from outside of her underwear to within, cupping her forcefully. He pulled his hand back up and then let his middle finger slide along her slit, delving past the outer folds to seek the heat within. Kate cried out, her fingers again leaving welts, and Damian seized the sound with his insatiable mouth. He couldn't get enough of her sounds, her touch, her lips. He'd spent too much time dreaming about them, wondering how they would taste, when all he had to do was just take…

Take her. Taste her.

Damian kissed her harder, slanting his lips over her own as he pushed a finger into her core. Kate whimpered, swiveling her hips from side to side. She pushed up and then pulled back, gasping as his thumb pressed against her clitoris. He began to flick it gently, swirling the pad of his thumb through her own molten heat. She writhed against the finger he had within her, kissing him back as fiercely as he kissed her, and in the next heartbeat Damian introduced another within. He retracted them in and out, in and out, working through her yearning to satiate her.

Kate ripped away from his kiss, turning her head to face the chaise though her eyes were closed. "Please…"

Damian looked down at her, abruptly trapped by the sensual flush that climbed her chest to her throat. He continued his ministrations with his hand, though he gradually slowed, enraptured by the bounding pulse just below her chin.

Yours.

Take.

He thought it was her voice that called to him. He *wanted* it to be her voice that urged him. He thought he felt in the seat of her soul that she begged him to *take*…

Kate's head thrashed to the other side, revealing a long column of beautiful, alabaster skin. Her pulse fluttered wildly, almost in tune to her subtle whimpering, to the way her flesh throbbed around his greedy fingers now relentlessly pounding into her. Damian's focus narrowed on the flutter, and he felt his fangs ache as they sharpened within his mouth.

Yours.

Take.

He struck—hard and fast.

Kate gasped on a scream, her release hitting his hand the moment he took his first pull of her blood into his mouth. She shoved her mouth into the pillow as she screamed again, pushing down on his hand as she twisted her hips for more friction, more pleasure. Her hands flew from his arms to the back of his head and neck, holding him to her as he drank in the sweetness, the enticement of her blood. Like the finest wine he was instantly drunk on her, consequently needing more. The swelling sense of sweet drowning within him surged, encasing her as well, pulling them to a place they couldn't retreat from.

Creator but she was divine. Complete and utter bliss. Her blood hit his stomach and subsequently altered him beyond his own comprehension. He'd never tasted something so fine, so luscious, so smooth, so heady. Something that made him avidly, without question, whole.

I am whole.

I am her.

She is me.

Us. Together.

Kate's hands fell from his head and neck, and with one last draw of her blood—*can't take too much*—Damian pulled back to look down at her. He had to blink past the stars in his eyes, through the scarlet haze that surrounded her melted form, and only when her eyes met his own did he smile, his lips coated red.

Kate seemed dazed. Damian reached down to her, moving a wisp of hair from her forehead, and Kate blinked slowly up at him, her eyes focusing on his lips. Damian cleared his throat to say something—what, he didn't know—but Kate's eyes suddenly flew open wide as she abruptly sat up, pushing him away. He fell to the chaise beside her, watching as her already pale skin sickened to a sallow hue, the brilliance of her blue eyes fading as she stared at her blood on his lips. With a hand that quivered she drew her fingers to her throat and when she pulled them away, she looked down at the appendages in pure horror.

She sprang from the chaise in the next moment, staggering over to her forgotten clothes. She scooped up her bra and sweater from the floor, carelessly throwing the latter over her head as she scampered toward the door. Damian watched her, shocked to silence, as she ripped open the entry and passed through, never once looking back.

"What...the fuck..."

Damian gawked at the door as if it would respond. Naked, depleted from the best blowjob of his life, and defeated in the wake of her leaving, he moved his gaze from the shining wood to the matching floor, staring at the space where he had just gotten said blowjob. A door slammed from down the hall, causing him to flinch, and with a keen ear he heard the latch shut tight. He could feel Kate's discord from his space on the chaise, so volatile that it stirred within him a comparable feeling. His eyes trickled from the rug on the floor to the moonlight that sparkled through the windows, the panes reflecting the glow from above.

What the actual fuck.

He couldn't help it; even in his discontent he rolled his tongue in his mouth to savor the last bit of her, closing his eyes as her lavender scent enveloped him as if she still held him in her embrace.

In a flash Damian's eyes flew open, his breath leaving him in a rush.

He looked back toward the windows, but not before his gaze snagged on the desk. The harrier hen, upset from where it had stood for years, glared at him from across the room in sharp revere. Unsettled, his eyes flitted over the grey curtains, picking up on the subtle glimmer some of the strands displayed in the low light of the moon. He saw every thread of the silver tethers that held them open, felt the draft from a slight wind beyond the panes. His eyes easily discerned the constellations from above, Canis Major and Cancer twinkling with white light. From across the room he scanned the bookshelves, reading the titles as easily as if he held them in his open palm. The wood carved by hand had been freshly polished, and if he concentrated hard enough, he could smell the pine scent of the chemical that had been used. He could feel his heartbeat thrumming in his throat, and if he held still enough, he could feel Kate's from down the hall as well.

Creator take me...

He swallowed thickly, this time his mouth as dry as a bone.

There is the truth you seek, his conscience hummed.

Chapter Twenty

Kate made a terrible mistake.

She knew she was in deep. Too deep to turn around now.

Creator. She closed her eyes to her reflection in the bathroom mirror, willing the bite marks on her neck to go away, before slowly reopening them one at a time.

But there they stood in all their glory: two bright, crimson puncture marks in an unmistakable location, no smaller than the day they'd been created, which was now two days past.

The night of the campaign's departure had come, and with it the sullen realization that Kate had a very sparse amount of turtleneck sweaters in which to hide the glaring reminder of what she let happen. As Asha liked to accuse, her closet bordered on "classy hooker", which was not serving Kate in her plight to hide her indiscretion from anyone—most importantly her father, who she'd (to his vast confoundment) avoided for the last two days. Thankfully she was able to feign needing "rest in order to recharge for the trip" and Talorc hadn't pushed the matter.

However little rest had been accomplished thanks to memories of her tryst. Kate (barely) successfully distracted herself by online ordering massive amounts of gear for their trip to the tundra and spending countless hours mapping and researching the area in which they were to be. Interspersed with some light yoga, meal gouging, and blood drinking, her time was well spent. Yet on the second day she remained locked in her room Asha came knocking to check on her, and her reaction to Kate's transgression had Kate wincing even now.

A trio of knocks startled Kate from her reverie.

"Kate?"

Kate's stomach twisted before dropping through the floor. She was perched in her window seat overlooking the grounds of the manor, lost in too many chaotic thoughts.

"Kate are you awake? Are you okay?"

Not ready to face anyone, let alone one of the females that knew her best, Kate said, "Go away Asha, I'm fine."

"I brought you breakfast. You didn't eat much yesterday. You need to if you're really going to leave with the rest of them. You'll need all the strength you can get. It's a five-hour flight and you've never flown before, so you don't know what to expect."

Kate simmered from across the room, glowering a pair of daggers through the wood. "I'll get something in a little," she lied.

"I'm not leaving until you open the door," Asha called, her light, melodious voice sharper than usual. "And I'm sitting with you while you eat."

Creator take me, *Kate thought, jumping up from her seat and hurrying into her closet. She began to push through her clothes, looking for something to cover her neck. But her turtlenecks were few and her outerwear was downstairs.*

"Kate, open the door." Asha knocked again.

"Hold on!" Kate snapped, her heart leaping into her throat. She threw all manner of clothes on the floor looking for something to hide the marks on her neck and when she couldn't find anything hanging, she moved to her accessory cabinet. Instantly she spied a yellow and blue polka dot handkerchief, one she used in her hair as a headband. It was small, too small to fully cover the marks and would look out of place with her current outfit of an olive-green shirt and black leggings, but it was all she had.

"If you don't open this door I'll get your father."

Kate swallowed a curse as she tossed the idea of changing her outfit. Feeling stupid and knowing she looked such, Kate tied the handkerchief around her neck, refused to look in the mirror, and went to open the door.

Her cousin stood on the other side, a tall wisp of a female, as thin as a willow branch. Her long, golden hair swept down her back in waves that Kate once longed for, and for a moment Kate was taken back to the days when the two had tied their hair in different braids and tried on dresses that were too big. Though she resembled her father mostly with her gentle and merry features, Asha's brown eyes were her mother's, and just as perceptive. She raked Kate from head to toe before her eyes flashed back up to her neck, ending Kate's whimsical recollection.

"What's that scarf on your neck? It's hideous." Her tone suspicious, Asha's eyes narrowed on the accessory.

Kate brought a hand up to adjust it, a flush starting just above her breast. "It's cold."

"So start a fire."

Kate glared, reaching for the tray of food Asha brought, to which her cousin retracted. "What are you hiding?"

"Nothing."

"You're lying."

Kate's eyes widened in a dull fashion, reminding Asha she'd also lied, and Asha returned the look with one of sheepish spite. They'd had their own reckoning over the last week, and though resentment lingered under Kate's skin, she'd forgiven Asha for her omission. Kate, in turn, had shared her own revelation, one that wasn't so much a surprise to Asha as anticipated.

"Just let me come in with the food." Asha took a step forward, leading with the tray.

"I'll take it," Kate said. Asha pulled the tray away again, staring pointedly at Kate's handkerchief. Kate huffed, moving a hand to adjust it once more, and consequently condemned herself into an inadvertent confession.

Asha's eyes widened and her jaw fell open, the tray of food in her hands slipping dangerously toward the ground. "What is that!"

Kate grabbed the tray before it clattered against the wood floor at the same time she wrapped a hand around Asha's wrist and dragged her over the threshold. "Shh! Will you shut up?" she hissed, slamming the door behind her.

"Don't tell me to shut up!" Asha nearly yelled, placing the tray on a nearby table and whirling to face Kate with an accusatory stare as Kate tried desperately to fluff the handkerchief. "What is that?"

"What does it look like?" Kate asked flatly, glaring at her in both embarrassment and irritation.

"Who bit you?" Asha gasped, and Kate swore dust fell from

the ceiling as her voice carried.

Kate shushed her once more. "Stop yelling! I'll tell you just...stop yelling." She plopped down on her couch, crossing her legs as she looked past Asha, the flush unfurling up from her chest to her neck as she ripped the handkerchief from her throat. Cornered and annoyed, she raised her eyebrows. "Well? Sit down. I'm not shouting it to you."

Asha hurried to the couch, closing her mouth as she went but unable to shed the look of shock on her features. She sat on the other end and stared at the bite mark until Kate squirmed in her own skin.

"It was Damian."

Asha drew in a breath and Kate was sure she would have shrieked if Kate didn't hush her once more.

"Stop! Don't say anything." Kate looked at the door as if someone were listening.

"Damian? Damian bit you?"

"Yes Asha. Creator, yes."

"What happened?"

The blush turned into a full bloom of scarlet as Kate cleared her throat but didn't answer.

Asha's eyes widened once more and she inhaled deeply before whispering, "You didn't."

Kate's eyes flicked to her, then away.

"You did."

"Not all the way," Kate said quickly, though why it mattered she didn't know. What Kate did with herself was her business, though the two did share almost everything with one another. They'd grown up together, only a few years separating their ages, Asha the elder. The female was no prude either, had run through her fair share of males while Kate lived vicariously through her, wondering what it would be like.

Not like that night, *she thought, the crimson flush hot on her face.* Definitely not like that. That night was...better than I could've ever imagined.

Both females knew Asha would be the first to know if Kate shared herself with another, as best friends did. She knew all of Kate's deepest secrets, and Kate hers. What Kate wouldn't admit to her, however, was that she didn't have a clue about what to do with a dick of her own. With Damian she'd just...run with it. Did what felt natural. What she wanted. *And Creator take her, but she felt more alive than she ever had in her entire life. Not only had it been enlightening and empowering but liberating as well.*

"I didn't mean for it to happen," Kate muttered, tucking a foot underneath her bottom as she turned toward the discarded tray and snagged the coffee that waited.

Asha was breathless, smiling. "So he knows then. You told him."

Kate didn't answer, sipping her coffee and looking toward the slumbering hearth.

"He knows, right?" Asha pushed, leaning toward Kate. Her slender hands gripped her white apron tightly, her khakis contrasted against the ivory.

Eyes dipping from the hearth to Asha and then back again, Kate replied, "I left pretty quickly. We...we didn't talk. After."

Asha lifted a hand to her mouth, covering her astonishment. "No. Kate you didn't. Have you talked to him since?"

He hasn't come for me, *Kate though dejectedly.* After everything he claimed and promised...

"No."

But there was little avoidance to be had now. The Guard would be arriving at the manor within the hour, Taryn, Lilith, and Fiona too. Ryder had spent the day here to go over everything with Talorc a final time, and the night before a convoy of SUVs had been driven in so the servants could begin packing their resources. And if she wanted to be a part of things like she had so adamantly pushed for, Kate knew she couldn't evade anyone any longer. Not Mora. Not The Guard. Not Damian. And certainly not her father. *Creator, I'm about to be within less than five feet of him for the next twelve hours. How am I going to hide this?* Kate groaned, dropping her head to look at the sink.

The strident determination in which she pushed for her plan to come to fruition cowered behind the fact that she let Damian bite her. Hadn't even tried to stop it a little bit.

Losing it over a dick. Kate picked her head up to stare at herself begrudgingly in the mirror of her bathroom. *I've come too far to lose it over* one dick.

It was a good dick though. She sighed as she arranged her pixie-cut hair to swoop to one side. Asha had trimmed it yesterday so it grew neatly, and paired with the dark jeans and skintight black top she wore, she looked kind of badass. She'd made Asha bring her winter clothes upstairs, and on her bed was a knee-length parka, scarf, hat, and gloves, all in black. *Hopefully that'll cover up any lingering scent of Damian on me.* Asha had also leant Kate all the turtlenecks she could spare (Kate may or may not have threatened her, hissing, "You owe me, *cousin*"), but between the two of them, the females apparently liked to reveal more than cover and the number only amounted to a measly four.

Maybe the bite will heal by the time we get to Winnipeg, Kate thought. *I just have to keep eating. Keep drinking.*

She faltered, her hands dropping from her head. *Drinking... Drinking of Damian...*

The better part of the night after their coupling Kate had laid in bed, staring at the ceiling, grinning ear to ear and replaying it second by second in satiated wonder. She'd vacillated between joy and shamefaced stupidity—*potentially enrage Father, sacrifice everything I've worked for, jeopardize the entire mission*—but Creator, she was *happy.* And selfishly, she didn't want to spoil the feeling she'd chased for so long. She felt *alive,* invigorated, for the first time in weeks. Months. Bolstered on his blood—his temperate, intoxicating, heady blood—she felt like she could do anything.

She closed her eyes as heat arose within her, the fire that would always burn when she thought of him. Which was often. *There really is no going back.* She was just... She had other things to do first. For herself. Damian and his promises would have to wait. Even though the notion was hard to dissuade when everything she had ever hoped for had matured.

Well, almost. Everything except...a future. That she couldn't have. Not now, anyway. She couldn't be clouded and distracted now. *Things to do. A Santiago to kill.*

Yet her badass façade would fall flat if her father put two and two together...two and two being her and Damian's matching bite marks. She would damn herself to another round of torture before she derailed how far her father had come. *Maybe he'll be too preoccupied. Maybe he won't notice. Maybe, if he does, he won't care.* In all her wildest fantasies, she'd never gotten as far as to think about the repercussions of a comingling with Damian.

Yet here we are. She stood up straight and reoriented herself with determination. *I'll just have to avoid Damian. Stay as far away as possible. Busy myself doing everything else. Ride in separate cars. Find the opposite of what he's doing and immerse myself in that.*

I can do that. She applied balm to her lips, smeared it into place, and pocketed the tube. *All I have to do is act and think like him.*

Or, at least, how he used to think... She huffed out a grunt, refusing to speculate on anything he said to be true.

Resolute, Kate nodded once and left her bathroom. The bag she packed had already been taken down to one of the SUVs by Mora, who suspiciously said few words and lingered little in the time she'd been to Kate's room. Casting her uneasiness and the hindrance it brought her away, Kate grabbed her outerwear, shoving her gloves and scarf into a deep pocket of her parka. Without a look back she left her room, stowing her cellphone on her person as she went.

Preoccupied by her churning thoughts still simmering with aggravation, Kate took to the faintly lit hall. She passed by vacant doors and watchful paintings, vaguely aware of her surroundings. She could sense her father in his room on the second floor sequestered in the far wing of the house, as Mora and the other servants busied about downstairs. She chewed on her lower lip as she heard Ryder enter the foyer, Taryn at his side, knowing the time was swiftly approaching in which she would have to face every last one of them. *I can do this,* she encouraged herself. *I'm an adult. I'm allowed to be myself. I don't owe anyone an explanation for anything. I've never been afraid of anything in my life and I'm not going to start now.*

In an effort to reorient herself, Kate patted her jacket, making sure her cell phone and—

Damian rounded the corner of the hall, storming toward her with all the force of hurricane. Startled, Kate faltered, her mouth falling open and her eyes rounding. She found she couldn't say a word, could only retreat, as he pushed himself into her space, a snarling vision of fury.

"You owe me an explanation."

"For what!" Kate cried, tripping over the runner as she backed away from him. She glanced over her shoulder, noting the door to her room was too far away.

Damian's harsh tone snapped her focus back to him. "For *everything*."

He changed direction and backed Kate into a door. Kate skimmed her right, her left, looking for an out, but for the life of her she couldn't recall what lay beyond the panels at her back.

Anything is better than him! She reached behind her for the doorknob, twisted it, and stumbled back over the threshold with every intention of putting space between them and shutting him out. Her plan, however, was thwarted when she realized she was in a closet.

By all that is holy—

Damian pushed her into the small linen closet, slamming the door behind him and blocking her only exit.

"What is wrong with you!" Kate fumbled about in the dark for a light switch. There were shelves on three sides of her, each with bed and bath linen stacked neatly on them, while Damian pressed hotly into her front. There was barely enough room to put three inches between them, and already Kate felt stifled in the close confines. Her parka had been abandoned somewhere in the hallway, and she wished with everything in her she had it now to shield herself from the wrath he was emanating.

"*Me*? You're the one I'm worried about. Aren't your secrets eating you alive?" Damian purred, though his voice held nothing but contempt. He wrapped warm, callused hands around Kate's upper arms and—*Creator spare me*—her body lit up in response to his touch, recalling the climaxes he'd wrung from her just three nights ago. Instantly, she flared in response, her core heating, her mind slowing, focusing on one thing: *Damian*.

"I don't know what you're talking about," Kate bit out with rapidly waning scorn, trying to thrust herself from his grasp.

Damian tightened his hold, pulling her chest flush to his. "*Yes, you do.*"

"No, I don't!" Kate squirmed from side to side, her breath coming out erratically, quickly. "Get off me Damian. Let me out of this closet."

"No."

"*Now.*"

"Not until you pay your due," Damian murmured, his breath fanning her cheek as he dipped his head to hover just beside her ear. "Tell me: how could you move on when those skeletons have their fingers so deeply in your flesh?"

Stomach rolling, thoughts crashing, heart pounding, Kate's mouth fell open, but no words came out.

"Angry little things, with bones as sharp as knives." Damian pressed his lips to the outer shell of her ear. "*How dare they hold you back.*

"I'm giving you one last chance." Damian's voice dropped to a dangerous level. "Spill your secrets willingly, or I'll draw them from you as torturously as I made you come. Remember when I did that Kate? Remember when I made you come?" He placed a hand above her on one of the shelves, and Kate leaned as far away from him as she could as he pressed into her. The other hand he dropped to her hip, squeezing her sensuously, slowly. "I can remind you if you'd like."

Kate closed her eyes, her heightened senses reeling. She could make out every detail of his face in her mind, feel every pulse of coolness he emanated. He was gorgeous, even as ireful as he was; truth be told, she loved his anger as much as she craved his laughter, his smile.

In more ways than one—than you want to admit—he's right, her conscience whispered to her. *You're angry because of what you've been through, and that's okay, but also because you know he's right and you're not willing to accept it yet. And your anger is holding you back.*

She could feel his copper eyes undressing her as he raked her from head to toe, locking on the spot where he'd sunk his fangs into her throat. His dark, curling hair framed his face and his body was hard, unrelenting as he accosted her with his presence. His seaward scent was overwhelming, but she inhaled it readily. Her mouth watered at the memory of his blood in her mouth, and she rolled her tongue as if she could taste it again. Her fangs ached as shamelessly as her core as she fisted her hands at her sides in an effort not to touch him.

But you need to move on, her conscience continued. *If you want to be a working part on the wheel that turns this situation, you need to focus your anger* there. *Not on Damian. It's misguided and ill-managed, doing nothing but causing you undue strife. He's only ever wanted to help—in his own, convoluted way. You know it, you've seen it, you've lived it. If you continue to direct your anger toward him, you'll do nothing but burn, just like he said. That fire within you will incinerate everything you have and want to accomplish.*

She clamped her teeth together hard, her jaw pinching, opening her eyes to glare up at Damian through the darkness.

No. I won't. It won't, she countered, but her conscience laughed low.

He told you exactly what you needed to hear: "Let me go with you". Why are you still digging your heels into the ground? He knows the truth of you both now. You know there's no going back.

She closed her eyes again, pressing her back against the shelving so hard the wood bit into her bones. Damian took the hand from above her and grabbed her chin, forcing her face to his.

I can't. I won't. I'm not...I'm not ready. I have things I need to do. Things I need to accomplish before...before...

Before you let him in? That's all you've ever wanted: to let him in.

It's different now, Kate thought. I'm *different now. I have other prerogatives.*

Kate swallowed, but the knot in her throat wouldn't dislodge. Damian's hand squeezed her hip again, the other tightening on her chin. "Look at me," he ordered of her, and his voice sent fire licking down each vertebra of her spine. Her pulse skyrocketed, sending her head spinning, making her world tilt as desire spread through her like wildfire.

Just crack the door, her conscience murmured. *What more is there to lose?*

Swept by heat, lust threatening to evade her reasoning, Kate's breath froze in her lungs, her fists uncurling. *Nothing.* In a flash her eyes opened, riveted to the fading mark she'd left on his throat.

I've already broken the barrier between us. I know there is no going back—

No, she thought, her thoughts pivoting as she began to

breathe irregularly, the warring within her mind too tumultuous to tame. *I'm too close to the end of all this. I need to see Santiago's end first. Close that chapter of my life.* Heal *from that chapter of my life.*

Her eyes flicked from one of his to the other before settling on his lips. She licked her own, and in response his parted subtly to reveal ivory fangs. His breath fanned her face, simultaneously cooling her heated skin while evoking within her insatiable need.

Fuck it.

It was with wild abandon glowing in her cobalt eyes that she met his own and said, "Take me."

His ragged breath stilled, his chest swelling and trembling. "What did you say." His voice fell like stone, an avalanche rumbling within.

"Stop talking and take me."

They stared at each other a moment more, not breathing, their thoughts colliding. Cool water and searing fire intertwining with one another to make the most perfect coalescence.

And then they were tearing at each other. In a flurry of movements hindered by their close confines, Damian lifted his shirt over his head as Kate began unbuttoning her jeans. She shimmied them to the floor, kicking off her boots as she went before Damian's hands found her face. He pulled her up to him for a kiss that had her head spinning, her feet stumbling, and she placed her hands on his bare chest to steady herself. The muscles beneath her fingers jumped at the contact, and Damian moaned into her mouth as Kate's hands slid down his torso to his jeans.

Damian thrust Kate backward, into the shelving of the closet, the wood whining at the contact. Kate didn't hear it, didn't feel the pain of it, as she drowned in Damian's seaward scent and the crashing waves of his emotions. Most potently was a desire that matched her own, spurring her frantic movements to see him unclothed and at her mercy.

Their mouths tangled in a rough and fevered kiss, his facial hair scraping roughly against her tender skin. Damian bent at the waist to slide his jeans down his legs, Kate bending with him as she was desperate not to lose contact with his mouth. Her hands helped push his pants away, pulling them until they got stuck on his boots. Kate gripped his shoulders and pushed her mouth harder to his, turning with his body until he finally discarded his clothing. Damian, naked and thrumming, pushed into her once more, his body fitting her every crevice, kissing her like the world around them didn't matter and the only thing that existed—would ever exist—was them.

As Kate's hands twisted in his hair she lapped at his lips, craving the lust he exuded, and his hands fell to her waist. He bunched the material of her lacy thong in his hands and ripped the material from her, casting it to the floor. His hands then swept up from her hips to her waist, taking her shirt over her head and throwing it down with the other pieces of clothing they precariously stumbled in. Her cry of protest once again obscured by his harsh mouth, Damian ripped Kate's bra from her chest and pressed himself into her before his hands flew to her thighs, lifting her from the ground. Kate eagerly raised her legs and wrapped them around his waist, her arms sliding around his neck as she kissed him with every suppressed, lascivious thought she ever had. She felt him release one of her thighs to grasp his cock beneath her, and she pulled her hips back to align with the head of him, suddenly realizing that she was dripping wet in anticipation of what was to come.

Damian rubbed the head of his dick along the slit of her pussy, causing Kate to throw back her head and moan. She didn't care about anything save this very moment. Nothing else mattered. Not her capture. Not her torture. Not their journey. Not Santiago. Her life was culminating in a rush—but she needed *more*.

She would always need more when it came to Damian.

She arched her chest into him before opening her eyes to cast him a look that reiterated her last spoken words. He was watching her with dangerous intent, and Kate saw and felt the restraint he used to torment her wane treacherously close to breaking.

"No going back," he said, his voice like thunder, indicative of the storm to follow.

And then he was in her.

Kate cried out, the tightness of her pussy instantly contracting around Damian's thick cock. She felt a pinch at the corners of her eyes as she closed them harshly, pain singeing a deep part of her she'd never felt before. Her fingers dug into his shoulders, sure to leave marks, and she hissed softly through her teeth as Damian paused, his breath coming out in heavy pants.

His voice was nothing short of a growl. "Are you okay?"

Kate roved her hips gently, allowing her body to adjust to the newness. She took a deep breath in and opened her eyes, her very soul on fire as she met his gaze. It was with a passion, a longing that had burned for years that she murmured, "Don't go easy on me."

Damian's eyes flared and his hands found her hips to help steady her on him. His tone was guttural as he replied, "I wasn't planning on it."

He pulled back his hips and surged forward. Kate tossed her head back again, striking it on a shelf, but unable to feel anything but pleasure. Damian moved his hips again, stroking places Kate didn't even know existed, starting a slow rhythm that had the pain she fleetingly felt receding. She could only clutch onto him for dear life to curtail her moans from suspicious attentions, but the feelings inside of her wanted *out*. She tipped her head down to look at him once more, and as her body burned with flame, she took his lips.

Damian quickened within her, thrusting her into the shelving, causing it to knock a little too knowingly if ears were to pry. Kate tried to move her hips to meet his rhythm and found that if she gripped the shelf above and behind her she could counter his moves to make a very satisfying groan fall from his mouth. Said mouth fell from her lips to the length of her throat, and Kate tipped her head to the side to reveal the marks he'd left to claim her. Doing so had him scraping the flesh with his fangs, as if he could hardly resist penetrating her again.

A swirl of her hips had his own head tossed, and his movements became frantic. A towel fell from above and Kate laughed, tossing it to the floor before a sigh overtook her humor. She urged Damian with little mewls, small words of encouragement, her body singing with pleasure. He grunted, driving her so hard into the shelving that she knew she would have new scrapes and bruises. She didn't care. She didn't even notice. She was floating in a euphoria only the two would ever be able to create, a yellow haze so bright that it stoked them with hedonistic joy.

That joy was suddenly overwhelmed by a surge of fire that

caused her core to pulse. Damian cursed in response, shoving himself harder, faster, into her, so much so that she felt the slap of his balls against her ass. Kate dropped her hands to his hair, curling her fingers within the strands, suddenly needing to hold onto him for dear life as ecstasy arced from a place inside of her that had never been woken. Her mewls turned to moans, her breaths to gasps, as Damian's thrusts turned from fast to purposeful, each heavier and more targeted than the last. A tingling began where his cock met her pussy, licking along her insides to reach that part of her which stretched, yearning to be released.

"Damian…" she whispered, her voice catching on a long groan.

"Say. It. Again," he commanded, pounding into her with each word.

"Damian," she breathlessly obeyed, her fingers drawing blood as they latched onto his shoulders.

"Again," he demanded, pushing into her so hard a sting of pain accompanied it.

Kate cried out, pulling herself up against him with her arms wrapped around his neck. The stretching within her spread, opening up a part of herself which had never been touched. She fell into the new sensation, swirling, suffocating, spiraling into a world of sensuality she'd never known.

"*Again*," Damian snarled, thrusting harder.

"Damian!" Kate cried, and she exploded with an orgasm that had her seeing stars even behind her closed lids.

At the exact instant she released Damian came within her. He caught her lips in a kiss to hide his own shout of relief, hot heat striking her in frantic pumps. He didn't slow his plunging cock, instead picked up the speed, driving Kate to gasp into his mouth over and over as she pushed herself into him, onto him, with everything she had.

It took a full minute, but Damian finally slowed. The kiss turned languid, sensuous, a slow lapping of their tongues as the other parts of their bodies stilled. Kate released her grip sluggishly, though not entirely, as Damian sagged into her, his body trembling. They broke apart on a rush of breath, sweat covering them both, Kate's own quivering legs unable to stay wrapped around his hips. Gently, Damian lowered her to the ground, his dick sliding out of her with slick heat that made them both shiver. His hands never once left her body as they traveled from her waist to her chest, her chest to her shoulders, her shoulders to her neck, before taking her face between them. He peered down at her, entire body flushed scarlet, lips parted in awe. Feeling the same, Kate could only stare back, her own hands flat against his chest.

Until Damian said, "You know we are beloveds."

Chapter Twenty-One

He felt Kate freeze, her breath halting on a sharp intake of breath.

"You *knew* we were beloveds," Damian accused, his chest constricting as his words bit with venom. His hands tightened on her face as he looked down at her, the pleasure he felt within warring dangerously with his wrath. Creator take him, but he wanted to kiss her again, fuck her again; it was all he could think about. His rage corralled him, coercing him to remember the deceit she'd cast over him…though the decadence she'd just shared with him cried to be merciful. To not fuck things up worse than they already were.

But Damian felt volatile. "From the moment you took my blood in the cabin in New York, you knew. And you've been harboring that information for weeks. *Weeks*. And I want to know why."

Kate didn't answer, and her eyes widened as her mouth parted.

Damian smelled it then: hollowing, sinking fear that pushed at his newly heightened senses with a cedar undertone. The last two days had him struggling with this intensely new identity, and he'd spent the majority of the time in his apartment, reeling with everything it meant for the future. It was only after a long drive through the winding city the night before that he found clarity: he was a beloved male with a beloved female he could no longer deny.

The truth was in the fact that he could see for miles, his eyes sharper than they'd ever been. He smelled wraiths as easily as if they stood next to him. He felt every twist of leather beneath his hand as he drove, every strand of fiber from his shirt as it rubbed against him. He tasted the notes of Kate's heady blood as if it still lingered on his tongue, which even now damned him to a lifetime of desire and vicious need. And the bond...that beautiful, effervescent bond between them, seen only by them, had finally, irrevocably tethered them together, allowing him a window into Kate's flayed, broken, and battered soul.

He now understood her in a way he never had before.

The mercy his conscience called for him to employ cried out again in light of everything he learned about her in those days of introspection. The veracity of their situation was mind-numbing, but also explained everything Damian had ever felt and wondered in the deepest, most darkened corners of his soul. *Everything makes sense now.* Through sharing her feelings, he understood her pain, her vacillations, her needs, her desires. Why she wanted to run but also to stay. He understood she barely had footing outside of the pit she'd crawled from, and still now the darkness called to her. He understood she needed compassion, empathy, and caring in a way he, as her male, craved to share with her.

I'm putting her first. Thinking only about her. No—it's always only been about her. But now...now I see it for what it was all along. Our bond. We are beloveds.

The bond had always been there but was now awakened fully because they'd exchanged blood. He'd been a damn fool to try and push her away. Provoked by wild uncertainty—for years—he'd tried to uproot it all, but never again. He would deny her, nor himself, no longer.

After I get my answers. Because while he may have a beloved, he was still a prideful male, and parts of him would always be hot-blooded, defiant, and arrogant.

His enhanced senses allowed him to see the fear that enveloped Kate in a rusted hue, overwhelming the blush that beckoned their shared pleasure. He willed himself to calm a measure, to not scare her further, but his fury felt limitless and unrestrained.

"You're not denying it," he hissed, eyes narrowing. "Now would be the time."

In a flash the fear and passion disappeared, replaced by a bright orange flare of anger. "What's the point if you know the truth?"

Damian snapped his teeth together to keep from answering

her fury with his own. His body still trembled in the aftermath of their lovemaking, and while he didn't want to spoil the euphoric feeling, he couldn't let Kate redact and retreat from this. *She's run away enough.*

"I want to hear you say it."

She glared at him.

"*Say it, Kate.*"

It was with no small amount of ferocity that she said, "It's true. You are my beloved."

Excitement, resentment, thrill, wonderment, apprehension …they all swelled and ebbed, churning like a crashing sea as Damian met Kate's unwavering gaze. Her shoulders held strong, upright, as she dropped her hands from his chest; he immediately felt the withdrawal and grabbed her wrists, forcing her to him once more. Their bodies collided, their feet tangling in their discarded clothing, Kate making a small sound of protest.

"Damian what—"

He captured her mouth in a kiss that had her melting against him. He grabbed her shoulders to hold her to him, so tight he would always remember the way she felt against him at this moment.

Kate ripped away from him a heartbeat later. "Damian—"

"You thought I was persistent before? In my denial of you?" Damian uttered boldly. "You'll know my pursuit now, which is actively and eagerly more potent than that."

As if she didn't hear him, Kate only stared at his lips.

"I'm not going anywhere," he echoed his earlier statement, though now instead of dumbfounded he was determinedly resolute. "I still don't care how long it takes for you to yield to me. *You will.* Make no mistake."

Kate's eyes flipped to his own. "Why," she whispered, then cleared her throat. "For so long you denied me—"

"Never again," Damian warned, both himself and her. "I was callous, stupid, heartless. I won't be again. For a while I suspected that we were beloveds and—"

Kate reared back as if struck, her head banging against one of the shelves. "*You suspected?*" she asked incredulously.

Damian wavered, his words falling short.

"You thought I was your beloved, but you *rejected me?*" Her heated voice rose, and then fell dramatically to utter a hushed,

"How could you be so cruel?"

Damian suddenly didn't know what to say, his own anger receding.

"You kept that from me, selfishly holding back the happiness we could've had." Kate pushed him back, but in the small limitations of the closet he didn't go far. She shoved at his chest again, forceful in both tone and touch. "*You pursued other females* while actively believing that I was your beloved? *How could you?*

"You dislike me so much to reject me?" Kate whispered, her eyes turning glassy, though the fire with which she spoke didn't dim. "You would rather lead a life of emptiness than be with me?"

"I was scared, Kate." Damian admitted, finally revealing the core of the truth. "I was scared of how it would shape my future, how my relationship with Talorc would change, how my position in The Guard would change, how my life would change..." he trailed off, eyes creasing with choking pain. "I was scared of *you.* Of being overtaken, completely and utterly, by you. Except it's too late. As soon as I met you it was too late. You took over my entire life with just a tilt of your lips. I just...I didn't know how to accept it. I thought I was going to lose myself, when in reality if I'd just...done *anything* different, I would've realized a lot sooner that I would've *gained* so much more than what I feared losing."

Kate snarled like a caged lion. "The Creator can take your hypocritical self-righteousness and shove it up your ass! You stand there and dare accuse me of hiding the truth? When you suspected all along? For how long, Damian? Huh? How long?"

"At least I didn't *know.* And continue to pretend I didn't. How dare *you* stand there and pretend you never even thought once about it before actually knowing."

"What did you expect me to do?" Kate tossed her hands up between them. "I threw myself at you constantly only to be shut down. For so long you denied and rejected me. *Fucked other females.* I thought you had completely cast me aside. Did you expect me to confess my feelings for you and risk being rejected? Come on, Damian."

"There was no one else," Damian confessed, his voice firm in its accuracy. "It's been that way for a while."

"Bull. Sh—"

"I mean it," he cut her off harshly. "I can't stand to be around other females, other women, for more than an hour. They make my skin crawl. I get restless, bored; I'm always wondering what you're doing and thinking. I constantly count the seconds until I can come back to you. They don't smile like you, laugh like you, tease me like you. They aren't *you*."

"How do you drink then?" Kate said pointedly, as if catching him on a lie.

"Banks. I go as long as I can between feedings."

Kate sputtered, "Well it's too late—"

"Don't say that," he cut her off again, nostrils flaring, chest tightening to the point of pain. "It's not. And you know it. We've both wronged. You in your untruth and me in my mistrustfulness. But now we can make it right. Let's make it right, Kate."

It was with powerful conviction that he said, "I *need* you in my life. I know that I haven't shown it. I've been a total ass. I've hurt you in ways that I don't know if we can come back from, did and said things that will scar you. But if you just let me tend to the scars, Kate…the ones I made, and the ones Santiago made, and the ones your father made, and everyone else who ever wronged you…I'll do it. I'll happily spend the rest of my life lifting those scars. Because nothing…nothing else matters. Just you. Only you. Since I've met you it's only ever been *you*."

Kate didn't speak; he knew she couldn't. If she felt anything like he did, he knew it pained her to even breathe.

"I will change your mind. I won't stop until I do. I'm not leaving you, Kate. I don't care what anyone says or does or thinks. Nothing will stop me from changing your mind." He took her in his arms again and she weakly resisted until he continued, his tone softening, "Every minute we've ever spent together is my favorite; the next surpasses the last. Even these ones. And I want to make more of them with you. I want to make every memory we can together going forward. I know it's a lot. This—*us*—is a lot. I'll be here until you figure it all out. In the meantime, I'll grovel at your feet to hope to atone for the years I've spent damning us both."

Kate's glassy eyes shifted between his two, and her own nostrils flared. The salty sting of tears bit his nose, but Damian knew Kate was too proud to cry. However, he couldn't bring himself to read her emotions, too raw in his own need to understand himself.

Her voice wavered as she said, "I deserve so much more than that, Damian."

"I know," he whispered desperately, clutching her upper arms tightly. "Let me show you that I understand now. Please. Give me the chance."

Silence fell between them, the only sound their galloping hearts and unsteady breaths. Veiling her face in a look of both wariness and insecurity, Kate asked, "How do you expect me to give you a chance when I've barely learned to accept myself, to give this new part of me a chance? You want me to open myself to who I am now—to move on—*and* you? You ask too much."

"I'll wait. For as long as it takes, I'll wait," Damian said, his grip contracting. "I *want* to go with you on this journey."

"Do you?" Kate challenged, her voice sharpening. "I can learn to accept myself for who I am. I know where I need to go and what I need to accomplish to see myself whole. Can *you* see that? Through my eyes, with my ears, by my touch, do you know what I need? Until you are willing to accept and appreciate all facets of me," She pushed back from him and gathered her clothing, pulling on first her shirt and then shimmying into her jeans. "The old, the new, the broken, and the confident…"

"Don't place a hold on this." Damian watched as she bent to pick up her ruined bra and underwear. "There's no ultimatum. Fate has destined this, Kate. The watchers, the Creator, the very universe itself…"

Kate brushed past him, clutching her belongings to her body. She paused by the door to the closet, slightly turned away from him as she looked over her shoulder from under a shroud of uncertainty.

"Then show me. Make me believe it, too."

She disappeared into the hall, shutting the door softly behind her. It wasn't until Damian heard the gentle closing of her bedroom door that he snapped out of the stagnation of his thoughts while sentiments he'd never felt before threatened to drown him.

She's right, Damian thought, stooping to gather his own clothing. *She's not the naïve, innocent female I've known for years. She is changed, different—but not in a way that's unworthy. It is I who am unworthy.*

He pulled on his shirt. *I'll show her my worth. I'll show her…her worth. If I want to make her believe that I am fit to walk alongside her, I have to realize that sheltering her, coddling her, restraining her is not what she needs. She no longer needs protection; she needs support, guidance.*

He winced slightly as he tucked his throbbing member back into his pants before pulling on his socks and shoes. *I'll show her that I'm not against her. She needs it. She deserves it.*

Damian left the closet then, resolved in his thoughts. He glanced down the hall to Kate's bedroom door, sensing her brazen heat from within. As any beloved male would be, he was drawn to her, even took a step in that direction before he stopped. He inhaled deeply to steady himself but instead took in a lungful of her scent—*lavender.* Her frenzied whimpers from minutes before echoed in his ears and he felt himself grow hard again, painfully quick and severe. Realizing he couldn't look Talorc in the face with an erection brought on by the memory of his daughter's illicit moans, Damian determined a cold shower should set him to rights, as well as wash her scent from his person.

Beyond those thoughts, he knew a reckoning the likes of which he hadn't seen before was on the horizon.

Well that went as poorly as I imagined, Kate thought, feeling as though she hadn't slept in a thousand years while thrumming with an anxiousness brought on by the knowledge that she was preparing to save the vampire nation. The argument with Damian, though a long time coming, had drained her. She felt as though she could drink ten cups of blood and still not be sated. She felt agitated. Hollow. Eager. Animated. Frightened. The list went on, would never end, and over the last hour Kate couldn't arrange her thoughts into purposeful reasoning for the life of her. *But I have to focus. We're leaving for Winnipeg. This could be the faceoff with Santiago that I've been craving. I can't let Damian get in the way.*

Yet he was all she thought about, which she realized dismally was nothing new. And while the truth was out now, the weight of it lifted from her, what harkened in its absence was just as significant. *He's asking for a future together.* Kate huffed, checking the time on her cell phone as she paced her bedroom. 20:58. They were slated to leave in two minutes for the airport, but Kate couldn't bring herself to leave the comfort of her room. Because she couldn't bear facing *anything,* let alone a future with Damian.

I have to do this. I can *do this,* she thought, staring at the woodgrain on the floor as she paced. *What's done is done. What's passed is passed. I'll figure out the future later.*

A part of her wanted to deny him, though it warred with the guilt that stabbed her for hiding what she'd known. That same part of her wanted to hurt Damian as badly as he'd hurt her, for the years of strife he'd put her through. *What's another one, two, three, years of my life if I live to see the next hundred?*

You may not, her conscience warned, and Kate glowered at her bedframe before lashing out to smack it with an open hand.

Another part of her, the bigger part of her, reminded her that she wouldn't have made it this far *without* him. Everything the beloved bond had brought about since she'd opened it in New York—the auras, the smells, the sounds, the feelings—she reckoned were the only things that kept her alive the month after she came home. They grounded her. Through her despair and her gloom those things grounded her because they were rooted *in him.* She couldn't admit that to herself at the time. It was only marginally easier now.

With his words ringing in her head, she knew he'd already been with her all along. And if what he said about other females was true...

Ugh. What kind of thrill was Fate getting now that *Kate* was the one trying to reject him?

For what purpose am I even doing so? If this is what I've wanted for so long...

Her mind swirling, her heart throbbing, and her body aching, Kate snapped her head toward her door and walked toward it. *I have to think about this later. I can't hold up the group. I have to focus on my revenge and Santiago.* She opened her door, the wood creaking on its hinges. Her body hummed when it recognized the pull Damian had on her even from a distance, but willing herself to be distracted no more, Kate shut the door and began her trek down the hall.

I can do this, Kate thought, taking even, deep breaths as she followed the sounds of her travel party in the foyer. She could hear the deep rumble of Cyrus, the clipped words of Ryder, the easy chatter of Vadin as he exchanged words with Mora and Asha. Talorc was there as well, speaking lowly with Lilith, and as Kate rounded the balustrade above the vestibule, she saw the bright red hair of Fiona standing by the coat closet, in active conversation with Taryn.

With ease and in quickness, Kate's eyes snapped to Damian's form pacing at the foot of the stairs. She stumbled, a slight hesitation when their gazes locked, his tapering to her like a bird of prey. Heated memory seared her, to barely an hour before when she'd been pinned in a closet by a very naked Damian. Her eyes roved him now, from his booted feet to his wet hair, and her mouth dried.

I can do this.

Kate abruptly looked away, turning her eyes to her shoes. She wrapped a steadying hand along the rail, notched her chin back, and took the stairs swiftly, her hiking boots squeaking against the clean stone. She'd showered, changed her clothing, sprayed herself with perfume, and donned her outerwear, all in hopes that her scent would be as masked as well as her bite marks.

I can do this. Just avoid him. Don't make eye contact again.

Her body's humming hit a crescendo. Her breath held, frozen in her lungs. Her skin heated as tingling started in her toes. Her head began to spin, dizzying with the knowledge that *Damian was her beloved.* Creator take her, but it took every ounce of self-control to hold her head high and nonchalantly brush past him after descending the stairs. *Is this how it's going to be? When I'm near him?* Quickly deciding Ryder was the safest bet if she was to remain busy, Kate headed for him, desperately trying to shake off the shock of Damian's proximity.

"Need me for anything?" she asked Ryder as the conversations about the foyer lulled at her entrance, before picking up once more.

He glanced down at Kate. "I think we're almost ready." He

looked back at Cyrus, to whom he'd been speaking, opening his mouth to continue the conversation. Yet just as swiftly he looked back at Kate, his eyes flickering from her own to her neck. They narrowed there, to the neatly tucked scarf and zipped up parka, before moving to her hands which couldn't hold still from where they were jammed in her pockets. He met her eyes once more, nostrils flaring.

Creator save me, Kate hissed at herself. *He's a beloved male. He'll sense the marks, the claim they carry.* Though it was obvious to even males who hadn't been claimed, beloved males were more intuitive and had amplified perception. And Ryder was newly beloved, which meant he would pick up on Kate's new bling even faster.

Kate quickly turned away from him. Her eyes darted around the group: Asha would try not to bring attention to Kate but would actually do the opposite; Vadin didn't know how to keep his mouth shut to save his life; Kate didn't know Taryn nor Fiona well enough to make small talk; her father and Damian were to be avoided at all costs, which meant engaging with Lilith was out of the question…

She headed for Mora, who broke away from Vadin and Asha to capture Kate in her arms. She first grasped her forearms before pulling her into a hug, an embrace so tight Kate knew there was more beneath the surface than a simple farewell.

"I would see you well from this," Mora whispered, her mouth pressed close to Kate's ear. Kate inhaled deeply of her honeysuckle scent, the earthen undertone settling her chaotic feelings and thoughts, before pulling back from Mora and severing the connection.

"From all of it." Mora looked first at Kate before her eyes danced to where Damian stood, still at the foot of the stairs, and back. "Trust in yourself. In what you want. You cannot be guided to misfortune if you do that."

Kate smiled slightly as Vadin announced in the background that he was heading out. He grabbed a duffle and was the first out the door, Damian not far behind. He took his things from the closet and as he closed the door, he looked over his shoulder at Kate, his eyes clouded with too much to understand in the fleeting moment they shared. The auras that surrounded him were a swathing kaleidoscope of colors both natural and unknown, his sentiments too many to identify. Kate broke the contact by turning her attention to Asha, who approached from behind her mother.

"I threw some Aspirin and Meclizine in your bag," she said with a quirk of one side of her lips. "If you get sick on the plane."

Kate chuffed a laugh. "Thanks."

"Got to be prepared, just like a hangover." The reply earned her a stern look from her mother.

"Remember that one time we drank that whole bottle of whipped cream-flavored vodka for New Year's?" Kate asked, and Asha groaned in response as Lilith and Fiona left the foyer, Cyrus not far behind.

"Can we celebrate in a different way when you get back?" Asha asked, and Kate laughed again.

"We'll go to The Tomb," Kate said, referencing the popular goth-themed bar.

Asha waggled her eyebrows. "Barhop all the good places."

Kate reached forward to pull Asha into a tight embrace, inhaling deeply of her morning dew scent. "Start pregaming now."

"Be careful." Asha pulled back to look down at Kate. Her eyes skimmed the scarf at her neck. "I'm sure you'll have plenty of stories when you get back. But still. Be careful."

"*Piseag Bheag.*" Talorc's heavy hand fell to Kate's shoulder from behind, and Kate turned so quickly she caused it to fall. She moved back a full step from her father and if it bothered him, he didn't let it show. "Are you ready?"

Kate's hands gripped her gloves tightly in her pockets, twisting in the fleece-lined leather. "As I'll ever be."

"You have been absent the last two days." Talorc's eyes moved about her face, assessing her features. "Are you sure you want to go through with this?"

Kate arched a brow, the question going unspoken.

"Forgive me," Talorc amended, a slight bow curling his shoulders. "It will be a hard habit to break."

Kate smiled, surprising herself with how easily the gesture came. *Correlate much?*

"I already have, Father," Kate said, speaking of this moment and so many more which had passed. "Just do me a favor and try to keep up. Can't have your old self slowing us down."

Talorc glowered, snapping his own leather gloves in his

hands, his gray wool jacket stretched taut across his broad shoulders. His beard twitched only slightly, a subtle hint that he found joy in her teasing. "I will endeavor for such."

Asha and Mora stepped outside to bid the others farewell, and Kate made to follow after Ryder who was crossing the threshold. She took a few steps before a hand on her arm stopped her, and Kate turned to face her father once more. She swallowed roughly upon the realization it was just the two of them left, the other servants about the house elsewhere, and Noir having left for Winnipeg in the days past. *I can do this,* she reminded herself, though a small part of her hoped against hope that her father hadn't stayed her hand to ask further about her demeanor. *But as a once beloved male, as well as the world's oldest vampire—not to mention my father—I would be stupid to assume he doesn't have at least a clue. The only faith I have is that he can't already suspect, not so soon, not with so much else going on,* she told herself.

"Lend me some understanding." Talorc dropped his hand from her arm, his usually rumbling voice even. "I cannot leave this manor without taking a moment to wish you swiftness and health. While I am more than ready to have you by my side in this, you are still my daughter. I will worry for you. It is my hope that you do not hold that against me."

Her features softened. "I know, *Athair.* I won't."

Talorc took her forearms in his hands, squeezing gently. "I know what you seek through this, and I will help you wherever I can to achieve what you need. Just please...be mindful. Be thoughtful. Be vigilant. These enemies will stop at nothing, and you must be just as vicious."

Her jaw rigid, Kate nodded once. "I understand."

Talorc's brown eyes brightened as he held onto Kate, and then pulled her into a hug. Realization pierced her: It was the first hug they'd shared after everything that happened. *I missed this,* Kate thought as she sank into her father's form, drawing greatly of his wintry scent. She was instantly enveloped in a cool rush of icy wind, which both centered and exhilarated her, while the arctic bite of frost tickled her nose. Finding comfort in the sensations, she nestled her head against his shoulder and closed her eyes, letting herself get lost in memories of a time when things weren't so convoluted or complicated. While Talorc had been a distant father, he was never removed, and they had plenty of happy memories to share. Now, Talorc held her in a way that Kate knew those same memories took hold of him as well, and it was only after several heartbeats they separated.

Talorc held onto Kate loosely as he looked down at her, eyes still bright. "I love you, Kathryn. Do not ever think otherwise. It has always been with love that I act for you."

"I know, Father," Kate whispered, her own eyes shining. "I love you, too."

Talorc smiled, trailing a hand to her chin to chuck before pushing her hair out of her face. His eyes trailed her brows, her eyes, her nose, her cheeks, before trekking back to her eyes. In the next moment his hands fell from her person, and he stepped back, but Kate noticed he didn't turn away, and his eyes had gone from bright to sharp, acutely locked on her face.

"You sure you are well?" Talorc asked, and something chimed within Kate to warn *danger.*

Avoid. Separate. Move. "Yes," she hedged, stepping toward the doors and glancing over her shoulder. "Why do you keep asking?"

Talorc followed her, his tone questioningly pensive. "You seem…tired."

Kate shrugged, feigning indifference as her inner monologue chanted *shoot shoot shoot.* "Stressed, I guess." She pushed open the front door and moved onto the stairs, palms sweating.

"Nothing more?"

"Not a thing," Kate lied, skipping down the stairs.

A line of three large black SUVs circled the front of the manor, their engines warming the cold winter night. Kate hurried toward the first, noted Damian there, and veered to the second. Talorc came up behind her, reaching above her for the door she'd opened, and Kate moved to the side so he could take the seat. *Avoid. Separate.*

"You can take this one," she offered, backing toward the third vehicle. "I'll bring up the rear. Shouldn't have both royals in one car. Yikes. Asking for disaster."

Shut up, her conscience said dully. *You sound like a fool.*

"I would like to speak with you about our plans," Talorc

said, his eyes never leaving her own. Kate's blood swam hot, and she bit down on the inside of her lip to keep herself from squirming. "You have missed out on much these past few days."

"I'll catch up with Vadin," Kate said, snagging said male's jacket. A flash in the night drew her attention, but Damian was quick to hide his disdain, his sharpened fangs, at her thoughtless hold on another male. Kate instantly dropped her hand, clearing her throat. Vadin made a noise that sounded like a choked laugh from beside her while Talorc's eyes narrowed once more. If he had a thought to say anything, he kept it to himself.

"See it done." He disappeared into the middle vehicle, Ryder already at the wheel with Taryn in the passenger's seat. Damian, Cyrus, Lilith, and Fiona took the first, while Kate and Vadin deposited themselves in the last.

"Something on your mind?" Vadin chirped as Kate slammed the door.

"Nope." Kate yanked on her seatbelt, missing the clip twice before finally securing it.

"You *sure*?" Vadin drew out the last word as he grinned like a cheshire cat.

Kate closed her eyes, anchoring her head on the frosted glass of the window. "Just drive, Vadin. Creator, just shut up and drive."

His laugh reverberated throughout the car all the way to the airport.

Chapter Twenty-Two

On their arrival, the campaigners were directed toward the private flights entrance where they met the vampire pilot who would fly them to Winnipeg. The female had a thick Spanish accent and looked no older than thirty but cheekily assured them she'd been flying since planes were invented. She also had experience piloting all over the world, as she hailed from Guatemala and used to work for one of the cartels. Damian shot Cyrus a look of skepticism at the knowledge, wondering idly if this contact could be trusted, and Cyrus nodded once in reply. Implicitly, Damian knew Cyrus would never steer them wrong, but still he had his reservations—especially now. As he lumbered from the SUV his eyes caught Kate as she hedged herself against the cold, her own attentions purposefully elsewhere. Nevertheless, Damian promised the territorial male that had woken within him he would let no harm come to his female.

Bianca, the pilot, cautioned them that the weather in Winnipeg was brutally frigid this time of year and could bring turbulence. Damian again glanced at Kate, knowing she'd never flown before; the only overt sign that she was nervous was a slight flexing of her jaw. *Creator,* but she was beauty, and her fire reached out to him even as they stood as far from each other as possible. How he could feign her presence didn't singe him, razing everything he thought he once was to realign him with who he now needed to be, was beyond him. He'd barely made it out of the house without causing a ruckus. Nevertheless, he was eager for this trip to commence so he could move forward with his still-forming plan to win Kate to his side.

As if sensing his discord, Kate met his gaze, though just as quickly looked away. In that fleeting span of time three of her emotions seared him at once: spiteful anger, dizzying bliss, and shameless desire. The fragment of light that spanned between them, a bond only the two could see, pulsed with a pearlescent glow, like the moon wandering through the night's ascent. Damian inhaled deeply, the wind bringing to him a scant trace of lavender, and suddenly nothing else in the world mattered except for that tether between the two.

The party boarded the small charter plane and were in the air not more than an hour later, with a planned arrival in Winnipeg just after three in the morning. Talorc confirmed that Paavak, the head of the Winnipeg coven, would meet them at the airport, and the necessary arrangements had been made for their stay. The coven rested just outside of the city along a slight mountain ridge, which gave them privacy but also afforded them access to modernity; Talorc informed their party it had been there since the early eighteen-hundreds. Damian had never been to Winnipeg, but then again, his nomadic lifestyle had been centered around his contractor's needs.

The Guard's full plans hadn't been shared with Paavak and his coven as of yet, a precaution Ryder wanted to take until they knew what would welcome them in Manitoba. All Paavak knew was Talorc and The Guard were coming to speak with him about the state of affairs, with a plan to stay mere days before moving onto the next coven. Talorc was hoping his good relationship with Paavak could withstand the abbreviated visit, especially considering the fact he'd stayed much longer at the other covens he'd visited. Rumors were swirling thanks to Vadin's internet machinations, and Talorc had mentioned he was eager to bring Paavak up to speed because he knew he would be a staunch ally.

It had also been agreed upon within The Guard to withhold the information that Talorc reached out to the watchers but heard nothing in response; the ideal would only sour Paavak's palate, as it did Damian's now. *Leaving us on our own yet again,* he thought, his gaze locked on the night outside of his small plane window.

Two parallel rows of seats stretched into ten spaces, just enough for their party. Lilith and Fiona sat in the front, reviewing their latest medical cases, with Vadin engrossed in something on his cell phone behind them. Damian sat somewhere in the middle, and as often as he breathed his eyes would turn to Kate, who sat across the narrow aisle from him. For quite some time he let himself get lost in the feel of her fire from where she simmered, knowing that while she burned from their passionate rendezvous, she also burned with retribution yet to be claimed.

Your confidence and determination will see you through this, Damian thought of Kate, willing the slight haze of ashen uncertainty to lift from her form. *And I'll show you that you can depend on me too.*

The hours crept by, little changing about their behaviors. Conversations ebbed and waned, the participants varying, the topics flowing. Damian noticed Kate never indulged, her gaze always fixed to the pane of her own window. When snacks were passed around by Fiona, she didn't partake, and her countenance remained ambiguous and removed as the flight dragged on.

"Are you okay?" Damian finally asked, unable to sit next to her in disregard any longer. His new vulnerability toward her left him questioning himself on several fronts. And while he could easily reach out through the bond at any moment to know what she was feeling, her thoughts were still her own. Staring at her now he realized he would give anything to know them. Something had changed between them, and he felt as though he didn't know how to read her anymore. Or maybe he was afraid to. But he *wanted* to learn this version of her, was eager to understand and be near her more than ever before.

Kate glanced at him, her eyes trailing his face, before she smiled softly. That smile unraveled something within him, and his chest swelled. He couldn't take his eyes off her in that moment; captured by all that was her, he turned to face her more fully.

As if unaware that his attentions continued, she stifled a yawn and stretched her arms above her head. She'd tossed her outerwear to the floor, and he couldn't stop his eyes from tracing her booted feet, slim legs, and tapered waist. The tight top she wore highlighted the curves he had handfuls of not hours before, and his eyes wandered the places his mouth once roamed. Though she was still thin from her time spent in confinement, she now had color to her cheeks and her eyes glittered with the stars inherent within. Her short hair had a sheen of health to it and her voice carried strong. She appeared fuller, her reinvigorated confidence lending her resilience and splendor. The vainglorious part of him reveled in the knowledge that it was his blood alone that strengthened her.

Mine, an errant thought demanded, and he felt his fangs sharpen in his mouth. A need that hollowed his core swept him, churning with an unsatiated voraciousness he was sure would never be alleviated when it came to Kate.

"Do you need anything?" Damian asked to distract himself, his conscience reminding him who surrounded them and what his true focus should be, while the bonded side of him demand he provide for his female. "I can get you a water."

Kate smiled again, and Damian lost his breath. "No thanks."

The need within him to provide was strong. "You sure?"

"Yes, Damian. I can get my own water if I need to."

Checked by her words and the mundanity of the conversation, Damian retreated. *Retreated.* It wasn't a maneuver or mindset that existed in his being...*but here the hell I am.*

Sensing that she'd created some tension between them, Kate amended, "But thank you."

With all the wallowing emotions of a teenager, Damian nodded once and turned his regard back to the window.

I don't know how I'm going to get through the next couple of days, he thought. *But the life I was living before is nothing compared to what it is now. I need to be patient. Understanding. Focused on the end goal. Which is Kate.*

Pensiveness remained his companion throughout the flight, though he and the others did engage in some banal conversation. As they neared Winnipeg, Talorc gathered their collective attention, and they reviewed their plan a final time.

"Paavak will pick us up from the airport." Talorc unfurled a large, detailed map of Winnipeg and the surrounding areas, gesturing to the airport and then to the location of the coven. "It's about a forty-five-minute ride."

"Jean-Luc and Roberta are planning to leave within the next day or two," Ryder added, rubbing a hand over the stubble on his chin. "They've recruited who they can in such a small amount of time. In total we should see about forty from their combined numbers."

Damian winced at the small sum.

"Heath stayed behind to watch our respective covens." Talorc tapped a finger on the map he'd opened. "But is sending who he can spare. Another ten to twenty, I believe. Noir reported a fair reception from Paavak when he arrived, and relayed he probably had another twenty vampires willing to fight. But the numbers from Ruskill will be less, if any at all. Snow Lake... Noir said he could not garner which way they swayed when it came to their loyalty in his conversations with Paavak."

A few gazes were exchanged, though no one spoke.

"I will have Noir leave for Ruskill as soon as possible; they most likely lean toward our side because of their close relationship with the Winnipeg coven. Damian, you are to go to Snow Lake. Vadin, I will need you to monitor all modes of travel, looking for large parties entering the area or patterns that do not fit the usual trajectories."

The protectively territorial male in him growled its disdain, quivering with spite. *Shit.* Damian held his breath, unsure of how to get himself out of leaving Kate's side whilst knowing he couldn't toe the line between him and Talorc much further.

"It may not be wise to send Damian north until we have a chance to lock down Ruskill," Ryder muttered, almost to himself. "And I don't know if sending Noir ahead alone is the best plan. What if there's a trap waiting for him there?"

Damian's breath eased out of him, but he held it tight once more. His eyes swung to Ryder's quickly, only to find the male locked on Talorc. *Newly beloved, and no fool is he...*

"On the contrary: we do not have the time to spare if we are to hold the upper hand," Talorc replied. "Damian is known for his travels, could act as an ambassador of sorts."

Vadin muttered, "But if we've miscalculated and Santiago is already waiting for us..."

"We'll need all the hands we have."

Damian released his breath fully at Ryder's firm rebuttal, thankful the noise of the plane drowned it out.

"Let us hope that is not the case," Talorc said, bolstering what courage he could spare for the time being.

"I don't think it is," Vadin said. "Even though we've put the word out that you're on the move I made sure to scramble the timeline a little bit. In Santiago's mind, you won't be in Winnipeg for another week."

"Smart," Kate murmured.

"But you forget he's probably tracking us," Ryder insisted, sitting back in his chair restlessly.

"Maybe. Maybe not. Maybe he's too preoccupied with his diabolical little plans." Vadin shrugged, stretching back in his own seat. "We just have to hope we have the leg up."

"So Paavak picks us up from the airport, we settle in Winnipeg for a day or two, then head up to Ruskill. By then, Santiago will have learned of our true motives, but we'll still be one step ahead. It will take him and his army just as long to get to Ruskill as it did us. Unfortunately, we can't do anything largescale while he's traveling; it would draw too much attention. Vadin's done some extensive mapping of the area around the cabin and reports it's dense enough that civilization won't be interrupted. We have a place to stay and enough supplies to equip a full battalion. We have Lilith, Fiona, and Taryn on standby, and whoever else Paavak may recommend." Cyrus summarized. "Maybe we can convince Paavak to send some correspondence to Snow Lake on our behalf. It would be better than losing a Guard."

Vadin tipped his lips in a downward fashion, raising his brows the opposite way. "Not a bad idea."

"I can see to it when we get to Winnipeg," Ryder offered.

Talorc nodded. "Bianca is on standby?" he asked Cyrus, who nodded once.

"She can take us home at a moment's notice."

"So long as you're paying!" she chimed, thanks to her impeccable hearing, from the front of the plane.

"And her loyalty?" Damian rumbled sardonically.

"Stands," Cyrus replied.

"*Et tu, Brute?* No' my thing," Bianca called again, her accent thick. "For no amount of *dinero*. Besides, flying for the king is my coolest job yet."

Vadin guffawed and Taryn snorted, earning dull looks from their comrades.

"What's Plan B?" Cyrus, ever the doomsayer, asked. "If this doesn't pan out how we want?"

A few looks were exchanged, though no one knew what to say.

After an ill-timed bout of turbulence, Kate responded, "There isn't one. This has to work."

Damian's eyes flipped toward her, and he was surprised to find her looking at him. He sat up a little straighter and said with a confidence he lent from her, "We have to trust in ourselves. We know what we're doing. Fighting isn't new to us. Shitty weather isn't new to us. Enemies aren't new to us. Cyrus knows every type of explosive known to man and Noir can work a set of knives like no one has ever seen. Vadin knows a gun like the back of his hand and Ryder is a master of it all. We're *all* experts at what we do or else we wouldn't have made it this far."

"That is it then," Talorc said, shifting back in his chair and sighing, a hand absently stroking his graying beard. "See it done."

Kate couldn't get off the plane fast enough.

The door to the plane was barely open before she plowed through it, and as her boots met the tarmac, she couldn't be more thankful not to have to fly for another few days. Bianca hadn't been lying when she said there would be turbulence, and Kate knew she was tinged green as she slid her parka onto her shoulders and sucked in a breath of arctic air. The chilling rush steadied her head and settled her stomach almost immediately, though the bite was admittedly frigid.

And so it begins.

She imagined Winnipeg to be like Warwick, except colder. Kate had watched through her plane window as the city sprawled out beneath her with metropolitan characteristics she knew boasted of the best modernities life had to offer. Through research in her time of feigned reprieve, she'd learned Ruskill, on the other hand, was known for its polar bear sightings and Northern Lights and had more bed and breakfasts than abodes. She was surprised a coven of vampires chose to inhabit such a small, glacial place; the population didn't even reach a thousand. With a stretch of coastline that could hardly be considered a beach, one baseball field, a health center, and a single police barrack, Kate supposed it was a working town well enough but could never picture herself so...isolated. In contrast, there was so much to do and see in Warwick. She rarely went to the same restaurant twice and had her choice of the finest liquor, entertainment, and food at the flick of her wrist.

She was enthralled all the same. Having never travelled before, Kate was blown away by the fact a metal box with fixed wings brought her roughly sixteen-hundred miles from home in a matter of hours. She was excited to experience the weather, the people, the buildings, the food; the different scents, tastes, sights, languages, and cultures that were sure to abound. Even though her time in Ruskill and Winnipeg would be short, and her focus had to be on Santiago, Kate made a silent pact with herself to take as many mental notes as she could and come back as soon as possible. Travelling was always something she'd wanted to do. She yearned to see the beauty of the Northern Lights. Experience the history of Stonehenge. The awe-inspiring Cliffs of Moher. The sheen of the Eiffel Tower. The enormity of the Taj Mahal. The sprawl of the Great Wall of China. The vibrancy of the Maldives. The list went on and on and on.

At the same time, it had taken a lot of internal encouragement and reassurance to get herself here; she spent the entire plane ride convincing herself to push forward. Not only was it the very first time Kate had ever been on a plane, but it was also her very first time being out of Warwick. She'd never experienced anything beyond the city limits to her home, and while it was remarkable and wondrous, it was also overwhelming. A new world had opened for her, which was simultaneously debilitating and invigorating. Anyone could be waiting at any moment to snare her, or a single threat could uproot their whole plan. The smells, the sights, the noises and the unnerving fear they brought with them…it wasn't something she'd experience before.

I can't think like that, Kate prompted herself for the umpteenth time. *I didn't make it this far to be derailed by 'what-ifs'. I deserve this moment. I need this moment. I can't afford to falter. Not now. I am worthy of this and everything that sits before me. I'm allowed to be afraid, but I have to push forward.*

Shaking herself internally, Kate raised the hood of her parka to protect against the swirling snow and bitter wind and thought, *focus.* They'd landed at the airport right on time outside of a small, private plane hangar adjacent to others that stretched on as far as the eye could see. Kate was awed by the size of the airport, which sparked with different colors and sounds she'd never heard before, while planes, vehicles, and people moved in all directions. *Unfathomable that someone came up with a way to make this all work.*

She glanced over her shoulder to see Damian debarking from the plane, followed by Ryder and then her father. The others filed out as well, Bianca bringing up the rear. Noir's tall, slender frame loped from a nearby car, and Bianca approached him to converse about unloading their cargo. The duo was joined by Cyrus and Vadin, the males exchanging terse handshakes. Ryder steered Talorc toward the hangar, and Kate fell into step just behind her father with Damian to her left, both listening intently as Ryder spoke.

"Paavak should be in here waiting for us." The droning sound of the airport would've made it difficult to discern what he was saying, but Kate's hearing was near immaculate now in light of the bond. She was keenly aware of the others trailing behind her and Damian, their own reservations simmering just below her own. "It shouldn't take us long to get to the Winnipeg coven. The snow doesn't seem to be sticking."

"The storm just came in," Kate said, stopping behind Ryder as he paused by the keypad next to the gargantuan garage door. "I've been following it."

"Did the ride suit you?" Talorc asked her with a small glance over his shoulder, and Kate's look turned sheepish, knowing the tint of green still lingered on her face.

"Flying will grow on me."

Talorc smiled in return. "I hope so."

Ryder gripped the handle to the door, sidling himself in front of Talorc while Damian pressed into Kate from the side. Kate heard the unmistakable brushing of guns against leather and fabric, and a chill slipped down her spine that had nothing to do with the weather outside.

"Stay close to me, just in case," Damian whispered to her, and the chill Kate felt a heartbeat before readily turned into a warming caress. She swallowed thickly, trying to dispel the ache of want that pulsed through her at Damian's proximity and his oceanic scent, and walked into the bright hangar after her father.

The space was wide and echoed with the closing of the door. Glaring white lights shone down from the soaring ceiling above, interspersed with steel beams that made up the structure of the space. The sounds of the airport became muted, allowing Kate to focus her senses on what was now before her: a rolling toolbox, a small TV, a cot, and another door. Precluding those things were three large SUVs parked in an arc, guarded by the hardened faces of two males and a female. Their countenances did not make Kate feel warm nor welcomed, and she felt Damian tense beside her. She kept her eyes on the trio, who were dressed entirely in black and made no move of greeting.

"Where's Paavak?" Ryder called, the space between their respective parties at least twenty feet.

Kate's eyes narrowed as her heart began to pound. *None of those beings are Paavak?*

The door which Kate just walked through swung open again, and she flinched as it *cracked* against the neighboring wall. Distinct clicking sounded, warning Kate weaponry had been pulled, and the heavy presences of Vadin and Noir permeated the space behind her. She felt Damian press his shoulder into her, placing himself slightly before her frame, while Ryder shielded Talorc with his body. Cyrus, she guessed, stayed outside with the other females, no doubt having been alerted to danger.

The tallest of the individuals by the SUVs, a thin, pallid male with black hair that fell into sharp hazel eyes, moved quickly to the side. More than one gun swung up to pin him at his sudden movement and he paused, calculating a risk versus benefit assessment only he knew the attributes of. Kate's heartrate increased, her eyes fastened on the male, wishing she had something to defend herself with. *Getting into the game so soon? Didn't see that coming.*

When no one moved for a full minute, the male must have deduced he was safe to continue. That didn't stop Damian from loading a bullet into the chamber of his semi-automatic handgun and Ryder from growling. They all watched, wading in tension as thick as quicksand, as the male reached a leather-gloved hand to open the back door to the middle SUV, his long black duster swirling with his movements. His other two associates took simultaneous steps back, and several sets of eyes fixed on another form as she unfurled from the confines of the SUV.

"Trigger happy your boys are."

Kate's eyes flared at the hypnotic lilt that belonged to the most beautiful female she'd ever seen. Layered red hair fell over a petite frame to tickle her waist as she came to her full height, and when the female lifted her face, it was to shine in the light of the hangar despite its starkness. Warm, brown eyes sparkled with mirth as she smiled, not yet to reveal the fangs beneath, as she came to stand in front of the tallest male. She was dressed in luxury clothing, and though the black was monotonous it was a spectacular contrast to her natural coloring. An upturned nose nestled between high cheekbones, and a pointed chin and cat-like eyes sat in an oval-shaped face. Her shining stiletto boots clicked along the concrete floor as she moved toward Talorc, the others falling into a V-formation behind her.

"Gíselle," Talorc said, his tone friendly and relaxed. Hearing it caused Kate to calm slightly, though her eyes remained on the female she'd never seen nor heard of.

"Talorc." Gíselle reached forward to clasp Talorc's forearms. The two shared a brief embrace before breaking apart, while the beings behind her bowed at the waist to Talorc.

"Lower your weapons," Talorc called to The Guard, and though they hesitated, they obeyed.

Gíselle nodded toward Ryder. "Always good to see you." Her eyes meandered over the others, and if she had any thoughts her striking features kept them mute. "Vadin, Damianos, Noir. It is wonderful to see you as well."

The males said nothing.

"Please excuse the absence of my beloved," Gíselle continued, her countenance softening with mild regret. "He remains at Blackwood, our coven on the mountain. He will greet you there, and most eagerly awaits your arrival."

Sensing her confusion, Talorc gestured between Kate and Gíselle. "This is Paavak's beloved, Gíselle. Gíselle, this is my daughter Kathryn."

Kate felt a little jolt, as if she'd been shocked by static. A sudden sense of familiarity swept through her before dissipating. *Impossible. I've never met this female. Father never included me in any of his business dealings nor invited me to meet people he knew in times past.* She tried to shake away the feeling, assessing the female with a calculating gaze.

"Kathryn," Gíselle breathed in wonder, her smile widening to indeed reveal fangs. "The elusive daughter of Talorc. You are quite the mystery to our kind, and I am honored to be in your presence. Furthermore, I speak on behalf of my entire coven when I say we are happy to hear of your safe recovery, and I am most obliged to be able to open my home to you."

Mystery to our kind? Kate thought, not allowing her confusion at the female's choice of words show.

Astonishment dawned on her, however, when she realized their meaning.

I've never been outside of Warwick. No one outside of my immediate family and The Guard has ever met me. They don't know my life, how meaningless and starving it once was. I can go forth on a new slate, create a name for myself. A name that means something, that holds weight.

Purpose. Intent. Choice. Independence.

The notions she sought, from so long ago, thrummed a beautiful chord within her very soul.

"Yes, I'm Kathryn." Kate stepped forward to take the female's outstretched hand in her own. She clasped it tightly, enveloping one with both of hers as she met Gíselle's eyes with firm yet congenial engagement. "It's a pleasure to meet you as well."

Chapter Twenty-Three

L et's not tarry." Gíselle nodded kindly before turning toward the middle SUV. "While the sunrise is far off, the weather can turn inclement without much warning. Talorc, I would have you and Kathryn ride with me so I may brief you on the tides of the times. Though I'm impatient to ask: I'd heard that you were removing yourself from your campaign?"

"A decoy," Talorc responded, moving after Gíselle. "A necessary one. There are things happening that even I have a hard time comprehending and staying ahead of."

"After centuries of friendship, Paavak and I are more than inclined to help in any possible way."

Centuries? Kate thought, momentarily stunned.

"Indeed," Talorc responded with a hum of humor, but it was Ryder's rumble of disapproval that had them stopping.

"We don't readily engage in a trusting relationship with those we haven't been introduced to," he said darkly, and Kate thought she'd never heard him so belligerent. She glanced at him to note his eyes were swiveling over the three bodies behind Gíselle. "It's hard to decipher friend from foe these days."

Gíselle arched a perfect, sloping brow, but did incline her head slightly. "If you would be so persuaded to bring the others in, I would show you, Captain, there is nothing to fear."

Ryder, his body as tense as a brick wall, didn't move from beside Talorc. Kate watched as his jaw twisted from one side to another before he finally called, "Cyrus."

A moment later Cyrus opened the door, leading the other females in from the cold. Lilith was directly behind him, and then Fiona and Taryn, followed by Bianca, who looked less than fazed.

Cyrus tucked the females tightly behind Vadin and Noir, and it was with a flick of her wrist that Gíselle pointed toward those she had brought with her.

"Mikom, Olivia, and Yann. Members of our coven and highly trusted."

It was with no small amount of disparagement that the members of The Guard regarded Gíselle's security.

"I'm sorry in this day and age we must doubt each other so much."

"Lilith," the female called, boldly identifying herself. "And my colleague Fiona."

Gíselle dipped her head in reception, and Taryn introduced herself next, followed by Bianca. When Ryder relaxed by a minuscule amount, Gíselle stepped back and opened her palm in a gesture that encouraged Talorc to board the vehicle. Ryder went next and Kate followed, with Damian behind her. With a quick goodbye to Cyrus, Bianca punched in a code for the garage door and slipped underneath it as it rose, and then boarded her plane to begin breaking it down. Cyrus and the females went to the first SUV while it was decided that Noir and Vadin would remain behind to load their supplies into the last. Kate didn't miss the look of meaningful conviction Ryder struck Cyrus with before the car door closed behind him, and the latter male nodded in a way that Kate knew he understood the cargo he carried was dear.

No going back now, Kate thought, settling against the warm leather seat.

Peculiarly, she wasn't afraid. Emboldened by the possibility of creating a new version of herself and excited at the thought of experiencing a different city, she relaxed into the third row of the vehicle while unzipping her parka for comfort. Damian settled next to her, leaving not an inch of space between them, which both irritated and soothed her. Yet it was the slight brush of his hand against her thigh and then the squeeze of her knee that had her melting all over the place, so much so that it took several deep breaths and a fixated gaze out the window for her to refocus on the present.

How can I want him again? So quickly? And so strongly? Kate dragged in a slow breath through her nose and held it, knowing he could feel her desire for him. His own called to her, inciting a burning hunger she'd only just begun to appreciate and was eager to explore further.

Not the time nor the place, she chastised the shameless trollop inside of her. She forced herself to think of the long road ahead of them, from getting to Blackwood, to Ruskill, and finally confronting Santiago, but her desire stubbornly simmered beneath the surface, fervently ready to learn everything she'd been missing out on about the male she'd fantasized about for years.

"I trust your journey went well?" Gíselle said as Mikom guided the car out of the airport and onto a freeway.

"Uneventful," Talorc responded, his and Ryder's frames struggling for dominance in the middle seat; both were egregiously large males. "Which is the best thing I could have hoped for."

"I sense unrest from you all." Gíselle's eyes reflected in the rearview mirror, flickering with the light from the streetlamps overhead as Mikom picked up speed.

"Perhaps some."

"Do you know what you're getting into, Talorc?" she asked, and it was not an unkind statement, but a firm one nonetheless. She turned slightly in her seat to address him head on. "Have you thought about the consequences of your actions, both positive and negative, and how far they could stretch?"

Talorc tipped his head back, and Kate felt the smallest bite of icy wind at the question. "Overwhelmingly so. We have talked of little else for months."

"All angles?"

"Every one."

Gíselle's eyes skimmed over Ryder, who returned her regard with indifference. Kate couldn't gather anything from the dynamic between the two, their emotions locked down tight. When Gíselle's eyes swept to Damian, however, anything she could've felt was overpowered by heated jealousy.

Hello darkness my oldest friend.

"Damianos...The Wanderer," Gíselle remarked passively, a smile curling her lips. "I see you have found yourself at Talorc's side for the time being. Is it the call of battle that has you stayed?"

"Damian now. I've been in Warwick since two-thousand-seventeen." His tone stayed neutral, but his eyes held fire. "I plan to stay."

Kate's heart flipped, and she tried desperately not to think about what that meant for her own future.

Not the time. Not the place. Not the time. Not the place.

Gíselle settled more comfortably in her turned position as she addressed the males. "Only those newly made haven't heard of The Guards of Nightfall, and even then, they're quick to learn. Your reputations precede all of you, and your longevity speaks well of your experience. You were once a Byzantian-Greek solider. And you, Ryder, the last of the Vikings. Never known for your mercy."

Damian nodded once, and Kate sat still, listening as Gíselle continued. She didn't know much of Damian's early history because he didn't speak often of it…and, shamefully, she rarely asked. *I was always too wrapped up in myself. But he's lived countless lives before coming into mine. What was he like before?* A sudden thought struck her, so forcefully it rendered her breathless. *Did he…know my mother?*

"Damian, your battle-mongering never went unnoticed. You were ruthless, hungry for blood in a way most found repulsive. You were once great with a spear, could throw it a hundred and twenty meters to skewer a victim. I doubt your prowess has decreased." Gíselle hesitated, but her words were steady when she asked, "Although, there are a lot of us who wonder: if The Guards are the strongest, most cunning, and the bravest of our kind, why did it take so long to retrieve Kathryn? How could you let yourselves be thwarted so thoroughly so many times?"

A flush swept Kate from her chest to her forehead, and her blood roiled torridly. *How dare she?* She felt Damian shift beside her, the swift sting of violence cutting between them.

Ryder's growl was leaden with imminent danger. "It was no fault of our own—"

"You don't owe anyone an explanation," Kate cut him off fiercely, her eyes like ice shards as she glared at Gíselle. "Especially to someone who didn't lift a finger on my behalf."

"I only wonder what others will ask. The answer will come easier to a friend than a foe, for it is I who will have more understanding and empathy. Don't take offense to my question; prepare for worse from others."

Kate's eyes narrowed further. *She's…right.*

Damian shifted again beside her, his body rigid with

tension. "It'd been a while since we fought seriously."

"These times are different," Ryder all but snarled. "The modern weaponry, the technology we have to avoid. Everything changes at the drop of a hat. Cell phones are everywhere. Humans get in the way. We have to be more careful than ever."

"And if there was anyone to blame, it was my own self," Talorc said, his voice holding not an ounce of the disdain the other two males were emanating. "I held them back for a long time. From a lot of things. We had forgotten who we once were—me most of all."

Gíselle looked at him inquisitively, though didn't say anything.

Talorc continued, "I am working to make amends with not just the covens, but my family as well. For a long time I let darkness win. It is through these amends that I am taking control back—of my life, my sense of self, and my nation."

A single brow rose, and a slow smile spread across Gíselle's lips. "Talorc *'An Claidheamh'* MacNehhtonn admitting he isn't flawless? I never thought I would see the day."

Talorc rumbled a low laugh, dissipating some of the tension.

"Disappointments notwithstanding, I'm glad we have your individual capabilities on our side." Gíselle removed her gloves to reveal perfectly manicured hands, and the largest emerald-cut yellow diamond Kate had ever seen. Her eyes bulged before she righted her features, clearing her throat of her shock. Though it wasn't customary for vampires to marry or procure rings for their beloveds, some, like Gíselle and Paavak it seemed, adhered to the human tradition.

"I don't hold the same reservations as some of my peers do," Gíselle finished strongly, assertively. If there was any doubt before on where she stood, her tone brokered no argument. "We have all waned in our competencies over time. We all have dues to pay, things to answer for. But I have no doubt that you will lead us to victory, to stability, to peace, as you always have."

Kate turned her face back to the window, struggling to grapple with her tumultuous emotions and those of the others in the car. Even after a month of learning to deal with the enhanced feelings, auras, senses, and emotions, she still found it difficult when her own were agitated.

"And you, Kathryn," Gíselle called to her, drawing Kate's reluctant regard. "Tell me about yourself. I daresay I am the first to get to learn about the enigmatic daughter of Talorc from her own mouth."

Gradually festering with unease, Kate didn't know what to say. *Admit that I used to be a shopping and reality-TV addict until I was mercilessly tortured by the enemy? That I was obsessed with my monthly hair appointments and changing my nail color to match my mood before I was forced to redefine who and what I was? Not the best conversation starter.*

"Father just recently began to involve me more in decisions involving the vampire nation," Kate started slowly. "Before then I was training with Ryder in combat." *Not a lie. She doesn't have to know I was the worst student.* "My aunt Mora raised me with compassion and empathy but also pressed me to learn the *Elden Edicts* thoroughly; I can recite most any law by memory. I can speak Latin, Spanish, Gaelic, and French fluently. Though I rarely leave Warwick" —*Okay that's a lie but an inconsequential one—* "I am motivated to learn more about the world and what it has to offer." She left out: *because I was vilely made to suffer on the brink of death for days on end and desperately want the bloodiest of revenges.*

"What changed?" Gíselle asked, and Kate got the sense she would never hold back from what she wanted to know or say.

"It would be a lie if I said my time in captivity wasn't the catalyst." Kate didn't shirk from the truth of the matter, and she refused in this moment to be restrained by the memories anymore. "I couldn't sit by idly anymore. Our world is in danger, and I want to fight for it."

Gíselle nodded once, her eyes bright with what Kate liked to think was respect. "I know the feeling well."

"She is learning more every day," Talorc interjected. "And I could not be prouder of all she has accomplished."

A fist seized her heart, and Kate basked in the pride that swirled from her father and wrapped around her tenderly.

Gíselle's brown eyes softened. "I see it: you're very proud. Herja would be too."

That static feeling jolted her again, and a distant, dreamy laugh carried on from the wisps of a memory she didn't fully experience or understand. Frowning, plagued by both comfort and pain, Kate asked, "Did you know my mother?"

"Of course," Gíselle replied with a radiant smile. "I fought at her side for more than two hundred years."

At her urgent and eager behest, Gíselle regaled Kate with stories of Herja for the rest of the car ride. Just as excitedly, Gíselle promised to show her the armory at Blackwood where she kept an impressive repertoire of the ancient weaponry she and Herja once shared. Talorc listened distantly from the middle seat, Ryder and Damian also remaining quiet, as Kate fired questions at Gíselle with all the subtlety of a machine gun, absorbing everything she could.

Gíselle, who astoundingly neared six hundred years old but barely looked a day over forty, met Herja when the two were travelling through northern Europe in the early fifteen-hundreds. Gíselle had been roaming with a small band of archers, and Herja, who'd been on a crusade separate from Talorc at the time, hired them to help with a nearby battle. The two formed a swift and firm friendship with their shared love of arms and horseback riding, and in the fortnight it took to see them victorious, they became inseparable. When Herja inquired whether she wanted to join her forces, Gíselle, an archer without equal, didn't hesitate to accept. She'd stayed with Herja until the mid-seventeen-hundreds, when Herja and Talorc finally decided to settle in North America, leaving Gíselle to turn her sights to Canada and the booming trade empire. She actually knew The Guard very well but hadn't seen or communicated with them in years.

Kate learned Paavak's and Talorc's friendship started after Herja passed. Paavak and Gíselle—newly beloved at the time—had travelled to Warwick to see the male when word began circulating he was becoming a recluse. Gíselle had the idea to remind Talorc he was the vampire king and needed to act as such; she could be brash, just like her dearly departed friend. However, Paavak was a new face, and brought with him a gentler, more understanding tone. Whatever transpired between Paavak and Talorc at that time was enough to create a lasting friendship, one that transcended the different courses of their lives.

The looming structure of Blackwood rose before them as Kate's questions dwindled and her riotous mind quieted. The woodland chalet was tucked into forestry so dense and so removed from civilization that Kate couldn't be convinced they were outside the bustling city of Winnipeg if she didn't just traverse the milage herself. Carved into the cliffside, a rock quarry spilling not far below, the monstrous manor gleamed with golden lighting, lending stark shadows to the dark wood façade.

As they ascended the asphalt drive, snow drifted softly around them, lending a softness to the strict vertical planks. A six-car garage made the first level of the abode, and the second was a rounded structure carved into the mountainside made entirely of windows. On a flattened level of cliff above was the main home, which boasted of a convex structure with varying levels of deck that overlooked the forest, quarry, and sparkling city of Winnipeg. Kate could not hinge her mouth shut the entire time Mikom steered the SUV up the drive. She was slow to make her way from the car, having to tip her head back to appreciate the entirety of the home.

"I can give you a full tour after we have dinner," Gíselle said, smiling at Kate's slack-jawed appearance. "But there's still more for you to see."

Distantly aware that the latter statement was vaguely leading, Kate grabbed her suitcase from the back of the car and followed Gíselle into the garage. The expensive vehicles within eluded Kate's appreciation as she distractedly asked Gíselle, "How many live here?"

"Nine of us in the coven," Gíselle replied, punching a code into the keypad that allowed them into the warmth of the house. "Three families, including Paavak and I. We have staff to run the home as well, but most don't live here. The vampire population of Winnipeg reaches over five hundred."

Kate knew *coven* was an antiquated term which stood for a cohort of vampires who lived together. In times past, vampires cohabitated due to kinship, necessity, a sense of uniqueness, and unbreakable bonds; it was the way of the vampire. Nowadays, not all vampires in an area lived within the same walls and *coven* was interchangeably used to denote a vampire presence in the area as well as those who lived together. Generally, where there was a large vampire presence there was a coven, with the members having voted a single vampire who spoke for the whole of that specific community. Each vampire, irrespective of their home or stature, ultimately deflected to Talorc.

Usually, Kate thought, tugging her bag up two stairs into a mud room.

In smaller towns, like she suspected Ruskill to be, it was common for the vampires to share space or at least a plot of land. Each coven had its own name, discerning them from others. Some areas didn't have covens or vampire populations at all, like the entire landmass of Greenland. *There aren't a lot of vampires being borne or made anymore,* Kate thought. *And covens are deteriorating.*

The weight of her bag suddenly lifted, and Kate looked over her shoulder to see Damian taking it with ease. She smiled slightly, dipping her head to hide her girlish pleasure, and continued to follow Gíselle into the lower level of the house.

The small hall off the mud room opened into a spacious living area. "You may leave the bags here." Gíselle indicated with her hand a stretch of open floor. "Mikom will disperse them to the rooms you will be staying in. Dinner has been prepared and will be served shortly. But first, Paavak eagerly awaits you."

Kate barely had the time to look around her, but the woodland feel of Blackwood was darkly mesmerizing. Fur rugs spread across wooden floors, the décor neutral in black, greys, and wood tones. The lighting was low, lending amber warmth to the cavernous ceilings and stone-faced walls. Elaborately carved archways led to rooms with different purposes, and as they passed by a doorway larger than the others, Kate noticed the flooring rose in level to expose an entire separate wing of the massive house.

"One of the families inhabits that area entirely by themselves. The other two are upstairs in the main house with us," Gíselle said, turning a bend in the corridor which consequently revealed a swirling set of wide stairs. There was an elevator tucked into one corner Kate noticed, but the intricate, life-sized set of howling wolves carved at the base of a staircase captured her astonished attention.

"Mikom's doing. He is a talent when it comes to carpentry."

Kate's thoughts took her elsewhere as they began walking up the pristinely polished pine stairs. "Are there children here?"

"Only one," Gíselle replied. "In the family that inhabits the separate wing."

Falling into a small stretch of silence, Kate followed the curved staircase up to the main house behind Gíselle. The space opened into a wide foyer, one with an enormous antlered chandelier and an entire wall of taxidermized waterfowl, wings spread in flight. The foyer boasted two other staircases on opposite sides, which Kate presumed led to an array of rooms on the upper level. Between the two staircases was a sweeping doorway that opened into a space vaster than the last, where she could hear voices murmuring in quiet conversation.

Suddenly, Kate got an uneasy feeling low in her stomach. She stopped walking abruptly, which caused Damian to place a hand at the small of her back and inquire softly, "What's wrong?"

The others stopped behind her, and Gíselle paused to address the group while standing not four feet from the doorway.

"Come," she called, but Kate's feet wouldn't move. The sinking feeling grew, threatening to swallow her whole, and she glanced over her shoulder at Damian.

"I don't like this. Something's wrong," she said to him quietly, though she knew everyone heard her. The rumblings from within the space before her faltered, and Kate looked beyond Gíselle where the feeling of dread was siphoning from.

"There's nothing to fear," Gíselle said to Kate, removing her jacket from her shoulders to reveal a black, form-fitting midi-dress tied at the waist with a black silk ribbon. The wide neck spread open to reveal her shoulders and the delicately freckled skin of her chest, a stacked yellow diamond necklace to match her gargantuan ring on full display. A servant materialized seemingly out of nowhere, taking her jacket before disappearing once more. "Come. You'll see."

Talorc brushed past Kate with determined confidence, though little would sway her father to act in any other way. Ryder was close behind him, and Damian urged Kate forward with a small push at her back. The unease grew to an almost nauseating level, but Kate forced herself to walk forward, not to show everyone how capable she was, but to prove it to herself.

There will be worse things to face in the coming days.

As she crossed the threshold into the room, the unease steadily grew, stirring panic within her. Damian hadn't moved far from her back, and his touch was soothing, grounding, and quelled the apprehension from clawing at her throat.

Kate quickly looked around the space to search for the cause of her disquiet, but so much grabbed her attention at once. On one side, a wall made entirely of windows looked over Winnipeg in the distance. A lively fire crackled in a stone-faced hearth that spread from floor to ceiling on the opposite side of the extensive space, which Kate figured was at least the size of a basketball court. Wooden-beamed ceilings soared overhead, at least twenty feet high. The right side of the room housed several doorways that Kate was sure led to other busy areas of the house, while the room they came to a stop in appeared to be another living space decorated like the last, but much grander.

However, it was those who stood in the center of the room which caused her to gasp aloud in surprise, her feet nearly stumbling over one another.

Watchers.

Chapter Twenty-Four

A massive male with skin the color of coffee and an enormous set of ebony wings grabbed her attention first. He watched the group move into the room with volcanic eyes swirling with the colors of embers. Long hair touched his back, twisted into locs which framed an angular face sharpened in a look of malice Kate was sure never left his features. Behind him were three other watchers of varying uniqueness, similarly dressed in black flowing robes. Ethereal yet undoubtedly lethal, Kate immediately knew the unease she was feeling stemmed from the most dominant of the watchers before her.

"Oleander." Talorc bowed slightly at the waist. The Guard fell into like poses, the females doing the same.

Kate's eyes flared in wonder. *The celestial deity of fire.*

The *Elden Edicts* claimed there were eight watchers who were there at the start of the universe, each with their own powers and intuitions stemming directly from The Creator: Imra, Oleander, Adhamh, Xypher, Hydra, Undulane, Bara Khan, and Raham. Kate knew from her readings that Oleander was made to capture The Creator's drive, determination, volatility—his *fire*. Other watchers were created after the First Arc, including a middle tier who helped control and monitor Earth, though they and all the others were considered subordinates. They each fell into one of three factions of watchers: celestials, who had diverse abilities that ranged from tricks of the mind to camouflage, to sensory ruses, and other untold gifts; healers, whose talents were self-explanatory; and warriors, who were artfully skilled in battle, weaponry, and strength. The First Arc, however, were powerful to the point of limitlessness, with unfathomable wisdom, knowledge, and intrigue. Internally shaking herself back to reality, Kate realized she should respect

Oleander as was his due.

"Talorc," Oleander rumbled, his voice so low Kate had to strain to hear it. "It is good to see you."

Talorc stood straight, the others following his lead. Kate's eyes flicked to the other male behind Oleander and the watchers, who she quickly gathered was Paavak as Giselle came to stand beside him and he wrapped an arm around her waist. A tall, broad male with skin the color of bronze and black hair which flipped into light hazel eyes, he dipped his head in slight greeting to their group but remained silent as Talorc addressed Oleander.

"I must respectfully disagree," Talorc said, and the uneasiness Kate felt doubled. "For your presence means war is on the horizon."

"We believe it to be so." If Oleander took offense to her father's statement he made no show of it. "Some of us have gathered. Further discussions have aligned our cause with yours."

Kate's dread was suddenly replaced with stinging shock. In all her two hundred and twenty-one years of living, she'd never heard of such a thing. In fact, she'd never heard of the watchers embarking into the twentieth century and beyond, let alone found herself in the same room as one—not just one, but *four*.

"But not all?" Talorc asked, picking up on what Oleander had omitted.

"This is true."

"Then you cannot act."

Kate's dread flashed to the forefront again.

"A matter we are working through." Oleander's eyes blazed with the contempt he so easily shed. "I come here tonight to bring the others news of your plans. Speak now, Talorc."

Talorc recanted the events that had brought them to this exact moment, leaving no detail spared. The watchers listened, their faces neutral, while Kate tried to swallow the discordance she felt slithering between her bones. Damian remained at her back, a steadfast hand never far from her person, and she used his presence to control her wayward emotions as she was quickly realizing only he could do.

Talorc finished his story with the plans they had strung together in just a handful of days, and it wasn't Oleander who replied but Paavak as he said, "We remain at your side, Talorc. No matter what, you have the backing of our coven."

A slight nod at Paavak from Talorc had hope swelling from her father, so bright a yellow that it matched what Kate thought sunshine looked like.

"What you have arranged is good, but remains high risk," Oleander interjected roughly. "And with no back up plan…"

"Fool's play," one of the watchers murmured, causing a rumble of agreement from the others, and Kate to feel both viciously defensive and discomfited.

"Santiago knows you have traveled north and has gathered a large contingent of wraiths and vampires to act against you." Oleander dishearteningly confirmed what they'd suspected. "I would not discount humans either. Furthermore, Santiago has means to get his allies where they need to be in one fell swoop."

"He can disappear," Kate muttered, and Oleander nodded.

"Yes. He can. With just a thought he can leave one place and appear in another. A trait given to him by his watcher. In doing so, he has the ability to transport others."

"It's not possible," Cyrus mumbled, his voice like rolling stone.

"You didn't see it," Vadin said, his tone annoyed as he eyed his comrade.

"It is, and he can. But the ability is limited and can be impeded to a degree."

"We can't fight humans," Ryder growled, his ire obvious, as he brought the conversation back around. "It's against our laws."

"You scarcely have enough bodies to form a defense," Oleander said, and Cyrus sneered.

"How do you know what we are capable of?" His tone held years of accusation and distrust, and while that was just generally Cyrus, Kate inwardly cringed at his hostile tone. "And how do you know so much about what Santiago is planning?"

Oleander fixed him with a stare that would have felled a lesser male. "A spheros."

Kate inhaled a slow breath. The First Arc had each been given a spheros in order to keep watch over what they protected, as it allowed its user to see anything they desired.

"What are your numbers?" Oleander asked Talorc.

Talorc glanced at Vadin, who after a quick tally responded,

"Maybe a hundred."

"He has double that," Oleander said, and Kate let out the breath she'd inhaled on a rush as defeat numbed her mind.

"However, your strength lies in your expertise," Oleander continued. "Santiago has collected mostly wraiths, which means his army will be relatively mindless. The vampires he commands are young and inexperienced. They do not know much of the ways of battle. Show them why you are superior. You have warriors, some with hundreds of years of practice. Be smart. *Be strategic.* Use the land to your advantage. The weather. You still have time on your side. And Santiago will expend much energy to get his army here."

"But the humans," Vadin said, the frown on his face evident in his voice. "What do we do about them?"

Oleander's eyes trailed from Vadin, past Kate and Damian, past Cyrus, to another in their group. Kate glanced over her shoulder to find Lilith staring at Oleander just as intently as he was staring at her, and her memory blazed from their conversation that felt like so long ago:

"*...the night I awoke as a vampire on earth I found those who betrayed me and slaughtered every single one.*"

Kate had a sudden thought: through her schooling, she knew the *Elden Edicts* stated, "*As intended by The Creator, there shall be duality: Within contrast there shall be balance, and it shall be like for all things.*"

"Duality," Kate whispered, and Oleander turned his ember gaze to her.

Kate continued excitedly, "There's a loophole: duality. The concept that there needs to be two contrasting things in order to maintain balance. Our beliefs, the totality of The Creator's existence, is based on duality and balance. If that balance is tipped one way, it needs to be amended. If a *being* is wronged, it is only right to balance the scales. In the *Elden Edicts* it also states, 'no harm by the hand of one should befall another, lest they aspire to know the same pain'. It never specified *who* had to be wronged; we just always assumed it meant vampires couldn't act against humans because that technically goes against why we were created. But in certain instances..."

"Balance," Lilith answered softly.

"Do no harm…" Ryder started.

"But take no shit," Taryn finished with a laugh.

Oleander neither confirmed nor denied, but his eyes flared with the fire that naturally resided within him.

"Our goal is to nullify Santiago," Talorc said. "When he falls his militia will crumble."

Oleander's face darkened, his eyes falling to shadow. "Not necessarily."

The temperature in the room fell a degree, and Kate looked at her father as the dread within her surfaced once more.

"We have reason to believe that Santiago is acting by Adhamh's hand."

The fire crackled from across the room, and remained the only sound as Kate clamped her jaw tight enough to splinter bone.

We already figured as much, she thought bitterly. *This large of a contingent, how fast wraiths are being made, their increased presence in the last year…*

"We thought it, but did not want it to be truth," Talorc said.

"How?" Cyrus asked, his tone biting. "He's imprisoned, held by one of your own."

"The ability Santiago has to disappear is inherent in Adhamh." Oleander's answer was pulled through clamped teeth. "However the ability also allows the originator to call upon their subordinate at any time. We believe Adhamh has been utilizing this power to relay his whims upon Santiago."

"Adhamh can make wraiths *and* vampires," Ryder said. "He's figured out a way."

"Yes."

Just like we thought. Kate tried not to visibly wilt, but the visit with Oleander was souring her stomach further.

"Have you used a spheros to confirm this?" Ryder asked.

"We have tried, but our timing has been ill," Oleander said. "And we do not use the spheros lightly. With one missing…"

"Anyone could be watching," Kate finished weakly. She knew that using the spheros came with a price: what the user was doing, where they were, who they were with, and what they were feeling while exploiting the spheros, anyone else with a spheros could experience. It was a countermeasure set in place to make sure that no watcher plotted against another. However, when Adhamh

314

fell from grace his spheros was lost, and no one knew where it went. Which meant that anyone could be watching at any time, waiting for the watchers to reveal something they did not want to be revealed.

"Adhamh's powers are vile, and could be endless," Ryder said. "If he were to ascend..."

"We are making efforts to make sure he is contained as he should be," Oleander said, his tone firm. "Without the full support of the First Arc, we are limited. But we—Imra, Raham, Hydra, and Undulane—know and are apprehensive of the threat Adhamh could bring. Our actions require time, but we are well aware time is rarely on our side. But we need the effort from many to make a cohesive decision for change. We must tread carefully. Once our motives are set to action, the course of the world—the very universe—cannot be changed. And it will change. If we were to truly get involved, you know what it would bring."

Kate had never heard of such a thing, so she assumed it meant the apocalypse.

Yikes.

"We figured all of this out without you," Cyrus said bitterly, his thick arms crossed over his chest. "We needed your help months ago. We could've been ahead of all this."

More than one set of wary eyes glanced at the male who could not be bothered to give one fuck. Even when Oleander pinned him with those unnatural eyes, Cyrus held his ground.

"We would have intervened if we could. But it was not our time or place."

The scoff Cyrus gave echoed throughout the room. "So you say."

"Your faith is challenged; truthfully, it has been since you lost your brother," Oleander said with more patience than Kate thought he had. "I urge you to find a way to put your trust back in us. We are here now. We plan to be for the future. We will not let our nearsightedness hinder us anymore."

Kate watched Gíselle glance up at Paavak, who pulled her to him tightly. Talorc said nothing, but the icy gust of wind that swirled from him told enough of his thoughts.

"Our presence here tonight is to reconfirm our alliance with the vampires and lend what we can without directly getting entangled in this mess. We have faith you can handle this uprising on your own, as you have so many times before. Know we are watching, and let us worry of things in the Ether," Oleander said, his eyes grazing over them all, before settling on Talorc. "While you maintain control on Earth. You are on the right path, Talorc. Know that you are supported in all your decisions."

Oleander turned to face Paavak and Gíselle, who presented a unified, determined front. "Thank you for opening your home to us. We will take our leave."

Paavak broke from Gíselle to walk toward the doors that led to the deck attached to the room, and the watchers followed. All were silent while Paavak unlocked the door and then pulled it open, letting in artic air and drifting snow. With one last look over his shoulder, Oleander gazed over their group.

"We will not let you fall."

Robes billowing, the watchers took to the deck and were gone in the blink of an eye.

Paavak shut the door slowly and then turned to face their group, masking the foreboding cast to his features with a smile of welcome. "Come. Let us dine. We can talk more of what's to come when the sun rises."

Exhausted and trying not to feel completely overwhelmed by all she'd experienced in the last twelve hours, Kate closed the door after being shown to her guest room by Mikom. Turns out his haunting façade was just that: he smiled quickly and spoke openly. She enjoyed their conversation on the way to her room and was happy to hear he was a staunch supporter of her father, which he talked about at length.

Kate sighed heavily, leaning against the door as she rubbed her face with her hands. She blinked to clear the bleariness from her vision as she looked around the room: a king-sized rustic bed with beige linen was framed by matching bedroom furniture to the right, a TV with a small sitting area was to the left, a door which Kate guessed led to an adjacent bathroom was tucked in a corner, and a small balcony prefaced by sliding doors lay across from the entry. Kate pushed off from the door to close the heavy curtains to bar herself from the outside world, as the sun would be rising fully soon.

The sky was already a lightened gray, muted by the snow, which had picked up thickly. Kate lingered in her gaze of the wintry landscape before tying the curtain shut, thinking she couldn't wait to go outside tonight and listen to the tranquility of the snow-covered forest before the inevitable chaos ensued. *So much could happen.* She stilled with her hands on the curtain ties. *Things could change so drastically...*

The hollow pit in her stomach put there by Oleander's presence had yet to dissipate. His words—sporadic bits and pieces—had played over and over in her head as the others caught up over dinner. *Disappearing vampires. Can wraiths disappear too? The spheros...what can it show? Testing duality. Have we erred all along? Has the balance been tipping in our disfavor for years? How, in all of the Creator's world, can we impede Santiago? This all seems so...unobtainable. Here, now, faced with these otherworldly problems...*

Paavak and Gíselle shared their thoughts as well. *And most of it wasn't good news,* Kate thought of their talk of the surrounding covens. Paavak revealed he knew little of their loyalty to Talorc. Gíselle had a close relationship with the leader of the Ruskill coven but hadn't spoken to her in months. Snow Lake, a small coven quietly nestled on the western side of Manitoba, kept to themselves. Their leadership had recently changed, and Paavak hadn't been out to speak to the new coven head. Talorc had little to shed on the knowledge either, which left Vadin volunteering to do some digging.

Sighing again, Kate glanced at her luggage sitting by the seating area and immediately decided she was too tired to break it down and instead headed for the bathroom. She reached for her scarf which she'd kept donned throughout dinner, feigning a chill, now eager to relieve herself from the confines. A long soak in the tub she hoped was there sounded ideal, and coupled with a glass of wine—

A knock on the door had her pausing, and Kate bit back the groan of annoyance at being disturbed already. She feared what small amount of sleep she could get would be futile because of her roving thoughts, though at the least she'd hoped for solace and time for pensiveness. She needed the introspection; it was all she'd had for months, and the saturated immersion back into reality was overwhelming at times. Less than twenty-four hours ago she'd been an untainted, untraveled, uninformed foof with a haphazard plan to save the world. Now, she didn't know what to think or how to feel. *Could use a little boost of confidence now, mother. Anytime would be great.*

Instead, she found herself walking back over the pine floors and wolfskin rug to the plain door, twisting the knob before pulling it open. Her father stood in the hall, the golden light from the recesses above portraying him with a false aura of warmth and happiness. She knew better, could sense better, even if he refused to show it: Talorc was unsettled.

"I want to let you know I am down the opposite hall," Talorc said, his outerwear draped over his arm. "If you find yourself unable to sleep, I am most likely in the same boat and could use the company."

Kate smiled, a small huff of laughter expelling from her nose. "I was hoping to find a bottle of wine to be my sleep companion."

Talorc rumbled his own laugh. "Perhaps I could do the same."

"I would've expected you to stay downstairs and catch up with Paavak and Gíselle," Kate stifled a yawn from overtaking her features with a scarred but healing hand.

"It is my plan to go back downstairs, but I wanted to collect myself first. And check on you. The night was long, and you experienced much you had not before."

You don't know the half of it, Kate thought, clearing her throat and briefly dipping her eyes from her father's regard. "I'm okay. Just tired."

Talorc's gaze was steady on her, as if he expected her to say more. When she didn't, he said, "I would offer for you to come downstairs as well, but I fear the conversations Paavak, Gíselle, and I would have would be tedious to your ears."

"Maybe that would put me to sleep faster than the wine," Kate joked, and Talorc smiled.

"I find it comforting to know you retain your humor." Kate felt herself soften in the happiness that he exuded, igniting her own. "To know that all was not lost in the time you were gone."

As introspected as she had been as of late, the notion hadn't crossed her mind. "There are pieces of me that remain, just like there are pieces of me that have changed."

"For the better, the stronger," Talorc reminded her, and Kate softened further.

"You will have to be strong, Kathryn," he continued, his tone gentle but with intrinsic determination. "While you have experienced much that is new to you, there is still a battle to come. While I would never think to remove you from the frontlines now, I ask that you proceed with caution. Even I do not know what to expect. But I do know one thing: I will not let anything happen to you, even at the risk of my own life."

"Don't talk like that," Kate said, a little too sharply. "It won't come to that. Oleander said we can do this. To have faith."

Talorc did not seem resolute. His eyes looked between her own as if memorizing their color, their shape, their luminescence.

"My faith is in you and the others. I still wish to find it within myself."

"*Athair,*" Kate whispered, reaching out to brush her hand down her father's arm. "It's in your path that we follow. Don't stop now."

"I am not," Talorc said, though his voice was low with uncertainty. "I am just having difficulty discerning which path is the straightest."

Never had he talked like this with Kate before, and she squeezed his arm to lend him the strength she barely held within herself.

"If there's anything I've learned lately, it's that the path doesn't have to be the straightest." Kate squeezed again before she dropped her hand. "Sometimes it's not the easiest path. Or the least dangerous. It just has to get us to the end."

Talorc looked at Kate with eyes that shined with pride, their brown depths fathomless. "Your wisdom gives me courage." He dipped his head in respectful regard. "May sleep find you well, *Piseag Bheag.*"

"You too, *Athair.*"

Kate watched her father walk the way he came and then shut the door once more. With a twist of the lock she hoped no one else would bother her, and she turned toward the bathroom while kicking off her boots and removing her scarf. She tossed the latter haphazardly to the floor and then reached for her sweater, pulling the clothing over her head and tossing it just as thoughtlessly. She moved into the doorway of the bathroom while tussling her hair and fighting off another yawn, flicking the switch to light the surprisingly large space. There was a sink and toilet to the left, a shower stall to the right, and across the stone floor beneath the floor-to-ceiling, now heavily tinted, window was a gloriously large soaking tub stocked with—

Kate stifled her scream, shielding her nearly bare chest with her hands as she stumbled to a stop.

"What are you doing in here!" she cried, her eyes widening in shock. "Have you been in here the whole time?"

Damian reclined leisurely and fully clothed in the tub, grinning like a youngling. "I was surprised no one heard me cursing under my breath when Talorc wouldn't stop talking."

Kate grappled for a nearby towel to cover herself up with as Damian raised a brow. "You can't be in here." She flushed from head to toe. "How did you even get in here?"

"Balcony," Damian answered simply, tipping his chin toward the doorway. "Took you long enough to get up here."

"I thought you went up with the boys."

"I did. Then I left."

Kate groaned, closing her eyes. "Why won't you just leave me alone? I want to be alone."

"No you don't." Damian hopped out of the tub with ease, eyeing the small hand towel she'd grabbed with a smirk. "A little late to be covering it up, don'tcha think?"

"Get lost," Kate snapped, whirling back toward the bedroom to recover her sweater. It was the last thing she wanted him to do but she wasn't about to let him know that. "Jumping up and breaking in through the balcony like a juvenile..."

A creak on the mattress told her Damian was making himself comfortable while she pulled her sweater back over her head, and a look at said furniture a moment later had her suspicions confirmed. He was sprawled on the bed like it was his own, legs crossed at the ankles and back propped up on the pillows with his hands laced behind his head. He kicked off his boots under her judgmental gaze, not put off in the least.

"Damian, you can't be in here. You can't *stay* here," she

said, crossing her arms as she glared at him. When his eyes dropped to her chest she ditched the pose, and he scowled.

"Why not? I just came to check on you." His smile was lazy as his eyes very blatantly scaled her from head to toe, deviously suggesting his intent lay on the darker side.

"What's Vadin doing?" Kate hemmed impatiently. "Go find him."

"They all turned in. Ryder and Taryn are probably trying out their guest mattress. Cyrus is off being Cyrus. I helped Noir and Vadin bring all the supplies inside. Talorc is talking with Paavak and Giselle. And I don't care about any of them half as much as I do you, so here I am."

Kate's face heated at his openness, but she remained firm. "You have to leave. What if someone finds out you're here?"

"They won't think anything of it. It's not any different from the millions of other times we've hung out."

"Ryder suspects something," Kate said, beginning to pace. "And none of the others are stupid; they'll figure it out eventually. We have to stay separate. Apart from one another."

"Not doing that."

Kate shot him a glower, though her traitorous mind recalled Damian saying, *"You thought I was persistent before? In my denial of you? You'll know my pursuit now, which is actively and eagerly more potent than that."* The ideal had her shivering, and her body came alive, fire striking in the pit that had once been hollow.

"Seriously Kate, I wanted to check on you," Damian continued, moving his hands from behind his head to his lap. "I know you haven't traveled before. Been on a plane before. And now you're going to head right into battle. Not to mention what we did together. It can be a lot. It can be overwhelming. I'm worried about you."

She flushed at the mention of their intimate tryst, knowing the color on her cheeks was a bright crimson. Two sides of her instantly warred: she wanted to vaporize with gooey, girly admiration while the more savage side wanted to remind him, *I don't need no man.* She settled for silence while the fire inside her blazed.

"I wanted to talk to you on the plane," Damian said, his gaze nor his words faltering. "But I didn't know what to say. I wanted to hold you but knew I couldn't. I wanted to do anything to take your mind off things, but I didn't even know where to start. Do you know how much it pained me to see you so uncomfortable for five long hours and not do anything about it? It felt like I was failing you. I never want to fail you again, Kate."

The fire within her snapped with crackling flame, and Kate's heart rate increased. She tried to tamp down on the emotions within, but knew she had little control when it came to Damian. Coupled with the fact that he already knew her so well, there was barely any way to hide her true feelings.

And really, that's okay, she thought. *I know I can be myself around Damian. I can trust him. I have for years. And in light of all that we've experienced, there's no difference. I can still trust him. I can still go to him. I can still seek solace in him. Because he was my friend before anything else and we have that foundation.*

She vacillated quickly, her skin pricking with the turning of her thoughts. *And now he can be more. I just have to let him. I want to let him. I want what he has to offer.*

But I can't, I can't...

But I can...

Kate continued as if he hadn't spoken. "I have to focus on Santiago. On this fight. I can't be distracted. I already feel all over the place and honestly, Damian, you complicate things for me. This entire ordeal is complicated. There's so much to think about, to do, to see.

"Trust me—I want to focus on so many other things. I mean, never in the two hundred years of my life have I been outside my *home city.* I'm trying not to get distracted with everything the world suddenly has to offer because my very life depends on focusing on our plan. But do you have any idea how badly I want to run to the nearest store and grab a camera—or even a journal—and document everything I see so I don't forget it? I just know pictures won't do it justice. I need to express what I'm feeling in the moment, about *everything.* Write down my mood, the auras I pick up on, learn what makes me happy and makes me want to cry. I want to try all different types of food and experience everything the cultures in the area want to share. I want to see the Northern Lights. A polar bear. I want to see wolves and whales and what a beach covered in snow looks like.

"But even if I did get to do all that stuff," Kate finished sadly, stopping her pacing to look at Damian. "I can't make those things a priority. I need to put all my attention into bringing down Santiago. I won't be able to live with myself if we don't succeed in annihilating him."

Damian was off the bed in an instant. "Don't talk like that," he growled, grabbing her arms maybe a little too forcefully. "Don't talk about…"

Kate wilted, only slightly shameful. "I didn't mean it like that. I've transcended that place in my life." And she meant it. *She meant it.* By all that was holy, she meant it. "I need this, Damian. And I won't let anything—or anyone—get in my way. Including you."

Damian squeezed her arms in his warm hands, and Kate couldn't help but heat at the molten look in his eyes.

"I know. And that makes you all the more hot."

Kate rolled her eyes and broke out of his grasp, but not before Damian grabbed her arm and whirled her to face him once more.

"Listen, I know you think you're past everything to a degree, but speaking from experience, what happened will always be there to haunt you. And while that's expected, sometimes it can cloud your judgement, and you'll need a little help to keep going." He pulled her to him once more, closer than before, his hands on her upper arms. "I understand you need to overcome this. I get it. We all do. I want to support you in this and everything else. Just…ask for help, Kate. Ask *me.* It doesn't make you weak. I know you think you have to prove something to all of us, but no one could do this on their own.

"And when all this is over," his voice dropped to a low level, holding more resolve than she'd ever heard before. "I want you to let *me* be the fight you'll have for the rest of your life. Because I will never be who I'm supposed to be without you."

Kate knew the mood of the moment changed not just from the softening of Damian's features but from the whisp of a fuchsia aura that swept them both into its embrace, strengthening the ethereal tether between them.

Well, that and the absolute smothering sensation of *need.*

"Why do I want you so badly?" Kate whispered, and she

watched as his fangs descended from between parted lips, making her instantly wet. "Why can't I control this?"

"It's the same for me," he responded, sweeping his hands up her neck to cradle her head as he tipped her face back. "It's always been like this for me."

Ever the fighter, she tossed her head slightly, though not enough to break from his hold. "But you resisted me for so long."

"And I plan to make up for every moment lost."

Chapter Twenty-Five

They kissed fiercely, an ardent meeting of sensuality. Kate fell into Damian's grasp and his hands moved from her head to her back while hers did the same to him, clutching tightly. He maneuvered them to the bed, pulling at her sweater as he went, while her hands grappled with his belt and jeans, the garments falling to the ground. He held her face in his hands as he sat on the bed, she bending to finesse her own pants and socks from her legs. She clutched onto his shoulders as he kicked his pants and socks away, his hands moving from her face to her hips as she crawled into his lap, a knee on either side of his thighs.

"I told you it was too late for this," Damian said, pushing her sweater up and over her head. When it fell to the floor he groaned, unable to help himself from cupping her breasts in her crimson lace bra. The fact that her panties matched...

Creator take me, he thought, pinching her nipples through the material, causing her to throw her head back and moan. He buried his face between her breasts and began to kiss her there, scraping his fangs along her flesh in the wake of his lips. His coarse facial hair left her skin reddened, but Kate didn't seem to care as she thrust her hands into his hair and pushed her chest to his mouth. She sat in his lap, aligning her core with his cock, and began to rock back and forth, back and forth, causing Damian to hiss and dig his fingers into her hips to still her.

He nipped her clavicle, pressing his mouth to her neck as he said hotly, "Don't."

Kate dipped her hands down his back, gripped his shirt, pulled it over his head, and flung it behind her as she swiveled her delectable hips once more. "Don't what?"

Damian slammed her into place on his lap, shoving his hips up to push his cock against her almost to the point of pain. "Move."

Kate laughed, a sensuous sound of torment. "I like moving against you." She leaned forward and nipped his chin, knocking his head back with her nose to run her lips, and then her fangs, down his neck. "I've been thinking about moving against you for a very long time."

Fire snapped from where her mouth was on his neck all the way down his flesh and back. Her words physically pained him in the sweetest, most damning way. "Likewise," he croaked as he moved his hands from her waist to her ass, finding her underwear was not only transparent but deliciously made to not cover her fully. The subtle swells of her flesh molded to his hands as if they were made for him, and he pressed her down onto his dick as he leaned back fully on the bed, closing his eyes in barely restrained yearning. He began to knead her skin as she kissed his neck, his chest, down his torso to his navel.

He stopped her, his hands moving to her shoulders and pushing her upright. She barely had time to protest before he rolled on top of her and then pulled her to the center of the bed, pressing his hips into her own. He grabbed his cock with one hand and ran it the length of her slit, pushing against the thin fabric that separated them. He could feel her wetness through her underwear, his senses overcome with the essence she exuded, and he shuddered as he nudged her clothed core. He caught her gasp with another fervent kiss, his skin searing with fire as her hands again found him.

"I'm so happy you don't wear underwear," Kate murmured with a laugh against his lips, her fingers dancing along the rigid lines of his cock as it strained for her touch. She leisurely ran one fisted hand down the length of him while the other cupped his balls, squeezing to elicit a sound of constraint from him.

"And I'm so happy you do," Damian said, pulling back to appreciate the length of her slender form, pulling his cock from her grasp. She gazed up at him, flushed in the face and across her chest; her starlit eyes, alabaster skin, and ebony hair was a vision against her scarlet undergarments. Damian felt himself throb painfully as he stared at her breasts, her nipples dusky and pouting from his touch. "You're absolutely stunning."

He couldn't resist kissing her again, and she cupped his face to hers as he did so. Her hands slid from his neck to his shoulders, then down his back, over the dips and crevices of his honed body. He felt appreciation waft from her, a warm caress that had him swelling with male pride. *Mine. My female.* He was reminded in that moment of the jealousy he felt when her hands were on another, and he couldn't stop himself from pulling away from her with a growl.

"Don't ever touch another male again," His copper eyes flashed brightly with the tsunami he felt raging within. "When you touched Vadin…"

She laughed languidly, sensually. "Sorry."

He met her lips for a kiss once more, pulling her tongue into his mouth to suck on. His jealousy faded, replaced with desire, as she mewled gently, her claws leaving welts in his skin. The more she touched him the more torrid he became, his body falling victim to how hard she burned. All because of *him.* The notion sent him to the edge of where he needed to be, and he let their tongues twine a final time as their bodies rolled against one another, lust coursing through him like rapids, while pulling away.

"As much as I like seeing you in lingerie and can't wait to see what else you have in your collection…" He reached between them and popped open the front clasp on her bra, releasing her breasts from their confines. He swept his mouth down her chest, licking each nipple languorously, before sidling down her body to hover just above her mound. "I like seeing you *without it* even more."

With his teeth he took her underwear down her legs, and the scent of her called to him as wantonly as it was eager. She bent her knees to assist his movements, slinking out of her bra and tossing it to the side as well.

Damian kissed one ankle then the other, one calf and then the next, before nudging her thighs apart with his desperate mouth. Kate moaned breathlessly, her denial lost as he licked the top of her pussy, burrowing his face in the depths of her flesh. Her legs fell open in the next moment, and Damian didn't hesitate to taste her, his hands snaking underneath her to cup her bottom. Her essence coated his tongue at the first delve between her folds, and his body quaked with barely restrained desire. He growled into her pussy, causing her to moan again, and her thighs squeezed his head as she gripped the bedsheets. He pushed his tongue inside of her, retracting it only to repeat the ministrations until she turned positively breathless.

"Please, Damian," she whispered, her voice desperate in its imploration. "Please don't stop."

He answered her with a sumptuous lick down her slit, and then flicked his tongue against her clitoris until she writhed. When she tried to pull away from him, he sealed his lips around her bud and sucked, causing her to lift her hips from the bed. He dug his fingers into her buttocks and pulled her back down onto his mouth, making her whimper a futile denial.

"You can't do that…"

Damian lifted himself from between her legs, gazing down at her with hooded eyes. "Then I'll do this instead."

With hands that shook, he grabbed her hips and flipped her so she lay on her stomach, and he nearly spilled himself then and there at the sight of her perfectly petite ass. He kneed her legs apart with his own, pulling himself up her body while leveling his weight on one hand and gripping his cock with the other. Kate's head was turned to the side, and she panted feverishly against the mattress as she clutched at the linen with trembling hands. She lifted her hips as if she were unable to stop herself, effectively baring her sweet pussy to his starving gaze. He nearly stumbled, his grip on his dick tightening as he regained his stance. *Merciful Creator, if I die here…* Damian pushed his cock to her opening, gliding the head against her hot, slick flesh, before sliding into her in one fluid motion.

They both groaned and closed their eyes, Kate wilting beneath him as he turned rigid atop her. She maneuvered so her ass was in the air and her face was down, pushing herself fully onto him as she whimpered unintelligible demands. Damian had to pause to collect himself, but not a heartbeat later he began to move inside of her, addicted to the friction only her body could provide. He gripped her hips tightly, knowing he was going to leave bruises but uncaring; all he thought about, all he tasted, all he knew…was *Kate*. He began a rhythm that left his body simmering, set to roil by the female who had captured his soul in its entirety.

The pounding Damian started sent her spiraling; he felt the fall as well, but he wanted to feel more. Deeper. *Swifter.* Harder. He grabbed her waist and forced her into his lap, falling onto his ass on the bed with his legs bent beneath him. Kate's legs folded neatly beside his hips, and he held her to him as he drove into her from behind, his arms wrapped across her chest to hold her shoulders. She turned her head to gasp against his wrist, clutching his forearms with her hands, using the leverage to meet his thrashing pace.

He wasn't expecting it when Kate's fangs pierced his skin, but the shockwave it sent down his arm went straight to his groin, nearly making him come. He thrust into her fiercely and then stuttered to a stop, almost falling atop her. *Creator, she cannot be this divine,* he thought as he started back up again in earnest. He fought the urge to spill, needing to feel her more, more, *more.* Kate began to drink from him, and he readjusted his hold on her chest so she had easy access to his lifeforce. She began slow pulls, and the moans that ensued made him pulse within her as he lifted his hips to thrust even more mercilessly. Her mouth broke from his wrist a few moments later, when his plunges became so intense she could do little but hold onto his waist for dear life.

Damian threw her forward, forcing Kate to her hands and knees. With the taste of her core lingering on his tongue and the vision of her before him, he allowed the pressure at the base of his spine build as the tide within him swirled with heat.

"Damian, please..."

She didn't stop her wicked begging as he slammed into her, over and over again. Not even when the pitch of her voice changed and her pleas became incoherent murmurs of pleasure. Damian gazed down at her in wonder, his hands tight on her flesh as he strained against releasing his own orgasm, before he couldn't resist her encapsulating rapture any longer. With a roll of his hips, he pushed her to the mattress roughly and laid his lips to her neck before wasting not a second more and impaling her flesh with a ravenous taste for her blood.

Kate drew in a sharp breath but before her scream could loose, Damian clamped a hand over her mouth. Her orgasm contracted her pussy around his cock in abandon and coupled with the exquisite savor of her blood, he fell over the edge as well. He grunted against her neck as he came within her, pushing so hard into her hips that she mewled in protest, weakly straining to pull away from him.

Mine.
A savage part of him that he was just starting to recognize snarled in territorial fury, and he clamped his mouth around her harder and pulled deeply of her blood. Kate shook with another orgasm, and the sensations of her squeezing him wrung the last of the ecstasy from his body. He pulled away from her neck a moment later, and his thrusts slowed; once, twice, three times, before he stopped altogether, though remained fully seated inside her.

Damian opened his eyes to stare down at her, watching as Kate rolled onto her back and threw her arms above her head, opening her own eyes. Their gazes clashed, hooded and content, their breath mingling. So much passed between them in that moment. So much that couldn't be said, or expressed in any way; not now, and maybe not ever. Damian couldn't think about any of that right now. Anything he wanted to focus on was replaced by her.

He rolled from overtop her, lying beside her on the bed. He reached for her, and she let him pull her to him, curling into his side. Their sweat-slicked bodies slid until finding the perfect spot, and it was with her head tucked beneath his chin, ear to his chest, leg looped over his thigh, that he closed his eyes once more, a smile on his lips. Within five minutes they both fell asleep, with Damian thinking this was the most content he'd ever been.

Sometime later, when the day was past midpoint but there was still sun to be had, Damian and Kate found themselves lounging in the soaking tub in her bathroom. He rested serenely with his back to the tub with her sprawled languidly between his legs, warm water waded up to their chests. He was tracing the fresh mark on her neck with an idle hand while she did the same to where she had bitten him on the wrist. They'd hardly spoke, using only the words necessary to get them to where they were now, however the silence around them weighed heavily on Damian's shoulders. The unspoken utterance that fell between them during their time together still lay unnamed, unclaimed, and untamed. Somewhere between those words—and the feelings they brought forth—Damian realized he had a sudden and very visceral urge to tell Kate he loved her.

The ideal both absolutely terrified him and quelled the most desperate part of his soul. He knew she wasn't ready to hear it, and he wasn't too sure he was ready to speak it. He idly wondered when he would be, or more importantly, when she would be. He settled on knowing that in this moment she was happy, and he couldn't remember a single time when he had been so at ease. Even with the future so unknown, at least they had this moment together.

He relished basking in all that was her. In fact, that's how he intrinsically knew she was just as placated as he. He felt resiliency surging within her, fortitude and determination extracted by the wonders he'd shared with her. He noted her satiety, as it was the color of scarlet and wrapped around her every plane like the whisper of a lover's touch. He felt her happiness; it was sunshine, the feeling so abstract to him that it left him speechless for a moment. Yet with her to remind him of what it felt like, what else did he need? She felt so much, grounding him, anchoring him to the present with her vivid vivaciousness... *Creator, but I almost lost her. So many times, I almost lost her...*

Needing to touch her, to swallow the fear that suddenly enshrouded him, he brought his untethered hand up to her shoulder to knead gently. "Are you okay?"

"Fine," Kate murmured, her voice heavy with exhaustion, telling him otherwise.

Guilt immediately stabbed him, the blade sinking thickly in his gut. "Are you sure?" His conscience *hmm*ed, reminding him that he'd taken her virginity and drank from her twice in one day. He said lamely, "Today has been a lot."

"Fine," she muttered again, sounding even more tired than before.

"Kate." He had a startling impulse to see her, even though he could just as easily feel the bond between them and discern her state. He shifted restlessly, uneasily, and she protested unintelligibly when he tried to turn her face.

In answer to his volatile tone, Kate tipped her head back onto his shoulder, displacing his hand, and he was relieved to see a lazy smile tugging at the corners of her mouth. "I'm okay. I promise."

Damian swallowed, his mouth feeling dry as he readjusted himself in the bath in order to see her better. His cock throbbed in response to her naked skin sliding against his own, but he tamped down on the desire with a keen bite.

"It's just…" He watched Kate yawn, but as she did so she brought her hand up to his mouth and began to trace his lips as if she couldn't help herself. His cock immediately responded by twitching, and the fire between them, since waned after their lovemaking, flared once more.

Damian hurriedly stammered out what he'd been about to say to dissuade himself from pulling her into his lap and taking her once more. "I-I know you haven't been with another. With everything else that happened, all the travel and the stress and the times we were together, I just want to make sure you're okay."

"Damian," Kate mumbled, trailing her index finger over one of his fangs and then his bottom lip, her eyes drowsily trailing the movements. The motion had his skin rippling, his mind spinning. "Shut up."

"Kate," Damian said earnestly, trying desperately to resist taking her finger in his mouth, lancing her flesh, and taking from her again. "I'm serious."

Kate paused, lifting a brow as her eyes left his lips to meet his eyes. "You are? I couldn't tell."

He glowered at her, and the resulting laugh did something strange to his insides. They contracted, swelled, then the pressure released, and pleasure undulated through him not born from what they'd just shared. It was a different pleasure, one he hadn't experienced before. It went deeper and touched parts of him that yawned awake, basking in the light of her joy.

"I'm okay," she amended. "Just sleepy." She resettled against him, nuzzling his shoulder and then his neck. "And I'll be okay going forward. We have another half night of travel, remember? That's plenty of time for me to recover."

"I wish it was longer," Damian mumbled. Their plan to take the rail—which would've meant another two full days of traveling—had been turned over during dinner, knowing they needed the extra time to get to Ruskill before Santiago. Cyrus had called Bianca then and there, who confirmed she could get them to Ruskill no problem. Kate had been a little sad at missing her first train excursion Damian knew, and he made a mental note to arrange a ride for her as soon as all this was over.

"Besides, we're staying at Blackwood through tonight and into tomorrow. Mikom will have reached Snow Lake by then.

Hopefully he brings good news."

It had also been decided at dinner that Mikom would be their ambassador to Snow Lake, saving them from sending a Guard. "Hopefully," Damian said, his mind distractedly elsewhere. He just...he couldn't stop thinking about Kate's wellbeing.

"Are you...sore?" He lifted his hands to run them from her thighs down to her knees to divert his guilt into his attentions for her.

Kate shrugged. "Maybe a little."

Damian couldn't help it: his cock stirred further at the memory of what they'd done, and then again as he murmured, "I was your first." He squeezed her thighs with calloused hands, feeling both pleased and tortured by the notion; while he never wanted to cause her any harm, he was immensely satisfied with the ideal that he would be the only one to ever have her.

He felt her vibrate with laughter. "Yes Damian. Does it make you happy to hear it?"

"Yes," he admitted, a smirk curling onto his lips. He turned his head to place his mouth to her head, muttering, "I'm sorry I can't say the same."

Kate moved her head so she could eye him once more. "Ew. That's weird to bring up. And makes me think of every other woman or female you've been with." Her face clearly said *way to go, butthole.*

Damian squirmed internally and fought with his body not to elicit the movements. He brushed his hair out of his face as he said, "Sorry. I just... It makes me feel...less than. Less than you deserve. I know I did a lot to hurt you. To drive you away. I didn't mean to bring up the reminder, I just—"

Kate smiled, and he knew the front to be a devious one. "You're rambling."

He glowered, and Creator strike him, he felt his cheeks heat. "Well."

"Well, what?" Kate said with a small laugh. "If it bothers you that much you can make it up to me with lavish gifts."

He rumbled his own laugh. "Don't you think people would really start to suspect then?"

"The way I shop?"

He laughed again, and Kate pecked a small kiss to the

underside of his jaw. The contracting and swelling within his chest amplified, and he suddenly had the very moving thought that this is what he'd been missing in all his years of his denial of her.

Utter happiness. Radiant, blissful happiness.

"You're not less than, nor have you ever been. A little misguided, but you're here now."

Her words left him dumbstruck. In them was a forgiveness he didn't know he needed nor thought he would ever receive. He cleared his throat to rid it of the tightness and, while he was on the trek for clemency, he decided to continue, "I'm sorry for that. For a lot of things."

Kate whispered softly, smiling still, "I know."

"I'm sorry I was rough with you, too. I'll be gentler. Next time." It felt like a lie, leaving his mouth dry as cotton.

"That was rough?" She turned her head back to look at their intertwined legs as she ran her hands down his arms and finished coyly, "I didn't think so. I liked it."

The pure delight in her tone left him throbbing.

"I left marks," he said weakly, trying not to focus on the way her touch sent sparks down his limbs.

"So? They'll go away."

Damian groaned. "You don't know what you're getting yourself into by talking to me this way."

Kate laughed, squeezing his forearms. "Sorry. I'll stop."

His rebuttal was fierce, "No. Don't ever." *Fuck it all, but I'm doomed.*

And I am so looking forward to it.

"I do have to ask." Damian decided he was already too far down this path now to turn around. "How did you ever learn to move like that?"

"Porn."

His dick instantly shot hard, and Kate laughed aloud at the feel of him against her back. He flushed with heat, his internal stillness rippling with scorching desire.

"You didn't think I was totally innocent, did you?" Kate turned in the bath to face him with a coiling smirk. She moved to the other side of the tub, bending her legs to hide her breasts. "Do you have any idea how many times over the years I touched myself while thinking about you?"

Damian slammed himself away from her, so hard his back cracked against the tub. "Kate... Don't... We can't..."

"Here you go, telling me what to do again." Kate raised an eyebrow as she continued to smirk. She lifted a foot and trailed it up his calf, to his thigh, and then back down, water jostling around them. "Don't act like you don't want to."

Damian's chest heaved with barely restrained yearning. "Didn't you say you needed to focus on other things?"

Kate's eyes dipped below the water, to where his member stood proud and ready for another achingly deviant bout of pleasure.

She looked back up at him, her blue eyes bright. "I am."

He was on her in the next second, and then everything else was a blur.

Kate stood near the door to her borrowed room, watching as Damian collected the rest of his things. He did so slowly, reluctant to leave her. They'd spent the remainder of the sun's hours together in wondrous rapture, and then a deep, albeit short respite, before sharing a shower and then admitting they had to part. The rest of the house would be waking soon, and if they wanted to remain secretive of their changing relationship, he knew they had to separate.

"You'll come down for breakfast?" Damian slid his shoes onto his feet before walking over to the door. Kate was dressed in a white guest robe she'd found in the closet, her short hair mussed from the sleep he'd just dragged her from, but otherwise appearing well. She'd drank from him again, as he had encouraged her to do so, and the knowledge that he both satiated and pleased her would fortify him for whatever was to come.

She hummed a *hmhmm* and Damian placed a hand on her cheek to kiss her deeply. She folded into him, her hands on his chest, before he pulled away to look down at her. Her face was flushed across her nose and cheeks, and her breath heaved out of her in huffing breaths.

"Don't do that," she said, though she didn't let go or step away.

Damian stared hard at her, his throat so tight he couldn't take a breath. She was absolutely stunning, and it physically aggrieved him to leave her.

"I can't think when you do that," she whispered, and finally, one finger after another, she released his shirt. But she still didn't move away.

Damian's eyes narrowed, both dangerous and hungry. His appetite had been whetted again—though he knew he would forever be this way around her. There was no dulling his need for her, even though he'd claimed her several times over the course of the last day. The floodgates had been opened. Especially when he knew how she felt, deep in the depths of her soul. Especially in the light of their shared bond—*my beloved.*

"This change between us," she said, wonder in her tone. "I don't know how I feel about it."

He cleared his throat, a nervous sound. "What do you mean?"

"This sudden...*want.* I'm...insatiable. I need to be around you. All the time. More than ever before. I want to know what you're doing, what you're thinking. When other females look at you a vicious jealousy overcomes me. I can't stop thinking about you. It wasn't so long ago that you were doing everything you could to get away from me. Now...now we can't keep our hands off one another. I like it. I want it. But it's...it's so different than where we were. It makes me wonder...how...what changed." She shook her head, and confusion pulsed from her like waves from an earthquake.

"Kate," Damian interjected swiftly, feeling himself spiral into madness along with her. Everything she felt he reciprocated to a frightening degree. Distantly, he realized her abduction put him *exactly* where he needed to be: in this moment, realizing his full potential as a male. He also realized their current situation could be limited. *No.* He'd lived too long and worked too hard to be robbed of the best years of his life.

"From the instant you whisked through the doorway in the kitchen you've been in my every waking thought and plaguing my dreams. I've wanted you since the moment I saw you; the only thing that has changed is how *much* I want you now. I remember wondering how one female could exude the entire universe with just a smile. How is it possible that you hold all the stars in your eyes? I couldn't stop thinking about it, and now I have my answer.

It's because you're *my* universe. The entirety of who I am and will become."

She shook her head as if unable to comprehend. "There's just so much—"

"The thought of losing you," Damian found himself confessing sharply as he took her face in his hands once more. "For good. That's what changed. It changed everything.

"When you were taken, I realized that life could change—*does* change—in the blink of an eye. But I still wasn't ready to accept everything your capture altered between us and within myself. I was still trying to make excuses or pretend like things could remain the same. But my world was already shifting; even then there was no going back, no turning from the future. I wasn't myself when you were gone and I'm still not whole now. Your absence affected me more than I'm willing to admit. Now that I have you, I won't just let you go. I can't. *You* are my chance at happiness. At *life*. I'm going to show you that I can give you the same thing: a reason for being and the happiness that comes with it. Because you *are* my reason for being, Kate. What's changed is that I can admit it now. I'm not afraid anymore."

He saw her eyes shimmer with unshed tears and felt a wave of despair sweep from her so cold that it stole his heartbeat for a moment. *Why?* Yet while the organ shuddered the bitter sheen of ice from its ventricles, the despair still lingered.

"Why this sadness?" Damian whispered, his thumbs tracing her cheekbones.

"I don't...I don't know," she responded, her eyes so vivid.

Damian stared at her with all the desperate want he possessed. *You mean more to me than my own life. How do I show you? How do I tell you?*

He said to her, "I'll help you figure it out. Cast it aside. And then I'll replace it with everything you deserve."

She closed her eyes and turned her head toward the floor and Damian's chest ached at the gesture. He tipped her chin back up so he could drink in everything she was feeling, though it was still too much for him to comprehend. They stared at one another for a long while, lost in the swirling abyss that was the unknown.

"You're going into the city tonight, right?" she finally asked him softly, her eyes trailing his features.

"Yes, with the others. Ryder wants to scout the city."

She nodded once. "I'm going to stay here with father and Paavak, to go over what's to come now that things are fully in motion."

"The rest will be good for you," Damian told her, continuing his gentle caress. "Promise me you'll take it easy."

"I promise." Kate's fingers curled along his pectoral muscles. "Promise me you'll be safe tonight."

"I will." The statement felt final, their parting goodbye, but neither moved. "I'm just down the hall if you need anything."

"Okay," Kate said, and he caught the tail end of her breath with another savoring kiss. They broke apart slowly, their lips lingering, before Damian kissed her forehead and she opened the door for him, leaning against it. He glanced back at her one last time after he crossed the threshold, and with a smile he didn't feel, he departed from her.

Despite everything in him calling to forever remain by her side.

Chapter Twenty-Six

The plane ride to Ruskill was less eventful than the one to Winnipeg, and Kate tolerated it a little better. She wasn't queasy as she disembarked from the plane, but then again, she could focus on little else than the biting weather that greeted her on arrival. *How can it be this cold?* She clamped her teeth together to keep them from chattering, rounding her shoulders inward. *Creator, how can anyone stand anything this cold?*

The airport in the small seaside town was less than a quarter of the size of Winnipeg's; a single, two-story building and some scattered hangars greeted them. Bianca informed them the airport was rarely without a fine layer of snow, and the weather had indeed turned from their favor immediately upon landing, with the intensity and volume increasing. Bianca also told them the brusque winter storm wasn't to decline anytime soon, and Kate was glad for the warm enclosure of the SUV as her party hurried in from the cold.

The Ruskill coven, a home on Isobel Lake, was where they planned to spend less than twenty-four hours before Talorc travelled to the cabin near the park. *Hopefully,* Kate thought, as Noir had brought word back that his initial correspondence with the coven's leader, Uru, had been vaguely apathetic. The notion made Kate suspect she toed the line regarding her loyalty to Talorc, however she was a great friend of Gíselle's. They planned to use the tie to their advantage and the female traveled with them now, as did Paavak.

The vampires who lived at the Ruskill coven were indigenous to the area, with a heritage that traced back to the peoples who'd lived on the landmass for thousands of years. Kate learned through Vadin that Uru had been in her seat of power for just over a generation, and the coven itself was a small one named after the lake it bordered. A family of seven made up the entirety of the vampire population in the town and surrounding area; it used to be larger, Kate also learned, but harsh times caused their numbers to decline.

The drive to Isobel Lake would take a little over twenty minutes but only included somewhat of a road. Kate gathered from her research that tarmac didn't suit the area well, and most of the roadways were dirt and winter debris. She glanced at the car's dashboard as she settled into her seat with Damian beside her, noting the temperature outside to be negative twenty-five degrees Fahrenheit. *Frigid temperatures are not my thing,* she thought as Ryder took to the driver's seat, Talorc to the passenger's. *And I'm about to find out if off-roading is or isn't, too.*

Strangely enough, glacial coldness notwithstanding, Kate felt more invigorated and energized than ever, with a strength in her marrow that wasn't there before. *It has to be Damian's blood.* His life source was like high octane fuel to her body, and she'd healed from his bites and the lingering bruises from Santiago in no time at all. Coupled with the sleep she'd been getting and the meals she'd been provided, her cheeks weren't as hollow, and her bones didn't grotesquely stick out from her skin anymore.

Paavak and Gíselle climbed in to settle in the third row, and with a goodbye to Bianca they were off into the night. The moon was almost impossible to see overhead, muted of its waxing gibbous phase by the snow, and Kate watched the night go by through arctic swirls as Ryder navigated them slowly over slippery roads. *No polar bears or Northern Lights tonight,* she thought, sighing gently. Damian, hearing the sound, pressed his knee into hers, and she glanced at him as a small smile bent her lips.

He had indeed returned safely to her, having spent most of the night before in Winnipeg with the rest of The Guard. Noir had taken them about the city, trying to garner any patterns of movement from the transit centers or deduce if there were areas heavy with wraiths. Their recon was unremarkable, which made each of them more apprehensive. If there were no wraiths in the city, they were certainly elsewhere.

Kate, in contrast, had stayed behind at Blackwood. She'd met with several heads of households as they'd flooded the coven to converse with Talorc, promising their aid in the fight to come. Each vampire that pledged their hand to Talorc assured him they had their own method of travel and would arrive at Ruskill the night to follow this one. Furthermore, calls came in from covens far and wide pledging their allegiance. More than a few were inquisitive of her, and Kate found herself emboldened by the knowledge that she could continue to create a new version of herself. But as the time loomed closer for Talorc to go to the cabin, Kate realized how little of it they had left.

One being they hadn't heard from was Mikom, which unsettled Talorc and Paavak alike. He was due to arrive in Ruskill in the coming hours, and Gíselle blamed the poor weather for his lack of communication. Vadin was having trouble with his laptop this far out from civilization and couldn't confirm any information on him. She wouldn't say it aloud, but Kate didn't have confidence that Mikom would return with good news, if he did at all. He'd spent more time flying than on land in the past twenty-four hours, and with the weather as inclement as it was, Kate was sure he wouldn't be joining them for the fight to come.

The coastal road they took to get to the Ruskill coven was unlined and covered in snow, and the only reason Kate knew the bay was near was because of the briny hint of salt in the air. The land around them was vast and empty, without houses, stores, or even utility poles, with a thick layer of snow hiding its true nature. Ryder turned off the bumpy, dirt path onto a smaller, similar one directed inland, and Kate watched the land change from merely snow-covered to that and dotted with trees. The trees became denser the further Ryder drove, and it was under the cover of tall, thick pines that Isobel Lake was revealed.

The property was less grand than Blackwood, but still striking. A beautiful two-story home made of wood sprawled in either direction, prefaced by a wraparound porch with thick timber columns. Warm light spilled from the home, golden glows in every window, yet it was the lone figure who stood on the porch wrapped in a patterned blanket that captured Kate's attention as she disembarked from the vehicle. A female with long hair plaited in two ropes on either side of her head, her tanned skin untainted by the sun, watched them in stoic regard. She had dark, knowing eyes and stern features, and her greeting was clipped as the rest of

Talorc's party huddled around the entryway to the home.

"Come in," she offered, though her stance was as frigid as the night around them. The words she spoke next bordered on antipathy, as if she wished the opposite. "So as not to freeze."

She must be Uru, Kate thought, her eyes keen on the female. She attempted to pick up on any auras the female portrayed, but she was startlingly and confoundedly neutral.

Gíselle and Paavak led the way, each exchanging a brief embrace with Uru after they topped the stairs to the porch. Ryder and Taryn followed next, and then Talorc with Kate. Kate watched as Uru tilted her head back, elongating her already slim face, and narrowed her eyes at Talorc. Talorc nodded his head in welcome and the female declined to reciprocate; her brown eyes were less than hospitable, and she showed no deference to his title. Kate, in turn, tapered her own eyes, but followed her father into the home, nonetheless. The others who made up their convoy trailed through the carved wooden door, and it was Uru who shut it before moving into the large living room to take her seat next to a fireplace.

The space was lit by the candles in the windows and a handful of towering floor lamps. A crackling hearth sparked from one end of the room, while a wood stove radiated heat from the open kitchen. The seating was cozy, a large brown sectional and two matching chairs, and the décor reflected the woodsy characteristics of a log cabin, though not nearly as opulently as Blackwood.

As Kate took a seat on the sectional, she noted halls and doorways branched off from the living space to lead to other places in the house. Down the lengths, Kate could sense others inside, but they remained quiet and removed. The odors of pine and smoke were heavy on the air, yet underneath, Kate could still discern a trace of Damian's soothing saltwater scent, and she drew a deep breath in order to steady her racing heart.

Uru settled her wrap around her shoulders and indicated the chair opposite her own. "Sit," she said to Talorc, and after removing his outwear he did so. Ryder stood behind him with Cyrus, while the females in their group took to the couch next to Kate and the males stood scattered behind them. When no one spoke, it became pristinely evident tension held their tongues.

Kate encouraged herself to be brave and speak first. "You

open your home to us, though it's obvious it's done reluctantly."

Uru tipped her head to look at Kate, her face void of feeling. Yet the first sighting of an aura suddenly permeated her presence: auburn anger glowed warningly, and if she delved further Kate could sense hostility coiling just underneath her skin.

"When your lackey reached out to me to ask for shelter and aide, warning of dire times, I was not eager to acquiesce."

Kate heard Noir shift somewhere behind her, though her father remained stationary.

"We don't do so lightly," Kate continued, her tone bordering on sharp. "We would apologize for the brusqueness of our arrival, but there isn't time to delay."

"According to whom?"

Is she for real? "Us. The ones spearheading all this."

"What, if you care to divulge, is even happening? All we hear are rumors. The vampire nation has been kept in darkness for so long I'm not sure you even know we exist."

Kate felt her blood begin to roil, aggravated by the female's hostility. "That's why we're here," she snapped, as her father remained rigidly controlled beside her.

"Who are you to speak to me in such a manner?" Uru's voice dripped with acid as readily as her expression.

"My daughter," Talorc said, his voice a low rumble.

"My name is Kathryn," Kate answered for herself, her eyes stayed on Uru. "I won't bother you with pleasantries, as it seems they have little effect on you. We came here to ascertain your loyalty. Noir told us his initial contact was less than appreciated, even with the knowledge of what's transpiring and what has happened to bring us here."

It seemed as though she responded through gritted teeth when Uru said, "It would be beneath me not to express my apologies for your suffering; no one should have to go through what you did. While I recognize The Guard, I didn't know it was you who traveled alongside Talorc. There are many of us in the vampire nation who don't know your countenance. I ask that you forgive my words, as I'm very much taken by surprise. Though I will warn you my enmity for this entire situation runs deep."

Kate, knowing she had to curb some of her animosity, nodded once. "Thank you."

"Uru," Gíselle said, her petite hands folded in her lap. "It's with earnest that we come here. We're sorry to encroach, but you know we wouldn't do so if things weren't grim."

Uru said nothing, but her eyes flashed as her anger intensified.

"Oleander came to Blackwood," Paavak supplied.

"You lie." |

Paavak, with a deep frown, replied, "I would never on such a matter."

"The watchers are distant. Couldn't be concerned with what we're doing."

"On the contrary: he warned us the tide is changing. He confirmed the vampire nation, humankind as well, is in danger if we don't act. We know you are somewhat up to speed, so believe me when I tell you this: Santiago needs to be stopped. And going forward, to eliminate what could linger afterwards, Talorc needs our support."

Uru looked at Talorc, who remained silent but listened intently to the exchange. "There are many who are upset by your lack of action. Many who would be less welcoming than I."

You call your reception welcoming? Kate thought, and almost opened her mouth to say so. *Dignified,* she reminded herself, *be dignified.*

"And we're afraid that has caused a veritable rift, one that has even influenced some to side against Talorc," Paavak said. "But the vampire nation cannot afford to be so divided."

"An uphill battle," Uru murmured, her eyes darkening. She wore a thick bracelet made of bone and red and black beading, with dangling earrings to match, and the jewelry made subtle noise as she placed her hands in her lap.

"I will always be the first to admit that I have made appallingly near-fatal mistakes over the past years," Talorc said, his eyes fixed on Uru. "Only recently have I realized how disastrous my actions have been, and how my reluctance to fortify and embolden our nation has caused its near collapse. I am not without fault, but I am also not without contrition. If I could change how I handled things I certainly would, but I cannot. I am here now, however, to show you that I am ready to make amends and unify us once more. To do that I need your help in this; I need all the coven leaders to my side. We need to combine our strengths and fight this would-be usurper." His own gaze grew dark as he finished, "It has been confirmed that Santiago is working under the hand of Adhamh."

Uru said tightly, "Adhamh?"

Talorc nodded, Paavak's mien shadowing with strain in the wake of it.

"Not likely." Uru dismissed the notion easily. "Besides: you want to take on a watcher? One who is rumored to be vile beyond measure, calamitous in nature, with powers untold?"

"If we stop Santiago it won't come to that," Ryder said. "Adhamh can't amass power if he has no one to do his bidding."

"Yet you said Santiago's reach is limitless," Uru argued. "Implying there will always be someone else."

"We have the opportunity to get ahead if we seize the moment now," Talorc said.

Uru's nostrils flared and she leaned back in her chair, her face masked in icy stoicism. "No. I refuse to believe this could be Adhamh's doing."

Gíselle started once more, "Uru—"

"Why should we help you when we were left to rot for decades?" Uru's hands coiled around the arms of her weathered chair as she leaned forward to snarl at Talorc, "Our coven has dwindled, and though our numbers were never large, we could have used outside aide time and time again to see us through harsh winters and long summer days. Do not make me count the times foes came to our doorstep hoping to catch us unawares. This is all barring the fact the *nation* itself has declined; my coven is not the only one that's suffered from your slackened hand. Do you even know how many vampires still stand? You have done *nothing* to see us flourish in the past two centuries. Never once reached out. To any of us. Countless have died by *your* idle hand. All you did was sit in your home, continuing to demand your due, while we struggled to survive. I would argue that your presence now is too little, too late. And you come asking for support?" Uru's hands relaxed and she leaned back in her chair, her back straight, her eyes gleaming with loathing. "Why should I help you remind the others why you deserve to be king?"

"Show your respect," Ryder growled. "Or you will be

replaced with someone who knows how."

Talorc lifted a hand, and the captain of his Guard bit back on the rest of his response.

"You are lucky I care deeply for Gíselle and Paavak or I wouldn't be entertaining this conversation," Uru continued, her lip curling as she looked down at Talorc with disdain. "You couldn't even be bothered to reach out to me personally."

"There wasn't time," Talorc said, maintaining his calmness while those around him smoldered; it was all Kate could do not to interject with a well-timed *fuck you.* "Although the conversation I needed to have with you I wanted to do in person, I thought it would be better received if I sent word ahead in caution."

"You were wrong," Uru said flatly, her countenance hinting she was almost done with this conversation.

"I advise you to think about what you're asking, Talorc. Not only are you in need of assistance to scourge the Earth of this tyrant, but you are wanting to reclaim your place as *king.* What have you done to prove that you're worth such a seat? Have you even asked yourself why you want the throne? It can't be because you think your tie to the watchers proves your significance; they have been of little help, if at all. Is it money? Because as our numbers fall there will be less of that to have. It can't be only because you think you deserve it, have earned it from your years of battle prowess— that means nothing in this day and age." Uru turned her face away slightly, her eyes narrowed and sharp on Talorc. "You may be the oldest vampire, but that doesn't mean you are fit to lead any longer."

The room rang with silence, as even the fire seemed to falter.

"Who would you suggest then," Talorc asked, his tone unreflective of how he truly felt; Kate sensed his disquiet. "To take my place and the burdens it carries?"

Uru's nostrils flared once more. "Maybe we don't need a leader anymore. We have survived this long without."

"You bemoan that you struggle to stay afloat as the waters churn," Cyrus rumbled, causing Uru's eyes to flash to him. "What happens when they begin to drown you? You'll need an ally then, too."

"We're already drowning," Uru snapped, her fangs glinting.

346

"You think that ally is you?"

"There are others who side with Talorc: Jean-Luc, Robertha, and Heath are only some who have spoken their support. Uru," Gíselle interceded, repositioning her hands. "Please, have heart. You know what Talorc has gone through. There are not many who stand among the living in the wake of losing a part of their soul."

"That's two hundred years passed." The cruel tone in which she said it had Kate bristling. She bit her tongue to hold herself back, but the action was becoming futile.

"I'm sorry you lost your beloved," Uru said in a tone that suggested she wasn't, looking at Talorc once more. "And in such a tragic way. But you are blind and deaf if you think that hasn't been happening to hundreds of other vampires. We are hunted, with even our own turning against us, for promises of power and wealth. *Our own kind,* Talorc. The Hangmen still exist. And the wraiths are getting smarter, stronger. Do you know there is another vampire working with Santiago, one who is just as powerful? Who has an even more voracious appetite for supremacy? By all the Creator possesses, we just want *peace.*"

Kate's eyes widened, the knowledge chilling. *Another? There can't be. I thought Santiago was the top of the totem pole.*

"If you defeat Santiago, are you ready to move onto this foe next? This battle you seek, it doesn't end here in Ruskill. It will linger, for years to come, and encompass so many more, taking lives across the globe. You will have to stretch your campaign overseas. Too thin it will make you. Are you ready for that? Do you know what it entails? Is that what you want?"

Uru finished, "I will ask you this again: what makes you think you deserve to be king?"

A hard silence fell over them all, and Kate felt more than one shard of animosity concentrated on Uru. She was among the throng, but she knew her father had to speak for himself in this moment; Uru would respect and accept nothing less.

"As much as I ask for forgiveness and assistance, I am also asking for understanding," Talorc began. "I know I have wronged you. I have wronged many. There is no reneging on my idleness. I cannot change the past. But I *can* change the future. I *want* to. I want to see the vampires succeed, to crush the wraiths, and

347

Santiago, and Adhamh. Those abominations have no right to our world. This is not about money or notoriety. This is about survival. If we do not stop the wraiths and their allies, the world will change in unimaginable ways. The watchers cannot intervene without shifting a cosmic balance, which is why it is up to us to unite and see the end to this diabolical fiend.

"You ask why I deserve to be king?" Talorc continued. "I do not have an answer for you. Not right now. But I would ask: do you know of many who would take my place and try to make amends? To fight for what is good and what is right? To lead a gathering to stabilize the world on its axis, as it tilts toward chaotic disarray? What is happening is well beyond you and I both, but together, with the rest of the vampire nation, we can fight for the peace and serenity we deserve, that we in turn lend to humankind. Earth is our home, and I will fall into madness before it is taken from us. I am in agreement with you that things have gone untended for too long. I want to make it right. I want to see things balanced. And while you may not think I deserve to be king, I am one of the only ones that has the courage to do what needs to be done. I have not lived for more than a thousand years for it to end like this."

"What is your goal, then?" Uru asked.

"Deliverance," Talorc responded. "For those who desire it and those who deserve it."

Uru held her quiet, staring hard at Talorc. Kate sensed she was vacillating. She also sensed the female was inherently good and loyal, but years of disservice had corrupted her.

"I know my father has a lot to accomplish in the face of absolution," Kate started. "But you'll only hinder the entirety of the vampire nation if you don't unite with us. Because we *will* be victorious in this. If you continue to be a roadblock, we will trample you like one. My father may not deserve to be king in your eyes, but there is no better leader in mine. Find me another who has travelled the lands and the seas as well as he has. Find me another who can recite and uphold the *Elden Edicts* as well as he knows the pommel of a sword. Find me another with friends across continents, who would die in his name. Find me another who would lay down his life for what's right, what's true, and what's owed, without a question or a doubt. *Find me another.*

"I'll ask *you* this, Uru: do you want to be part of the

solution, or the problem?"

Uru turned her stoic façade to Kate, who refused to shrivel under her relentlessly ruthless gaze.

"Tell me why I should bow to you too, daughter of Talorc."

"I'm not asking you to bow," Kate almost snapped, but pulled back on her anger with shaking hands. *Dignified.* She softened her tone from brittle to one of heartened persuasion as she said, "I'm asking you to walk alongside us."

No one spoke. For a long time, no one spoke. No one moved, and even the breath in the room became still. The fire crackled hotly, spitting embers onto the stone floor before it.

"This talk of an attack," Uru said, her voice steady. "You're planning for a large one?"

"Yes," Talorc replied. "I am to head to the cabin that belongs to Paavak to draw the interests of Santiago there."

"There's a park there."

"On the edge, yes. Near Morton Lake."

"You will draw much attention to the area."

"On the contrary," Kate replied. "We've done our research. The land has dense patches of trees with a lot of lakes and marsh-like areas. The weather will work in our favor as well; the water should be frozen, and the snow will make it difficult for them to track us. There is no electricity and no cell service. The area isn't habitable for humans, so they won't be a problem."

"You are aware that the weather here is well below freezing at night."

"We're immune to such things."

"You can still get cold. Frostbite can still occur, even though it may not linger."

"We have medical staff," Talorc gestured toward the females with such a background. "And there are more on their way."

"And you have acquired vehicles to get you to the cabin?"

"Yes."

"And you know the times of sunrise and sunset? Have accounted for the changing of the weather? Have weaponry and means of survival in the wilderness?"

"Everything we could think of," Talorc replied steadily.

Uru hesitated, remaining pensive as she said, "There is one

thing you don't know well."

"And that is?" Kate bit out, the words clipped; she had enough of the female's resistance. *She's making it more than clear where she stands.* She felt a hand on the couch behind her and heard the scrape of Damian's boot as he neared her.

"The land," Uru responded, her eyes first on Kate and then Talorc. "I would be willing to show you the easiest routes, and how to avoid the most dangerous areas."

Kate immediately felt her fury dispel, and a huge weight lifted from her shoulders.

Yes. Yes!

"Does this mean I have your backing?" Talorc asked, his tone one of caution.

Uru narrowed her eyes as she said, "Through this, help me remember why you should retain your place as liege, Talorc. Show me you can triumph and are still the male of legend I know. If you succeed, I promise you will have a loyal ally in me once more."

Immediately after their conversation, Uru secluded herself in her study with Talorc, The Guard, and Paavak, leaving the females to bring in the supplies necessary to see them settled. Kate found herself impressed by all that Cyrus was able to procure in such a short period of time, and with it all piled in the garage, Kate's hope surged once more. *We can do this. We have to do this.* She helped Lilith, Fiona, and Taryn create a makeshift treatment area in the dining room, and while they worked, she caught more than one set of curious eyes peeking around darkened doorways. Harsh whispers would draw them away, but their presence confirmed to Kate there was more than one child in the house. The notion left her ill at ease; though the fighting would be far removed from Isobel Lake, she wanted to put no youngling at risk.

With three hours to spare, Uru took Talorc and The Guard out in her personal vehicle to survey the land near the cabin. Kate used the time for respite, though there was little to be had. *How could anyone sleep under these circumstances?* Kate thought of her roiling emotions. With battle looming, she knew the apprehension and unease that came from it would keep most of them from repose. Just so, those left behind found themselves huddled around the hearth after all was said and done, conversing lightly of nothing in particular.

After a while, a young female named Sesi came to the adjoining kitchen and offered to make hot coffee and tea for everyone. She introduced herself as Uru's sister and revealed the prying eyes to be her niece and nephew from a brother long passed. She exposed the other members of the household as her cousins, one with a beloved, and disclosed delicately that any elders were no more. Her cousins, twin brothers with long sweeping hair and traditional Inuit tattoos on their faces, came forward to introduce themselves as Kalliq and Tulok. Shortly after, the remaining household members came forth, making for good company as they waited for the reappearance of the others.

Kate was sleepily sipping hot tea and watching the fire dance when the scouters returned, ice and snow caked to their outwear. Her eyes immediately focused on Damian, and she straightened in her seat while putting aside her mug. She stood and walked to him, reaching to assist with shucking his outwear. With so many others doing the same their exchange went unnoticed, and they were able to enjoy a brief moment of silent relief the other remained safe.

As Kate slipped Damian's jacket from his shoulders, they slowed in their actions, eyes locking, lost in one another. Kate felt a surge of elation through the bond they shared, noting the golden glow of happiness that became him. She smiled slightly, a gentle tilt of her lips, before the flurry of movement swept them apart. She turned to hang his jacket on a post by the door, however when she glanced at him again, Damian's eyes were still on her, and the pretense he gave her was one of sincere affection and fiercely unwavering devotion.

Uru showed The Guard to their appointed guest rooms before excusing herself to get changed and warm up. As much as she wanted to follow Damian to his room, Kate knew she couldn't, and it was with a wilted smile that she bid him a quiet, secret farewell. The younglings had long been put to bed for the day, and Kate watched with a yawn as Sesi and Gíselle began to draw the curtains to bar the sunrise. Kate helped and then retired shortly thereafter, her heart heavy and her thoughts only on what was to come.

Chapter Twenty-Seven

The snow finally stopped falling, and as Kate walked out onto the porch at Isobel Lake the next night, she inhaled deeply of the bitter air. Needing a moment to herself before the anarchy unfolded, she looked up to appreciate the clear, sparkling sky. *I've never seen stars shine like this.* So endless in their beauty, she had difficulty tearing her gaze away. The fallen snow lent a quiet to the land she'd never experienced before, muffling the very sounds of the earth and cosmos beyond. It made her feel serenely alone. It was a humbling sensation, yet as the house behind her bustled with commotion, it was a staunch reminder she was to be anything but in the coming hours.

The plan for the night had been dissected nauseatingly throughout the day because, of course, no one had slept. Talorc, Kalliq, Uru, and The Guard were to head to the cabin while Kate and the others waited at the airport to converge with those who were due to arrive. Though no one liked the idea of such a small party embarking on their own into the wilderness, any more would be suspicious to watching eyes, as would Talorc going on his own. *We have to draw Santiago to the cabin. It's our only chance to get this right.* Calls came in all day with updates from those who promised to be there to show their support to Talorc, however Mikom and the Snow Lake coven had yet to respond.

Refusing to think about the upcoming separation of their group, Kate turned her eyes outward, to the trees dotting the property. Snow layered the branches heavily, almost as much as she was burrowed in winter clothes. Even so, she felt the bite of the cold against her face and pulled her scarf to cover her nose and mouth. *Who knew I would ever be standing here, in this exact spot, to appreciate all this?* She continued her projections, trying not to think about how she secretly feared this could be the last time she would have such time. She brusquely tossed the notion away, negating the ideal that they would leave Ruskill as failures.

I've come so far in so little time. From the broken, battered female with a future blacker than the sky above to who I am now. From worthless, pathetic, useless, disgraceful, hopeless, dark, morbid, plaguing, defiled, hateful, disgusting, and woeful to resiliently transformed into a worthwhile and stalwart female. Everyone was right—I am beyond who I was in Santiago's clutches. But I needed to go through what I did. I had to get here to realize it.

I'm proud of myself no matter what happens tonight, she thought, just as the door behind her opened. She knew it was Damian by his soothing seawater scent, and she glanced over her shoulder to confirm such as he came to stand beside her. As she gazed into his shining copper eyes, she finished her musings with: *I've overcome the worst of my demons; anything to come, I can most certainly handle. I've made it to the other side, and it's time to bring forth the reckoning. I'm ready.*

Shifting the duffle bag he carried to the ground, Damian smiled wolfishly at her as he asked, "Ready?"

Kate drew in a breath as she pulled down her scarf. "As I'll ever be."

"Weapons?"

"Four guns, eight magazines, each extended. Although I know shooting really won't kill vampires, it's a good distraction," she said, reciting what Ryder drilled into her. She patted her boots, "Two daggers," and then her hips, "Two knives. Got my bulletproof vest on underneath all this. A tourniquet somewhere. Walkie-talkie too."

"And?"

"Play on my strengths," Kate answered. "I'm fast, I'm agile, and I can blend. Use surprise as often as I can and ask for help when necessary. As Ryder likes to say, 'don't be a hero'."

Damian winked, and Kate's stomach flipped. "There's my girl."

Kate took him in slowly then, drinking in his presence. His square jaw and narrow nose gave him a sharp countenance, yet when he smiled, the severity disappeared to reveal the most handsome male she'd ever laid eyes on. And the way a smirk came to his face before his laughter rumbled out of him, as if he couldn't control it? She lived for those moments.

She wished he would put his limber arms around her so she could feel his muscles rippling against her, feel his heartbeat twining with hers. *Because when he does nothing is wrong in the world, and right now, everything is tipping toward wrong.* She turned to face him then, needing the solace his body provided. She reveled in the fact that his frame easily towered over her own, broad and muscled. She liked to think he was made for her—that Fate had chosen him specifically for her. *Which, if lore is true, she has. The other piece of me, of my soul.*

Kate yearned for the way he encompassed her wholly: mind, body, and spirit. She allowed herself to get lost in him now, in the heartbeat's worth of time they shared, because a small part of her cried that it could be the last. She felt her chest constrict with pain as she lamented for all the time they'd missed because of miscommunication and unshared thoughts. As if he knew and shared how she felt, Damian's face softened with a furrowed brow as he turned to face her as well. He lifted a hand to her face, then hesitated, as if it would shatter the moment.

After this, Kate told herself as she reached to capture his hand in her own. *Get through this night and the next and you can have the future you've wanted for so long. The future you deserve. The future you are* worthy of.

She stepped nearer to him, drawn by his strength, staunch determination aligning with bloodthirsty vengeance. Beneath the outer shell, however, was the same raw pain she felt in the wake of their impending separation: he was just as hesitant and fearful as she. Yet he quickly buried the fear under the visage of the man he used to be before he became a near-immortal male of retribution. The being that peered down at her now would not accept failure this night, or any night to follow, because, she knew, he wanted exactly what she did. Maybe even more than her. He kissed the back of her hand, and then her palm, before she tenderly stroked the coarse hair of his face.

She used his confidence to inspire her own, and she said to him with gusto and a grin, "Let's do this."

Damian lifted his hand to chuck her chin, his calloused

fingers lingering. A flush rose from her toes to her cheeks, but the moment was severed when the door opened again and Ryder appeared, Taryn close behind him. The others followed, no one speaking, before piling into the trucks that awaited them. Uru said goodbye to her family, and Kate tried not to listen to the muffled crying from the younglings who stayed in the house. Her heart split, however, when the beloved female tried to soothe them, her own voice edged with weeping.

You have to block it out. Put it behind the wall, her conscience warned her. *It'll drag you down if you don't.*

Resolve settled in her bones as their vehicle lumbered off Uru's property and onto the coastal road, the sky a glorious, deep navy hue of night. She was thankful the turbulent weather waned, for it allowed the moon to shine in a way she'd never been able to appreciate before, even though its face was near to new. A distantly small part of her still wished to see the Northern Lights, but it fell silent, suffocating in the anticipation of what was to come as they neared the airport.

When they arrived, their vehicles pulled into an arcing formation alongside an unfamiliar plane. Talorc got out of his car to greet the newcomers, and the hatch of the plane opened. Kate recognized Jean-Luc and Robertha, bringing with them as many bodies as space would allow. She watched from her tinted window as they deferred in respect to Talorc, the conversation between them short because of the biting cold. They walked to the hangar where everyone but Talorc, Kalliq, Uru, and The Guard would wait for more reinforcements, and Kate abruptly knew the time had come. She unfurled from her own seat, huddling against the cold as she slipped from the vehicle. She approached her father, who stood near the truck he'd come out of, matching his austere gaze.

Anything less and the emotions she'd placed behind her internal wall would raze it.

"Be careful," she told him, her hands in her pockets, her face uncovered. The wind, though gentle, nipped at her skin, instantly flushing it scarlet. "Don't slow the others down."

Her teasing tone made Talorc smile, but only fleetingly. "I shall endeavor not to, dearest daughter."

His manner seemed subdued, and the cadence of his voice proved forlorn. Kate lowered her own to softly ask, "Are you having doubts?"

She was suddenly ridden with guilt. *Did I push too hard, too fast? Did I ask for too much? Was he not ready?*

"There is no room for doubt, Father. We're in too deep and we've come too far. If what Uru said got under your skin, don't let it. You deserve to be king because you have *heart*. You want peace for the vampire nation, you want to see things right instead of falling into the chaos, even in the face of all that you've gone through. You are the strongest, most intelligent male I've ever met. There is not a soul on this planet who could fill your shoes as the vampire king."

"It is the unknown," Talorc confessed gruffly, reaching out to cup Kate's cheek. She closed her eyes for a heartbeat, drawing in her father's wintry scent, and then mustered a feeble smile as she lifted a hand to place over his own. With a gentle squeeze, he released his hold. "It has been a long time since I have trod such a path. It pains me to bring others down it with me when I do not know what waits around the bend."

"We want to be next to you, father," Kate said vigorously. "Me, The Guard, Lilith, Paavak... The list goes on. We *want* to take this path with you."

Talorc's eyes dimmed. "If I only tread it for you to prevail, that is all I could ask for."

Kate's stomach bottomed out and her voice weakened as she said, "*We* shall prevail, *Athair. We.*"

Talorc hesitated too long, and Kate's stomach sank further.

"This night and the next will be telling of where we stand, how far we can truly take this." He dipped his head and turned from her, toward the all-terrain vehicle.

Kate caught his arm and pulled him to her, clashing their bodies together in a tight embrace. Talorc swept her into his arms, tucking his face against her head, before pulling back to look down at her. He clasped one of her hands to his chest, pushing firmly on the back of it as he whispered, "I keep it with me still."

Swiping her head to and fro slightly with a small frown, Kate replied, "What?"

Talorc smiled, squeezing her hand. "The stone you gave me."

Kate's frown deepened before her eyes flared, surprise

causing her voice to pitch. "From all those years ago?"

Talorc nodded once. "Mayhap it holds the courage I need to see this through." He leaned forward to kiss her forehead before pulling away, breaking their hold. They both knew if he didn't do it now, they would've held on for the rest of their lives. He turned away from her for the last time, heading for the truck.

"All my faith I lend to you," Kate called after him, her voice catching at the end as her eyes burned with sudden tears.

Talorc stopped, only turning his head to look over his shoulder. His face, weathered and weary, was unreadable. "And I, to you," he murmured, before turning to continue his course.

It was Damian who threw open the door for Talorc, and in doing so caught Kate's attention. Immediately arrested, Kate's heart pounded as her eyes clashed frantically with his, her father's figure disappearing as he settled in his seat. She refused to believe this could be the last time she would see either of them and instead drew all the strength she could from Damian's fortifying regard. The bond between them crackled, glowing under the night ascending, and through that tether, Kate appreciated exactly what she needed to see this through.

Reverence. Complete and utter reverence.

Her breath caught on a despairing gasp as he shut the door, and the vehicle sped off into the night.

Damian.

Keep my father safe because I have to focus on Santiago. Bring my friends back to me, too. But most of all, please, please, please come back to me. Please don't leave me after I...we...

A single tear fell, scorching her raw skin, before she felt a pull on her elbow and a gentle voice say to her, "Come on, Kate."

Kate looked at Taryn, her brown eyes glittering with her own unshed tears. Understanding was shared between the two, and together they walked into the hangar.

They waited more than half the night.

After Jean-Luc and Robertha, they were joined by several other North American covens, who arrived by their own means of transportation. Even though she'd been prepared for such, Kate was still surprised when they looked to her for guidance. *Your lineage speaks for you; use its weight wisely,* her conscience reminded her.

Under Tulok's penetrating gaze, she took the reins, filling in everyone on what had transpired while organizing those who continued to filter in. From beyond the borders of North America came others, the Dublin and London covens each separately divulging they wouldn't miss a fight like this one. Beijing, Sydney, and Cape Town provided vampires from the furthest stretches of the globe, though their combined numbers weren't more than ten.

"Talorc has been there for us time and time again," the leader of the Dublin coven, Darragh, said in a brogue so thick Kate had immense difficulty deciphering the words. "His loyalty saw our ancestors through the roughest times. We would never think of deserting him now."

"Did he ever tell you about the Crusades? Or Agincourt?" the London leader asked. When Kate shook her head, she continued, "You'll have to ask him about it. He was glorious. The finest of warriors. And the most vicious."

"He hasn't mentioned Bannockburn? Never knew him to be modest about that," the Edinburgh coven leader said, pausing in counting the spears he'd brought. *Spears*, Kate noted in awe. *He brought spears. Actual spears. And swords too.*

Kate made mental note after mental note as people approached her with similar stories, small tidbits of information she stored away to inquire about when this was over. *Because it* will *end.* She glanced at her cell phone that was only intermittently good for receiving calls and texts. The time read a little after one thirty, and she knew they would have to begin the journey to the cabin soon. They had one satellite phone for the entire group, and instead would rely on walkie-talkies for communication; the other satellite phone her father had taken with his group. She'd heard nothing from them thus far and worked to swallow the trepidation that came with that fact.

She brought her gaze up, surveying vampires she'd never encountered before and only distantly knew by name, all crowded in a hangar a quarter the size of the airport itself. *A glorified tool shed,* Kate thought, biting back the laugh that wanted to bubble up from her throat. *Sheltering some of the most badass beings to ever exist and more weapons than I've ever seen.* Creator help her, but laughing would be easier than the alternative, which was cowering in fear with having to decide what to do next.

Because the more she looked around at the vampires, the more they looked at her. *To* her. She knew what they wanted to know: what the next step was.

Dignified. Strong. Worthy.

I can do this.

She inhaled a deep breath and cleared her throat to address the echoing room.

"We don't know the exact whereabouts of Santiago," she started, and the din reverberating throughout in light conversation seized. "But we have means to believe he's arriving tonight in Ruskill. There's a slight chance he's still a day behind. We might have to turn in before the sun rises if that's the case. But at least that gives us more time to prepare. We want our defense to be as much of a surprise as possible."

"Our home is open," Tulok said. "And there are plenty of places in town to disperse to."

"Enough vehicles have been rented that they should fit all of us if we cram," Kate said, her eyes flicking over the group; every last one of them looked ready, eagerly awaiting what was to come. Not one set of eyes was wary or frightened. "We know where this is headed, and I speak on behalf of my father when I thank you wholeheartedly. We know what you've sacrificed and left behind to be here."

There was a short stint of silence and then a chipper voice said, "So what are we waiting for?" Darragh rubbed his gloved hands together. "Let's get this show on the road."

Damian was less than thrilled when the sun began to rise, and Santiago hadn't bothered to show up.

Forced to endure another day in this dismal place, he thought sourly, looking around the small hunting cabin. They'd just settled into Paavak's cottage for the day, shedding their outwear after spending the night canvassing Morton Lake. They'd decided to post on the far side, which was thicker with trees and would allow for more coverage so Cyrus could man his explosives. The lake was covered with snow, which Uru assured them would start to melt throughout the day if the sun were to be unhindered by clouds, but would refreeze closer to nightfall. The snow from the previous night reached just over two feet, and the males spent the last hour before sunrise creating a trench around the cabin and a path to the front door. Uru took the time to make some phone calls with the satellite phone, confirming to the other half of their party they were alive and well and continued to wait on the enemy.

Cyrus finished stoking a fire in the wood stove, the only warmth to the open space as there was no electricity to the cabin. Kalliq sat on the small twin cot to take off his shoes while Noir rummaged through the kitchenette. Ryder checked behind a door which revealed a small space for a toilet, and Damian sat in one of the two chairs in front of the stove. The other bodies littered around the space in various states of respite, rubbing aching feet or trying to warm stiff hands. It was only Talorc who stood attentive, gazing through one of the windows until he couldn't anymore, the ultraviolet rays of the sun too much for his sensitive eyes and skin.

Damian watched as Talorc lumbered over to the other chair, his enormous frame swallowing the seat whole. Little had been spoken between the lot of them, each simmering with their own fears, their own angst. *I hope Kate is making out all right.* It was the only whim he allowed himself because if he thought too often of her, he couldn't concentrate on the task at hand; with little sleep and high tension, it was hard enough. *When this is over, I can think about her—touch her, know her, feel her—all I want. She has to see this through.* We *have to see this through.*

As his eyes drifted to Talorc, he felt compelled to speak against the concerns he knew his liege held. *This perception is something,* he thought of his newly heightened senses.

"It just gives us more time to prepare." Damian's words drew the male's intense gaze upward. "It's good that Santiago is still behind."

Talorc grunted, relaying he didn't feel the same.

"This place isn't so bad," Damian said, contrary to his personal beliefs. "So what that there's no food or running water. We have plenty of snow to melt. Could fill up on that."

Vadin snorted from where he lay on the floor, an arm thrown

over his eyes.

"Maybe there's a meal delivery service," Damian continued, trying to lighten the dour mood. "What do you think they specialize in here? Polar bear or seal?"

Kalliq chuckled. "There's actually a pretty good pizza place in town."

"See." Damian gestured toward Kalliq good-naturedly. "Nothing to worry about. You like pizza."

Talorc didn't smile. His tone was low as he replied, "I do not like to linger in this state of nescience."

"How is this different from what you've been doing?" Uru called from her place on the cot next to Kalliq, her eyes never leaving the line of the wooden spear tipped in bone she sharpened.

Damian's foul mood dissolved further at her abrupt and caustic retort. It was difficult and went against everything he felt, but he ignored her…

"This state isn't different than the one you've sat in for decades. I would think you're comfortable in it." She slowly, almost threateningly, slid the file down the bone of her spear. "And you: you sit there and mock our culture, the way we live, for your own idleness."

…for all of two seconds.

"Just trying to pass the time." Damian narrowed a glare in her direction. He tolerated her presence thus far because she'd been helpful, but it was never without a condescending or pessimistic tone. Throughout the night she disrespected Talorc as often as she could, throwing in jabs about his legacy and how there was little hope for them to pull through. She may be helping them because she knew it was the right thing to do, but she wasn't happy about it, and she made it clear. Her negativity was draining, but no one said anything even though the anger brought about by her mood was evident to them all.

"He means no harm, Uru," Kalliq responded, nodding at Damian.

"I tire of his mouth. All night he speaks light of things when war is on our doorstep."

Damian's temper hit the bottom of the barrel of his tolerance. "And I'm tired of your attitude. You volunteered to come with us. To show us around. *To be here.* Remember?"

"Damian," Ryder warned, ever the mediator.

"Only in an effort to make peace," Uru replied, her eyes never leaving her steady strokes. "The peace we deserve, that was taken from us, and then kept from us. It's as if *he's*—" She gestured toward Talorc with a jerk of her chin, her voice like venom. "—wanted it that way all along. So our coven would fall, lost to history. After all, what do we matter? We are but—"

"Uru," Kalliq interjected, his dark brow heavy across his eyes. "Why are you acting like this?"

"It's unnecessary." Damian's glare turned downright hostile. "And distracts us from what we need to focus on."

"So stop speaking."

Damian's nostrils flared. As he was never the one *not* to have the last word, he said, "If it shuts you up, gladly."

Silence fell heavy on the air, though not heavier than the tension. Ryder watched Damian until he was confident he wouldn't speak anymore, and Damian took his eyes off Uru only when he knew she wouldn't retaliate.

Her derision sits ill with me. He tried to settle in the chair for comfort, but his eyes flicked back to Uru, his irritation festering. *The fact that she's so eager to share her disdain for Talorc tells enough of her character.*

But she is helping, and honestly, we wouldn't be able to navigate this Creator-forsaken land without her. Damian sighed heavily, closing his eyes, vying for rest. A draft of frigid air had him shivering, and he bit back the grumble that wanted to pass his lips.

One more day.

Two at the most.

Chapter Twenty-Eight

Talorc's allies were forced to diffuse about the town and to Uru's at the threat of the sun. Kate sent correspondence to her father relaying such, and his reply that he remained safe and the cabin untouched came shortly thereafter. With little else to do, Kate tried to get some sleep. When it eluded her in longevity, she did a workout with Taryn and then helped Sesi—who was immensely more tolerable than her sister—make meals for everyone. After a quick shower, she rechecked her backpack, confirming the supplies she'd stowed remained in place. When the sun finally set, she went over the vehicles with Darragh and Tulok, reviewed the makeshift infirmary one more time, and then rounded up those who stayed at Uru's. Kate split their convoy of rented vehicles between going into town to pick up those who'd stayed overnight and to the airport to begin loading the rest of the supplies.

The clock neared midnight when Kate, with the help of Darragh and Tulok, deemed them ready. The last of those who said they would make the journey arrived, and the vehicles had been packed to the best of their ability. Their combined number topped one hundred and thirty. *Still no word from Mikom or the Snow Lake coven,* Kate thought, trying not to let her disappointment show. *Even with the extra time it wasn't enough. But that's okay. We can do this.* She took a deep breath, strapped her pack to her back once more, and bid them begin their trek east.

The path was winding, challenging even for their behemoth off-road vehicles made to conquer mounds of snow and thick patches of ice. Engines cranked loudly in low gears, whining against the frigid cold, puffing out clouds of diesel smoke that clogged the crisp air. Kate kept covered from nose to toes despite the confines of the vehicle, as the measly heater barely warmed her hands. *It hasn't gone above twenty today,* she thought miserably. *I definitely don't like this weather.*

"All's well?" Tulok's voice crackled through the walkie-talkies they were using for communication, and Kate clutched it with stiff hands to reply, "We're good here."

The others who made up their convoy replied similarly as Kate checked her backpack from where it was tucked between her knees. The idleness of riding passenger as they bumped along the not-a-road had her restless, though Darragh's lively humming from the driver's seat did cast a smile to her face for a brief moment. *He really is excited about this.*

Her eyes traveled from the Irishmale to the night beyond the window, where the sky stretched on for miles in deep tones of indigo. Tulok was careful in his navigation of the open land interspersed with shallow marshes glazed over with ice, and Darragh was close to follow. Kate herself had done her best to memorize the surrounding territory after tirelessly reviewing it by map with Tulok; she refused to be stranded with no idea of where to go if something happened. She'd learned there was a field station about five miles northeast that was uninhabited this time of year, and they'd passed several deserted buildings and a polar bear excursion lodge on their way.

I will admit, Kate thought as they dipped and veered and swerved over the rocky land. *Manitoba is beautiful in a wild frontier sort of way.*

Still, Kate regarded the winter forestry with wariness. She knew anything less would be foolish. *Santiago could be anywhere waiting to strike.* The others in the vehicle seemed to carry the same sentiments for no one spoke, though the majority of the auras projected were thick with determination. There was some fear; Kate knew it wasn't only about what was to come, but where their actions would take them after tonight. *If we are victorious, where does the road lead next?* Kate tried not to dwell on an intangible future, knowing she had to focus on tonight.

Because tonight I will finally get my revenge.

It will be over.

I will move on.

They traveled for almost forty minutes before Kate smelled a different kind of smoke on the air. Smoke tinged with the acrid scent of death.

One of her worst fears was confirmed when the bright orange glow of flame flickered from between thick spruce trees. *The cabin.* Kate reached down to grab her bag, throwing it across her shoulders. She reached for the walkie-talkie, pinging the side as she said, "Fire ahead. It's the cabin. Proceed with caution."

A resounding affirmation met her, and her gloved hand wrapped around the door handle as Darragh stopped the truck behind Tulok's. She glanced at the others as the vehicle idly rumbled, watching as they gathered their belongings and weapons with ease and efficiency.

"Ready?" she asked, tucking her walkie-talkie in a side pocket of her bag.

"Go forth," Darragh started.

"For mayhem and bloodshed," Eliza, the London coven leader, added.

"And the victory that comes with it," James, the Edinburgh coven leader, finished.

For victory, Kate thought, taking a deep breath. *For peace, deliverance...*

But most of all vengeance.

She opened the door and jumped out of the vehicle, crouching low in snow that covered her knees. She rose slowly as the opening and closing of doors told her the others joined her, her eyes scanning the forest. Darragh came up to her side with a shotgun in his hands, his own face covered against the harsh temperature as he surveyed the clearing beyond the few trees that separated them.

The cabin was raging with fire. It burned violently, the flames licking high into the air. The space around it had been packed down with vehicle tracks and cleared by hand, and Kate confirmed it by picking up on traces of Damian's saltwater scent. However, the tracks were the only sign there had once been life in the area, because the cabin was quickly crumbling by incineration. She bit back the dread that sat ill within her, burning as hotly as the sputtering timber of the cabin. *The others...did they...*

She swallowed hard, reaching for her walkie-talkie. "I'm

going to circle the cabin from the right. Stay vigilant. They may have moved on from this area, but there could be stragglers."

They made it out. I would've sensed otherwise.

Tulok disembarked from his truck, jumping into the snow. He checked the area cursorily, seeming to find no immediate malintent, and nodded once to Kate before he took to the other side of the cabin. Kate watched him disappear around the corner before drawing one of her guns and beginning her own trek through the snow. The others scattered, moving quickly and quietly for such a large group, looking for clues to what transpired. With their heightened agility, sight, and strength, the snow was more of a nuisance and less of a deterrent, but still proved to slow them down. Additionally, the plague of cold and heavy foliage muddled Kate's sense of smell, and as she neared the burning structure, the scent of fire became overwhelming.

Focus.

The inferno raged, a towering wall of flame that singed her exposed skin. She squinted her eyes against the light, instead turning her gaze back to her path. As she strained for more clues to what transpired, her gaze scattered over the ground, and then the cabin, and then the forest beyond. *The lake.* Her eyes flared when she saw snow trampled at the edge of the forest line, and her eyes followed it back to the cabin. Her lips parted under her covering when she picked up on the increasingly nauseating scent of blood, and her eyes homed in on the streaks she just then noticed in the snow, leading into the forest. *They left the cabin to go to the lake.*

She was raising her walkie-talkie to relay her findings to the others when she faltered, hearing the snapping of thick timber. Her gaze jerked to the cabin as one section of roofing fell in, casting a wave of embers toward her. She raised an arm to block her eyes from the distracting onslaught, and in doing so didn't sense the approach of danger.

The assault was swift and had Kate face down in the snow before she could even catch a breath. In the next, her pack was ripped from her, lost to the tundra, and a gnarled hand pushed her face further into the snow. Knees jarred her spine, pinning her body so thoroughly she knew the wielder thought to suffocate her. *An inconvenient obstacle.* She wouldn't die, but she would be hindered. *Can't afford that.* Remembering her gun, Kate lifted it over her shoulder—*upside-down and backwards so let's hope for at least one shot landing*—and fired off two rounds, which was enough to displace her captor.

She rolled to her back, popped to her feet, and spun to face a wraith. The wide gape of the decrepit creature howled its disdain, spittle and blood dripping from its jowls. Ragged clothes hung from its emaciated body, so little that it hardly covered what sallow flesh was bared. The telltale sign of ligature marks across its neck confirmed how the creature had died, most likely after being promised immortal life. *That's how he snares them. Promising them life everlasting. Despicable.* Rage anew flared within Kate, for this creature who had once been human, with a life and thoughts and feelings and purpose. Now it only existed for blood.

And it was bent on hers.

Kate sprung toward the trodden snow, needing to get away from the wraith. *If I can get to the trees I can blend easier, and it won't be able to find me,* she thought, pouncing from one mound to another. While she moved through the snow, she recalled wraiths were relatively straightforward to kill, and thankfully the bodies disintegrated as soon as they perished. If she encountered a vampire, however, the means to see them defeated would be less easily accomplished, and their bodies only disintegrated under direct sunlight.

She neared the forest, though the dexterity of the wraith that trailed her was something she kept a keen eye on. She heard the cry of the other warriors over the roaring flames and knew they were being engaged as well. *An ambush. They were waiting for us. But my crew will hopefully outnumber the enemy; I brought a hundred vampires with me. I need to focus on getting to Santiago.* She grappled for her walkie-talkie, at the very least needing to let her party know where to go.

"Get to the lake!" she shouted into the device. "They've gone to the lake!"

She grunted when she was tackled once more, her walkie-talkie flying completely out of her grasp. Her gun jostled, fell, as the wraith who had been trailing her took her down in a deep mound of snow. Kate propelled her legs to her chest and then out, launching the wraith from her body, and then rolled to her feet to a ready stance. She barely had time to think before the creature roared and launched itself at her again, lashing at Kate with massive, jagged claws. She leaned back from its reach, ducking this way and that as the creature swiped and lunged, swiped and lunged. Kate reached into her jacket to produce another gun and fired off four shots into the wraith, though none were aimed precisely enough to kill. It did, however, give her enough time to spin and dart toward the tree line, while a quick glance around her revealed her walkie-talkie was long gone, lost to the heaps of snow.

One gun down. No means of communication. Pack gone. Creator take me—it hasn't even been ten minutes. Kate grappled over an enormous fallen log, pulling herself up against the ice-slickened bark. *Need to focus on what I can do: run and blend. Not time to be a hero. I just need to get to Santiago.*

She pushed herself up and over the log and began her jaunt through the trees, directing her focus on her ability to blend. The gift didn't necessarily make her invisible, but it did dilute her scent and the sounds she made, while casting an aura about her that would chameleonize her presence. She'd been borne with the skill and doing so came naturally to her, as she'd been practicing ever since she realized she could steal cookies from the kitchen without anyone noticing. It was an easier feat to accomplish when she was at full strength, which thankfully with Damian's blood in her system she nearly was.

And it's a good thing I do all that running and hiking, Kate thought of her activities at home as she leapt over fallen trees and through heaps of snow. *I wouldn't be so nimble if I'd been a complete couch potato.*

The journey to the lake wasn't long, but Kate heard more than one wraith in pursuit of her the further she travelled. Regrettably, blending couldn't hide her tracks in the snow. The grunts and snarls of the wraiths were close at her heels, sometimes even above her in the snow-capped trees, but she kept pushing, regulating her breathing and forcing her heart rate to steady. The more she travelled, the thicker the blood on the air became, and she began to hear the sounds of battle raging: gasps, shouts, hissing, the *shing*ing and popping of weapons.

With a cry of success, Kate broke free from the tree line and slid down a small, snowy embankment before skimming onto the frozen surface of Morton Lake. She crouched low, steadying herself on her hands and digging her cleated feet into the ice, before coming to a stop. Her gaze was immediately drawn to the sight before her, and as she stood to her full height, her eyes widened in shock.

Across a distance that spanned about a mile, Kate could see fire burning brightly from the opposite shoreline. Trees were arcing flames into the sky, fueled by the potency of gasoline. There were large, dark smudges scattered across the ice, while several bodies were engaged in hand-to-hand combat. There were at least fifty figures, moving and not, and if The Guard, Uru, Kalliq, and Talorc still held strong, that meant they were fighting on severely limited odds. *The others will be here soon,* she thought of the comrades she left behind.

Gunfire rang out, echoing in the emptiness of the night, and another fire leapt to life after a small explosion trembled the land, illuminating the ridge that bordered the lake opposite her. *Cyrus.* He was an expert in explosives, carried them readily wherever he went. *It has to be Cyrus.* Hope bloomed, and Kate latched onto it with both hands.

A snarl drew her attention and Kate whipped around to face the sound. Three wraiths slithered toward her, stooped low on the ice, their eyes alight with murderous intent. Kate took a step back, and then another, pocketing her gun in her jacket. She knew it would serve her little purpose against three foes; close-range against one was a different story. To take down multiples with well-aimed shots? *I'm not that skilled.* Instead she reached for her daggers, taking them both from their holsters and holding them up before her face. *But I can stab and slash with the best of them.*

Adrenaline coursed through her, heating her blood, and she narrowed her eyes at the beasts as they lumbered toward her. Seething with the knowledge this was a part of her revenge, Kate ripped down her scarf to bare her teeth, inciting one of the wraiths to howl its disdain.

"The princess," it hissed, and Kate snapped her fangs.

"That's right," she called, continuing to slink back along the ice.

"*He* will want her back," another whispered, and Kate's spine pricked with warning.

Fuck. That. She wasn't letting anyone get their hands on

her, least of all Santiago. *I am not his plaything. Not his minions' disillusioned toy. I am a fiend, a fighter, a foe to be reckoned with.*

"No—*kill*," another jeered, a heap of skin falling from a gored chest.

Kate snapped her fangs again. "You can try." She twirled one of the blades, the light from the stars catching briefly. "But it's you who will see its end."

All three wraiths sprang at her at once, and Kate ducked low to the ice, jutting both blades in front of her. The wraiths dodged, and so she turned to the left, catching one in the side. When she struck flesh, Kate pushed all her weight into her blades and gutted the wraith clean from its chest to its abdomen, spoiled organs spilling out onto the ice. The creature bayed, falling onto its side, scrabbling to gather its tissue as blood sprayed across Kate and its companions. Knowing it wouldn't recover, Kate swirled to the other two but was too late as one knocked heavily into her knees. She fell jarringly to the ice, her jaw cracking against the thickness, and she lost one of her blades in the process. It spun away from her, and the greedy hands of one of the wraiths grabbed it, siding with its ally to stalk her once more.

These wraiths aren't the wraiths I've heard of for so long. They're smart. They're quick. They talk. No wonder the boys have their hands full.

Kate switched her remaining blade to her dominant hand, narrowing her eyes and swiveling her jaw to dislodge the pain that had settled there. The wraith wielding the dagger lunged at her, but it was a feinted move as the other swept for her legs once more. Kate dodged, dancing back along the ice, and the two continued the offense, first one and then the other. When the second went to take her down for a third time, she swept her blade down and then up, catching it along its gaunt face. It howled, bringing skeletal hands up to staunch the blood, and the other with the blade dove at her with it held high above its head. Kate spun backward and arced her blade up, flinging her arm behind her, and was able to catch the wraith in the lower part of its abdomen. It wasn't a deep cut, but it was enough to slow it down, and Kate tramped back over the ice to take in the two wounded beings.

Heaving breaths, she watched as the creatures staggered to their feet, growling with contempt. They wasted no time in dually hurling themselves at her, and the speed at which they did so had Kate faltering. She tried to duck, to spin, but the cleats from her boots didn't catch the ice and she landed flat on her back. Her teeth rattled in her mouth and her ears rang, and she had no time to shake herself from the upset as both wraiths converged on her at once, the captured blade forgotten.

She scrambled to lift her dagger, but it was ripped from her grasp, cast to the side, and she felt jagged teeth sink through her sleeve to her flesh. She grunted as she tried to kick her legs with all her might, but the other wraith sat on them to hold her still, claws penetrating her skin. She raised her free fist to punch the creature who held onto her arm one, two, three times, but just as quickly remembered her knives and moved to grab one from her hip. She lifted the steel blade and slammed it into the temple of the wraith, and with a screech it disintegrated into wisping smoke.

Kate lifted her upper body from the ice and locked eyes with the wraith that had her pinned. The creature unhinged its jaw and bellowed, leaping at her face with claws extended. Kate caught the wraith by its shoulders and used its momentum, along with her feet, to clear it over her head in a feat that caught both of them by surprise. The wraith cracked against the ice, spinning as it grappled for leverage, as Kate jumped up to brandish her knife. As the wraith gained its footing it looked left, then right, and Kate followed its eyes to find them locked on her forgotten dagger.

She dove for her dagger at the same moment the wraith did, and they collided in a tangle of limbs. The wraith bit at her, scraped at her, catching her cheek with a twisted hand as they rolled along the ice. Kate began to stab vehemently, and it was only when she switched to her nondominant hand that she was able to catch the wraith off guard. She first caught it in the stomach, then below the clavicle, and with a thrust she buried the blade to the hilt in its throat. The wraith disintegrated into nothingness just as a cry pierced the bitter night, and Kate jerked her gaze to the right to see a bloody Darragh thundering from the tree line, leading a host of vampires. He slid to a stop next to her, reaching down to help her to her feet as blood coursed from a wound on his temple, the others continuing onward.

"You okay?"

Kate nodded once, then pointed across the width of the lake.

"They're on the other side," she huffed, pulling her scarf back up over her lips. "I didn't have time to count, but it looks like there are around fifty."

"More than the ambush," Darragh supplied, wiping his forearm across his face. "The others in our party aren't far behind. We didn't lose any that I know of." He handed her the gun she'd lost in the snow and Kate pocketed it with a thank you. They nodded at one another and then took off across the ice, the thrill of the fight coursing in their veins.

The veil of night parted to reveal a battle of epic proportions. Fire swept to towering heights along the bank of the lake, eating trees despite the layer of snow thanks to the gasoline she scented on the wind. Swords clanged and gunfire sparked while the earth quivered with sporadic explosions. A thick wave of wraiths were actively engaged with her allies, and as the vampires she brought with her converged on the battle, a sense of relief and triumph swathed her. *We can turn the tide!* Spears flew and guttural yells split the night as her team began easily annihilating the wraiths—just like Oleander said they would with their experience and skill. Kate desperately scoured the area for her friends, her family, pausing in her plight to do so.

She first caught sight of Kalliq and Uru decimating a trio of wraiths with perfectly aimed shots from their handguns. Behind them Noir was fighting a wraith in hand-to-hand combat, one of his eyes swollen shut. Her eyes skipped to the forest beyond, and Kate saw Cyrus crouched low to the ground, his hands busy with what she assumed was another explosive, while Vadin brought supplies from an all-terrain vehicle tucked in the trees. Her gaze drawn back to the lake, she saw Ryder kneeling below a wraith as he drove his blade into its face. As the wraith disintegrated, Ryder's eyes quickly diverted to who Kate recognized as her father, who was battling two wraiths with a sword. Her eyes widened as one parried him, the other sliding along the ice to attack from behind.

Damian suddenly appeared with a cry of contempt and a blade of his own, bringing it down to sever the arm from the assailing wraith's body. The creature howled, frozen in pain, giving Damian the time he needed to decapitate it.

Thank the Creator they're all alive, Kate thought, propelling herself toward Talorc.

"Father." She grabbed onto his outerwear with shaking hands, and briefly they embraced before Talorc pulled back to look down at her. Blood was smattered across his face while a scrape to his forehead trickled blood, however his grip was strong and sure. Kate couldn't see much else wrong given his clothing, and a quick assessment of Damian, who came to stand beside Talorc, revealed the same. Kate swallowed the hysterical bubble of elation that threatened and instead cleared her throat to reorient herself to the present.

"You are...well?" Talorc asked, his words winded.

"Fine. How long have you been fighting?"

"An hour, give or take," Damian responded. "They waited in the woods at the cabin in an attempt to lower our morale before they got bored and drove us out with fire."

"Vampires too?"

"Just wraiths," Talorc replied, his eyes flicking over the scene that played out before him. His face remained impassive, but Kate sensed dread, like a curtain of thick grey smoke, overcome him.

"Any sign of Santiago?" Kate asked, her voice no more than a serpent's hiss.

"None." Damian spit blood onto the ground, wiping his mouth with the back of his gloved hand. His eyes bored into her, but Kate didn't—couldn't—give him her regard. *Not now. Not with so much on the line.* She knew if she did, she would weaken.

"Which means the night has just begun." Talorc lifted his sword once more.

As if conjured by his words, a riotous cry took the night, and the battle waned to confront the sound. A wave of wraiths descended from the darkness to the north, carrying torches and gleaming metal weaponry. Kate counted those in the first line, and by the time she got to fifteen her heart began to sink, as row after row of bodies continued to appear.

There has to be at least a hundred, she thought, another cry piercing the night.

She looked to her right and saw another wave of adversaries appear, leaping from a small outcropping of land jutting from the middle of the lake. Her senses peaked and her eyes sharpened when she realized these were no wraiths.

These were vampires.

Ten...Twenty...Thirty... More kept coming.

All Kate could think was, *Oleander was wrong. There's so many...so many more than what he said,* as bodies continued to appear out of thin air. Her eyes widened, her breath leaving her body on a wavering gasp.

Santiago. He's bringing them in.

Kate tightened her grip on her knife and extracted a gun from her jacket, her brow falling low over her eyes as a retaliatory snarl coated her fangs.

That means he has to be here.

With a shriek she began running toward the enemy vampires, ready to see her vengeance through. Santiago was close. He had to be. There was no other explanation.

This was it.

She headed for the narrow crop of land that nearly halved the lake. She ducked and swiped, waylaying those she could, using her ability to blend with the other bodies to her advantage to stay her course. With each length of distance traveled, she recalled how *easily* Santiago tortured her, how *sure* he'd been in his callousness, and how *intense* he'd made her suffering. In turn, her steps were sure, her eyes were intensely focused, and she increased her speed easily, driven solely by retribution.

She noted the outcropping was riddled with pools, and she readied herself for a frigid dousing if the ice wasn't as thick as the lake itself. The thought of catching frostbite made her grit her teeth, but she wouldn't be swayed from this path. She *needed* to get to Santiago, felt the shrill knell of reprisal calling to her, pushing her onward. It intertwined with another voice, and she knew her mother was with her in this moment, spurring her on from above.

The voice was cut short when Kate was thrown off course, sliding across the ice not twenty feet from the outcropping. Her trajectory took her away from the main area of battle and the funnel of vampires appearing, and she spun to a stop with anger alighting every fiber of her being.

What. Now.

She lumbered to her feet, still holding onto her gun and her knife, and came face to face with—

"Uru. What are you doing?"

Chapter Twenty-Nine

The female twirled a staff headed with a tip of bone, her dark eyes narrowed on Kate. She wore a caribou hide across her shoulders overtop her outerwear, her dark hair draping down to her waist. "Daughter of Talorc, you tread on the side of failure."

Resentment and fury burst hotly within Kate before being overpowered by an impending feeling of doom. She kept her gun and knife in front of her, rewrapping her fingers around her weapons to keep them from trembling. "Excuse me?"

"You'll fall this night, as will your father and The Guard." Uru walked closer to Kate as the fight raged on behind her, backlighting her frame like the villain she suddenly was. "A new power will rise and see the vampires to the absolution they desire."

Kate knew exactly who that sounded like, and her eyes flared along with her nostrils as she breathed, "He sank his talons into you too?"

Uru stopped, striking her staff onto the ice with malice. "I side with the one who speaks the truth, not the dribble your father sputters," she said, her voice acidic. "*He* promises safety. *He* promises wealth. *He* promises prosperity. Talorc does *nothing* to promote any sort of wellbeing or longevity. He demands his payments, his taxes, and respect he doesn't deserve while our family falls deeper into desolation. He comes to *my land* and usurps it for his own purpose, *destroying* everything in his wake without thought or consideration.

"Do you have any idea who we are? Who we used to be? Isobel Lake was *strong*. Almost a hundred vampires helped settle this land and kept it safe—a haven—for centuries. It is on this land that my parents hunted, hiked, surveyed, and survived. It is on this land that my ancestors did the same, for years and years and years. But our prosperity brought prying eyes and heavy hands."

This is personal for her, Kate thought, even though the notion didn't soften her toward the female or her tainted way of thinking.

"Santiago will see us rise once more, to become the coven my parents—my grandparents and their parents—built from the ground up. The coven my brother singlehandedly saw through the roughest of times after we were abandoned by Talorc—and then suffered for it by losing his own life. Santiago has promised us freedom, to take the retribution we deserve with the backing of a new nation. He's promised not to abandon us like Talorc. He's promised us *belonging*; to not feel like outsiders, or like we're forgotten." Uru swung her staff up, pointing it at Kate. "And so it is on this land that I will see you fall, and then strike your father down, crumbling the empire he thought he had."

"How long?" Kate asked, needing to know the answer. "How long have you been working with Santiago?"

Uru laughed, a malicious sound, twisting her features vilely. "Does it matter? Maybe it's been weeks, maybe it's only been a day. What matters is his army is in the precise location to bring you down, and he knows exactly what you will do before you do it: how you will strike, how you will move, how you will retaliate."

Kate's breath halted in her lungs. *She shared our plans. She told Santiago everything we have up our sleeves.*

Brutal fury lanced Kate, but before she could move, Uru lunged. Kate dove to the ice to her left, sliding across it on her chest. She flipped onto her back and fired off shots from her handgun which didn't so much as graze Uru. The female jumped at her again, her staff poised to strike, and Kate rolled before leaping to her feet, swinging around to face Uru once more. As she did so, Uru slapped Kate's hands with her staff, a hard *thwack* that had Kate spitting curses and loosening her hold on her knife. Uru began to jab at her, brusque stabs that had Kate dodging until Uru caught her in the thigh. Kate fell, pressing a hand to the wound, and then collapsed fully to avoid another decimating strike.

Run. Need time to think. Kate leapt to her feet and began to lope away from the fight, glancing down at her leg. *Need a plan.* The wound seeped readily, oozing crimson through her clothing and onto the ground. The more pressure Kate put on her leg to walk the more it bled, but she didn't have time to put on her tourniquet. Blending would be impossible to accomplish in a vast open space with little furnishings, and there was no one around her for Kate to piggyback from, either. *But if I can reach the trees...*

Kate growled, paused, and spun, raising her gun up to train on Uru. The female stuttered to a stop as Kate lit the night with all the bullets in her magazine, though with her poor aim and Uru's agility she didn't hit her at all. Uru launched at Kate again, a fierce cry tearing from her lips as she brandished her staff.

Kate tossed the gun to the side without thinking and instead caught the staff in her hands. *Not the plan I was going for.* Uru jerked the staff, but Kate held on, yanking it back her way, causing Uru to stumble. She pulled again, tugging Uru along with her, and when the female fell before her, Kate lifted a cleated boot and slammed it into Uru's face. The crunching of bone threatened to take Kate back to a memory best left forgotten, however when Uru's grip loosened, the memory faded. Kate ripped the weapon from her hands and held it at her neck to keep her in place. On her hands and knees, Uru looked up at Kate from beneath her raven-colored hair, her shoulders quaking.

"You're a traitor," Kate snarled, jabbing the head of the staff into Uru's neck until skin broke. "I should take your life now."

"Then do it," Uru bit, her fingers curling against the ice. Her smirk was patronizing as she lifted her head and hissed, "Go on. Show me you can do it. Prove to *yourself* you can inflict pain on someone like Santiago did to you."

Kate tried not to flinch, but Uru was sharp; she preyed on Kate's hesitation.

"You remember, don't you? How he had you tortured? I've heard the tales. I wonder if you still carry the marks?"

Kate's heart faltered, tripping in its beats.

"They say he drowned you. Burned you. Starved you. Suffocated you. I wonder which was worse?" Uru chuckled, the gesture causing her neck wound to bleed more. "I could hear it straight from the horse's mouth. Tell me Kathryn: which plight did you fear the most?"

Kate's voice quivered with piercing anger. "None will compare to what you'll experience."

Uru tsked. "Don't show me mercy now, *princess*."

Kate's eyes narrowed, her heart still beating erratically. "I'm showing you neither pity nor mercy," she said, forcing her voice to steady, as her shoulders heaved with her labored breaths. "But I want you to look my father in the eye when you admit to him your deceit. *Stand up.*"

Kate retracted the staff and then plunged it into Uru's shoulder, causing the female to cry out and crumple in a pathetic heap. Kate cracked the staff across her bloodied knee and then tossed the ruined weapon away, looming over Uru. She kicked her wounded shoulder, causing the female to scream and roll onto her back.

As Kate opened her mouth to leer a taunt, she was cut short when Uru pulled her own handgun from beneath the folds of her caribou hide and trained it on Kate with precision. Kate's eyes widened in shock. She had little time to dodge and took two bullets to the shoulder, which effectively levelled her to the ground. In the distance, she thought she heard a pained roar.

Searing pain tore through her, and Kate moaned as she rolled onto her stomach, clutching her shoulder. Blood poured through her fingers as she forced herself to her knees, blinking through the agony as she lifted her head. *Creator that hurts.* She squeezed her eyes shut to dissipate the stars and opened them to meet the odorous muzzle of Uru's gun not a hairsbreadth from her forehead.

"I'm showing you neither pity nor mercy," Uru mocked, her face stricken with hatred as she loomed over Kate. "And you will look *me* in the eye as I take your life."

Her finger tightened around the trigger and Kate curtailed a ferocious growl. She knew she wouldn't die from a direct blow to the head, but it would be incapacitating enough that Uru could effectively finish her. *What do I do? What can I do?* She couldn't reach her remaining guns, and her shoulder was screaming in pain. Her blades, save one, were lost.

I need my revenge. I need to get to Santiago.

She allowed the growl to blossom into a yell of fury as a tremble overtook her, and Kate reached out with a bloody hand to snag the gun's barrel as Uru pulled the trigger. She swung the gun off course and the shot missed Kate, but the two began to grapple for it in a flurry of twisting limbs. Kate, still on her knees, reached forward and sank her claws into Uru's forearm, and Uru fired the gun again, but Kate had it pointed down toward the ice. Her grasp still on the barrel, Kate retracted her hand from Uru's forearm to slam it into her wrist, eliciting a crack of bone. Uru screamed and dropped the gun, her hand limp. Kate stumbled to her feet and then back as Uru cradled her hand to her chest, forgetting about the gun Kate immediately kicked away from sight.

"You *bitch*," Uru seethed, her fangs bared in a nasty snarl. "You think you're so—"

Uru's words halted, and both she and Kate looked down at the blade that suddenly protruded from her chest. Uru gasped and then choked as blood bubbled from her parted lips, her face instantly draining of color. She lifted her good hand to touch the blade, to discern the reality of the situation, and by the look on her face she knew.

A stake through the heart.

There would be no healing, no coming back from such a blow.

The blade retracted and Uru fell, her knees striking the solid surface of the lake to reveal a menacing vision of Talorc.

He said nothing as he watched her collapse fully onto the frozen lake, his downturned sword dripping with her lifeblood. Uru looked up at Talorc with eyes that quickly glossed over, and Kate watched as death stole her final breath, effectively seeing the female to The Abeyance.

"Thank you." Kate lifted a hand to her shoulder to check her wounds. One shot, thankfully, had been a graze and only slighted her flesh. The other had gone through skin and bone, and unfortunately still bled.

"I was suspicious." Talorc's lip curled as he looked down at Uru in distaste. "But I did not see such a betrayal coming. I thought she was merely angry and using her voice as an outlet."

"I didn't particularly care for her," Kate confessed, glancing down at her thigh. The wound still oozed, and Kate reached for her tourniquet tucked in her jacket as she continued, "But neither did I."

Talorc watched as Kate looped the tourniquet over her foot and up her leg, tightening the band until the bleeding stopped. The application was painful, but Kate couldn't afford to lose blood when she still had a fight to see through. After she secured the tourniquet in place, Kate looked up to her father to see his eyes on the battle beyond.

"We are outnumbered." His voice was soft against the stricken sounds of war.

"But we are stronger, better, faster," Kate said, checking her person for the rest of her weapons. She found three guns and a knife and reinforced them securely. "And once I take the head, the body will crumble."

Talorc's jaw tightened, and his eyes were bright with fire when he turned to look down at Kate. "See it done."

Kate nodded once, then took back off across the lake.

She headed for the narrow outcropping, focusing on nothing else but finding Santiago. *I know he's there. I can sense it.* Whether she wanted to admit it or not, she held a cruel tie to her captor, and the pungent smell of his peppered scent carried over the arctic wind to her. She concentrated on the draw, ignoring the pain of her shoulder and the bite of the tourniquet around her wounded leg.

Everything I've done has come to this, she thought, clearing the embankment in a single leap. She began sprinting once more, the spice of his scent acrid to her nose. *Everything I've wanted to accomplish is going to come to fruition. I may be injured. We may be outnumbered. Uru may have told him our plans. But I am going to kill Santiago despite all that, and we'll win this fight.*

She wasn't surprised when Santiago appeared out of nowhere.

Kate slid to a halt, snow and mud kicking up behind her. Santiago peered at her with keen brown eyes as his goateed face curled in a malevolent sneer, his long black hair pulled back in a ponytail. He wore outerwear like the rest of them, and Kate knew under the clothing he wore his gold jewelry: loops of necklaces and rings on nearly every finger. The dagger tattooed alongside his left eye was bold, and his countenance held a sanctimonious arrogance that threatened Kate's courage.

"Hey, Little Kitten." His wiry voice coupled with the private endearment only the closest to her used sent chills throughout her entire body. "I see you're well."

Kate said nothing.

"I also see you've brought your friends." He indicated behind her with a tip of his chin, but Kate refused to take her eyes from him. "I brought mine too, and more are on the way."

The chills turned to dread, and it wrapped skeletal hands around her heart and pulled at the strings.

"Did you think this was all I had?" He smirked, the movement twisting his features. "You know better, Little Kitten. You know what I'm capable of."

As if to bolster his words, a shrill cry split the night, joined by another, and another. Kate spun on unsteady feet to look over her shoulder, over the lake that had become the battleground.

She watched in morbidly crippling astonishment as an entire battery of soldiers emerged from where she'd come from. They brandished swords and stakes and infused the night with rapid gunfire. Screams tore from her team as they were ensnared by the onslaught.

She whirled back to face Santiago, her face stricken with terror.

Santiago laughed. "Don't worry. They're just humans. But they know enough. They know how to kill."

"Why?" Kate whispered, her voice almost lost to the mayhem.

"You know why. You've figured it all out."

"The throne doesn't belong to you." Kate's voice quivered with hatred as she closed the distance between them to ten feet. "It belongs to my father."

"And let me guess—you'd rather die than see me on it?"

"No," Kate snapped, withdrawing her last blade. "I'd rather *you* die."

She launched herself at him then, a hasty move that didn't get her anywhere. Santiago disappeared and reappeared several feet to her left, and Kate spun wildly to attack him, but her hastiness cost her: a small pool lay there, and with all the traffic that had plunged over it, it was no longer frozen. She fell in up to her knees, the chill instantly sluicing to her bone. The nauseating cold spiked directly up to her thigh wound, and Kate gritted her teeth against chattering as Santiago watched her pull herself from the water, laughing all the while.

"You don't have it in you," Santiago said, hands tucked in

his pockets as Kate faced him once more, brandishing her knife. "You never had it in you. Honestly, I'm surprised you're standing here to face me now."

Kate knew he was trying to notch her down little by little; it was a tactic that worked on her when she'd been in her weakest state. However, now in her strongest, she pulled down her mask, ripping back the attached head covering as well. Santiago narrowed his eyes slightly, and Kate knew he wasn't expecting her show of courage by the gentle hitching of his breath.

"I will never cower before you again," she said, straightening her spine. She could feel her pant legs beginning to freeze, the fabric icing, but she disengaged it as she moved into a ready stance. "You own no space in my future."

"Pity," Santiago said in a relaxed tone, reaching into his jacket to produce two long daggers. The black steel glinted under the starlight as he moved them with expertise and ease. Kate forced her trepidation behind the wall she'd built, using it now as a fortress against her greatest enemy. "I thought we could play some more."

Memories surged like rapids after a storm, and Kate drew a deep breath in before letting it out slowly. *No.* She repeated the measure. *Remember everything you've done to get here: your lessons with Mora as a youngling, your hiking and running and exercising, your sessions with Ryder, your nights on the streets, all the time you put into practicing with weapons, the mental hurdles you grappled with...* She took in another breath and held it, her eyes narrowing. *None of it is going to go to waste.* You *are not going to go to waste. Don't think of that very short span of your life when he had control.*

He doesn't now, and he never will again.

With a cry Kate leapt at Santiago, and he held up his blades to parry her strike. He pushed her away, but she didn't go far, and when she sprang at him again, he seemed surprised that she was so quick to retaliate. She swept up, down, from the side, but Santiago matched every assault. She drove him back from the main battle, trying not to focus on the increased sounds of pain and despair. She focused solely on Santiago, swinging her blade from various directions to keep him engaged.

It didn't take her long to figure out he was entertaining her to wear her down. *He's waiting me out. He knows I can't go all night like this.* With each swipe of her blade, he simply raised a dagger or two and deflected. He made no move to start an offense or to stop her from driving him further from the battle. He never once looked toward the mêlée violently clashing behind them. *He has to be tired,* she thought of his expenditure in transporting a third of his army to be here. *But if he is, he's not showing it.*

I have to do something different. Change it up.

As if sensing her internal thoughts, Santiago's last block was rapidly followed with a swift push that almost sent Kate to her bottom in the trampled snow. Santiago revealed his intentions with the maneuver that came after: he reached for her, but Kate didn't have her footing, and he missed, his hand closing around thin air.

He means to take me away, Kate thought, sidling back several feet. *He wants to kidnap me again.*

The idea burned in the pit of her stomach, and she snarled a vicious sound more beast than being. Santiago, knowing he had erred, chuckled and looped his blades in a show of finesse rather than confrontation. His face, however, sharpened ever so slightly with ire, and if it weren't for the aura of bright orange that surged around him briefly Kate wouldn't have known he was displeased.

Kate propelled herself at him again, and they clashed brutally, causing Santiago's chuckle to die abruptly. She slashed downward and reached into her jacket for a gun, raising her blade at the same time she aimed the weapon at Santiago's midsection. Before she could pull the trigger, however, Santiago wielded his dagger in an arc that slit her hand to the bone, and Kate cried out as she dropped her weapon, cradling her bleeding appendage.

Shoot. She darted back several paces, dodging once-frozen pools as she went. Santiago followed, picking up her gun, and didn't hesitate to unload her own magazine in pursuit. Kate tried to dodge the onslaught better than the pools, but a bullet caught her arm and her chest, and though she wore the bulletproof vest it still took the wind out of her. As she fell, another grazed her cheek. *Creator.* She was more thankful for the sound of the magazine emptying a second later than the sodden mud that cushioned her fall.

She scrambled back from Santiago, panting and dragging her bad leg with her. They were almost at the tip of the outcropping of land, and Kate made the mistake of looking over her shoulder at the battle instead of focusing on Santiago.

Her heart sank to the core of the earth.

Her team was almost overrun.

Bodies littered the ice, more than Kate could count. Some were on fire. The ones that were upright were being overtaken by two or three foes, and barely holding their own. Her gaze turned stricken as she watched a vampire get beheaded, another stabbed through the heart with a spear. She couldn't locate her father and her tether to Damian was weak, almost nonexistent. She saw no one else she recognized, and her heart screamed with anguish.

We've failed, she thought, grinding her jaw to keep her whimper of defeat. *We've failed and it's all my fault...*

She felt the press of a knife at the base of her skull, and Kate flung herself away from Santiago, irate that she'd let him get so close in her moment of despair. She rolled until she was back on the ice, and her cleated feet held strong as she pulled herself to standing, gripping her last blade with vengeance. He stepped onto the ice as well, as unperturbed as anything, his eyes sparkling with malice.

No. We won't fail. We can't. I'll take Santiago down still.

I have to.

"I grow tired of these games, Little Kitten." He swung his blades so they flashed with their own malevolence. "I'll put an easy end to it: come with me willingly and I'll make you my partner. You can live to hate me for as long as you like."

Her response was a bite: "*Never.*"

"Then we'll have to do this the hard way." Santiago's body stiffened in a way Kate knew he was readying to disappear. She tensed to leap away when a tremendous resonance halted her, eviscerating the night.

BOOM.

The frozen lake beneath her feet trembled before a giant *crrrrraaaackkkk* splintered the air. Kate swung around, but found her footing unsteady, and she lowered her body to her hands and knees as she took in the sight before her.

An explosion caused the lake to explode. Macerated bodies flew through the air, chunks of ice soared overhead, and the once frozen lake rippled in angry waves. Fires flared and then were doused, and fearful screams rent the air anew. Kate desperately grappled toward land but was brought to her chest as the lake heaved and the berg she'd settled on broke from the shore. She dug her toes into the ice and used her knife to hold her place as she watched others not able to tend the same fate. Countless beings—mostly wraiths and humans—howled their disdain, slipping between floes before subsequently getting crushed by the massive pieces, while others fell into the glacial water to drown in its depths.

Kate veered her gaze over her shoulder, back to Santiago. He'd lost his footing and was rolling from his back onto his stomach, rassling to gain ground on his own bobbing floe, his daggers lost.

What the actual fu—

Kate's attention was not meant to last as another sound gradually overtook the night.

A slice of stark light from an enormous military-grade helicopter cut through the darkness and began to descend on the bank where Kate had first encountered the battle on the lake. Another shard of light appeared before a second helicopter flew overhead, coursing to the north side of the lake. A third headed south.

By the sudden potency of Santiago's fury, she knew these were not enemy reinforcements.

Hope surged within her, and as her iceberg settled, Kate rose to a standing position. She flipped her gaze back to Santiago, who was watching the helicopters descend with a façade that crumbled into bitter, spiteful misery. Her gaze flashed beyond him, to the steadiness of land. She wasted not a second more before leaping to it, darting from one slab to another.

She felt Santiago's eyes burning into her like rays from the sun, and she heard his yell of wrath a split second before a bullet tore through her calf. She fell hard to the ground and rolled onto her back as Santiago disappeared from his block of ice to reappear at the edge of the churning water. The maneuver seemed to pain him as sweat beaded on his brow, and he gasped a heavy breath as he pulled himself through the mud, his boots trudging slowly through the soaked earth.

He's slowing, Kate thought, the hope within her surging.

"You won't...win this," he said through gritted teeth. "Not tonight. Not *ever.* You all will know...I will show you all that *I* am the rightful vampire king. Talorc doesn't deserve his seat. He never has. He let us fall. Crumble. We were once proud, the vampire nation. We had *purpose*.

"A new night will befall the vampires. And I will be their leader. I have *earned* the seat of power. It is through *him* that our purpose will be renewed. While I may have gotten off track, at least I've proven to *him* that I am worthy of the seat and that it should belong to *me*."

Enraptured by his ramblings, Kate asked, "Prove to who?"

The answer melted from curling lips, "*Adhamh.*"

The hope Kate felt faltered.

"I wanted to take from Talorc...everything he had," Santiago continued, advancing a step onto land as Kate pulled herself to trembling feet. "I wanted to hurt him where I knew it would the most: *you*. I got carried away, but I was having so much *fun*. I know I should've just killed you, forgotten The Guard, but knowing I was breaking Talorc one bone at a time...

"Maybe Adhamh was right." Santiago forcefully chucked the gun into the water to be lost to the waves. "Maybe I should've done exactly what he said. Maybe I wouldn't be here if I had. But I refuse to lose. I will be the victor tonight. And if I'm not there will be another. And another. And another. There will always be someone else—there *is* someone else—who is just as gluttonous for power as me."

He sprang at Kate and she pulled out one of her remaining guns, firing off as many rounds as she could before limping out of his reach. Santiago's body quivered with each penetrating injury, and he fell back onto the muddy ground. Kate's retreating path took her to the water, yet she knew with a bleeding calf wound and a tourniquet around her opposite thigh she wouldn't fare well on a floating block of ice. *What do I do? Blending won't help on this stark land...*

As if she were physically drawn, Kate looked to her right, to the ebbing waters. Near the bank, floating just there was a steel spear. It lurched with the advancing and then receding waves, knocking into debris before bobbing under the water. She crouched, biting her tongue against the pain, and grabbed the weapon. It felt... true in her hands, in a way she couldn't make sense of. *But I'm on the right path.* Her body shuddering, she whirled to face Santiago.

He'd rolled onto his hands and knees and was climbing to his feet, his lips split on a bloody laugh.

His form grew hazy before it disappeared entirely; Kate noted again the trick seemed to cause him physical pain. Still, she barely had time to spring out of his grasp when he reappeared. He fell to the ground once more, and as Kate huffed heavy breaths, she knew the veracity of the situation.

Santiago was waning. His strength, his valor, his might, *his ability to disappear* was diminishing right before her very eyes.

Oleander's words cut back to her, the memory of his omnipotence flaring in a bright orange burst of volcanic flare.

"The ability is limited..."

She tightened her grip on the spear, watching as Santiago tried to get up once more. Roiling water from the lake lapped at her boots, and as a chunk of ice nudged her, briefly drawing her regard, an idea sprang to life.

"...and can be impeded to a degree."

Impeded.

Impaled.

She looked from the spear, to Santiago, then to the ice.

Worth a shot.

She drew in a deep breath and leapt back onto the lake, launching herself from one ice floe to the next as fast as she could. The waters swayed from the rotors of the circling helicopters and the aftershock of the explosion, and a time or two she lost her footing and had to use the spear to keep her anchored. But she had to draw Santiago as far out to the lake as she could, and she focused only on that task as she pushed herself past what she thought she was capable of.

For vengeance. So I can finally move on.

Santiago appeared before her on the same ice floe, stumbling to a knee. Kate noted with surprise that he bled from several places on his chest, and she wondered fleetingly if she'd been successful with her shooting but also why he hadn't worn a bulletproof vest. *Does he really rely on his power to keep him safe that much?* If so, his narcissism had just become her ally. Her wonder dissipated as he rose to unsteady feet, his face pale but his eyes focused entirely on her.

"Going for the heart of the beast?" he taunted, nodding

toward the spear.

Kate didn't let the smirk of victory curve her lips like she wanted, but she absolutely relished the idea this would be the last time she would ever have to hear his voice.

"No." She restructured her grip on the spear, her hands steady. "For the head of it."

Shrieking, Kate drew her arms back like a designated hitter and swung with all her might at Santiago's legs. The force of her strike sent the ice tottering as Santiago crumpled and then began to slide toward the water. His face, once full of smug triumph, fell starkly to stuttering fear. He grappled to gain a hold on the berg, but his legs wouldn't work, and his hands slipped frantically along the surface. He tried to disappear but couldn't. In the next heartbeat he slid into the water and then under the floe, and Kate knew the moment had to be taken or she would lose it forever.

She raised the spear high above her head and with another scream she drove it through the ice and Santiago's abdomen, pinning him underneath the water and to the floe. She yelled again as she pulled the blade up, only stopping when his body caught on the other side. With her remaining strength—fortified by the knowledge that *this was the end*—Kate bent the end of the spear, effectively trapping Santiago to his doom.

Duality. Balance.

Kate let go of the javelin and jumped back onto another iceberg, staring at the weapon as breath painfully heaved from her lungs. Her body shook, her wounds bayed, but she *had* to make sure Santiago was unable to break free from her skewer. Weak from the fight but thrumming with adrenaline, she fell to her knees, then to her hands, watching with widened eyes as the ice floe bobbed and shook. If she listened hard enough, straining against the sounds of battle that raged just at her periphery, she thought she could hear Santiago's gurgling wails.

When he didn't appear above water for a solid minute, she knew her idea worked.

His ability to disappear has been impeded, and in his weakened state he can't recover. He'll drown repeatedly until morning when the rays of the sun take him.

She choked on a sob as tears burned in her eyes.

Duality.

Balance.
The tears fell as she thought, *may Otherworld shirk you and The Abeyance cast you to the depths of Hell where you belong.*

Chapter Thirty

"Open the door!"

Damian thundered up the stairs to the porch, bellowing with all his might.

"*Open the goddamned door!*"

Sesi appeared a second later, throwing open the entrance to Isobel Lake. Just over the threshold beyond, her family hesitated, their visages pale with dread. Damian nearly barreled over them all, carrying Kate through the entryway of the home while roaring for Lilith.

"Lilith I need you in the dining room!"

Absolute pandemonium erupted. Bodies spilled out of still running vehicles, some alive, some toeing the line between The Abeyance and Earth. Vampires shouted, grunts and cries abounded, blood arced and dripped, and weapons and belongings fell to the driveway without care. Ryder was quick behind Damian assisting a limping Talorc, who he deposited in a chair in the dining room before running back outside, trailing blood and mud in his wake. They'd made it back to the coven with little time to spare against the sun thanks to the all-terrain vehicles, which mercifully hadn't been tampered with.

"Kate, Kate," Damian said frenziedly, placing her down in another chair as Lilith went to Talorc, pulling at his clothing. She pitched forward, breathing erratically. Damian had his own wounds to tend to, but nothing on this earth would take him from Kate's side before he knew she was safe and well.

"Kate," he said roughly, pushing her to sit up straight in the wooden chair. He knew she lived, but *damnit* her limp form had him shaking badly enough to rattle his teeth. She hadn't said much on the ride to the coven, had barely opened her eyes when he plucked her from the waters of the lake, and her paling skin brought him back to a time he didn't want to remember.

When I almost lost you.

Fuck.

"*Kate.*"

Thankfully, blissfully, Kate moaned, her head falling to the side and then her chest. Damian clamped a hand around her shoulder to hold her upright, and she hissed in pain, her eyes flaring open.

"Careful." Her voice was hoarse, grating with discomfort. "Gunshot wound."

"Where else?" Damian choked, his hands trembling as he patted her from head to toe.

"Calf, thigh." Kate lifted a battered hand to pull her mask from her face as bodies poured into the room, into the house. Chaos ensued and Taryn began shouting to bring order to the force.

"Scrapes here and there." Damian's quaking hand found the tourniquet wrapped tightly around her leg. He caressed her gently, unable to stop himself, and his skin inadvertently jumped at the contact. "But I'm okay."

Kneeling before her, Damian lowered his head to his chest, squeezing his eyes shut, his hands falling to her knees. His heart shuddered, the organ finally coming to life after being on the precipice of shattering throughout the night.

"I'm okay Damian," he heard Kate say, and her shaking hand fell to his head, brushing through his hair. Her voice twisted his insides, and he clamped his eyes shut even more tightly as his throat worked vigorously to keep his emotions at bay.

He lifted his head, copper colliding with cerulean, and through bloodied lips he said, "*You did it.*"

Kate smiled, a wondrous smile that had his heart, his very soul, surging with vitality.

With love.

"We did it," she replied, her hand brushing his hair back from his bloodied, frost-ridden face. "I couldn't have done it without you. Without everyone."

"This is your win." Damian clutched her knees as his heart swelled, and swelled, and swelled. "And I can't wait to hear all about it. Is it good?"

Kate laughed, and his soul wept in reverence. "It is."

He couldn't help it: he swept up to her then, pressing his lips fervently against her own. She gasped when he pulled away, her hand falling to his chest. He pressed his forehead to hers and Kate cupped his cheek, laughing on an abbreviated sob. If it wasn't for Taryn who appeared with a pair of trauma shears and a roll of gauze in her hands, he would've completely forgotten anyone else existed.

"I'll help her, you go to the others." Taryn pushed in front of him, separating the two. Begrudgingly, Damian rose to his full height and stepped aside so Taryn could help Kate pull off her soaking outwear. "Dawn is coming. There's not a lot of time to get everyone to safety."

Thunderous boots clamored into the dining room, and Damian noted a male with red hair matted with blood and a bushy beard throw a wink at Kate as he gently placed a moaning female on the floor. Fiona rushed to her side to triage her as Damian began to growl, but the sound was cut off as the male said, "Glad to see you made it. A wee Valkyrie you were."

Damian's growl rumbled throughout the room, but the male was unphased by his show of dramatics. Kate, on the other hand, somehow managed to glance up at Damian with a tempering look before turning to address the male. "Thanks, Darragh."

This *Darragh* grinned at Kate, revealing bloody teeth. Damian felt himself draw back as if to strike, unable to contain the wrath he felt coiling within him. The male—who was either stupid or belligerent—didn't notice Damian's animosity and instead jerked his head in his direction after a terse survey of his form. "To help, are ya? Come on now."

"Who the hell is that?" Damian asked as the male disappeared. He stared hard after him, his eyes narrowed, as jealousy coursed through him. *Jealousy.* He hated how it tasted, how it felt crawling on his skin. But he couldn't help it. *After the way he looked at Kate?*

Me. Jealous. Didn't think I'd see the day...s.

"Darragh, the Dublin coven leader. Don't you know him?"

Damian's eyes narrowed further, his chest tightening. "How do *you* know him?"

Kate flicked his hip, drawing his attention. "Had to play

diplomat."

"Why is he winking at you?"

"*Damian,*" Taryn interjected. "Go. Away."

When he didn't move, Kate flicked him again. "Go. I'll be here when you get back."

Not keen on being around Darragh but knowing he had to help, Damian turned his heated gaze to Kate. His eyes softened, his voice almost a whisper as he asked, "Promise?"

"Always."

He lifted a brow and quirked a half smile. "No more running?"

Her eyes sparkled as she returned the gesture. "Never."

Dawn did indeed arrive swiftly, but thankfully everyone was able to be moved inside and situated so they could receive care. Their number after the fight faded to just under a hundred; even bolstered with the reinforcements that had indeed come from Mikom, it meant they lost over fifty vampires—not counting the enemy. It was with a heavy heart Talorc thanked the leader of the Snow Lake coven and the additional ally from the singular Saskatchewan coven for coming to their aide. Without their helicopters and the support Talorc wouldn't have been victorious, though it was admitted by Mikom that he didn't think they would make it in time.

The unofficial medical staff had their hands full, as they were joined by only five others with advanced training. They were able to direct others to fulfill their needs, and no one went without the proper tending to. Though it took the better part of the day, everyone was made comfortable inside the house, appropriately triaged and treated, then finally fed and watered. Ryder made the decision to return to Morton Lake later that night to retrieve any abandoned weaponry and make sure no bodies remained. He gained the support of a few of the less wounded vampires, and in under an hour they had a safe plan to return to the battleground. Others made plans to return to their various covens, though Sesi and her family made it known their home would be open for as long as anyone needed.

Sesi took the news of her sister's demise better than Damian thought. Though she wept for the loss, he noted she seemed to share none of Uru's apprehension and distaste for Talorc. In fact, it was evident to Damian the betrayal sat ill with the entire Ruskill coven. Later in the day, when The Guard, Talorc, Kate, Kalliq, Sesi, and Tulok were gathered in the kitchen while the rest of the house slumbered, they apologized profusely for her deceit.

"Uru didn't handle it well when our parents were murdered by Hangmen," Sesi said, wiping the tears from her face as she stared into her steaming mug of tea. "And then when our brother died… It doesn't surprise me she wanted revenge. But I didn't think she would take it in this direction."

"You had no idea?" Cyrus asked, his voice suggesting he was skeptical.

Sesi shook her head, lifting her gaze to him, and then Talorc. "No. I… We didn't speak about politics. I thought she was happy here. Living the way we were. I thought she wanted what was best for our family."

"We did too," Kalliq answered for his brother. "She never said otherwise."

"Maybe she thought what she was doing was best," Kate replied, and Damian considered the comment to be way more mature than how he felt about the female coming for Kate's life.

"In her own way, maybe." Sesi's voice was barely a whisper. "She wasn't a very charming or forthcoming being."

"What happens now?" Vadin asked, scrubbing a bandaged hand down his battered and swollen face. "To the coven?"

Sesi looked at her cousins, and their gazes were steady, sure. The pensive exchange was brief, and it was Sesi who answered with her hazel eyes trained on Talorc, "We will maintain, and be faithful and loyal to you. We don't share the same vision as Uru. We know the true way to peace is through you, Talorc."

"Why?" Damian asked, suspicion in his voice.

"Santiago's mindset was based on greed, on the whim of one of the most evil beings in lore," Sesi replied, and though her voice trembled with grief, her hazel eyes were sharp. "Talorc, though somewhat negligent, has only ever yearned for peace. For prosperity and unity."

"We will do whatever we can to sway others to your side," Kalliq confirmed.

"You won't have to worry about us," Tulok finished. "And

you can call on us whenever you need."

Their mellow camaraderie lasted through the day, other vampires coming and going as Sesi and Tulok's beloved maintained revolving courses of hot meals. Damian was exhausted even though he still thrummed with adrenaline, not for what was accomplished but for what would come next. *Kate.* He could finally focus all his attentions on convincing her he was worth what she'd been waiting for. *I know I have a lot to atone for. I need to get started now.*

He watched with a gaze that lingered when Kate retired closer to sunset. He felt her exhaustion through the bond they shared, and he realized distantly his own fatigue was just as pungent. He wanted to follow her but knew he couldn't, even though he was more than aware Talorc had seen him kiss her in the dining room after the battle. *I'll cross that bridge shortly,* Damian told himself. His liege said nothing to the fact, his face impassive and his tone neutral throughout the day.

Even after she'd gone, Damian's regard tarried on the empty doorway. *I'm ready. I want it. A future with her is where I was always meant to be. I'm not afraid of what's to come anymore.*

Well that's not true, he thought with an inward smile, finally turning his contemplative gaze to the table at which he sat. *What I'm afraid of is missing out on spending every second of the rest of my life happily by Kate's side. I've wasted too much time as it is. She deserves everything I can give her.*

And Talorc will just have to be okay with it.

Ryder and those he took to Morton Lake cleared the majority of evidence of any wrongdoing. The sun was strong in the days to follow, melting the snow that lay saturated with blood, and any vampires left for dead dissipated under its rays. However, it was evident a large number of wraiths and possibly humans had escaped. Whether they survived the frigid Manitoban frontier was another story, but no one thought lightly of their future motives; anything was possible anymore. It was also concluded if there were more vampires who could disappear at will, they'd probably escaped as well.

The separation from Isobel Lake, Paavak, and Gíselle was bittersweet. Kate knew her father wanted to return to Winnipeg, but his call to duty was pulling him back to Warwick to regroup. They left on cordial terms with their allies, with Gíselle promising to show Kate around Winnipeg on her return, admitting she hoped it was soon. Kate mirrored the ideal, and with a warm and heartfelt embrace she promised to keep in touch as often as she could.

Two days after leaving Ruskill, The Guard and Kate were gathered in Talorc's study in various states of healing and comfort. The first of March was behind them, and the start of the month brought with it a stunning sky of gold and cobalt that could only be appreciated as the sun dipped behind the trees. Talorc walked with a cane as his once-broken femur was still mending, and he sat with a heavy sigh behind his desk, the leather chair groaning under his weight. He pulled a notebook to him and grabbed a pen, his brown eyes shrewd as he looked about the room at them all. Kate and Ryder were seated before the desk in brown leather chairs, Ryder's arm in a sling. Damian stood behind Kate while Cyrus looked out over the manor grounds. Noir stood next to the crackling fireplace, his gaze pensively on the flames, while Vadin poked at the books on the shelves.

"Where do we stand?" Talorc asked, clicking his pen into action.

"We're in the middle of tallying the numbers of the covens," Ryder said. "To see how tall our nation stands."

"We should continue the tour once we recuperate." Talorc earned himself several dull stares and a grunt of disagreement with his statement, and he ignored them all. "It is evident that there is work to be done in the name of diplomacy. I cannot have what happened at Morton Lake happen again."

"Uru's betrayal isn't the first and won't be the last," Kate said, and no one was confident enough to say otherwise. She herself had healing yet to accomplish, and it was with no small amount of effort that she sat in her father's office now. Her body wasn't as slow to heal as it was a month ago, but her wounds still ached and throbbed. Even so, she was ready to embark on her next adventure and tackle the mountain of work to be done. She wasn't a fool to think that an uphill battle didn't await her; even though Santiago and his coalition had been defeated, she knew the threat wasn't conquered.

"We need to pull together if we are to truly defeat Adhamh," Talorc continued. "We cannot overcome him if we are not united."

"Have you updated the watchers?" Cyrus asked.

Talorc shook his head. "I plan to reach out after we form a strategy."

"Where do we even start?" Vadin asked, his tone relaying the fatigue he felt.

They were all tired. Over the last week they'd traversed a great number of miles and trudged through brittle tundra to fight ancient enemies. They'd all been challenged in ways they couldn't have imagined, and while the drive to push forward was there, a reprieve was needed as well.

We have to keep up the momentum, Kate thought, clearing her throat to speak.

"I agree with father," she said, and she felt Damian's hand grip the chair behind her as he stepped nearer. "We should continue the campaign to gather allies to our side, weed out those who aren't, and unify the nation. That's where we start."

"But there's only one of Talorc," Ryder countered. "And some of the coven leaders don't even respect him as it is."

"Then we will have to expand our reach." Talorc's eyes flicked from Ryder to Kate.

And stayed on Kate.

Her own widened. Her tone conveyed her shock as she asked, "Me?"

Talorc nodded. "You could travel to Europe and begin a separate campaign while I continue on in the Americas."

Kate's jaw fell open, shut, then opened again. "Me?" she asked stupidly.

Talorc's lip twitched as he fought a smile. "You know the *Elden Edicts.* You are my heir, which means you speak of my legacy. You have conquered your fear of planes, correct?"

Kate nodded once, still stunned.

"Would you mind the travel?"

"No but—"

"I'll go in her stead," Ryder interjected. "The covens know

me as well as they do you. There's no need for Kate to leave Warwick."

"I need you here," Talorc responded, his eyes pulling back to Ryder. "To keep the operation running smoothly from Warwick while running the coven and handling the city. I need to reach as many covens as I can and if I have you at the helm, guiding me, I can accomplish the task efficiently and effectively.

"It was evident when we went to Winnipeg others were intrigued to meet Kathryn and respected her as my heir. They do not know she has lived a life of reclusion, and you must admit it hardly showed. She spoke directly, with confidence and aplomb. She thought things through and proved to be a steadfast leader in the times when it was necessary. She accepted those who approached her and remained cordial, but firm. I trust her to do the same with others. I know she will do well."

Kate fought the smile that threatened to take over her face as her father regarded her with esteem. His expression clearly said, *your mother would be proud—as proud as I.*

"She has no experience in diplomacy," Cyrus said. "She doesn't know her way around and has no contacts overseas."

"Then Damian will go with her."

Kate's jaw fell open and stayed open. Through the bond she felt the sharp whip of Damian's astonishment.

"Who better to navigate the land? Damian knows it from his time as a contractual mercenary, and his contacts are endless. Together they can travel coven to coven, speaking on behalf of myself to unify the vampires once more."

Vadin was flipping through an old volume of the *Elden Edicts* as he said, "I see you've thought this through, boss."

Kate closed her mouth as her father replied, "I have had a lot of time to ponder."

"You've found your path then?" Kate asked, referencing their conversation before the battle.

Talorc smiled. "The most tortuous one possible." His eyes roved over The Guard as he said, "But I know with this team I will prosper. It will require all your own unique expertise. Cyrus and Vadin will come with me on my quest, while Noir scouts the cities and covens ahead. Ryder will stay here and navigate our separate ventures while keeping watch on the ebbs and flows of the enemy, protecting the manor and the population of Warwick."

"There are more foes than friends," Ryder rumbled with distaste. "Not only do we have to worry about disloyal vampires and unchecked wraiths, but humans too."

"The Hangmen were never completely disbanded," Noir said. "They're still scattered about, mainly in the States."

"We need to find out if what Santiago told me holds any weight too," Kate said, leaving her father's bombshell on the table for her to decipher later. "He warned there was someone else who was going to take his place in the struggle for power. Someone worse than him."

"Vadin can work on that as we journey." Talorc jotted down notes as he talked. "We can tackle both tasks at once. One may lead to the completion of the other."

"After unification, then what?" Cyrus asked, his eyes firm on his liege.

"We go after Adhamh," Talorc replied. "Hopefully after we accomplish the alliances we need, we will have the full support of the First Arc and can take Adhamh down with their help as well."

"If you do not enter the tiger's cave, you will not catch its cub," Noir murmured, his eyes fixated on the dancing flames.

"Okay, Confucius," Vadin jabbed.

Noir looked at him dully while snapping his lighter on and off. "Confucius was Chinese, asshole."

Kate chuckled, feeling more lighthearted than she had in months.

"Take two weeks reprieve," Talorc told the group, turning his double-monitored computer on while closing his notebook. "That will give us time to heal and formulate our next steps. I will reach out to Oleander promptly and begin sending addended missives to the covens we have yet to speak with, and updates to the others."

They all nodded and made to leave, sensing the meeting had ended. Kate glanced at Damian and their eyes locked briefly. They'd had little time together over the last couple of days, and none of it private. *Maybe I could sneak away now,* she thought. Their separation had given her clarity, and she had so much she wanted to say.

She broke the contact so as to not draw attention to it and

stood from her chair to leave. Damian was a pace before her, Ryder before him, Vadin and Noir still bantering, while Cyrus growled at them to stop.

"Kathryn, Damian, a word," Talorc called, effectively halting both beings in their tracks.

Well shoot. Kate lowered herself back into her chair. Fear speared her, sending a jolt of lightning through her body. *Don't panic. It's nothing to worry about. He just wants to talk about sending us to Europe.*

Vadin uttered a low, crescendoing *ohhh* as he walked out of the office, Cyrus pushing his head with a snarl. Noir shook his head as he brushed past the both of them, and Ryder lingered on the threshold before pulling the door shut. Damian cleared his throat as he took the chair next to Kate, and Kate propped herself as far away from Damian as possible as she settled her hands in her lap. Talorc turned to face them, leaning back in his chair, folding his own hands.

His eyes were no less shrewd than before, and his tone was low as he said, "I would have you speak the truth of your relationship."

Kate flinched as if struck while Damian froze.

Nope. Doesn't want to talk about Europe.

"It is apparent that I have missed much," Talorc continued. "When it comes to the both of you. I would endeavor not to be so unmindful in the future."

Kate didn't know what to say and Damian didn't seem to have a clue either.

"Speak," Talorc intoned, and they both jumped. The faintest twitch of his lips told Kate that he found their squirming amusing, while she on the other hand felt a flush starting to rise on her chest.

"Well we—"

"It's complicated—"

They both spoke at once and stopped abruptly, sharing identical looks of embarrassment.

Talorc barked out a laugh, startling them both.

"I have no desire for the details. I simply want to know where things stand. Did I err in assuming you wanted to journey together?"

"No!" Both Damian and Kate yelled at once, and Kate

glanced at Damian as she continued, "No, that's not it."

"Then?" Talorc prompted.

"It's just...that...we..."

"You are beloveds, are you not?"

Kate's flush rose and turned into the brightest crimson she'd ever wielded while Damian stuttered out a sound like he was choking. Again, neither knew what to say.

"Having once been a beloved male myself, I know the signs well." Talorc paused then, as if gauging what to say next. It was with a tinge of sadness to his tone that he continued, "However once the bond is severed, if one part of the soul should linger behind the other's, the remaining part succumbs to darkness. For a time there was little left inside me except for emptiness and sorrow. Color faded and warmth seeped from my bones, leaving my world veiled. Too veiled to see what was right in front of me, causing me to miss much of your life, my daughter."

Talorc's eyes brightened, and his voice rumbled like falling stone, thick with emotions he rarely shared. "I will never get those years back. I have much time to make up for, just as I have much to make up for in the vast realm of the vampire. With new purpose now I rise, and as the veil lifts, I can see plainly now what I should have stoked from the beginning to contribute to your happiness. To add to my regrets is the fact that he could have stepped in where I faltered."

Kate's throat constricted as tears rimmed her eyes. *"Athair..."*

"It wasn't time," Damian said, his own voice gruff. "We weren't ready. And Kate..." He looked at her then, his eyes softening. "Kate had to find herself first. Not saying that she had to go through what she did, but after... She deserved to learn to love that part of herself before she could learn to love anyone else. And I respect that. I had my own growing to do, too. My own acceptance on a lot of accounts. And to be honest, I didn't know how you would receive us...together."

"Why would I not want one of my finest warriors protecting my only daughter?" Talorc asked rhetorically, and an enormous weight suddenly lifted from Kate's chest. She felt Damian's relief too as Talorc went on, "You are of my greatest friends, and one of only a few beings I trust implicitly. I could never ask for anyone better for my Kathryn."

Oh these cretans, Kate thought, blubbering out a hideous sob.

"Well, so long as you plan to do right by her." Talorc raised a brow, causing Kate to laugh as she brushed away happy tears. "You forget I know all sides of you."

Damian's eyes were only for Kate as he said, "It's only been her for a long time."

Kate couldn't stop the ugly crying from fully taking over, and Damian had her in his arms in the next heartbeat.

Neither would see the vampire king smile softly from his chair, his eyes bright. "Then see it done."

Damian and Kate nestled in his bed in his penthouse, watching the city sparkle beyond the windowpane as the moon wandered across the sky. Both were content in the aftermath of their lovemaking, enjoying the solace each other's arms offered.

"I can't believe we're here, like this," Kate said, her head cradled on Damian's shoulder. She had one hand splayed on his chest, a leg thrown over his own, while he had one hand wrapped around her shoulder and idly stroked her thigh with the other.

"After all this time." Damian nuzzled her hair to plant a small kiss on her head. "It feels like a dream."

"It does." Kate smiled, taking her eyes away from the cityscape to look up at Damian. "We've come a long way."

"*You've* come a long way." Damian pulled her closer, his grip tightening briefly. "In the beginning, when you were gone, I kept thinking I failed you, that I had to save you. What I didn't realize is that you were capable of saving *yourself.* You've always been more capable than any of us gave you credit for. I'll never doubt you like that again, Kate. I should've seen it sooner—like a lot of things. Your drive to live, to come out on the other side, was more important than my selfish need to save you or force you to change your way of thinking.

"If you still need time to figure things out, I get it. This kind of shit doesn't happen in a day. I meant what I said when I told you that you deserved to find yourself first. I promise I'll wait until that time comes. When you're ready to accept me—"

"Isn't it obvious that I've *accepted* you?" Kate pushed her body into his with a sly smirk.

Damian pushed back, rolling into her to bury his face in her neck and put his body between her legs, a calf clasped in one hand. Kate squealed with laughter as he growled next to her ear, "You know what I mean."

She pressed at him until he pulled back, and braced on one hand Damian looked down at her. Kate lifted a hand to his bearded cheek while saying, "I accepted you a long time ago. Everything about you. Your stubbornness. Your arrogance. Your hotheadedness. Your humor. Your courage. Your inability to let anyone else have the last word. The not-so-resentful look in your eyes when I ask you to help carry my Amazon boxes. *Everything.* I love you, Damian."

He swept in to kiss her, taking her next breath. Kate met every stroke, every caress, with a radiant smile on her lips.

Damian receded from her embrace, raising a hand to brush down her temple, over her cheek. "I love you too, Kate. With everything in me, I love you. And I promise to love you for as long as I live, and then beyond. You are my world, my life, my universe. I exist because of you. Only you. *Always* you."

Kate's eyebrows scaled her face. "Now *that's* what I call professing your love for me."

Damian grinned, all fang, only fleetingly remembering the night of their first kiss, before the memory whisked away for another time, another place. "Good right? Been wanting to say that for a while."

Kate pulled herself to him and they kissed again, finding themselves lost to the passion that so easily enraptured them both.

…Until Damian pulled away and shuffled hurriedly out of bed.

"I forgot I have something for you," he said, walking naked to the dresser by his door.

Kate watched his every move, fascinated by the way his muscles rippled. *Hot dang,* she thought, unable to stop the devious smile from painting her face as he rummaged around in one of the drawers. She sidled up in the bed, pulling the brown satin sheets up and over her chest, still smiling wickedly as he turned back toward her with a wrapped package in his hands. In an effort to not appear like a complete trollop, Kate pulled her eyes away from *his* package as he sat on the bed, instead turning her regard to the parcel in his hands.

"What is it?" she asked as she reached for it. It was rectangular in shape and thin, only slightly bigger than the entirety of her hand.

"I think it will be perfect to take to Europe with us." Damian watched as she pulled the knot from the string that kept the brown paper wrapped around it.

Kate set aside the string and opened the paper to reveal a brown, leather tome embossed with a bouquet of wildflowers. She flipped through the blank pages, her heart swelling. "A journal," she said gently.

"For you to start writing down your travels."

Kate ran her fingers gently over the pattern before looking up at Damian with a smile so bright that it rivaled the moon above. "You remembered what I said."

"With every step you take," Damian started, leaning toward her. "And every move you make…" It was only when he was a fraction of space away from her lips that he finished, "I'll be—"

Kate groaned, shoving his chest and flopping back on the bed. She moved the journal to cover her face as she said, "You *ruined* the moment!"

Damian laughed, the sound echoing across the bedroom. He moved after her, stopping to look down at her with a wily grin. "I couldn't help it. I had to."

"You suck."

"So do you. Very well actually."

Kate removed the journal from her face to glare at him, and he laughed again.

"Sorry. Do you want me to tell you what I like about you to make up for it?"

"Endlessly. All the time. Every day."

His grin lingered as he moved a hand to trace the features of her face. "I love that you are an excellent baker. You look damn good riding a horse. Actually, you look good doing anything. I love your endless chatter. I love that you like to people-watch. I love your laugh. Your teasing. Your inability to stop shopping. I have to take over that burden from Talorc now, don't I?"

Kate nodded with a huff of laughter, and Damian kissed her before he continued, "I love your fire. Your bravery. The fact that you picked up a gun and blasted wraiths to the abyss and speared Santiago to an iceberg. Do you have any idea how far you've come? You have to know how proud we all are. Your father, too. Myself especially. And your mother. Herja would be the proudest of all."

"You knew her too, didn't you?" Kate asked softly, almost timidly.

Damian nodded. "I'll tell you everything I know about her."

"Someday." Her smile was sad as she added, "Thank you."

He brushed his thumb along her cheek. "You constantly surprise me, Kate, and I live for every second of it. I can't wait to be surprised for the rest of our lives. I know you know, but to come from the female who lounged by the pool drinking all night to the one that lies before me now is both aspiring and inspiring."

"The old Kate would be proud, too, I think," Kate said pensively.

"There is no old Kate." Damian brushed wild hair from her forehead. "There's just *Kate*."

Kate's joy knew no bounds. She couldn't find the words to respond, but through the bond they shared she knew he felt her bliss.

"I hope you know that. I hope you know the version of yourself that pulled you through those terrible times was always inside of you; you just had to find it. You've become your best self, and I am beyond happy to be a part of your life, to know *all* sides of you."

Kate smiled, revealing pointed fangs. "Tell me more."

Damian took the journal from her hands and tossed it away. "I could go on for days."

"Please, don't let me stop you."

Damian rumbled with laughter, moving to kiss her once more. Kate sighed into his embrace, her fingers curling around his biceps.

And for a time, all was right in the world.

The End

About the Author

Natasha is a full-time registered nurse who is malingering in her thirties and lives on the Northeast coast of the United States with her wonderful husband, perfect daughter, chaotic dog, and three spoiled cats. When she is not chasing after aforementioned family, she is enjoying her coffee, appreciating nature, changing the radio station between death metal and classical piano, or diligently working on creating an alternative universe to run away to. She wouldn't have life any other way—although a tropical island doesn't sound too bad.

You can find more information on Natasha and keep up with all the latest from The Guards of Nightfall by following on social media:

Website: natgalauthor.wixsite.com/natasha-galan

Instagram: natashagalan_author

Facebook: facebook.com/natgalauthor